In memory of my mother,
who never stopped believing in me

Behold, I have refined thee...in the furnace of affliction.
-—Isaiah 48:10

For He is like a refiner's fire... He will purify...and refine them like gold and silver...
-—Malachi 3:2-3

Prologue

Mid-Atlantic Ocean
December 28, 1853

Cigar smoke swirled through the after cabin of the clipper packet *Caroline*. It was two o'clock in the morning. A gale was blowing outside, sending all but the hardiest of stomachs to their bunks. Two men remained.

A. Jackson O'Rourke squinted across the table at his opponent. The game had started with a table of seven some four hours before, and Jack had played it straight thus far, content with the dealer's fifty-six-percent advantage inherent in the card game Ace-Deuce-Jack. Then the other players drifted away to their staterooms, and it became apparent this naive but tenacious fellow would be an easy mark. Too easy to pass up.

He was a soft-faced, round-bellied Englishman making his first crossing to the Americas. A recently widowed earl of something or other, he had all the trappings of aristocracy: Savile Row cutaways, four-in-hand silk cravats, a gold watch and looping fob, the requisite monocle and walking stick, and a healthy dose of arrogance. Not to mention seemingly endless supplies of English pounds, many of which were already piled on Jack's side of the table.

The fellow was growing restless, his color fast fading with each roll of the ship. It was almost time…

Jack shuffled the deck and offered it for him to cut. Took it back and said, "Place your bet."

The Englishman slid a five-pound note into the center of the table. Jack matched it, then turned over the top three cards one by one: a queen, a ten and a seven. His opponent grunted his satisfaction and reached for his winnings, saying in his clipped, precise accent,

"This seems an opportune time for me to bow out. You have had the best of me tonight, old chap. The colonies win again, what?"

He scooped up his remaining cash and started to rise.

"I regret any distress I might have caused such a distinguished visitor to my country," said Jack. "So much so I am moved to offer amends. What do you say we each put our entire stake on the table? One hand. Winner takes all."

The earl sat back down, as much from a violent lurch of the ship as his own volition. He eyed his remaining bankroll, still several hundred pounds strong but much reduced from what he had brought to the table hours before. His gaze shifted to Jack's much larger pile.

"Mm-m. Tempting, but—"

"My dear fellow, you have taken the last two hands. You will have all the cards except my three. Who could ask for better odds than that?"

A lie given the deuce Jack had palmed earlier.

"I do not think—"

But Jack was already reshuffling the deck. He pushed his stake into the middle of the table. Handed the deck across to be cut and waited to see whether the fish would bite. The pudgy white hand fidgeted, then reached for the deck.

Jack made a show of squaring the cards and placing them precisely in front of him. He stretched his fingers as if to loosen them, in the process bringing the card in his sleeve down to the base of his wrist. He slid the first card from the top of the deck. Turned it over. An eight.

A little sigh escaped the Englishman's lips. His eyes remained riveted on the deck as Jack slipped the second card off the top and flipped it over. A three. The earl bounced in his chair, tension and excitement tinting his face pink. Jack reached for the deck, index finger extended while his little finger stretched backward to retrieve the winning card. In a fluid motion honed over many hours of practice, he pulled it forward.

He had executed this move dozens of times without the gull being any the wiser. This time the ship shuddered and pitched, tilting his arm enough to expose the descending card. The Englishman jumped up and shouted,

"You are a cad and a cheat, sir!"

Jack inwardly cursed the vagaries of nature that had caused this difficulty. He checked the cabin's five stateroom doors in case some curious passenger had heard the commotion and decided to investigate. All remained as before, the only sound that of the rain lashing the skylight overhead.

He spread his hands and put on his most disarming grin. "Zounds, my lord, you have caught me out. Surely you cannot blame an enterprising Yank from trying." He pushed the pile of cash across the table. "The pot is yours. Take it, and we shan't speak of this again."

"Bloody hell I will! You have breached the code of honor by which I live and breathe. I shall meet you on the hurricane deck at dawn. Pistols at ten paces. Until then, I bid you goodnight!"

He spun away, staggering sideways on the rolling deck. Jack was around the table and in his path before he could regain his footing.

"You are making much ado about nothing, to quote your revered Mr. Shakespeare. I apologize for offending your sensibilities. Take the money, and let us be done with this."

"I do not accept your apology, sir. You may care nothing for your honor, but in my country it is everything. There is but one way to settle this!"

"To duel over a small indiscretion is ridiculous."

"Nonetheless, nothing else will satisfy me. The hurricane deck at dawn."

Jack had honed his instinct for survival under a variety of situations spanning his thirty-one years. A public duel on an exposed deck on the high seas? He did not like the odds. Worse, news of what had happened this night would gush like floodwater from captain to crew to all the passengers. He had left New York City under a cloud two years before and gone into self-imposed exile in England. Although he had managed to escape scandal there, his recently sagging fortunes had prompted him to return to a new life in the American West. Now his future was threatened with disruption once again.

He saw in an instant how he could extricate himself from this impasse. Hardly a sure thing, but he was, after all, a gambling man.

"Why wait for dawn?" he said as he reached into his breast coat pocket and withdrew the short-barreled muff pistol he had purchased in London and always carried with him. It was a single-shot weapon designed primarily for defensive purposes. Which was the exact circumstance in which he now found himself.

The Englishman saw the gun and froze, eyes bulging. "What the devil…?"

Jack did not hesitate. He pressed the muzzle into the earl's soft aristocratic midsection and pulled the trigger.

PART ONE—BUCKING THE TIGER

Chapter One

Charleston, South Carolina
February 3, 1854

Salvation came in the person of Andrew Jackson O'Rourke. Or so it seemed to Lizzie Hamilton. The past fifteen months had seen a plague of Biblical proportion descend on her life. She had begun the month of October, 1852 as she had every other in her nineteen years of living as the pampered youngest daughter of a prominent South Carolina planter family. A much-sought-after belle whose heart had been captured by a handsome and dashing young gentleman from a nearby plantation. With her future thus secure, she had been in no hurry to shed the excitement of the single life for that of matron.

Then catastrophe struck.

Lizzie would never forget the raw, stormy late-November day when the telegram arrived. She and her mother were already on edge due to the prolonged absence of Lizzie's older brother Nathaniel, who had assumed control of the ancestral plantation Rocklands after his father's death ten years before. His wife, a beautiful Northerner whom he had married against all reason a year and a half before, had betrayed them all by running away with two fugitive slaves. Instead of divorcing her, he had chased off after her, leaving his family virtually defenseless against what was to happen.

Within days of his leaving, they discovered the escape had been orchestrated by none other than one of their own, who unbeknownst to them all had been spiriting local slaves north to Canada via the abominable Underground Railroad. How a seemingly true son of the South could have hidden his treacherous abolitionist tendencies from his entire acquaintance was beyond knowing. Yet even this horror paled before the realization that all the while Lizzie was being courted, her beau had been nurturing an illicit alliance with Nathaniel's faithless wife. Shock and shame had so inflamed Lizzie that she thought herself beyond the reach of any further calamity. How wrong she was!

On that fateful November day, she and her mother were sitting in the family sitting room when a telegram arrived. It was addressed to Nathaniel, but as acting head of Rocklands, her mother hesitated only a moment before opening it. Her face paled. In a near swoon, she allowed it to slip from her hand. Lizzie snatched it up and read the contents for herself.

Creditor's patience exhausted STOP Rocklands in immediate foreclosure STOP Hired manager currently en route STOP Meanwhile all assets frozen STOP Family may remain pending arrangements. The sender was one Benjamin Hanley of the Merchants Bank, New York City.

Creditor, foreclosure, assets—the words meant nothing to Lizzie, who had no head for business, but her mother's reaction left little doubt something dire had happened.

"What does it mean?" she cried.

Each one of her mother's forty-nine years sat heavily on her face. "It means we are ruined."

Lizzie gaped. "Ruined? What—"

"Silly girl, is it not obvious? Nathaniel has squandered his birthright and left us bereft of home and livelihood. We are destitute!"

Lizzie was unsure which shocked her more, her mother's harsh tone or the incomprehensible idea her words conveyed.

She shook her head. "Impossible. Nathaniel knows his duty. He would never jeopardize our well-being in such a way."

Her mother seemed not to have heard. She rose, hands clenched together. "We must go to Roland. He will know what to do. We shall leave on tomorrow's train. Go and see to your packing."

Roland Townsend, a successful lawyer in Charleston some eighty miles southeast of Rocklands, was Lizzie's older sister Sarah's husband. Mention of his name brought Lizzie immediate relief. Yes, Roland would consult with his many contacts in the business and political realm and find a way to make this terrible situation disappear. Her spirits restored, she went in search of her lady's maid so the packing could commence. On reflection, she even welcomed the opportunity to escape the confines of the estate for the bustle and excitement of Charleston. Life had become unbearably boring of late. No parties. No gatherings among the young people of the neighborhood. Only humiliation and isolation. In the social whirl of Charleston, she would prove she cared not a fig about her former beau's perfidy. Confident of her charms and her ability to attract new suitors, she hummed beneath her breath as she chose which gowns she would take with her.

This fantasy lasted only long enough for the train to reach Charleston and Roland to read the telegram. His grim features told the tale. He would telegraph Nathaniel and urge him to return posthaste. Which, as it happened, was not to be. Within days, word arrived that Nathaniel had been killed in a duel. Lizzie's mother collapsed under this news, and her poor heart never recovered. Two weeks later, she was dead.

All semblance of normal life vanished. Lizzie was forced to move in with Sarah and Roland, not even being allowed to bring her maid since that personage now belonged to the new owner of Rocklands. Dependent on her only remaining relatives, she was disgraced, unmarriageable, and bereft of even the slimmest chance of happiness.

She had never paid much attention to the celestial Being. Oh, she had participated in the required trappings of religion as any good southern lady would do, attending church every Sunday, suffering through family devotions before breakfast every morning, reciting her prayers every night. It was something one did, like dressing properly and observing the edicts of etiquette. Beyond that, she had simply assumed she occupied a position of favor in God's eyes. It had never occurred to her to question her own worthiness. Or to worry that He might one day have the temerity to withdraw His favor. Now her anger over His betrayal knew no bounds.

Nevertheless, she still clung to the illusion that sometime, somewhere He would send a knight in shining armor to rescue her from her fate. It was in such a frame of mind that she entered the parlor one early-February evening to discover Roland had brought a guest home for dinner, a client whom he was currently defending before the bar.

He was handsome. Dark like her former beau but slighter of stature, impeccably dressed, and sporting a neat moustache. Lizzie was immediately struck by his eyes. Deep brown, almost black in color, they fixed her with an intense gaze that seemed to cut through to her very soul while projecting an air of supreme confidence. He was a man to be reckoned with, and his obvious approval upon being introduced to Lizzie resonated throughout her body.

She could hardly remember the last time she had been openly admired by a member of the opposite gender. Now she saw herself through this stranger's eyes. Lush reddish-brown hair. Piquant face with lively green eyes, delicate features and a milky complexion broken by a light spray of freckles across a pert nose. A slim form with a pleasingly full bosom. That he took it all in with interest rather than the pity to which she had lately grown accustomed came like a blast of warm air on the coldest winter day. She returned his greeting with a candid smile and lingering glance that found its mark in a slightly raised eyebrow. She ignored her sister Sarah's disapproving look and accepted the arm he offered by way of escort into the dining room.

He seated her at the table and took his place directly across from her. She sat tall and straight as the soup course was served, absorbing the gentleman's approving glances and forgetting her desperate circumstances for the first time in months. Then he spoke, and the bubble of self-delusion burst.

"Allow me to express my condolences over your recent difficulties, Miss Hamilton. Your brother-in-law has told me of the deaths of your brother and mother, as well as the calumny of your...
" A delicate pause. "... *friend's* betrayal. How such behavior could have been directed against such a charming young lady is beyond comprehension."

Lizzie's face flamed. How dare Roland reveal their dirty secrets to a total stranger! She tossed her head and said, "I assure you I am quite recovered. The young man was little more than an amusing diversion to me, and I have all but forgotten him. I only regret he is not facing justice for his crimes. Unlike you, although I can only assume you are innocent given Mr. Townsend's decision to bring you into our midst. Of what are you accused, if I may be so bold as to ask?"

She was rather pleased with herself for turning the tables on him, but her sister Sarah was not amused. She scowled fiercely from her seat at the foot of the table. Lizzie kept her eyes locked on the unbowed Mr. O'Rourke, who smiled with dancing eyes and said,

"I admire a bold lady, Miss Hamilton. Therefore, I am happy to oblige your request, although it may not make for the most delicate of dinner-table conversation. As it happens, I am charged with murder."

Lizzie's jaw dropped. It was not unusual for Roland to bring a client with whom he felt a particular affinity home for dinner. Their cases usually involved some civil issue such as a property dispute or inheritance matter. But murder? This was a first.

Sarah was sitting wide-eyed with her hand covering her mouth.

"There is no cause for alarm, my dear," said Roland. "Mr. O'Rourke merely defended himself against a disgruntled passenger who meant him bodily harm. Once the facts are out, he will be duly acquitted of any wrongdoing."

"But such a serious charge. How is it that he is not... not... "

"In jail?" offered Jack O'Rourke. "I most assuredly would be languishing there this very moment were it not for your husband's eloquent plea on my behalf."

"We must credit your ability to post bail over any eloquence on my part," said Roland. "Nonetheless, in this instance, justice was served. It would have been a travesty for an innocent gentleman such as yourself to be confined in that foul place."

Sarah sent her husband a fond smile. "As you have so often said, our legal system is the bulwark of the innocent. And you are a most valiant gatekeeper."

"I could not agree more, Mrs. Townsend," said Mr. O'Rouke, turning the full force of his charm in her direction. "My fate is quite assured as long as it rests in your husband's most capable hands. That he has found me worthy to share this meal in the company of his delightful family humbles me more than I can say."

Sarah blushed and murmured, "Our home is always open to those in duress through no fault of their own."

Lizzie studied her sister. Once every bit as beautiful as Lizzie herself, marriage and the bearing of three children with yet another on the way had added inches to her waist, lines to her face, and mundane cares to her spirit. These very changes were the reason Lizzie had been content to delay her entrance into matrimonial bliss for as long as possible. That, of course, was in the days when she had had her pick of available suitors. Now that her family's disgrace had diminished her prospects, she found herself envying Sarah's secure position and wondering whether she could ever hope to emulate it. Several of her former friends had aging maiden aunts living in their households, and the possibility she might be reduced to such a permanent situation sent chills through her soul. Was the instrument of her rescue sitting across from her this very moment?

She smiled and said, "I admit my curiosity is piqued, sir. How did an innocent man come to be in such a perilous circumstance as yours?"

"A fair question. Count boredom as the primary culprit. A transatlantic crossing provides little in the way of entertainment. Certain gentlemen were in the habit of engaging in a little friendly gamesmanship of an evening. An Englishman and I were the only ones remaining one night when my extraordinary luck led my opponent to accuse me of cheating. I tried to reason with him. Even offered to give him the entire pot, but he was not to be mollified. He pulled a gun, we tussled, and the gun went off. The unfortunate fellow fell dead at my feet."

"Horrible! But surely a regrettable accident."

"Exactly. However, there were no other witnesses. And he happened to be a member of the British aristocracy. An earl, I believe. The British embassy has made a stink, giving your local authorities no choice but to pursue the matter." He shrugged. "As Mr. Townsend has already said, I shall be vindicated at trial. Until then, I am in his keeping, so to speak."

"But what of your family? Your name tells me you are of Irish ancestry, but I hear no brogue in your voice and therefore assume your home is here in America."

"Indeed. I emigrated to this country by way of Canada when I was but four years old."

"Canada?" She said the word with distaste, that country being the magnet that had set their family troubles in motion that fateful October.

"I did not have the privilege of being born into a wealthy old family such as yours, Miss Hamilton. My parents, being of peasant stock, did not have the four-pound fare required to reach New York City. Canada, however, offered a subsidized fare of fourteen shillings, which we were just able to afford. My father died during the crossing, and my mother and I walked across the border. We made our way to Boston, where my mother found work as a scullery maid in the household of a prominent Bostonian. I rose from those humble beginnings to become a self-made man. An attribute, I am told, much admired by America's colonial forefathers."

Lizzie looked him over with new eyes. Given his stylish but expensive attire and courtly manners, she had imagined him to be the scion of a successful northern industrial family. She laid the image aside and replaced it with the sad, squalid little tale he had just told. Despite her disappointment, she could not deny his point that much value was made of American individualism. He did appear to be prosperous, and for someone in her position, that counted for much.

"And your mother?" she asked.

"She died of a brain fever when I was fifteen, God rest her soul, leaving me to make my own way in the world. Which, as you can see, I have managed to do rather well." A grin. "Excepting, of course, my present circumstances, which I have no doubt will soon be resolved to my credit."

Such crass boasting about his financial situation was the first sign she had seen of his crude beginnings. Before her ingrained training could stop her, she said, "And what exactly do you do to earn your livelihood?"

She knew the question made her equally culpable of employing bad manners, but she disregarded her sister's frown and waited for his answer.

"I shan't bore you with the particulars. I shall simply say I am a man of business whose ventures have brought him across the Atlantic to his adopted homeland. And very glad I am to be here."

Lizzie detected her sister's and brother-in-law's discomfort over the turn of conversation as well as their relief over the timely arrival of the main course: fricasseed chicken, rice, and boiled pumpkin along with their cook Bessie's best biscuits. She retreated into her meal, anticipation tickling her senses. She had no rational reason to believe anything had changed as far as her future prospects were concerned. Nonetheless it was there, a strong feeling that something had shifted in her favor. She smiled to herself. It was about time.

Chapter Two

Lizzie saw no more of Mr. O'Rourke in the week that followed, although she thought of little else. She had hoped he would call again and perhaps request her company for a stroll along the Battery, but he remained secluded in his room at the fashionable Charleston Hotel. She understood how a gentleman's sensibilities would keep him distant from a lady as long as he was under such an ugly shadow of suspicion. That knowledge did not dampen her impatience. She made subtle inquiries of Roland, but her brother-in-law remained tight-lipped, no doubt due to the notoriety of the case. She read the newspaper accounts and listened to rank gossip and speculation when she was out and about. Otherwise, she kept her aspirations to herself.

The case was scheduled to be tried on Monday, the thirteenth. Lizzie mentioned her desire to attend at dinner the day before. Sarah was nearly apoplectic in her refusal to even consider it. Roland agreed it was not suitable for her to be seen amongst the newsmen, curiosity-seekers, and general riffraff that would fill the courtroom. Their objections, far from dissuading her, merely stiffened her determination.

After Sarah retired for her afternoon nap on the day in question, Lizzie dressed in the mourning clothes she had been required to wear for a year following her brother's and mother's deaths and pulled the veil down to her chin. She passed Bessie in the downstairs hall. The cook, a heavyset woman whose yellow turban and snow-white apron were a stark contrast to her coal-black skin, stared at her in astonishment, no doubt remembering her oft-stated relief when she was finally able to lay aside the drab black clothes. She ignored the look, swept past, and went out into a gray gloomy day.

She crossed the piazza that stretched across the lower facade of the Townsend's red-brick, two-story house and descended to the front path. She had always thought it a rather grand residence until she saw the palatial home her Cousin Charlotte now occupied as the wife of the prosperous Captain Arthur S. Riddleston. Roland's house was located on Friend Street a block south of Broad Street amongst the homes of other professionals and men of commerce, whereas the captain's was at the very apex of the Charleston peninsula and looked out across East Battery Street to the harbor—a distinction that placed the families in two entirely different strata of society.

Not that it mattered to Lizzie. Her fate had been sealed by her brother's flagrant mismanagement of the family fortunes, and nothing would change that unless she took things into her own hands. She opened her parasol against a light drizzle and set out toward Broad Street.

The courthouse was a three-story Neoclassical building on the corner of Broad and Meeting Streets. Roland's prediction of the chaos that would attend the trial proved to be accurate. Access to the courtroom's lower floor was impossible, but Lizzie climbed the stairs and sidled her way through the crowd surrounding the balcony doors, nose wrinkling at the rank odor of so many warm bodies crammed into such a small space. Her mourning clothes bought her a modicum of deference, allowing her to finally claim a spot against the rear wall where she could look down on the proceedings.

The judge, a solid gray-haired personage in a flowing black robe, sat behind a mahogany bench on a balustraded dias beneath a large American flag. The clerk and his assistant occupied a desk beneath the bench, the county solicitor a table opposite. The twelve jurors were seated along the right-hand wall, their attention riveted on the small pale figure now occupying the witness box.

He could not have been more than fifteen or sixteen, a callow youth with protruding teeth and an unkempt tangle of black hair. Roland Townsend paced in front of him. He was a medium-sized man with light-brown hair and an expanding belly who wore spectacles and a frown of concentration as he said,

"Tell me, Robert, in the course of your duties as cabin boy aboard the *Caroline*, did you have occasion to enter the defendant's stateroom?"

Noticing the boy's confusion, he added, "The defendant being Mr. O'Rourke, whom you see sitting over there." He pointed to where A. Jackson O'Rourke sat looking suave and handsome in his impeccable gentleman's attire.

In a high, squeaky voice, "Yes, sir, your excellency. I 'uz in there lots of times."

A condescending smile. "'Sir' will suffice when you address me, young man. Now, when you say you were in the cabin 'lots of times,' how many do you mean?"

"Don't know exactly, sir. Ever' day we was at sea."

"Every day without fail?"

A vigorous nod.

"You need to answer me out loud, Robert."

"Oh. Yes, sir. Every day, sir."

"And what was your purpose in going into that particular cabin every day?"

"Just doing my job. Straightening up, emptying the chamber pot." He shrugged. "The usual things."

"And during all those forays into Mr. O'Rourke's cabin, did you ever have occasion to see... " He strode over to the solicitor's table and picked up a small, brown, blunt-nosed pistol. "... this gun among his effects."

"No, sir. Never, sir."

"But the gun is not completely foreign to you, is it?"

An open-mouthed frown.

With controlled patience, "I am asking if you have ever seen the gun before today."

"Oh. Oh, yes, sir. I seen it in Cabin Number Four."

A rumble of surprise rolled through the courtroom. The judge banged his gavel until silence was restored, then nodded at Roland, inviting him to continue.

"And who occupied that particular cabin?"

Grinning, "That there highfalutin' duke from England. That gun was his, for sure."

Roland turned to the jurors. "As previous testimony has already established, the passenger who occupied Cabin Four was none other than the deceased, Alfred Harley, Sixth Earl of Oxford and Earl Mortimer." Back to the boy, "Is he the gentleman to whom you refer?"

"He is, sir."

"Thank you, Robert. I have no further questions."

The Charleston District Solicitor rose for cross examination, but despite his imperious demeanor and aggressive verbiage, he was unable to shake the boy's story.

When the youth had stepped down, the judge leaned forward and said, "Do you have any further witnesses to call, Mr. Townsend?"

"I do, Your Honor. The defense calls Mr. Andrew Jackson O'Rourke."

Another murmur rippled through the room as the defendant walked to the witness box, swore to the truth of his testimony, and took his seat. Lizzie's legs were tired from standing, and she was sweating in the heat of such close quarters, but she would not have left the courtroom if her life had depended on it.

Roland stood to one side so the jury would have an unobstructed view of his client and said, "You understand the gravity of the charges against you, do you not, Mr. O'Rourke?"

"I most certainly do."

"Murder in the first degree, sir. You understand the severe penalty to which you would be subject should you be found guilty?"

"I do."

"Given that fact, would you not agree that any man in your position would enter a plea of not guilty?"

"Absent a particular desire to face his Maker, he would indeed."

"And was that motive paramount in your mind when you entered your plea?"

In a voice that rang throughout the room, "No, sir. I pleaded not guilty because I am, in fact, not guilty of this crime."

Roland surveyed the jury with a look of mock surprise. "Not guilty, you say. Did you not shoot to death one Alfred Harley, Sixth Earl of Oxford and Earl Mortimer, on the twenty-eighth day of last December?"

"I did."

More muted reaction quickly silenced by the smack of the judge's gavel.

Roland spread his hands in a gesture of incomprehension. "Then how do you claim to be not guilty of murder?"

"Because I shot the poor soul in self-defense. Had I not done so, he would be the one facing this jury today while I rotted in my grave." A rueful smile. "An unattractive prospect from my perspective, as you might imagine."

A few chuckles quickly suppressed by a frown from the judge.

Roland continued, "Before we get to the particulars of that fateful incident, allow us to learn a bit about who you are and why this jury should believe your version of what transpired."

At this, the solicitor rose and said in a tired voice, "I object to this proposed line of questioning, Your Honor. We are not interested in this man's character. Only in his actions on the night in question."

The judge pursed his lips and looked at Roland, who said, "To the contrary, Your Honor, character has everything to do with this case. There were no witnesses to the shooting in question. My client's testimony is the only account we shall have from someone who was actually present in the ship's after cabin that night. The jury must decide whether or not he is telling the truth. To do so, they must know enough about him to assess the sincerity of his words and demeanor."

The judge nodded. "I shall allow it. Please proceed."

Triumph flitted across Roland's face before he continued, "Now, then, Mr. O'Rourke, your surname is one often associated with Ireland, the fabled Emerald Isle. Was that the country of your birth?"

"It was."

"You are not, then, a natural-born citizen of these United States?"

"No. I was naturalized at the same time as my mother, God rest her soul, when I was nine years old."

"I am curious to know how a gentleman of Irish birth and heritage came by the decidedly American first and middle names of Andrew Jackson. Can you explain that anomaly to the court?"

An engaging grin. "Most happily. I was christened Aindreas James. When we arrived here, my sainted mother, who held a fierce love for her adopted country, anglicized my given name to Andrew and changed my middle name to Jackson in honor of the then President of the United States, whom she greatly admired."

A murmur of approval told Lizzie Roland's tactic was working. Many Southerners were deeply suspicious of foreigners, especially

Irish Catholics, but Roland had effectively cast an aura of respectability over his client by invoking the name of the slave-owning, states-rights advocate, Andrew Jackson.

Sensing this, the solicitor rose and said, "All very interesting, Your Honor, but I fail to see what the defendant's mother's political views have to do with this case. My opposing counsel seems to be accomplishing little besides wasting the court's time."

The judge nodded his head. "I tend to agree with you. Let us move along, shall we, Mr. Townsend?"

Roland bowed and said, "Very well, Your Honor." To his client, "Bearing in mind the court's interest in expediency, tell us about your family. You are your mother's only child?"

"I am. My father died before our ship ever reached these shores, leaving the two of us bereft and defenseless. We settled in Boston, and my mother found employment in the home of the great philanthropist, Mr. John Amory Lowell." A fond smile. "He was a kind and gracious man who encouraged my studies and made a place for me in his employ as well."

He gave a heavy sigh. "Alas, it was not to last. Mother passed from a brain fever when I was a youth, and I decided to go out into the world on my own rather than remain in menial toil. I was fortunate enough to catch the attention of a good man who schooled me in the ways of business. I prospered in a modest way until I received word two years past that my maternal great-uncle on my father's side, a man with whom the family had lost contact, wished me to come to London and keep him company during the final years of his life. He was a man of considerable fortune, which he left to me when he passed into the Lord's arms. Having no reason to remain in England, I decided to come home to the country I love."

"Which is how you happened to be onboard the *Caroline* on the night in question?"

"Indeed."

"Now, sir, perhaps you would give us your account of events as they happened. Events that led to an unfortunate loss of a life."

"I am most eager to do so, Mr. Townsend. The evening began as many others had with a group of congenial gentlemen engaging in a little friendly wagering. All but myself and the aforementioned earl eventually drifted off to their bunks, leaving us two to continue on. The cards had been favoring me all evening, and the earl had wagered more than was perhaps prudent. Out of frustration, he finally suggested we each risk our entire earnings on one final hand. I demurred, but he insisted I give him this chance to win back what he had lost. The cards were played, and I was once again the winner. This final loss drove him beyond the edge of reason. He accused me of cheating and drew his pistol."

He pulled a face of deep sadness. "I tried to calm him, but he became more intransigent with every word. Just as he seemed bent on pulling the trigger, a fortuitous shifting of the deck caused him to lose his balance, giving me the opportunity to spring at him and attempt to disarm him. The weapon discharged as we struggled, and he fell at my feet. I was horrified, as you might imagine. I attempted to revive him, but it was no use. The shot must have taken him straight in the heart. He was quite irretrievably dead."

Roland paused to allow the room's stentorian silence to impress itself on the jury. Then he said, "Let us be perfectly clear, Mr. O'Rourke. Did you at any time bear malice of any degree toward this gentleman?"

"Most certainly not! We had spent many hours conversing about these fair United States. He was most eager to experience its wonders for himself, and I am deeply saddened he will never have that opportunity."

"Very well. I have no further questions." He bowed and returned to his seat.

∞∞∞

Jack lifted his eyes to the gallery as the solicitor rose from his seat and lumbered around the table toward him. The lady in black leaned against the back wall, her shifting stance evidence of her discomfort from standing for so long. A mourning veil covered her face, but he had seen enough when she raised it to pat at the perspiration on her brow to know it was the Hamilton girl. He smiled up at her, and she started in surprise. It pleased him she had come, proving what he had already surmised about her. She was desperate enough to be unconventional. To take risks. And beautiful in the bargain. Just what he needed.

He shifted his attention to the solicitor, who had stopped to scowl at him from three feet away.

"How much did you pay the boy for his testimony?"

Jack lifted his eyebrows. "I beg your pardon?"

"The police questioned the lad Robert three times in the days after the *Caroline* docked, and he said nothing about seeing the murder weapon in the earl's stateroom."

Roland Townsend shot up from his seat. "I object to this characterization of the pistol in question, Your Honor. There has been no finding of murder in this case."

The judge nodded. "The objection is sustained."

The solicitor sent Roland a less-than-friendly glare and said, "Regardless of how this weapon is characterized, the boy did not report seeing it in that or any other cabin on the ship. To what do you attribute his sudden recall some six-and-a-half weeks later?"

"The mental acuity of youth?" A shrug accompanied by a charming smile. "It is a mystery beyond explaining."

"Oh, it can be explained, all right. You have claimed to be a man of considerable means. Again I ask, how much did you pay him to commit perjury before this court?"

Roland started to rise, but Jack's indignant response beat him by seconds. "Your accusation is an insult to my integrity as a gentleman!"

"Be that as it may, I require an answer. Bearing in mind that you are under oath, I ask again. Did you bribe the lad Robert to assure his testimony?"

"No, sir, I did not. And I defy you to prove otherwise."

The solicitor turned to the jury and held out both hands as if to say, *What can one do with a liar such as this?* He whirled back and took a step closer.

"Is it not true you are a professional gambler?"

"A professional... I do not take your meaning, sir."

"It is a straightforward designation. Do you earn your livelihood at the gaming tables?"

He shrugged. "I have already told the court I enjoy a stimulating hand of cards. As do most of the other gentlemen present in this courtroom, I would wager."

"Wagering seems to be what you do best, Mr. O'Rourke. You heard the earlier testimony of two of your fellow passengers onboard the *Caroline*. They made clear their suspicion over your extraordinary luck at cards during the voyage. How do you explain your success?"

"I cannot, except to say that luck is fickle. Here today, gone tomorrow. I certainly did not cheat to obtain such results, if that is what you are suggesting."

"That is, in fact, what I am suggesting. You did not answer my earlier question. Are you a professional gambler?"

"I am not."

"This great-uncle in England whom you claim left you his fortune. What was his name?"

"William Brougham."

"And he lived where?"

"No. 50, Grosvenor Square, London, England," smiling as the significance of the address sank in.

The solicitor clenched his jaw, frustration burning hot on his face as he plowed forward. "This fortune of which you speak. Where does it reside?"

"In one of the safest places there is, the vaults of Barclay, Bevan, Barclay and Tritton's of London."

"And if we were to contact that prestigious institution, would they confirm that you are, in fact, a customer with extensive financial assets?"

"Of course. In fact, I urge you to do so."

A contemptuous sneer. "Easy for you to say given that any answer to our inquiry would not arrive until well after this trial is concluded. I have no further questions for this witness."

Chapter Three

Lizzie decided she had stayed as long as she dared. She slipped out of the gallery, down the stairs, and through the courthouse doors. The rain was heavier now, and she hurried down Broad Street beneath a parasol that was unequal to the task. She arrived at the house breathless, wet and chilled to the bone. She had hoped to find her sister still secluded in her room, but as she handed her cloak and parasol to head houseman Amos, Sarah's irritated voice called from the family sitting room,

"Lizzie? Come in here, if you please."

She sighed and opened the door into the sitting room. Sarah sat in a pale-green wing chair beside a blazing fire, hands clasped on her swollen mid-section. Her disapproving frown did not stop Lizzie from going to the fireplace and stretching her cold hands to the radiating warmth.

When she turned back into the room, Sarah pinned her with her eyes and slowly shook her head.

"You still do not seem to understand the peril of your situation. The gossip surrounding our family's disgrace is just now beginning to fade. With time, you might yet attract a husband of adequate means. But when you place yourself in common, vulgar circumstances such as a murder trial, you risk tarnishing your reputation beyond repair."

Lizzie tossed her head. "Unlike you, I am not willing to stand by while my future fades along with my beauty. Besides, no one recognized me. I was veiled the entire time."

Frustrated silence. Then, "I fail to understand your obsession with this... this *Irishman*. I admit he is handsome. But... the son of a penniless scullery maid? Surely you do not see him as a proper suitor."

"There is nothing improper about a man who rose from humble beginnings to make his way in the world. And his family connections are much more respectable than you think. If you had been there this afternoon, you would have heard him tell of his great-uncle, a very important personage in London, England who left Mr. O'Rourke his entire fortune when he died."

Lizzie delivered these last words in a triumphant tone and watched to see how Sarah would receive them.

Her brow clouded, then cleared. "Nonetheless, he is a stranger to us and our ways. And do not forget he murdered a man."

"Not so. He merely defended himself from certain harm. Just as he told us when he dined with us. Your precious Roland, or any other gentleman, for that matter, would have done the same."

"He was acquitted, then?"

"Well, I left before the actual verdict was announced. But if you had heard him testify, you would be as convinced as I of the outcome."

Despite her declared certainty, Lizzie waited with nervous anticipation for Roland to return home, hoping he would bring not only happy news but his triumphant client as well. She changed out of her dreary mourning clothes and sat with a piece of lace she was tatting until the fading light forced her to set it aside. Winter's dusk had fully fallen and the evening candles been lit before she finally heard footfalls in the entry hall.

She restrained herself, waiting with Sarah until the sitting-room door opened. Roland entered, announcing a favorable verdict as he came. Mr. O'Rouke was not with him.

Disappointed, Lizzie blurted, "Why did you not bring him home for supper? We could all have toasted his victory."

"I did invite him," he replied. "He chose to make his celebration elsewhere." He crossed to the fire, saying, "I, however, am hungry enough to eat for both of us. I trust Bessie will ring the bell soon."

Lizzie simmered with frustration all evening and wakened the next morning feeling peevish and restless. She snapped at Tilly, the upstairs chambermaid whom Sarah had assigned as her quasi-personal servant, for pulling too tightly as she dressed her hair. After breakfast, she was unable to abide the daily sitting-room debacle that passed for the attempted schooling of her undisciplined oldest nephew and returned to her room. It felt as if a thousand insects were crawling beneath her skin. She had to get out of the house.

As she came downstairs in bonnet and cloak, she heard Sarah cry, "No, James! That letter is a q, not a p. You must pay attention!"

She tiptoed toward the front door, wincing at each creak of a floorboard. She was almost there when Sarah opened the sitting-room door and confronted her, hands on hips.

"Just where do you think you are going?"

"Out. I need some fresh air. This place feels like a prison!"

Raised eyebrows. "We are not your jailers. But you must take Tilly with you if you wish to go out. Ladies do not wander about town unaccompanied."

Lizzie huffed. Returned to the bottom of the stairway and called, "Tilly! Come here!" not caring that the maid was in the midst of her morning chores.

Tilly appeared at the top of the stairs, her brown face pinched with exasperation over her demanding mistress.

"We are going for a walk," said Lizzie.

A barely-suppressed sigh. "Yes'um. Be there quick as a wink."

The day was fair but unseasonably cold, which did not stop the constant parade of the elites' carriages and open buggies from clogging the streets. The social season was at its apex. During February of each year, planters from the surrounding counties came to Charleston to indulge in an orgy of activities such as weddings, musicales, soirees, debutante balls, dances, masquerades, and parties sponsored by the town's most prominent clubs and societies. The sight brought a bitter bile to Lizzie's throat. Two years before, she had been in the midst of the fun, a beautiful belle garnering the attention of every available bachelor in town. She had missed the previous year's festivities because the family was in mourning. This year they could have participated, but Sarah's pregnancy as well as her unreasonable sensitivity regarding their recent family scandal had kept them at home. And no amount of wheedling had been able to change her mind.

Lizzie walked down Legare Street toward the waterfront, Tilly trailing behind. By the time she reached South Battery Street, fashionable people thronged the sidewalk, preening in their finery in a quest to be noticed. Lizzie did not recognize anyone but met their eyes without apology, secretly scorning their pride and arrogance despite the fact she had once been the most haughty of all. She came to King Street, where the finest shops and businesses were located, and was about to turn into White Point Gardens when she saw a familiar carriage coming toward her.

Her heart tripped as she waited for it to draw even, one gloved hand raised in greeting.

Her Aunt Jane sat on the near side, her plump face framed by an elaborate gray bonnet bedecked with ostrich feathers. Their eyes met briefly. Then, to Lizzie's astonishment, Jane looked away as if her niece were not even there. The carriage passed by in a clatter of harness and swaying springs.

Mortified by the obvious snub, Lizzie hurried on her way. Her Aunt and Uncle Hamilton owned the second half of the ancestral plantation across the public road from Rocklands. She had already surmised they were keeping their distance following the deaths of Lizzie's brother and mother. They had made an obligatory call the day after they arrived in Charleston for the season. Since then, nothing. Nor had any of their former planter friends bothered to call. She and the Townsends were pariahs among the people with whom their family had shared common interests for the past century or more. Lizzie could not even quantify the humiliation that swept over her at that moment.

She headed home, no longer interested in her walk. As she went, her embarrassment turned to anger. How dare they disrespect her in such a way? She stormed into the house and through the sitting-room door.

Sarah was consulting with Bessie about the day's meals when she entered. She sent her sister smoldering looks until she finally dismissed the cook and turned her way.

"It is not fair!" she exclaimed. "It is not my fault Nathaniel ruined us. Why am I being punished?"

"Please spare me the melodrama, Lizzie. No one recognizes more than I that you were caught in an impossible situation and are an innocent victim of our brother's excesses. And yes, that was not fair. But you will learn as you grow older that very little in life is fair. Things are as they are, and you will go mad unless you learn to accept it."

Lizzie flounced onto a settee. "I saw Uncle William and Aunt Jane today. They passed in their carriage and ignored me. Why do we tolerate them disrespecting us so?"

"Surely you misinterpreted their behavior. They probably did not even see you."

"Aunt Jane looked right at me, then turned away. It was deliberate."

A deep sigh. "I am sorry, dear. Time will change all. Meanwhile, we must try to look beyond this and trust the Lord to do His will."

Lizzie made a rude sound. "I am tired of waiting for some future deliverance. If we act like whipped dogs, people will continue to treat us as such. We must show them we are not intimidated by them. That is the only way to regain the respect we deserve."

"And how do you propose we do that?"

"We have not made a single social call in months. You and I should call on Aunt Jane at their hotel this very day."

"Oh, Lizzie, I... I do not—"

"How you have changed! You never used to be a coward."

Sarah's eyes flashed. "This has nothing to do with courage. It has everything to do with propriety and custom. And pride. I refuse to thrust myself upon people who do not desire my company. And that is final!"

"At least make Roland take me out into society once in awhile. I know you are somewhat homebound since your confinement is near, but why must I suffer because of it? The St. Cecilia Ball is Friday of next week. Roland is a member of the society and has every right to attend. Would it be so horrible for me to have an evening out and show those hypocrites we refuse to be bullied and ignored?"

Her sister rubbed her brow with a tired, defeated look. "We have had this discussion before, and I despair of ever making you understand. As of now, you elicit a modicum of sympathy among our acquaintances because of the dire situation in which you find yourself through no fault of your own. If you were to flaunt yourself before time has healed this wound, you would bring irretrievable disgrace upon yourself. I promise we shall ease ourselves back into society next season. But it is out of the question for this year. So please accept it and leave me in peace."

Lizzie rose and turned away, determination burning like fire in her green eyes. Sarah might be content to sit by and allow their reputation to rot like last year's potatoes. She was not. Somehow, someway, she would take her life in hand and make a future for herself.

Jack O'Rourke popped into her mind. Had she so misread his dark, all-consuming Irish eyes? Had her delicious daydreaming been for naught? She clenched her fists and forced back a scream of exasperation. She would think of something. She always did.

∞∞∞

Jack stopped in front of the house and took in its details. It had been nearly dark the evening he came for supper with Townsend, but now he saw that his impression of tired gentility extended to the exterior as well. It sat with its side facade nearly flush with the sidewalk, and its mortared red bricks showed early signs of neglect. The white shutters needed a coat of paint, and the long front portico sagged at one end. He walked through the gate in the high brick garden wall, down the path, and up the front steps to ring the doorbell. A wizened black man whose name he remembered as Amos opened the door.

He handed him his calling card and said, "Mr. O'Rourke to see Miss Elizabeth Hamilton."

The man bowed and bade him enter. He took his hat, gloves and cloak and ushered him into the parlor.

Jack warmed his backside at the fire, turned to check his grooming in the carved gilt-framed mirror above the mantel, then took a seat on a mahogany sofa whose red-satin brocade had faded ever so slightly. It was some time before Lizzie Hamilton swept into the room, cheeks pink from the exertion of what had surely been a hasty toilette. He had to admit the result was stunning: yellow silk morning dress with black worsted braiding around the skirt, lace at wrist and throat, and a black onyx broach above her swelling bosom. The fabric clung to her youthful body in a most provocative manner, the whole set off to perfection by her rich auburn hair, which was parted in the center and slightly puffed over her ears before being collected in a chignon at the back.

He went forward to meet her, bowing over her offered hand and lifting it to his lips. "You are the picture of southern beauty this morning, Miss Hamilton. So much so that it would be shameful for me to keep you to myself. Therefore, I propose a morning's stroll along the waterfront. Will you do me the honor of accompanying me?"

She tilted her head toward the bright sunshine streaming through the window. "The weather seems most propitious for a stroll, Mr. O'Rourke. I accept your kind offer with pleasure. Please excuse me while I instruct my maid to fetch my cape and bonnet."

She turned and went out into the hall. Moments later, she reappeared swathed in a black silk cape and matching bonnet decorated with yellow ribbon. He guided her through the entry hall, across the verandah, and onto the sidewalk, where she opened her parasol and took his offered arm.

"I must congratulate you, Mr. O'Rourke," she said as they headed southwest down Friend Street. "My brother-in-law informs me you have won the day where your unfortunate trial is concerned. Not that I ever doubted your innocence for one minute."

A sly grin. "So you found my testimony compelling?"

A deep blush suffused her face. "Well, I..."

He laughed. "No need to pretend modesty with me, Miss Hamilton. I was delighted to see you in the courtroom. It was most rewarding to know I had your support."

She abandoned her attempts at propriety, tossed her head and said, "Then why have you waited a week and more to call on me?"

The question pleased him. His perception of southern belles was not an appealing one. They tended to simper and bat their eyes, tease and then pull back in their attempt to find the biggest sucker with the most money in their quest for a life of ease and luxury. He had no use for such a woman. He needed someone who knew what she wanted and was bold in reaching for it. Who would fight and claw her way to prosperity rather than accept her straightened circumstances like a whipped cur. He sensed that Lizzie Hamilton was such a woman. Nonetheless, he knew he had to play his cards right in order to capitalize on tendencies he had already observed in her.

Which was why he had allowed so much time to pass before approaching her again. He wanted to fuel the interest he had observed during their first meeting. He wanted her eager, pliant, grateful. And he thought his ploy had succeeded.

"I have been exceedingly busy, Miss Hamilton," he answered. "I must soon be on my way, and I had much to arrange before my departure."

His words brought the expected response. In a barely-audible voice, "Departure?"

"Indeed. It was never my intent to settle in Charleston. In fact, I would probably not have spent a single night here had it not been for the unfortunate incident aboard the *Caroline*."

"But where are you going?"

"West. The American frontier offers opportunities of which you staid South Carolinians can only dream. I am no dreamer, Miss Hamilton. I pursue fortune wherever it offers itself."

She gave him an odd look. "Why must you pursue your fortune? I thought your great-uncle's death left you a wealthy man."

Damn, she was sharp. But he had a ready response. "True, but idleness is not in my nature. I crave the challenge of conquering new horizons. Any gentleman who spends his time in leisure pursuits, content to depend on ancestral wealth for support, is a depraved dullard, in my estimation."

A tiny frown told him she did not altogether agree with him, but she said nothing. They walked thus in silence until they reached South Battery Street and turned east.

"Are the streets always this congested on a Tuesday morning?" he asked at last.

"No, but the social season is upon us just now, and the population of Charleston has nearly doubled."

"From whence do they all come?"

"The surrounding plantations mostly. Even as far upland as Orangeburg District, which was my home."

"Mm-m. And what happens during this so-called social season?"

"Nothing significant," was her tart reply. "Just rank foolishness. Parties, balls... the type of thing you just described as dull and depraved."

He stifled a smile. So he was right. She had been excluded from the orgy of festivities that had been her due before her fall from grace and was bitter and angry as a result. He said no more and guided her into the large green space along the waterfront known as White Point Gardens.

A steady procession of fashionable swells clogged the pathways, which wound among towering live oaks and pretty flowerbeds of jessamine, narcissus, oleander and japonica. They looped around and up toward South Battery where it intersected with Church Street, passing a granite marker faced with a large bronze plaque. He stopped to read what was written.

Near this spot in the autumn of 1718,
Stede Bonnet, Notorious "Gentleman
Pirate", and twenty nine of his men,
captured by Colonel William Rhett,
met their just deserts after a trial
and charge, famous in American history,
by Chief Justice Nicholas Trott.
Later nineteen of Richard Worley's crew,
captured by Governor Robert Johnson,

*were also found guilty and hanged.
All were buried off White Point Gardens
in the marsh beyond low-water mark.*

"*Gentleman* pirate," Jack repeated. "What an odd epithet."

"They say he was a prosperous sugar planter on the island of Barbados when he took it into his head to adopt a life of crime. His acquaintances were never able to explain why." A wicked grin. "Perhaps he craved new frontiers as you claim to do. Take care, Mr. O'Rourke, or your ambitions will find your neck stretching at the end of a rope as did poor Mr. Bonnet's."

He laughed. "That assumes I am foolish enough to give the authorities reason to pursue me. Or to allow them to catch me should it come to that. Now come. There is a certain vendor on the High Battery that dispenses the most delightful ice cream your pretty tongue will ever taste."

He offered his arm, and they continued toward the battery promenade. After he had secured the suggested sweet, they sat on a bench and watched the harbor waters sparkle in the sunshine, sailing boats crisscrossing to and fro, several distant islands hazy blue smudges on the horizon.

He crossed his legs, folded his gloved hands across his knees, and said, "So, Miss Hamilton, I am told a rather significant ball is to take place at Hibernian Hall this coming Friday evening. Sponsored by a certain local social club. St. Lucia, is it?"

"St. Cecilia Society," she corrected.

"Ah, yes. There is rather a large amount of gossip about it in the lounge of my hotel. I believe only the most influential are invited to attend. Does that include your brother-in-law, who is surely one of the more prominent men of law in the city?"

In a haughty tone, "Of course he is a member and therefore eligible to attend. However, he has declined this year due to my sister's present delicate condition."

"And you? Will you attend?"

A cross look. "What a question, sir. I cannot attend without an escort, as you well know."

"And if such an escort were to materialize? Someone such as myself?"

Her eyes opened wide. "You?"

"Certainly."

"But... but one must have an invitation to attend."

He grinned and reached into his coat pocket, producing a gilt-embossed cream-colored card bearing the St. Cecilia emblem and made out in his name.

She stared at it, shock battling with excitement on her flushed countenance. "How did you...? I mean, you are new to Charleston. The trial... and..." Her voice trailed off in confusion.

He could have told her about his machinations of the past week, which had involved a certain member of the St. Cecilia Board of Directors and a particularly voluptuous lady of the night. Instead, he said, "Suffice it to say this is the same invitation issued to the highest of society. Legitimate in every respect. Now, will you or will you not accept my invitation to the ball?"

"Well, I must ask my sister. But—"

"How old are you, Miss Hamilton."

The question surprised her, but she did not demur. "Twenty."

"A grown woman, surely. Is your sister your legal guardian?"

"Of course not. But she and Roland are my only means of support." Bitterness crept into her voice. "I am not a gentleman who could go out as you have done and make his way in the world."

"Good heavens, I should hope not. However, I cannot believe your sister would deprive you of the opportunity for an evening's enjoyment. It is not as if I am suggesting a visit to a common dance hall, a proposition to which she would have every right to object."

Her green eyes sparkled. "You are absolutely correct, Mr. O'Rourke. She may fear for my reputation, but the truth is it is mine to polish or tarnish as I see fit. And I am exceedingly tired of cowering in seclusion because of my brother's perfidy. I accept your invitation with pleasure."

He took her hand and looked deep into her eyes. "We shall throw their snobbery back in their faces while enjoying all they have to offer on such an occasion. You have decided rightly and will not regret it."

Chapter Four

Hibernian Hall blazed with gaslight. The last time Lizzie had passed through the massive wrought-iron gates, it had been on the arm of her disgraced former beau, whose betrayal of his heritage had brought shame not only on her family but on the entirety of southern culture. Now she had an escort every bit as handsome and just as impressive in his exquisite evening clothes. Her own plum-colored velvet gown was not new, but it had been commissioned shortly before the Hamilton fortunes collapsed and was fashionable enough that she was not embarrassed to wear it. They continued on to the entrance steps.

This fourteen-year-old Greek revival building was the pride of Charleston. The front colonnade had six giant Ionic columns supporting the pediment above. They entered the large stair hall with its domed, three-story rotunda where circular balconies rose behind another ring of Greek columns. They joined the bejeweled throng making its way up the stairs to the second-floor ballroom.

The brilliant chandeliers and wall sconces, the din of conversation, the scent of overheated human bodies masked by a patina of perfume—Lizzie's head swam from her over-tasked senses. Jack O'Rourke guided her to a relatively uncrowded spot between two of the room's long windows and left her while he obtained her dance program. She took a deep breath and willed her hammering heart to be still.

It had been a difficult three days. As expected, Sarah had been apoplectic over the prospect of Lizzie attending the ball with Jack. To her surprise, Roland had not shared his wife's disapproval. Lizzie had eavesdropped in the hall outside their bedroom door as they argued the issue.

"Do you not care about our position in society?" Sarah cried. "This man is totally unsuitable! We must do everything we can to keep them apart, not facilitate their liaison."

"You are hysterical, my dear. Please calm yourself so we can discuss this in a rational manner."

"You do not care." This in a bitter tone. "You see her as nothing but a millstone around your neck, and you would do anything to be rid of her."

"Enough!" His bark was so sharp and unexpected Lizzie jumped back even though a solid wood door separated them. "I am sick to death of your whining over the fate that has befallen your family. I expended a year's income trying to bail your foolish brother out of his self-inflicted difficulties. When he lost Rocklands, I took your mother and sister into my home, gave your mother a Christian burial, and have supported Lizzie without complaint ever since. I might add that I am prepared to keep her for as long as is necessary, even if it means doing so until my dying day. So do not accuse me of not caring! I know my duty, and I shall fulfill it."

A length of silence during which Lizzie heard the soft sound of weeping. Then, a delicate blow of the nose and, "Please forgive me, Roland dear. I did not mean to impugn your character. Of course you have behaved with honor where Lizzie is concerned, and I am grateful. But she is my only sister, and it breaks my heart to think of her spending her life as a penniless spinster."

"Then you should welcome the attention she has attracted from Jack O'Rourke."

"But—but he is a foreigner. And infamous around town because of that trial, regardless of his acquittal. He is not the sort of gentleman who would assure Lizzie a life of acceptance among our social circle."

"True. But she is in no position to be choosy. And from what I can tell, she seems quite enamored of him. And he of her. If he has somehow managed to obtain an invitation to the ball, then he must have friends in high places. You would be doing a disservice to her as well as to me if you continued to stand against her accompanying him."

Lizzie's face flamed over the memory. She did not want to be someone's obligation. A nuisance whose value or lack thereof could be counted only in the funds necessary to keep her alive. It was intolerable, and she would not stand for it.

Jack O'Rourke returned with her program, and she was stunned to see he had written his name on each and every line. Her first reaction was anger. It was the height of rudeness for a gentleman to monopolize a belle in such a manner. On the other hand, she could not be certain of receiving other requests given her reclusive life of the past year and a half. Which was worse? Inviting gossip by dancing every dance with one man? Or sitting like a doorpost on the sidelines while the young gentlemen passed her by?

She gave him an uncertain look, but his return gaze was steady and intense—a simmering challenge that caused a pleasant tingle in her nether reaches. He said in a husky voice, "You surely did not think I would surrender you to anyone else this evening. You and I are going to heat this place up. And I am not referring to the temperature of the air."

She gave a slight shiver as the orchestra took its position on the raised dias at the far end of the hall. He led her onto the dance floor to an incomplete set, and they waited for the opening bars of the quadrille.

Lizzie began to notice the stares and whispered comments after the third dance of the evening. She spotted several former friends from the plantations of Orangeburg during the intermissions between dances. A few acknowledged her with the dip of a head. Her old school friend Betsy, with whom she had attended Miss Datty's Boarding School, actually smiled and waved. Otherwise, she was either ignored or ogled, neither alternative palatable.

As the evening progressed, she felt the effects of the heat and physical exertion. She had been idle much of the past year and was unused to such rigorous activity. By the time the supper intermission arrived, she was more than grateful to take Jack's arm and move toward the stairs. They had just begun to descend when a party fell in behind them. The sound of a braying laugh, as familiar as breathing, brought her up short. She turned and caught the startled gaze of her Cousin Charlotte. Charlotte's husband, Captain Riddleston, was at her side. Behind them were her parents, Lizzie's Aunt Jane and Uncle William, and their middle daughter Mildred, who was coming out as a debutante that season. All five fixed her with open mouths and uncomfortable gazes.

A jam of guests was forming behind them, and Jack pulled her arm to urge her on. When they reached the rotunda floor, she turned and reached for Mildred's hand, pulling her away from those who were continuing on to the banquet hall. She planted a brief kiss on the girl's cheek and said,

"How lovely you look, Cousin," the lie coming easily to her lips. Mildred was built like her mother, short and stout with hair the color of muddy swamp water. Her gold brocade gown was expensive but wasted on its plain, spotty-faced wearer. "I hope you are enjoying your debutante season."

The rest of the little family stood to the side, their expressions uneasy. Lizzie turned to them with a brilliant smile and greeted each by name. After a moment's hesitation, her uncle came forward to take her hand, and her aunt followed with a brief embrace. Captain Riddleston gave a courtly bow.

Charlotte had recently given birth to her second child in less than two years, and her youthful bloom was long gone. Once Lizzie's best friend, she now stared at her with ill-concealed spite. Why she should bear Lizzie any malice was unknowable. She was the one who had the wealthy husband and lofty social position. But Lizzie did not care. She would rather face mean-spiritedness than pity, a sentiment anyone would have the right to feel toward her given her present circumstances.

Charlotte said, "So you have come out of hiding at last, Elizabeth." Aunt Jane had the grace to rebuke her daughter's rude comment with an elbow to her ribs. Charlotte lifted her chin and continued, "How very nice for you." She turned an arch look on Jack. "May we have the honor of an introduction to your, er, *escort*?"

She spat the word out as if it had a foul taste. Lizzie answered with a sweet smile, "Of course. May I present Mr. A. Jackson O'Rourke, lately of Grosvenor Square, London, England?"

The prestigious address registered on her cousin's pasty round face, and some of her belligerence abated. Lizzie went on to complete the introductions, which Jack acknowledged with barely-concealed amusement. Afterward, Charlotte said,

"It is most pleasant to see you, Elizabeth. But I, for one, am eager for supper. Come, Captain."

She took her husband's arm and pulled him away toward the banquet hall. The others murmured their goodbyes and followed.

Lizzie slumped back against a massive column, the fight leached out of her. Suddenly exhausted beyond reason, she said, "Please take me home."

The last of the attendees were disappearing into the banquet hall, leaving them alone beneath the lofty rotunda. Jack stepped forward and took her in his arms.

"I have a better idea," he murmured in her ear. "Let us leave this wretched town for good. Come away with me."

She was not sure she had heard him correctly. She pulled away and said, "What did you say?"

"I believe you heard me, Lizzie."

His use of her Christian name added to the surreal quality of what was happening. He went on, "I propose we shake the dust of this infernal place from our feet and head west. You do not belong here. Your beauty is wasted in a culture that blames you for the sins of your brother. That isolates you and turns you into an old maid before you finish your twentieth year. The opportunities for someone like you are limitless. Let us discover them together."

"Now? Tonight?"

"Why not? What keeps you here?"

Speechless, she could only stare at him, her breath coming in shallow gasps.

"We can spend the night at my hotel and board the mail packet to New Orleans first thing in the morning."

Lizzie's heart was pounding so hard she feared she would faint. "I—I cannot just disappear. Sarah would be frantic with worry. I must go home and tell her. Pack my clothes... "

"Do you really want to attempt explaining this to the Townsends? Is there any chance they would understand and give you their blessing?"

He was right, of course.

"As for clothing, I shall provide for all your needs from this moment on. You will be taken care of, dear Lizzie. On this you may depend."

She covered her face to blot out his compelling image. She had to think.

Finally, she looked up and said, "Why must we rush like this? Sarah and Roland would not begrudge me a wedding of modest proportion. Afterward, we could go anywhere we pleased without a breath of scandal. But this way... Sarah's social standing would be irretrievably harmed."

"Why do you care?" He took a step back, and his expression turned frosty. "I am offering you a way out of your present circumstances. But I am not prepared to wait around while your family orchestrates some showy wedding. My plans are set. I leave for New Orleans tomorrow morning. With or without you. What is it to be?"

All the past year's humiliations rushed in on Lizzie. How often had she longed for deliverance? This was her chance. She would never again have to see the silent accusation in her sister's eyes. Or pretend to ignore the curious stares. The whispered innuendos. She would be free. Her own person making her way in the world, just as this man had done. She squared her shoulders and looked him hard in the eye.

"Let them rot in their hypocritical judgments. I am coming."

∞∞∞

The grand lobby of the Charleston Hotel was deserted except for a sleepy concierge behind the desk. Heart racing, mouth dry as cotton, Lizzie clutched Jack's arm and climbed to his room on the third floor. She knew she was breaking every rule of propriety and was grateful no one was around to witness it. Her bravado of earlier was fast disappearing. Was she doing the right thing? It was not too late. She could turn around and return home without raising any alarm in the Townsend household. Yet she kept climbing as if in a trance. Her life was taking an irreversible turn, and she felt incapable of stopping it.

Jack unlocked the door to a spacious, tastefully-appointed room. He took her bonnet and cape and hung them on a hook in the carved mahogany wardrobe. She noticed two large steamer trunks sitting side by side against one wall. He placed a light hand on her back and urged her toward them. He opened one of the lids. It was filled with female attire.

"As you can see, my dear, I have made accommodation for your every need."

She knelt beside the trunk and removed its contents. Dresses ranging from calico to silk, plain to fancy, all a bit more garish in color and immodest of design than she would have chosen for herself. Capes, bonnets, petticoats and undergarments, shoes, stockings. He had provided it all.

"This is merely a start," he said. "When we are settled, you shall shop to your heart's content."

For the second time in the past hour, Lizzie was speechless. She sank back onto her heels, stunned beyond thinking. At last she said,

"You planned this. You knew I would come."

A triumphant grin. "I am a good judge of character, my dear. I knew you were too vibrant, too irrepressible to remain behind in the life you have been living. A finer helpmate I could not have conjured had all the powers of sorcery been at my disposal. Together we are going to shake up the world."

He grasped her shoulders and pulled her up. "Come, now, it is time for bed. You look exhausted, and we must rise early to meet our ship."

She looked around the room, the canopied four-poster bed just now registering. "But... the bed. Surely we mustn't... "

"Whyever not?"

"We—we are not yet married. We cannot share a bed now."

With a gentle smile, he placed a forefinger on her cheek and drew it slowly down her neck, raising a shiver. "I shan't force you into anything you do not want to do, Lizzie. We shall lie side by side as celibate as a priest and nun should that be your wish. But it is a fact that there is only one bed. And I do not intend to sleep on the floor."

He turned her around and undid the hooks on the back of her gown. Then he pointed to the white linen nightdress lying on the bed and disappeared behind a dressing screen in the corner.

Fingers shaking, she removed her dress, petticoats, slippers and stockings, chemise and drawers, and drew the gown over her head. There was no maid to unpin and brush her hair, but a brush and hand mirror along with assorted ribbons lay on a vanity dressing table awaiting her pleasure. She loosed her hair and brushed it, then hastily wound it into a single braid and tied the end with a green ribbon. She was aware of time passing and wanted to finish before he came out. The water in the washstand pitcher was cold. She poured some out and splashed it on her face, drying herself with the linen towel provided. She scurried barefoot to the far side of the bed, the covers of which had been laid back by some unseen servant, and crawled in.

He must have been waiting for the creak of the bed ropes, because she had no sooner pulled the covers tight around her neck than he came out from behind the dressing screen. He turned the gaslight off. Soon she felt the bed give as he lay down beside her.

She turned away and curled in a tight ball. She felt his heat on her backside and nearly melted with the sensations it aroused in her. She lay there barely breathing, waiting to see what would happen. When nothing did, she was not sure whether to be relieved or disappointed. She was beginning to doze off when she felt his fingers on her neck, softly caressing in lazy circles. She could not keep herself from gasping, the sensation was so pleasurable. The mattress shifted as he inched closer, his body spooning against hers so she could not miss feeling his aroused male organ.

She and Charlotte had spent much of their adolescence speculating about the mysterious procreative process. They had seen animals in the field or around the farmyard engaging in this strange ritual, but the two girls had been unable to figure out how it all worked with humans. Lizzie had shared Charlotte's bed on her wedding eve, and Charlotte had repeated the information her mother had given her earlier, little though it was. They had giggled and painted scenarios from the ridiculous to the ethereal, but it had not seemed real to Lizzie then, nor did it now.

She tried to ignore him, reminding herself in a constant mantra this was not her wedding night. She was a maiden, and to give in to him now would be a sin of vast proportion.

Sin was not a subject to which she had ever given much thought. She had attended St. Mark's Episcopal Church with her family and been taught the Creed and the Ten Commandments. She had recited the words of confession with little thought that they applied to her because she had always regarded her personal behavior as above reproach. Now she faced a temptation that not even she could excuse away. Even so, she could not stop herself from breathing in spastic gasps or feeling the weak tide that washed over her body and made her yearn for his touch.

His hand wandered down her back, around her waist, and up to a breast. She nearly wept from the sheer pleasure the gesture evoked. Even as her mind screamed *no*, she lay still as his hand sought the bottom hem of the nightdress and inched it up until his hand moved on bare flesh. He turned her to face him. The inner voice receded into a haze of desire, and she received his kiss with a sigh of longing. There was no going back. She was lost.

It was not until it was over and she lay nestled in the crook of his arm, cheek resting on his soft smooth chest, that she realized the import of what had happened. Unease crawled up her spine. He had promised nothing would happen if she were not agreeable. Why had she not stopped him? Insisted they wait until they were legally wed?

As those heated moments flashed through her memory, she realized some important words had been missing. She bit her lip, thought about how to phrase it, then simply blurted, "Do you love me, Jack?"

A long silence. Then, "I have a weakness for all women, Lizzie. But I have never met one quite like you. You have captured my heart. On that you may rely."

It was not quite a declaration of love, but for the moment it would have to do.

"Could we please wait a day and seek out a preacher to marry us tomorrow?" A nervous giggle. "Now that I am a fallen woman, you are surely eager to make me respectable."

He absently stroked her hair. "You are respectable enough in my eyes, my dear. That is all that matters. As for delaying our departure, it is out of the question. Your sister and brother-in-law will be doing their best to find us, and we must be gone before they come looking. Now go to sleep."

With that, he released her and rolled away. Within minutes, she heard his gentle snores. A deep sense of foreboding washed over her. What had she done?

Chapter Five

The *SS Empire City* was a wooden side-wheeled steamer with three towering masts, a round stern, and a dragon head. Her two-story deck house extended from stem to stern, the hurricane deck supported by stanchions from the bulwarks to form a canopy for the promenade deck below. Lizzie stood at the bottom of the gangplank looking up, excitement warring with deep foreboding.

Until that day, guilt had been a foreign emotion to her. She had never engaged in any egregious behavior for which she needed to hold herself accountable. There had been small infractions, of course, but they had always been easily justified by whatever slight had provoked them. Now she could not avoid the knowledge she had done something wrong for which there was no excuse or expiation. She had sinned mightily. And must make it her first priority to hide that sin beneath the mantle of holy matrimony.

"Impressive, is she not?" said Jack at her elbow. "You will have all the time you wish to admire her once we are aboard." He urged her forward as other passengers jostled behind them.

This was Lizzie's first visit to the wharves of Charleston. The constant din, the rank odors, the stacks of cargo and mass of humanity moving it from place to place overwhelmed her senses. She raised a tentative foot and stepped onto the gangplank.

A uniformed purser greeted them, studied the tickets Jack presented, and led them along the promenade deck toward the stern. The after saloon was an impressive space with large inch-thick glass windows to the rear, ornamental columns with gilded Corinthian capitals, and tables and benches for the benefit of the passengers. A number of staterooms gave onto the saloon, but the purser led them past them all to a stairway leading upward.

They climbed into an even more grand ladies' reception hall. The rosewood furnishings were upholstered in purple and gold damask and included every possible appointment one would expect in the finest of hotels: settees, sofas, ottomans, Italian marble tables, writing desks. Even a pianoforte. The stateroom doors along either side were decorated with Hudson River scenes, one of which depicted the rugged Palisades north of New York City. The purser led them to this door and ushered them inside.

The room was small but elegant with a crimson carpet, white woodwork, a recessed berth on each wall draped with damask curtains, two washbasins and pitchers held in place by firm braces, and a small sofa beneath a round window looking out beneath the promenade overhang.

"Your luggage will be along shortly," said the purser. He took the coins Jack dropped in his hand and bowed out.

Lizzie eyed the two berths with gratitude. A repeat of the previous night's indiscretion must be avoided at all costs until they were properly married. That issue aside, she was experiencing something she could only have dreamed of days before, and she intended to take advantage of every moment. She turned to Jack, grinned, and said, "Let us explore."

He gave her an indulgent smile and offered his arm. They went forward past the galley and a long narrow social hall where a number of gentlemen already sat at the tables smoking and playing cards. They climbed to the hurricane deck, then descended two flights to the main deck, passed the waiters' quarters and walked through the dining saloon, off of which were more staterooms, their doors decorated with scenes from Washington Irving's *Sketch Book*. They passed the pantry and came to the after saloon where they had first entered the ship's innards.

More and more passengers were milling about the promenade deck, and the increased hustle and bustle told them the ship was nearing departure. They secured a place at the deck railing to watch. Soon a gong sounded the warning for all visitors to leave the ship. Deck hands pulled the gangplank aboard, and the ship's horn issued a series of throaty bellows. Stevedores on the dock untied the massive mooring ropes and threw them aboard. The deck vibrations beneath their feet intensified as the massive side wheels began to turn. The sails billowed. The great ship moved away from the pier, the passengers leaning over the railings and waving to those left behind.

Lizzie watched the city slowly recede. The shops of King Street. White Point Gardens and the Battery. St. Michael's Steeple. The lighthouse at the end of Sullivan's Island where she had spent so many carefree summers as a child. It was all slipping away. She turned aside, a sudden wave of panic washing over her. How did one weigh an unbearable past against an unknown future? Was she taking control of her destiny? Or surrendering it to a fickle fate that might destroy her in the end?

She became aware Jack was watching her, his mouth curved in an amused smile. She squared her shoulders, lifted her chin, and looked to the sea's horizon. The staunch pride of her native state swelled in her breast. For good or ill, she would survive.

∞∞∞

Lizzie was pleased to discover she was a good sailor. She remembered the stories about her sister-in-law's illness during her voyage from New York to Charleston after her marriage to Nathaniel. She regarded it as something of a triumph that her constitution was stronger than that of the woman who had brought disgrace and ruin upon them all.

She quickly settled into the routine of shipboard life, her only complaint boredom and loneliness since Jack spent most of his time gaming in the social hall. The ship stopped at Savannah late on the first afternoon to take on passengers, cargo and the United States mail. By the time she returned to the ladies' reception saloon that evening, they were far out to sea and completely isolated from the world she had known.

She had no needlework with which to occupy herself. Nor did the ladies' magazines scattered about interest her. She wandered over to the pianoforte and began to play a snatch of remembered music. She caught a blur of movement out of the corner of her eye but paid no attention until she heard,

"Why, it is Lizzie Hamilton!"

She stopped playing and turned to the stout young woman who stood smiling down at her. She had mouse-brown hair and a round pleasant face, but Lizzie could not immediately place her. The lady read her confusion and prompted,

"Clarice Dupre. You would have known me as Clarice Cooper of Hickory Grove."

The name registered immediately. The Coopers owned a plantation near Rocklands and had been the Hamilton family's closest friends. Their youngest daughter Clarice had married a sugar planter from New Orleans several years before, and Lizzie had not seen her since. Although never a beauty, the Clarice of old had had a rosy complexion, large brown eyes, and a compact figure bordering on the voluptuous but well within the bounds of modesty. The eyes were the same now, of course, but the rest of her bore the unmistakable look of a matron who had given birth more than once during the intervening years.

The two girls had never been particularly close, but they were of the same age and had always enjoyed one another's company. Now Lizzie was inordinately glad to see her old acquaintance. She stood and stepped into a generous embrace.

Clarice took her hand and led her to a vacant settee. Lizzie waited for the inevitable expression of condescending sympathy to which she was always subjected on encountering someone from her old life, but Clarice simply beamed at her with genuine delight and said,

"My gracious, what a splendid surprise to find you onboard! How far do you travel?"

Lizzie felt the color creep into her cheeks. How was she going to explain her presence here? For the moment, however, she read only pleasure and mild curiosity in her friend's expression.

"New Orleans," she said.

Clarice clapped her hands. "Perfect! That is our destination as well. You may remember my husband, Mr. Dupre, owns a sugar plantation near there."

"I do, indeed. You have been away from home?"

"Mama insisted we come for the season. Our first visit, as it happens. Every other year I have been indisposed at this time." She blushed. "Three babies in three years. I do not mind admitting it is a relief to be my normal self for a time."

The comment reminded Lizzie of the physical consequences of the behavior in which she had engaged the night before, and she pushed down a surge of panic. What if she were to find herself with child before they were married? Though she had little interest in the specifics of motherhood, she seized the topic and said,

"My congratulations on such a fine family. Are the little ones onboard with you?"

Clarice made a face. "Good gracious, no. They remain at home with their mammy. However, I admit I am ready to resume my maternal duties. I miss their cherubic little faces."

"Three, you say. What are their names?"

"William after my husband, Benjamin after my father, and Lydia after my mother. But enough about me. Tell me. What brings you to New Orleans?"

Here it was. Lizzie slid her ringless hands into the folds of her skirt, took a deep breath, and plunged in. "My husband and I are on something of a honeymoon trip. A one-way trip as we plan to settle in the New Orleans area."

"Marvelous! We are often in town, and you must visit us at Mulberry Hill. We shall be the best of friends, I am certain."

Lizzie was speechless to respond. There was nothing she could say that would not expose her lie. She simply smiled and nodded.

"We must sit together in the dining saloon tomorrow so our husbands can make each other's acquaintance. As for you and I, we shall be able to while away the hours in much more agreeable fashion now that we have found one another. What do you think of our ship thus far?"

Lizzie was grateful for the opportunity to steer the conversation away from personal subjects. They chatted for half an hour or so, and then she excused herself for the evening.

"I admit to being ready to retire myself," said Clarice as she rose. "Our stateroom is off the dining saloon. Sally is no doubt waiting to assist with my toilette."

She would be referring, of course, to the personal maid without whom no southern lady would travel. Lizzie was glad their staterooms were on different levels, lessening the chance Clarice would learn that, for the first time in her life, she had no serving girl to attend to her needs. They said their good nights, and Lizzie waited until her friend had disappeared down the stairs before entering her own stateroom.

She was glad to find she had the cabin to herself. She quickly rummaged in her steamer trunk for her nightdress, undressed, and pulled it over her head. She did not even bother to wash before hitching herself into one of the berths and drawing the damask curtains closed. She hoped this would signal to Jack she had no desire to enter into further intimacy until they were married. She deemed the message delivered when he came in some hours later reeking of cigar smoke and spirits, turned out the gaslights, and went straight to the other bunk. Now if her monthly flow would only appear on time, she would know she had escaped the consequences of her behavior and been given another chance to get things right.

∞∞∞

Lizzie's machinations to assume the mantle of maidenly modesty amused Jack. Late though it came, he did not mind. It had been important to take her virginity in order to insure his control over her, but he had no wish to land in New Orleans with a pregnant mistress. Nor did he need her in order to slake his physical needs. He had never had difficulty finding women for that purpose. No, he needed Lizzie for something else altogether, and he did not intend to spoil her for that over something as inconsequential as the sex act.

They went their separate ways after breakfast the following morning, and he was not aware she had encountered someone from her past until he escorted her to the dining saloon when the dinner gong sounded. As they proceeded down the long table looking for open seats, a plump, plain-looking woman raised her hand and beckoned them toward the two chairs next to her and her husband, whom Jack recognized as a Louisiana sugar planter from whom he had won twenty-three dollars only an hour before.

The planter had a slight build, thinning sandy hair, and a pompous demeanor that had added to Jack's enjoyment over besting him at the gaming tables. Now he frowned and turned to his wife, who wore a warm, welcoming smile. She said,

"Mr. Dupre, this is the couple of whom I spoke earlier. May I present Mr. and Mrs... ?" A confused look directed at Lizzie. "Oh, dear. In our excitement, I failed to learn your new surname."

Lizzie's face had turned the color of a ripe tomato, and Jack took note of her pleading look. He would have been happy, for her sake, to go along with her little subterfuge. There was one problem.

The conversation and banter in the gentlemen's lounge earlier that day had already made it clear he was traveling with his paramour, not his wife.

The planter flashed Jack a knowing, supercilious glance even as he rose and spoke into the awkward silence. "I have already had the pleasure of making Mr. O'Rourke's acquaintance, my dear. And I am happy to extend that acquaintance to his lovely lady. Please, join us."

∞∞∞

Lizzie reeled from the thoughts and emotions cascading through her mind. It was clear Jack and Clarice's husband had already met, no doubt in the gentlemen's social hall. She had not missed the subtle communication that had just passed between the two men. Nor the fact that Mr. Dupre had greeted her as Jack's "lady," not his wife. Now, however, he was unfailingly polite, rising to bow over her hand, then pulling out the chair to his right and seating her beside him.

She decided to put the best face on the situation. Calling on a lifetime of experience, she bent herself to the task of charming him with lively conversation and harmless flirtation, a skill at which she had always excelled. He rewarded her by parrying word for word, innuendo for innuendo while maintaining the overall respect any gentleman would display toward a lady. After the meal, he and Clarice excused themselves to their stateroom, and Lizzie thought she had pulled it off.

She was mistaken.

She did not see the Dupres at breakfast the following morning, but when she entered the

ladies' reception saloon later, she saw Clarice in conversation with two other ladies. Their eyes met briefly, and Lizzie smiled and waved. Clarice looked away without similar greeting. As Lizzie approached, she heard her friend say,

"Dear me, but I seem to have left my handkerchief in my stateroom. Will you excuse me?"

Before Lizzie had come within speaking distance, Clarice had turned and disappeared down the staircase to the lower level. Stunned though she was at this apparent snub, she decided to give her friend the benefit of the doubt and assume her rushed departure was due to an acute need of her handkerchief as claimed. She greeted the two remaining ladies and made small talk while waiting for Clarice to return. The conversation died away, and she moved to a solitary chair and leafed through a magazine. When an hour had passed with no sign of Clarice, she was forced to acknowledge she would not come.

The Dupres sat surrounded by others at both dinner and supper that day and made no attempt to acknowledge Jack and Lizzie. Lizzie's foreboding and shame surged. Even so, her native determination drove her back into the ladies' saloon that evening armed for battle.

A young woman of obvious talent was holding forth at the pianoforte, her expressive playing complementing her sweet voice. A sizable throng of ladies surrounded the instrument, among them Clarice Dupre. Lizzie eased in beside her, ignored her sudden look of distress, and leaned in to whisper,

"You have been avoiding me. How have I offended you?"

Clarice's eyes went wide, and the color drained from her face. She glanced around to see whether anyone else had overheard Lizzie's words. All eyes were on the performer.

Her hand flew to her brow and she murmured, "You must excuse me. I have a blinding headache and must return to my cabin." With that, she pushed through the spectators and disappeared.

Lizzie was not about to allow her to escape this time. She followed and caught up with her on the second step of the staircase.

She grabbed her arm and pulled her none-too-gently back up and aside.

"Now you listen to me, Clarice Cooper," she hissed. "I have known you my entire life and have never seen you behave with such ill grace. I demand you tell me what has caused you to treat me in such a manner!"

She was astonished to see tears spring to Clarice's eyes. "Please let it be. I bear you no ill will, but Mr. Dupre..."

Lizzie studied her. Nodded and said, "I see. Given our long history of acquaintance, will you at least have the courtesy to sit with me and explain Mr. Dupre's objection to our friendship?"

Her look of panic transformed into resigned submission. "Very well. I suppose I do owe you that."

They took seats side by side in a deserted area of the saloon. Lizzie kept her posture rigid and proud, refusing to be brought down by what she was about to hear. For her part, Clarice looked as if she would rather be anywhere else in the universe than where she was. Her eyes darted here and there, her lips twitching as if she were creating and discarding a constant stream of words. Impatient, Lizzie prompted,

"Just tell me, Clarice. Is it to do with my family's disgraced condition? Have your parents warned him to have nothing to do with anyone connected with Rocklands?"

Sincere amazement. "Certainly not. Our family has nothing but sympathy for you and your mother and sister. Surely you remember how deeply my mother regretted her own role in that business."

Lizzie knew that was true. Having befriended Nathaniel's wife from the moment of her arrival in South Carolina, Lydia Cooper felt partly responsible for failing to further this Northerner's education in the southern way of life and thinking. Had she done so, there might have been a very different ending to the affair.

"If not that," Lizzie persisted, "then what?"

"Well… it is your current… living arrangement. Mr. Dupre has been informed you and Mr. O'Rourke are traveling not as husband and wife but as…" Her face flamed. "Please do not make me say it."

Lizzie had suspected this was the crux of the matter. It was time to limit the damage done. "It is true we are sharing a cabin and are not yet married, although that will be rectified the moment we reach New Orleans. However, I assure you our current situation is quite respectable. The stateroom's sleeping arrangements are altogether separate, and nothing untoward has passed between us during this voyage. On that you have my word."

"But why are you sharing a cabin? Surely two separate cabins would be the proper arrangement."

"Of course, you are right. However, our departure from Charleston was quite hasty, and only one stateroom had been engaged. Mr. O'Rourke promised to preserve my honor, and he has done so from the moment we stepped aboard."

Not a lie, but neither was it the complete truth.

Clarice wet her lips, her expression troubled. "Regardless, you must realize it is not… acceptable for unmarried persons to occupy the same stateroom. Mr. Dupre is very much attuned to scandal and avoids it at all costs. He has forbidden me from having further discourse with you." More tears. "I am so sorry, Lizzie. If it were up to me…"

Lizzie knew well enough the power a husband held over his wife. It was one of the reasons she had been willing until now to postpone marriage. Clarice's misery was clear enough. She was a kind, gentle soul who would not willingly cause pain.

She sighed and patted her friend's hand. "Do not trouble yourself. It seems we are at an impasse that cannot be breached. I shan't bother you further."

She rose and returned to her cabin, where she remained except for meals until the ship docked at Havana, Cuba the following day. The weather had turned from warm and mostly sunny to overcast. By the time the gangplank was in place, a heavy downpour discouraged the passengers from debarking and sampling the city's pleasures. Lizzie had no desire to do so, in any case. She spent most of her waking moments reconciling herself to her plight, engaging little in conversation with Jack or anyone else. The storm persisted after the ship set sail again, and the rough weather finally sent her to her bunk with a churning stomach. By the following day, the sun was out again but the seas remained roiled, and she kept to her bunk with little will to think or move.

The seas calmed the following day, the last before their arrival in New Orleans, and she felt somewhat revived. She took food for the first time in three days and was resting after dinner when a knock came at the cabin door.

She opened it to Clarice Dupre, who darted inside, shut the door, and said in a conspiratorial tone,

"I have been wanting to come for days. Unfortunately, Mr. Dupre has taken to passing the time with me. It seems your Mr. O'Rourke is a bit of a card sharp who has used him rather badly, and he has lost more than he thought prudent. Today, however, he has returned to his old habits, giving me this opportunity to talk to you."

Lizzie was delighted to see her old acquaintance, which revealed how severe her loneliness over the past days had been.

"Please, sit with me awhile. May I ring the purser to bring tea?"

"Oh, no. I must not stay long." She sat on the sofa and patted the place beside her. "I have been thinking about your dilemma, and I believe I have hit upon a possible solution. I have made the acquaintance of a Mrs. Belfour whose husband is a minister of the

Methodist faith. She has suggested he would be most agreeable to performing a marriage ceremony onboard."

A triumphant pause. Then, "Do you not see? If you and Mr. O'Rourke were properly wed by the time we dock in New Orleans, no one ever need know you did not begin the voyage in that condition, and your reputation would be salvaged."

Lizzie's breath caught in her throat. Would it really be possible to undo her terrible mistake and regain a rightful place in polite society? Granted, Clarice and her husband would always know the truth. But unlike many women she had known, her friend had never exhibited malicious tendencies. She would keep the secret to her grave, of that she was certain.

As if to verify the thought, Clarice continued, "Just imagine. We could continue our acquaintance as I suggested when we first talked. You can visit us at Mulberry Hill, and we can share outings when we are in town. You and I can salve each other's homesick melancholy with reminiscences of our homes in South Carolina. What could be more perfect?"

Lizzie blinked back threatening tears. "Do you truly think it could be accomplished discreetly?"

"Whyever not? The ceremony could take place right here. Mrs. Belfour and I would be the witnesses. I am not certain Mr. Dupre would agree to attend, but I know once the deed is accomplished, he will have a change of heart."

Hope sent a barrage of thoughts tumbling through Lizzie's mind. What would she wear? What would they do about a ring? Most fundamental of all, would she be able to convince Jack it was the right thing to do?

Clarice continued, "Let me know as soon as you have discussed this with Mr. O'Rourke. I shall take it upon myself to make all the arrangements. But it must be soon. Either later today or tomorrow morning before we dock. Otherwise..."

Lizzie nodded. "I understand. I shall put it to Mr. O'Rourke forthwith. How shall I get word to you?"

"I plan to remain in the saloon outside for the afternoon. As soon as it is settled, you need only come out, engage my eyes, and nod." She squeezed Lizzie's hand, rose and went to the stateroom door. With a last encouraging smile, she let herself out.

Beside herself with excitement, Lizzie allowed several minutes to pass, then drew on her gloves and followed. She went forward through the ladies' saloon, passed the galley, and stopped in the doorway of the gentlemen's social hall. She squinted through the haze of smoke until she saw Jack sitting at a gaming table with five other gentlemen. He did not immediately see her. She cleared her throat, and one of his companions looked up and nudged him. His expression was not a welcoming one.

She beckoned, face aflame, and was mortified when he ignored her and continued his game of play. What seemed an eternity later, the hand concluded and he rose to approach.

Their relations over the past days had been a strange mix of polite discourse and benign avoidance. She had been truthful when she told Clarice he had been a perfect gentleman as to his physical behavior toward her. It was something of a mystery given his initial passion prior to their departure from Charleston. At the same time, she could not quantify her relief. Except for that one lapse of conscience in his hotel room, she had behaved as a lady of virtue, a mantle she hoped to retain henceforth. She put on her most determined expression and said,

"I need to speak with you."

A look of exasperation. "Really, Lizzie, can it not wait? I am in the middle of a most profitable game at the moment."

"No, it cannot wait. Please return with me to the stateroom."

He studied her, weighing her resolve. At last, he capitulated and gestured for her to precede him down the passageway. Once inside their cabin, he turned with an impatient frown.

"Now what is this all about?"

Lizzie could see he was not in a propitious frame of mind to receive what she was going to say. She smiled her prettiest and put on a coy face. "Must I make an appointment to pass a few moments with my intended? You have been neglecting me, sir."

He merely stared at her, eyes hard. This was not going well.

She grabbed his hand and pulled him down onto the sofa. Abandoning all efforts at coquetry, "I have important news to share. Surely it is not too much to ask for a few moments of your time."

A sigh followed by an indulgent smile. "Very well, my dear. What is it?"

"Are you aware my friend Mrs. Dupre's husband has forbidden her from consorting with me due to my status as an unmarried lady occupying a gentleman's stateroom?"

His eyebrows rose. "Indeed? The man is a pompous ass."

"Nonetheless, his opinion is shared by all polite society. In fact, I feel compelled to express my own misgivings. I deeply regret our... um... intimacy the night before we left Charleston. I cannot think what possessed me—"

"What possessed you, my dear," he interrupted, "was a healthy desire for physical pleasure. It is nothing for which you should feel ashamed."

"How can you say that? I am a ruined woman! And no one in respectable society would think otherwise."

"Respectable society be damned! You and I have no use for such foolish standards. We shall make our own way in the world and come out a good deal happier, I dare say, than those repressed hypocrites with all their fancy ways."

"But we cannot live outside the bounds of decency. You told me I had captured your heart. And you promised to see to my needs. All I ask is for you to honor your pledge."

"Am I not doing so? Are you not fed, clothed and housed at my expense? Am I not taking you to a new life where your natural talents will elevate you to planes never before imagined?"

Lizzie struggled to leap off the spinning circle of their discussion. "Please understand. I am grateful for the opportunity to leave a life that was increasingly unbearable for me. But you must give me the courtesy of acknowledging my concern over my compromised situation. And since I have just now discovered an avenue for rectifying that situation, I beg you to indulge me for the sake of your expressed tender feelings toward me."

He shook his head. "You are talking in riddles. What is it you wish me to do?"

"Marry me. There is a preacher onboard who is willing to perform the ceremony. If it takes place before we land in New Orleans, I will debark as a respectable married lady, and no one will ever be able to impugn my moral standing in society."

He stared at her for a long moment. "My, my, you *have* been busy. You took it upon yourself to approach this so-called preacher and query him about performing a ceremony before you even consulted me?"

"Of course not. It was my friend Mrs. Dupre's idea. But it is a good one, is it not? Hasty though it might be, we can be wed today or tomorrow morning. Then we can put any thought of scandal behind us and go forward into the future without fear of reproach."

Moments passed. Then he took her hands in his and said gently, "My dear Lizzie. I understand your current disquiet given the manner in which you were raised. But you made a complete break from that way of life when you agreed to come with me. The old ways of thinking no longer apply to us, and you must learn to adjust. Foremost, you must understand one simple fact. I am not a man who is inclined toward marriage. In fact, I never intend to wander down that prickly path."

Lizzie could scarcely believe her ears. "Never marry? But you promised! You said I would be your helpmate. That we would face the future as one. If not through marriage, then how?"

"I apologize if you mistook my meaning. I do indeed see you as my partner and helpmate. But in business, not in marriage."

"Business? *Business?*" Her voice took on an hysterical edge. "What... what on earth do you mean?"

"Have you not guessed the manner in which I earn my living?"

"I... I do not understand. Earn your living? I thought your living was assured through your inheritance."

A deep sigh. "The first thing you must know about me is that I will say and do whatever is necessary to reach a goal. It is the first principle of success in my chosen field."

She shook her head as if trying to sort his words into something recognizable. "Chosen field?"

"I am a professional gambler, Lizzie. And a skilled one, at that."

"Gambler? Are you telling me you did not inherit your uncle's fortune? That you live by tricking other people out of their money?"

For Lizzie, the subject was beyond painful. Her brother's financial decline and ruin had begun with a penchant for gambling. Most Southerners regarded betting at cards, dice and horse racing as harmless diversions for a gentleman. When practiced to excess, however, those activities were frowned upon. As for professional sharpers, they had no standing whatsoever in respectable circles.

"Sometimes I trick them," he admitted. "Most often, they are willing dupes. No one is dragged to a game of chance in chains, my dear. The lure of easy money is a weakness shared by all mankind. I merely take advantage of those natural proclivities."

"And your uncle's fortune?"

He looked at her as if she were a child first learning there are no such beings as fairies and unicorns. "I have no uncle. Much less one with a fortune. But cheer up. You and I have no need of some stuffy old Englishman's wealth. We shall create our own. It is the American way, after all."

Lizzie felt something shift inside her soul. Her aspirations of finding a new and rightful place in the traditional society of her youth had proved to be no more substantial than smoke. She must find a way to shut the door on what might have been as well as on the life she had left behind. A strange new world lay ahead. One she did not understand but must learn to conquer if she were to survive. And survive she would. She squared her shoulders, firmed her jaw, and said,

"And what is my role to be in this new venture?"

His eyes lit with admiration. "By God, I knew you would come around. As I said earlier, you will be my business partner and helpmate. Together we are going to buck the tiger."

Chapter Six

Lizzie had never seen a sight such as what awaited her when the *Empire City* steamed up the Mississippi River and docked at the port of New Orleans. The city lay beneath cloudless skies on a wide flat crescent of land formed by a loop in the great river. The surrounding waters were alive with every manner of watercraft—keelboats, barges, flatboats, brigs, schooners, sloops, ferryboats and tugboats as well as gaudily-painted steamboats laden with cotton bales and other cargo and handsome ocean vessels such as the *Empire City*. The levee and its associated wharves and quays bristled with a forest of masts and smokestacks, each vessel's flag waving in a warm gentle breeze. On the levee itself, mountains of cotton bales, grain sacks, barrels, hogsheads and every other manner of goods awaited the next leg of their journey to market. Most fascinating of all was the diverse mix of people visible in every direction: stevedores and sailors of every age and size, merchants conducting business, loafers in shameless tatters, gentlemen with their gold watch chains and satin vests escorting their ladies along the promenade. She was comforted by the large number of Negro laborers whose skin color ranged from coal black to a pale color uncomfortably near to white. Perhaps this place was closer in culture to Charleston than she had imagined.

Jack joined her at the hurricane-deck railing just as the gangplank emerged from below and settled on the levee. "All has been arranged," he said. "Come along."

He took her arm and led her down to the main deck and out onto the promenade deck, where a crush of passengers already waited to debark. She caught sight of Clarice Dupre, whose return gaze was one of disappointment and resignation. Not that she blamed her friend, who had no doubt waited in the ladies' saloon all the previous afternoon and evening for Lizzie to give her the signal to proceed with their matrimonial scheme. Instead, Lizzie had remained in her stateroom, not even emerging for the evening meal or that morning's breakfast. Instead, she had spent the time reordering her vision of the future.

She was not to be Jack's wife. Nor did he love her. To be fair, he had never made such a declaration. He had, however, demonstrated his physical attraction on the night before they left Charleston. She did not completely understand his abstinence since then, but she was determined to perpetuate that state of affairs. If he would not marry her, he would not have access to her body. As for his offer to make her his business partner in the distasteful world of gambling, she had accepted because she had no other alternative. So she would work with him, but she would not trust him. He had made it clear he cared only for his personal self-interest, which meant he would support her for as long as she was useful. Should her usefulness come to an end, she had no doubt he would discard her as he would a piece of trash. The hard truth was she was on her own.

To that end, she had decided knowledge was her best weapon. After he returned to his card game that afternoon, she had examined his luggage, which consisted of a tooled leather valise with sturdy handle and brass latches and his steamer trunk. She opened the valise first and saw a confusing array of strange items she could only assume were the tools of his trade. The trunk was more forthcoming. She rummaged beneath his clothing and found a small leather-covered box in a bottom corner. It was a handsome piece with tacks, handle, hinges and lock made of brass. She shook it and heard a muted rattle but could discern nothing as to the precise contents. She pulled up on the handle to no avail. It was locked.

She knew he carried the keys to their trunks on a ring in the waistcoat pocket opposite his watch. Had the ring also held a small brass key that might fit the box? She thought so. She lay awake that night until he returned to the cabin in the wee hours. She waited until she heard him fall into his bunk and begin to snore before leaving her own bunk and tiptoeing to the sofa where he had discarded his clothes in a careless heap. A nearly full moon outside the cabin window let in enough light for her to find his waistcoat, probe the pockets and retrieve the keys. Heart pounding lest he waken, she raised the lid to his trunk, cringing at the slight squeal of the hinges. She retrieved the box, slid the small brass lock plate aside and inserted the key. It opened readily. She suppressed a gasp. It was full nearly to the brim with paper currency. She wedged her fingers beneath the pile and felt the metallic surfaces of various-sized coinage.

She quickly locked and replaced the box, lowered the trunk lid, and returned the keys to his waistcoat. Back in her own bunk, she tried to assess what she had learned. No matter how nefarious his methods, he was indeed a wealthy man and one with whom an alliance could prove lucrative. She might not be bound for a life of honor and respectability, but in exchange for compromising her integrity, she would gain a material comfort such as she had not experienced since her days at Rocklands. For the moment, that would have to do.

Now she returned her attention to the crowd jockeying for position around the gangplank. When it was their turn to descend to the levee, she was struck by two strong impressions. First was the large diversity of languages she heard coming from every quarter. Next was the foul odor in the air. After days of exposure to fresh ocean air, her nostrils quivered at the miasma of dank river water, damp-rotted produce, horse and mule excrement, unwashed bodies, and open gutters clogged with sewage. They continued on, sidestepping the muddy areas where shells had been put down to ameliorate this nuisance with negligible effect. Small white lumps of cotton lay scattered singly or in clumps as if a snowstorm of large flakes had just passed through. Jack pointed and remarked,

"They call this the city of cotton. Most of the buildings up and down the levee have to do with the financing, storage, processing and sale of that commodity. Do you hear that hissing sound?"

Lizzie cocked her head to listen. Amidst the babble of foreign voices and teamsters' cries, she could discern an overarching and rather unpleasant sibilance. She nodded.

He said, "I am told it comes from the nearby cotton presses where bales purchased from the planters... " An image of the giant screw where the ginned cotton was formed into bales at Rocklands flashed through Lizzie's mind. "... are compressed into a smaller size by steam and hydraulic machines. Which allows more bales to be packed into the holds of the ships, thus making sale and transport more economical and efficient."

They had emerged on the far side of the levee, and the subject of cotton fled from Lizzie's mind. She tugged on Jack's arm, urging him to stop so they could admire the sight before them. A broad thoroughfare paved with square granite blocks and thronged with pleasure and commercial traffic stretched to left and right. Directly across from them lay an immense open square enclosed by a tall iron fence. Entry was by way of a three-section gate graced by four stately lampposts. On the far side of the square, a massive cathedral sent three cross-tipped spires soaring to the skies, the central and tallest of which was of a unique open-work design. Matching three-story buildings sat to either side, each of a heavy French style with Spanish arches and a mansard roof. The streets on both sides of the square had identical block-long, four-story, red-brick buildings with cast-iron galleries running the length of their second stories. It was an architecture totally foreign to Lizzie.

The square itself was a verdant delight. Evergreens grew in layered splendor around the inside perimeter of the fence. A plethora of flowerbeds preened with all manner of colorful plantings. In the center lay a large grassy circle enclosed within a crisp green hedge and transected by a pathway in each direction like the spokes of a wheel. Lizzie could already imagine herself whiling away a pleasant hour or two within those gates.

"Lovely, my dear," said Jack. "But we must be on our way. I have things to attend to once we are settled."

She already knew one of his gambling acquaintances had suggested a boarding house where they might lodge. They crossed what she would learn was Levee Street and turned left to follow the square's iron railing until they came to the next street, which was marked St. Pierre. They crossed it and turned right to walk along the red-brick building with its gallery overhang. She noticed once again the babble of languages coming from her fellow pedestrians. Strangest of all was the large number of darkies making themselves at home on the sidewalk. In Charleston, the sidewalks were reserved for the white population. Here, these impudent folk walked along as if they were the equals of their white counterparts. She had never seen so many people of their race dressed as prosperous citizens. Nor did they walk with heads bowed and eyes averted in deference to their superiors but boldly met her gaze. Some even smiled and lifted their hats in greeting. Discomfited, she tightened her grip on Jack's arm.

They passed a variety of shops and other commercial establishments, crossed Chartres Street, and continued on past the cathedral. At the end of the block, they turned left onto yet another granite-paved avenue named Royal. One block later, they came to a cross street named Toulouse, this one an ordinary dirt road still muddy from a recent rain. They crossed Royal and continued up Toulouse until they came to a three-story lavender stucco building with wrought-iron balconies and a sign that read *l'Hotel de Marie*.

They entered a small deserted anteroom. A dining room lay beyond an archway to their left. Soon a short rotund woman with an apron covering her modest attire came through the archway. She greeted them with a smile, which broadened when Jack told her they were interested in taking rooms for the foreseeable future. Lizzie hung back while he made the arrangements, the most pleasing aspect of which was his request for two rooms. He paid for a month in advance from a large roll of bills, which the woman eyed with greedy admiration.

"We have just debarked from the *Empire City*," he said. "I directed the porters to transport our trunks and other baggage to this address. They should be arriving shortly, and I would appreciate your sending them on to our rooms."

"Most assuredly, monsieur," she replied in a thick French accent. "I shall see to it straightaway."

She handed over two keys and directed them out the front door and along a narrow passageway between this and the building next door. They emerged into a large utilitarian courtyard paved in brick. Among the surrounding buildings, Lizzie recognized a stable, a kitchen, a wash building, privy houses, and a wood-frame building on the stoop of which sat two small black children. The slave quarters, she presumed.

The rear facade of the main building featured two arched loggias supported with pilasters along the entire length of the upper two stories. A wrought-iron stairway led upward. They climbed to the second story and proceeded along the gallery, studying the doors they passed until they came to Number Four. Jack opened it with one of the keys, and they went inside.

A narrow high-ceilinged room held a four-poster bed, a chest of drawers, a vanity table, a rosewood washstand, and a tall armoire. Beyond was a wide archway leading to a sitting area furnished with a small sofa, a rocking chair and lamp table, and two overstuffed calico chairs on either side of a carved box fireplace mantel. Light streamed in through tall French doors that led onto a balcony overlooking the street.

Lizzie's spirits lifted. It was no Rocklands, but it was a cozy, genteel place much more appealing than the cramped room she had occupied at her sister's house in Charleston. She smiled her approval at Jack, who returned the smile and said,

"I see the room is to your liking. I shall leave you to make yourself at home while I go out to pursue our business interests."

"Do you not want to see your room as well?"

"It is no doubt comparable to this one. I am more interested in taking advantage of the day to find a place where we may freely engage in our craft."

Lizzie was still unclear as to what role he expected her to play in this so-called craft. He had told her he would teach her what she needed to know in due time. Meanwhile, she tried not to think about it

She glanced at the mantel clock, where the time read fifteen minutes past the hour of ten in the morning. "Will you return for dinner?"

"You go down without me. And when our luggage arrives, you may direct the porters to leave my pieces here. I shall collect them when I return."

After he had gone, she removed her bonnet and gloves and wandered about the apartment, taking in any details she had missed on first perusal. She opened the French doors and stepped out onto the balcony. The street below bustled with activity, the rising stench somewhat dampening her enthusiasm for the out of doors. She was about to turn back into the room when the doors to the room on her right opened and a striking woman appeared on the balcony. She wore a lavender silk dress in the latest fashion. Her black hair was dressed so perfectly Lizzie assumed it had been done by a maid. Her skin was an exotic bronze color, raising the possibility she had come from the West Indies. Regardless, she was obviously a lady of some means and repute. She glanced over at Lizzie and offered a dazzling smile. Lizzie inclined her head in acknowledgment and went back inside.

∞∞∞

Lizzie was at odds with herself. The trunks had arrived, and she had arranged her limited wardrobe and accessories in their proper places. That accomplished, she had nothing else to do. She wandered the two small rooms, sat awhile, went out onto the balcony hoping for another glimpse of her neighbor, came back in and lay down on the bed in a vain attempt to nap. All the while, anxiety grew until it was a hard knot in her stomach. What would her life be like in this strange city? What would her role be in Jack's business? Would she be able to perform it well enough to ensure his continued care?

She sat up, nearly swooning from a sudden lightheadedness. Her stomach rumbled, reminding her she had not eaten since the noon meal the day before. The mantel clock told her it was half past one o'clock. Dinnertime.

She went to the small mirror over the washstand to assess her appearance. She had never been responsible for her own toilette, that service having been provided by her personal maid at Rocklands and then by Tilly at the Townsend house, and what she saw did not please her. Her hair had been less than shapely to begin with that morning, and now it was even more awry from lying down. She did her best to smooth and readjust it, then poured water from the pitcher into the washbasin and splashed her face. She shuddered at the jolt of the cold water, there being no servant to fetch warm, soothing water on demand. She patted her face dry with a small towel hanging at the side of the washstand and tugged her dress around from where it had gone askew, pressing out the wrinkles with her hands as best she could. In the old days, she would have changed from a morning dress into a more formal frock for dinner. Her current wardrobe allowed for no such distinctions. She sighed. One more reminder her life had changed irrevocably.

She donned her gloves, let herself out onto the loggia, and locked the door. She dropped the key into a small black velvet bag and turned toward the stairway. She descended to the courtyard below and took the passageway to the street. She went through the hotel's main entrance and into the dining room, where most of the tables were already occupied. The variety of diners, from ladies with small children to businessmen sharing a working meal, told her this functioned as a restaurant open to the public as well as a boarding-house dining hall. Her eyes scanned the room and caught the uplifted hand of her upstairs neighbor, who smiled and beckoned her over to a table by the front windows.

"Please join me," she said, waving a long delicate hand toward the empty chair opposite her. "There seems to be an especially large crush today."

Lizzie thanked her, sat, and removed her gloves.

"I am Celine Pelletier," said her companion, waiting with an expectant air for Lizzie to reciprocate.

She hesitated, somewhat taken aback by the informal nature of the introduction. Noting no wedding ring on the woman's finger, she finally said, "I am most pleased to make your acquaintance, Miss Pelletier. My name is Miss Elizabeth Hamilton."

"My ears tell me you do not live hereabouts. Georgia, perhaps? Or Alabama?"

"I live here now. But my home was in South Carolina. And you? There is a lilt to your voice as well, but one I cannot identify."

She laughed. "No wonder. We are the most unique of cities with our citizens' unparalleled diversity of background. What you hear is the manifestation of my Creole heritage."

"Creole?" A puzzled tilt of her head. "I am unfamiliar with this term."

Celine studied her with her golden-brown eyes as if she were gauging what to say. At last, "We are a very old, very proud people whose ancestry dates back to a time when this land was under French and Spanish rule. My grandfather was a port official prior to cession to the United States in 1803. We Pelletiers have lived here ever since."

That she was of aristocratic European heritage explained her refined manner and obvious education. However, her black hair and dark complexion, even more obvious indoors than it had been when Lizzie had seen her on the balcony, suggested something more alien.

"I do now recognize your accent as French," she said. "But I would more easily have guessed your family having come from Spain. Or the West Indies."

A delicate shrug. "I bear a strong resemblance to my mother. Beyond that, I cannot say."

"And where does your family reside?"

"Not far. On Washington Square in Faubourg Marigny."

A surprise to Lizzie. "You mean they live here in New Orleans?"

"Why, yes. As I said before, my family goes back generations here."

"But... " Lizzie searched for a way to express her thoughts without being offensive. In her experience, single ladies lived at home until they married. They certainly did not reside unchaperoned in a common boarding house. Finally, she settled on, "Surely it saddens your parents not to have you under their own roof."

"They are in full sympathy with my situation, I assure you." A knowing smile. "I expect you are wondering why I am here at *l'Hotel de Marie*. The truth is this is a temporary arrangement until my permanent residence, which is under construction, is completed. In the meantime, I find it a most agreeable alternative."

Lizzie was glad to see the black serving girl approach. This personal discussion was uncomfortable and, she knew, inappropriate. When the girl had taken their meal orders, the two women fell into a general discussion of New Orleans city life, Celine the instructor, Lizzie the eager student. This strange existence was her new reality, and the greater her knowledge of it, the greater would be her ability to survive and thrive. If she could count on a new friend to help her in that quest, all the better.

By the time she returned to her room, she noticed the door to Jack's room was standing ajar. He must have heard her approach, for he poked his head out and said, "Ah, there you are. I shall relieve you of my luggage, then we have work to do. I have had a successful morning and afternoon. As a result, you must be ready to take up your duties in a mere day and a half."

Chapter Seven

Lizzie and Jack sat on either side of a small round table in Jack's sitting room. He had already carried his trunk and valise from her room to this one. Now the valise sat on the floor at his feet. She waited for him to open it and reveal its enigmatic contents, but instead, he leaned back and fixed her with his compelling eyes.

"Our primary goal in our endeavors," he said, "is to put our punters at ease. They must—"

"Punters?" she interrupted.

"One of the many terms you will come to understand. In this case, a punter is a player. A man who comes to the table to make his fortune and hopefully goes away disappointed."

"If they go away disappointed, then what will inspire them to come back?"

"Ah, you have hit on the crux of the matter. A balance must certainly be struck. If we are overzealous in our, um, shall we say stratagems, we shall raise the alarm and do ourselves no good. It is a delicate dance of nuance and one with which I am rather skilled, if I may be allowed to boast. But none of that is your concern. Your job will be to act the gracious southern belle you, in fact, are and charm the very money from our punters' pockets. In addition, you will make certain the fellows are well lubricated with spirits from our patron's bar. You will also have a small role in facilitating my efforts as banker. We shall get to that in a moment. Primarily, however, you will be the distraction that allows me to ply my skills undetected."

A measure of relief washed over Lizzie. It seemed she would not be required to actually cheat these people. Granted, he would expect her to expedite his efforts to that end. But she would not be personally responsible for their fleecing. Whether Almighty God would give her a pass over this fine distinction she could not say.

Nevertheless, it brought some needed comfort as she listened to him continue with his instruction.

"Now then, our enterprise is faro, king of all card games and commonly known as bucking the tiger. This because the Bengal tiger is considered the presiding deity, if you will, of this game. Do not ask me why. It is simply the case."

He leaned down and snapped open his valise. He pulled out a heavy cardboard poster some twelve inches square whose bright colors depicted a snarling tiger crouched and ready to pounce. "Images such as this are used almost universally to indicate the presence of a faro bank within."

Confused over his reference to a legitimate entity in this less-than-legitimate context, she asked, "Bank?"

"Such it is called. And I am the banker since I provide the resources for the game." He leaned once more toward the valise and took out a beautiful mahogany box. He opened it and began displaying its contents.

"This is the layout," he said as he opened a flat hinged rectangle to its full size of two feet by one and a half and laid it face up on the table. It was covered in green felt on which a complete suit of spades playing cards had been glued and lacquered down. The cards were laid out in two rows with the ace through six on the lowest row, the eight through the king on the upper, and the seven on the far right midway between the upper and lower row.

"And this is the dealing box."

He produced a rectangular silver box that appeared to be about five inches by three inches and equal in depth. The top surface was cut away to within a half inch or so of the edge, and the back surface was open. He tilted it so she could better see the interior, and she noticed a strange contraption whose purpose became clear when he took out a deck of cards, depressed a plate sprung up against the top, and slid the cards face up inside. The tension from the bottom spring now held the cards in place so that no matter how many cards there were, they would be pushed snug against the top surface. He turned it around to show her the front edge. This one was solid except for a narrow slit beneath the slight overhang of the top surface.

"This is how the game is played," he said as he removed another small box that, when opened, revealed a collection of round numbered discs of varying colors. "These are the checks or markers which the punters purchase from me in various denominations before play begins. Each punter is assigned a different color. Before each turn, the punters place their checks on whichever card or cards they have chosen. When all bets have been placed, I begin with the burn off."

He placed his thumb on the card exposed through the top window of the box and slid it out via the slit she had just observed. "This is the soda card and is, of course, dead since its denomination has been observed by all. The next card to appear is a losing card, which means it loses for the punters and wins for the dealer. You see that in this case, it is a three. Whatever bets have been placed on the layout's three card belong to the dealer." He pulled the card and placed it to the right of the box. "The next card, which here is a jack, is called a winner because it wins for the punters. Anyone whose check is on that number keeps the amount of the check. And that constitutes a turn. Play stops long enough for punters to adjust their wagers, leave the table, or indicate their intent to sit out. Then play begins again with the next losing card." He slid the jack from the box to reveal a seven. The jack went to the left of the box, the beginning of a new pile of discards. "And so it goes through turn after turn until the entire deck has been exhausted."

"But... it seems so simple and straightforward. How... ?"

An engaging grin. "How do I make certain more funds remain with me than leave with the punters? I shall get to that in a moment. First, I want to familiarize you with the case keeper."

He removed yet another apparatus from the seemingly bottomless valise. Another hinged box opened to reveal the miniature likenesses of a suit of thirteen cards, seven near the left-hand rim, eight near the right. A wire spindle on which four button-like disks were strung in a fashion reminiscent of an abacus led out from each card. He slid all the buttons to the left and said,

"As each card is played, a button corresponding to that denomination is slid over to the right." He demonstrated by moving a button for each of the cards that had already been played in their mock game. "When all cards of a particular denomination have been played, all disks for that card will be on the right. This allows everyone to know which cards have been played and which are yet to be played."

He studied her to make certain she understood, then said, "It will be your job to keep the case during each turn."

Lizzie flushed, the sudden switch from the general to the specific catching her off guard. Still, it did not seem a particularly difficult task to perform. She nodded, and he continued.

"We shall spend considerable time practicing later, but for now you need only know the broad outlines of your role. Back to your comment about the simplicity of the game. You are correct in that a square game gives but a slight advantage to the house or banker. Certainly not enough to justify risking one's resources, not to mention satisfying the need to earn a decent living. Which is why I employ several techniques to tilt the outcome in my favor. First, the box."

He picked it up and rotated it in all directions. "This box is identical to all other dealing boxes except that it cost me ten times as much to purchase. That is because it has a very ingenious mechanism which allows two cards to pass through whenever I so desire. I merely press on this rivet..." He pointed to a small button that looked to be part of the box's construction. "... and an invisible plate on the face of the box drops so the space is enlarged enough for the extra card to be delivered beneath the top card. This works in conjunction with certain tell cards."

He removed the deck of cards from the box, squared it up, and handed it to her. "Do you see anything unusual about these cards?"

Lizzie turned them over in her hands and shook her head.

"Run your finger along all the edges."

She did as suggested, and her eyes widened. "I feel a slight projection along the right-hand side."

"Exactly. That is the tell card." He took the deck and extracted the card in question, a queen of hearts. As if by magic, a second identical card appeared in the palm of his right hand. "This is its twin. Once a deck has been counted and I am shuffling it, I use my expertise to insert this fifty-third card in with the others. I then place the deck in the box."

He did so, then began pulling cards singly through the aperture. Some ten cards later, he stopped and said, "There! Did you see the second rivet quiver when I pulled the last card? That tells me the card beneath it is one of the two queen-of-hearts cards cut with the projection. When it rose to the level of second from the top, it tripped a lever connected to the second rivet, giving me the option to play the card as usual if it will win for me or pull it through under the top card if it would lose for me. Of course, when the second tell card comes up, I must pull it through as a second if I have used the first one to my advantage. If not, I must play it straight so the number of queens shows as four on the casekeeper instead of five. It is a small benefit, but used with enhanced splits, it is enough to give me a considerable advantage."

Lizzie's head was reeling. "Splits?" she murmured.

"Yes, splits. I realize this is a great deal for you to take in, but this last bit is important for you to know. The only time the banker has a significant advantage over the punters is in the case of a split, which means that the losing and winning cards are of the same denomination. Two tens, fours, whatever. In that case, the house takes half of any bets placed on the number in question. Now, this happens in square play about three times in every two hands. If additional splits can be put up by manipulation, then my advantage increases. Do you follow?"

A weak nod.

"Very well, then. As the cards are played and placed in their separate stacks, one for winners, one for losers, I am able to place any card of my choosing in a slightly skewed position so it can be identified later. I repeat the procedure for a card of the same denomination that falls in the other stack. When I pick up the cards at the end of a game and prepare to shuffle them, I am able to strip the two cards, place them in an identical position in each stack, such as on the bottom, and then shuffle in such a way that they appear together in the shuffled deck. I mention this only so you will be aware of what I am doing. You will not, of course, ever observe me in this manipulation. If it were obvious to you, it would be obvious to the punters and I could expect a bullet in my chest forthwith. These machinations are the bedrock of my craft, and I have honed them to an art form."

He beamed at her as if expecting praise for what was, in her estimation, a sleazy, dishonest skill and one for which he should be ashamed. She did her best to summon the appropriate facial expression and was glad to see him nod, stretch, and stand.

"Enough for now," he said. "We shall meet again tomorrow afternoon for further instruction and practice. Prior to that, I wish you to spend the morning shopping for suitable evening dresses. In addition to the few I have already provided, you will need five or six to wear on a rotating basis." He went to his trunk and withdrew the small wooden box she had examined the previous night aboard the *Empire City*. He took out a number of bills and pressed them into her hand. "If more is wanting, you must let me know. You are to be as beautiful as nature and artifice can achieve. I shall join you for tea at seven o'clock this evening. Meanwhile, you may be at your leisure."

Thus dismissed, Lizzie returned to her room, her mind blessedly numb, exhaustion pulling her toward the bed. Could she perform this new role life had thrust upon her? The answer would have to wait. For now, she desired only the oblivion of a long nap.

∞∞∞∞

Lizzie stood outside Celine Pelletier's room the following morning, hand poised to knock. She had been wrestling with herself since waking about whether to further this relationship, especially in light of what she had learned the previous evening.

While taking tea with Jack, she had noticed Celine at a nearby table in the company of a prosperous-looking gentleman. He was tall and thick of stature with a full head of dark-brown hair and a well-trimmed beard. He wore an impeccable long black cutaway complemented by a colorful vest and cravat, his heavy gold watch chain of the highest caliber. The two chatted in what came to Lizzie's ears as the French language and crossed themselves in the Catholic manner when their food arrived. Throughout the meal, she saw nothing untoward concerning their behavior, noting only that the gentleman was besotted with his companion as his eyes never left her face. She assumed him to be an ardent suitor pursuing his quest for the lady's hand in marriage.

Later, however, she heard the rumble of a deep male voice through the wall separating her room from Celine's. It was shocking enough to realize Celine was entertaining the gentleman alone in her room. The sounds she heard much later in the night, however, took her well beyond any innocent interpretation of their liaison. These sounds repeated themselves several times during the night, and she did not hear the fellow leave until well beyond sunrise.

Given such obvious evidence of moral corruption, Lizzie had vowed to keep her distance from this new acquaintance. Then a small inner voice had forced her to acknowledge her hypocrisy. She herself had spent numerous nights alone with a man. Not only that, but she had succumbed on that first night to the very sin she now condemned. Celine was the only female with whom she had established even the most tentative of relationships in this strange city. In addition, her neighbor was a lifelong resident who knew the city inside and out. Did she serve her own interest by cutting herself off from such a valuable resource? Could she not swallow her pride and admit she had perhaps more in common with Celine than not?

She knocked and heard footsteps approach from within. Celine opened the door and smiled in recognition.

"Why, Mademoiselle Hamilton. What a nice surprise." She stepped back and pulled the door wider. "Please, come in."

Lizzie hesitated only a moment before stepping into the room, which was similar to her own except for a number of decorative touches suggesting more permanent residence. A dusky young servant wearing a blue-and-yellow calico dress bustled about the bedroom, affirming her earlier supposition that Celine had a personal maid to assist with her toilette, which was as impeccable this day as the day before. This realization served only to remind Lizzie of her own lack of the help every southern lady took for granted.

She had attempted to correct this deficiency that morning when a strong-looking black woman knocked at her door and came in to retrieve her chamber pot and empty it into the slop jar she was carrying from room to room. Lizzie had ordered her to stay and assist in dressing her hair only to be met with an astonished, imperious look and the comment, "Dat ain't my job, missus," followed by the wretch's immediate departure. Lizzie was still smarting under the audacity of a slave treating her in such a fashion. She had every intention of calling it to the proprietress's attention, which would result, she was sure, in the offender receiving the lashing she deserved.

Now she pulled her attention back to Celine and said, "I have come to ask a favor, Miss Pelletier. My circumstances require that I purchase a number of evening gowns, and I have not the least idea where to begin with such a mission in your fair city. I hoped you might be able to give me some guidance in the matter."

Celine's face lifted with obvious pleasure. "To shop is my favorite pastime. Of course I shall help you. As it happens, I was about to go out to watch the Firemen's Parade. Please join me, after which we shall have *un temps joyeux* with our shopping."

"Well... Firemen's Parade?"

"Oh, yes. It is quite the marvelous spectacle. Every Fourth of March, our fine Volunteer Fire Department comes out in all its splendor. It is a fitting tribute to those brave fellows who are the city's last defense against the devastating conflagrations that too often plague us. And since you did not arrive in the city in time to see our renowned Mardi Gras pageants, you surely would not want to miss this one."

Her excitement was infectious. Lizzie said, "It sounds most intriguing. I accept your invitation with pleasure."

Adequately bonneted with parasols in hand, the two emerged onto Toulouse Street and turned south toward the river. It was a glorious sunny day, but the ubiquitous malodor of animal droppings took the edge off its perfection. Nonetheless, the crowds of people progressing to and fro projected a festive mood that Lizzie found energizing.

A strange sight awaited them on the northeast corner of Royal and Toulouse Streets. A small bowlegged man with long unkempt black hair and a large moustache stood cranking a wooden box from which came tinny, ear-piercing music. On his shoulder sat a small brown monkey tethered to his wrist by a slender leather strap. As they watched, the monkey jumped down and began to dance and prance about the man's feet. Many who passed by paused to drop a coin or two into the man's hat, which lay crown down nearby. Lizzie thought to dig into her handbag for a contribution, but Celine urged her on, saying,

"We must not tarry or we shall miss the beginning of the parade."

Lizzie complied, aware of the growing throngs pushing eastward. They came to the widest street she had ever seen, identified as Canal Street by a sign on a corner building. A crush of people already stood packed along its verge in both directions, leading Lizzie to give up any hope of seeing whatever was to transpire. National flags and red-white-and-blue bunting hung from every building. Carnival-like energy fairly crackled in the air.

Celine took her elbow and steered her north behind the crowd until they came to a four-story brick building. They went through a narrow doorway and climbed a flight of wooden stairs to an inside corridor. Turned left and came to a door marked *Messrs. Girard and Laurent, Cotton Factors.* Celine knocked and entered.

They stood in a small anteroom where a pimple-faced young man sat behind a small desk piled high with paperwork. He looked up, smiled, and said,

"Go right in, Mademoiselle Pelletier. He is expecting you."

The rear wall had two doors. Celine opened the one on the left and ushered Lizzie inside. The same gentleman whom she had seen taking tea with Celine the prior evening rose from behind a massive desk and came around to greet them. He took Celine's hands and kissed them in turn, murmuring,

"At last, *ma cherie*. And not a moment too soon."

He turned inquisitive eyes on Lizzie. Celine said, "Allow me to introduce my neighbor at *l'Hotel de Marie*, Mademoiselle Hamilton. She is new to our city and has never witnessed the Firemen's Parade, so I brought her along." A dazzling smile. "I hope you approve."

He seemed to melt before the smile. "*Absolument!*" To Lizzie. "Welcome to my humble place of business, mademoiselle."

Lizzie dipped her head in acknowledgment, her face flaming as she recalled her knowledge of the intimate relationship between these two people. She wondered what they would think if they knew the extent of her awareness. Then Celine shocked her by turning and saying,

"Mademoiselle Hamilton, I am proud to introduce my paramour, Monsieur Francois Gerard. He has made his balcony available for us to view today's celebration." She cocked her head as the faint sound of band music filtered through the open balcony doors. "And it would seem we are just in time. Come."

Lizzie followed her out onto the balcony, her mind in a whirl. What was happening here? These two people behaved as if theirs were a perfectly legitimate liaison blessed by society and devoid of shame or the need for deception. She already knew this culture was far different from the one in which she had grown up, but could it possibly be so alien as to eschew all pretext of morality and propriety? She would like to have explored these issues but knew it would be the height of rudeness to do so given that she was this gentleman's guest. She turned her attention to the street below, where a great roar of approval rose up as the first glimpse of flags flying and horns shining in the sunlight heralded the first wave of the parade.

She had to admit it was the most incredible spectacle she had ever witnessed. Company after company of firemen passed by, each with its individual identity carried out in the design of its banners and flags and the uniforms of its members. Each engine had been polished and decorated with flowers and ribbons, its team of horses sporting braided manes, gilded hooves, and harnesses festooned with bells or other trinkets. Ropes twisted in complementary colors and attached to the engines stretched forward with the company members spaced along them in full regalia, their shirts and glazed hats wearing the company's identifying emblem. There seemed an endless number, each designated as an engine, hook-and-ladder, or hose company. Small black boys ran hither and yon carrying pails of water and ladles for those in need of refreshment in the blazing sun. A number of musical bands marched betwixt and between the companies, their rousing tunes contributing to the festival atmosphere.

Lizzie's attention began to flag after an hour or so. Her host had provided straight-backed chairs for the ladies' comfort, but the hard surface was taking its toll on her backside. The refreshing morning air had turned hot and sultry, and her parasol did little to protect her from the sun's relentless rays. Thus she was not unhappy to see the final company pass by and the street crowd disperse in disorganized mayhem.

She was eager to get on with her shopping, but when M. Gerard invited them to accompany him to an early dinner at one of the nearby restaurants, she could not refuse. Her stomach was rumbling with hunger, and she doubted there would be a place where two ladies could procure sustenance on their own. Besides, observing these two together for an additional period of time might help satisfy her increasing curiosity about their relationship.

As it happened, she learned very little of note, and it was left to Jack to clarify the situation when they met later to continue her education in faro. After telling him about the yards of fabric, the corded and ruffled petticoats, the shoes and bonnets and parasols and other accessories she had bought and her subsequent visit to Celine's dressmaker to arrange for the gowns to be created, she mentioned the scandalous liaison between Celine and M. Gerard.

He gave her an indulgent smile. "You have much to learn about New Orleans, my dear. You must eject all preformed notions of propriety and morality and approach the people here with new eyes. Not that they do not have their own very particular code of conduct to which people must adhere if they expect to travel in certain social circles. But there are some unique, hm-m, shall we say alliances rooted in the area's history that are generally accepted as benign and acceptable. You have stumbled onto one of them. It is known as *placage*."

A frown. "My schoolgirl French does not bring such a word to mind."

"As I said, this arrangement is unique to New Orleans. It refers to a union between a man and woman that is outside the law of marriage. They are known as *mariages de la main gauche*, or left-handed marriages. In general, a wealthy gentleman takes a society-sanctioned concubine and keeps her in a household separate from his legitimate wife and children."

Lizzie was about to express her outrage when he added, "These women are often of Negro descent and are known as *placees*."

Stunned, Lizzie thought back to her conversation with Celine about her Creole heritage. Could it possibly be that her dusky complexion reflected not a Spanish or other European background, but that of a common slave? Could a person of such refinement and beauty, a person who herself employed a black maid, be of that degraded race herself?

"I do not understand," she said. "How can a Negro, even one of such light skin as my new fr—" She caught herself and substituted, "acquaintance be so well-educated and elevated in social status as to go about in polite society as an equal?"

"I assure you, these unions are given a status close to marriage itself. The women are courted as any other young lady would be. Their families advocate on their behalf and negotiate a contract by which the lady and her illegitimate children have security for the rest of their lives."

Lizzie remembered Celine's insistence that her family was aware of her circumstances and approved them. Her statement that she was living in the hotel until her permanent residence could be built. Never in her wildest dreams would she have assumed from such statements that Celine was a kept woman.

Her mind drifted to the multitude of black people she had observed in the past days who did not comport themselves as slaves. Or even as free blacks did in South Carolina. Many dressed as ladies and gentlemen. They met one's eyes with brazen composure as they passed by on the street. Even the chambermaid that morning had met her request for assistance with insolence. This was, indeed, an entirely new world.

Chapter Eight

The remainder of that day and the majority of the next passed in a mind-bending assault on Lizzie's intellect as she struggled to master the game of faro and the role she would play as Jack's assistant. There was no room for the questions of a pesky conscience. With her debut performance but hours away, she fought to assimilate everything he said while denying the panic that hovered like a dark ghost in the shadows of her consciousness. She could do this. *Must* do this...

By the time the sun had set, she was dressed in the ball gown she had worn to the St. Cecilia Ball—could it have been just little more than a week before?—and was walking on Jack's arm the six-block distance to *La Chanceux Maison* on Carondelet Street. She noticed her companion's nonchalant demeanor, his stride relaxed, his face a mask of sophisticated charm as he nodded here, raised his hat there to those of seeming consequence whom they passed. They might have been the most respectable couple in the city out for an evening stroll before attending the theater or a debutante ball. She had never felt more an imposter than she did at that moment.

Their destination proved to be a brightly-lit place where everyone wore evening clothes and the lavish furnishings bordered, in her opinion, on the garish. Crystal chandeliers hung from the high ceiling. Seafaring oil paintings decorated the walls, and the long mahogany bar shone from prodigious polishing, the mirror behind it reflecting the room and giving the illusion of even more space. A long sideboard sat against the lefthand wall in expectation of the extravagant buffet supper that would be served gratis later in the evening. Gentlemen sat in soft chairs at a variety of tables, their card games already well underway, or lounged about the bar holding glasses of wine or other spirits, their voices rolling over her in a disjointed rumble.

At the moment, she was one of only three ladies present, if ladies the other two could be named given their high coloring and immodest clothing. She resisted the urge to tug upward on her own fashionable decolletage and swept past them without a glance of acknowledgment, a poorly-suppressed titter following her and causing her cheeks to flame. Let them mock her, she told herself. She was as elegantly coifed as money could buy, her toilette having been enhanced by the ministrations of a free Negro matron who had attended the city's elite at various times and was now hired to appear at Lizzie's door at six o'clock every evening to insure she emerged the quintessential southern belle when it was time to leave for *La Chanceux Maison*. It was not quite the same as having her own full-time personal maid, but it was better than having none at all.

Jack pushed through a pair of swinging doors at the rear of the large room and ushered her forward. He lifted his valise to a large round table to the right of the doors and instructed a hovering servant to light the brass chandelier overhead. He arranged his faro layout on the tabletop and affixed his "bucking the tiger" placard to the wall just outside the door. Soon half a dozen men were arrayed around the table, and play began.

That first night, she did not notice the sly, lascivious looks of the punters as she kept the case for each turn, took orders for drinks between games, made some inane but flirtatious comment whenever she caught the signal from Jack that he intended to use one of his sleight-of-hand moves, and kept her eyes peeled for sleepers, an additional task he had taught her to perform. This was the one honest tactic they could employ to make a difference in their profits. If bets appeared on the board that could no longer win because all four cards of that denomination had already been played, the dealer could claim those as his own winnings if he or his lookout spotted the bets before the player who had made them took them back. To take advantage of carelessness on the part of the punter was a legitimate ploy and one Jack insisted she keep in mind.

As the days passed and her faro tasks became second nature, she began to relax and take her new life for granted. She had little chance for outside activities or relationships, thus solving her quandary over Celine. They saw each other occasionally in passing, but Lizzie's late nights and midday risings precluded any meaningful interaction. Otherwise, the sameness of her nights came first as a solace, then a numbing monotony. The completion of her new wardrobe provided a fleeting excitement, and she thrilled to the appreciation she read in the eyes of her punters. It did not last, and boredom eventually drove her out and about during the afternoons, either alone or in company with Jack. As a result, she began to get a real sense of the city of which she was now a part.

She explored the fashionable shops of Chartres and Royal Streets: Woodlief's, Barrière's, Mme. Pluche's, Mme. Frey's, Olympe's millinery, Hyde and Goodrich jewelers. She familiarized herself with Canal Street, the wide thoroughfare down which the Fireman's Parade had marched. Originally named for a planned canal that was never built, its uncharacteristic width made it the city's main pedestrian and vehicular thoroughfare. Horse-drawn carriages and omnibuses brought citizens to this center of commerce from nearly every neighborhood of the city. A steady stream of wagons carried the goods of international trade to and from the port, a phenomenon that had prompted the construction of a Custom House, now an unfinished behemoth surrounded by a lacy skin of interconnecting scaffolding. She took the omnibus through the uptown suburbs and ogled the fine mansions and splendid gardens with their grassy fields and groves of live oaks, pecan trees and willows, evergreen shrubs, and blooming rose trees.

Her impressions were favorable for the most part, except for two incidents that reminded her in jarring fashion of the life she had abandoned. She and Jack were out for a stroll one Sunday afternoon when they happened on Congo Square, an open space beyond Rampart Street at Dumaine where the local slaves were wont to gather in order to while away their free afternoon dancing to frenzied African music. She had been accustomed to the weekend merry-making of the Hamilton slaves back at Rocklands, but never had she heard such primitive and frightening sounds as came forth from those strange instruments. Long, narrow, hollowed-out drums with animal skins stretched over one end, stringed instruments bearing fanciful carved figures depicting who knew what superstitious horror, clanging triangles, obscene jawbones taken from some poor dead animal and stroked to produce a jarring rattle—these made a hideous din and evoked such macabre human contortions as would never have been allowed by the white masters in her home state. Her flesh crawled with alarm, and she could not get away fast enough.

The second incident was even more unsettling in that it raised the first doubt she had ever experienced about the economic and social foundations of southern culture. She was walking along the balconied arcade that faced the block-long, four-story St. Louis Hotel, also known as the City Exchange Hotel, when she noticed a cacophony of sound coming through the open doors. The stream of people going into and out of the hotel piqued her curiosity, and she went inside.

She was in a beautiful domed rotunda framed by archways supported by squat marble pillars. The bedlam all around quickly overwhelmed any aesthetic virtues she might have observed. Masses of people milled from arch to arch, where auctioneers were attempting to sell their wares by outshouting their competitors, resulting in a din of unholy proportion. All manner of merchandise was being presented, but the blocks receiving the most attention were those where slaves were being sold. Transfixed, she moved to the nearest one where a family of four—husband, wife and two boys aged nine and six—stood on the raised dias while the auctioneer proclaimed their skills and physical virtues in English, then in French.

The sight was foreign to her. Nearly all of Rocklands' servants had been lifelong residents who passed down from her grandfather and father to her brother. She knew the occasional miscreant had been sent away to be sold or punished at the whipping barn in Charleston, but for the most part, discipline had been handled on the farm, and the entire property had functioned in peaceful harmony. It had never occurred to her to wonder how slaves were acquired to begin with or what happened when they were sent away. She had certainly never seen them auctioned off like so many head of livestock.

Interested parties were poking and prodding the current merchandise, opening mouths to inspect teeth and gums, squeezing arms to test muscle strength, examining feet and hands and backs for telltale scars that would indicate rebelliousness. Through it all, the four stood stoic, their faces impassive, their eyes fixed afar, their jaws bunching whenever a particularly intrusive pawing occurred. She watched until they had been sold, each to a different buyer. Witnessed their anguished cries and desperate clinging as they were pried apart and taken away. They had been a family. Now they were—what?

She swallowed the bile that rose to her throat. It was the way of the world, was it not? Their world, at any rate. And these four were, after all, only Negroes whose sensibilities and emotions were not as keen as those of whites. They would get over their moment of sadness and make new connections in their new homes. They would be cared for and would thrive so long as they were obedient and hard working. Why, then, did she carry the sound of their weeping with her when she turned away and went out into the street?

The incident lingered in her mind for days afterward, her attempts at rationalization useless until a new catastrophe drove all other thought away. It began about the time of the fire. She had been noticing an unusual weariness of late, so much so that she had difficulty staying awake at her faro duties. Yet once home, she often could not sleep due to a strange unsettling of her stomach. In the wee hours of Thursday, March 16, she was drawn out of a fitful sleep by the persistent wild peeling of church bells. She rushed out onto her front balcony in time to see several men emerge from doorways below and race down the street pulling their suspenders over their shirts. She sniffed and detected a faint odor of smoke but saw nothing to indicate the direction from which it came. Fire was a danger never to be taken lightly, and prudence drew her back inside and out to the courtyard loggia, where she saw an eery orange glow in the sky to the southwest. It appeared to be far enough distant that she need not worry about being in immediate peril, but the odor of char and smoke was stronger on the loggia, and her stomach rebelled. She leaned over the railing and lost what little she had eaten at the buffet supper the evening before. Horrified, she retreated into her room before anyone could attribute the resultant disgorgement to her.

The odors grew stronger as the night progressed. She closed her balcony doors against them, but it did little good. By morning, she had vomited several more times, although there was little left in her stomach to come up, and she lay in a heap of misery.

She improved as the day progressed and was able to take tea and a light meal in the early afternoon. While she ate, she read that morning's article in the New Orleans Picayune describing the fire. It had been a dire affair destroying thirteen fine brick buildings near the intersection of Magazine and Natchez Streets. One brave fireman had lost his life when a wall collapsed on him, and a number of others were badly injured. The financial losses were in the hundreds of thousands of dollars.

The fire was the prime subject of discussion at the faro table that night, but its only residual for Lizzie was her peculiar physical response to the odors she had experienced. In addition to these, she was noticing other troubling signs that indicated something strange was happening to her body. Her queasiness at various times of the day, her excessive tiredness, swelling and discomfort in certain unmentionable parts of her body—a suspicion was building that she fought to ignore. It was not true. Could *not* be true.

She had never paid much attention to the female rhythms of her body, but as each day passed, she was acutely aware that her monthly flow was overdue. She looked for the telltale stains each time she availed herself of the necessary facilities. Each time she was disappointed. Finally, she was forced to confront the possibility that she was with child.

Her common sense railed against the notion. One indiscretion. A mere matter of minutes before it was over. How could this have resulted in the beginnings of a baby? She remembered her former sister-in-law and the months and months during which she had prayed for a child to no avail. Lizzie knew it had not been for lack of trying. Sounds carried throughout the old house at Rocklands, and she knew her brother had been diligent in his visits to his wife's bed. No, it not only made no sense, it was grossly unfair. Was God punishing her for her years of cavalier refusal to acknowledge His power and influence over her life? Was He mocking her lifelong belief that she could control her own destiny without any help from Him, thank you very much?

Whatever the reason, she knew it was now her problem and hers alone. She considered telling Jack and demanding he do the right thing. What she knew of him and his lack of moral virtues quickly disabused her of the notion. If he had a true gentleman's honor, he would have married her before bringing her on this venture. No, she could more readily believe he would abandon her on the spot than that he would take sympathy with her plight and make an honest woman of her. She must work this out for herself.

Her first task was to stop thinking of what was inside her as a baby. She recalled her three nephews back in Charleston. They had become insufferable brats as they grew from infancy to youth, but in the beginning, they had been adorable beyond compare. She could feel the warmth of their little bodies as she had cradled them against her. But they had not begun that way in their mother's womb. They had been nothing but a glob of bloody matter, something she had once seen firsthand. She had been quite young, probably no more than twelve or thirteen, when she happened onto a grotesque scene in the basement weaving room. A servant not much older than she lay on the floor attended by Aunt Josephine, the plantation's slave nurse, and Lizzie's mother, who shooed her away but not before she saw the mess that she later learned was the remains of a baby that had been expelled before its time. She owed no sentiment or allegiance to an obscene mass such as that. A mass she must shed from her body as soon as possible. But how?

There was but one person she could think of who might have the answer. She made a point of appearing in the hotel's dining hall at dinnertime on the following Monday even though the smell of the prepared food made her stomach churn with nausea. She spotted Celine alone at a table by the window and went toward her, praying she could make it before her stomach rebelled.

Her neighbor offered a genuine smile and said, "Mademoiselle, how good to see you! Please join me."

Lizzie grasped a chair back and said through gritted teeth, "Thank you, but I am feeling unwell. I merely wanted to inquire whether you and I might have a private word this afternoon. At your leisure, of course."

Concern clouded Celine's beautiful face. "Of course. I shall come to your room immediately following my meal."

Lizzie thanked her and retreated. When they were seated later on either side of the fireplace in her sitting room, Celine gave her a piercing look and said, "I see you are in difficulty. Your pale complexion, the dark patches beneath your eyes, the gaunt hollows of your cheeks—what is troubling you, my dear friend?"

The time for prevarication was over. "I am with child."

No judgment. No condemnation. Simply, "Ah. The gentleman next door?"

Lizzie had never spoken of Jack or their business arrangement, but Celine had no doubt seen them coming and going in each other's company. Nor did she feel compelled to explain things now. She merely nodded.

"Am I to assume you do not wish to carry the child to the end?"

Another nod.

"Well, then, I believe I can help you. May I have pen and paper?"

Lizzie rose to acquire the necessary implements. Celine dipped the pen in ink and scratched something out, then handed it to Lizzie. It read: Madame Laurence, No. 501 Marigny Street.

"This person," said Lizzie. "She knows how to, uh, bring my female parts back to their normal state?"

"Without a doubt. There will be a fee, of course, but it should not be exorbitant."

A fee. Lizzie mentally counted her earnings, which Jack doled out in regular if less than generous increments. Would it be enough?

"You have used her... services yourself?" she asked.

"Oh, my, no. M. Gerard has contracted to recognize and care for any children we might have together. I look forward to a large and happy family in the home he is now preparing for us."

Impotent anger surged over Lizzie. This person and her illicit lover were flaunting every depravity known to humankind, behavior that should result in disgrace and isolation from decent society. Yet here she was, expressing confidence in a secure future free from want or recrimination. It was not fair!

She jumped to her feet, fingers closing on the slip of paper and crushing it.

"Thank you, Miss Pelletier. I am grateful for your suggestion."

The soft brown eyes held hers for a time, weighing, assessing. Was that pity she read in them? Then she rose with grace, tipped her head, and said, "You are most welcome, mademoiselle. If I can be of further service, do not hesitate to ask."

And with that, she was gone.

∞∞∞

Lizzie made the required journey the following afternoon. She said nothing to Jack, but she had begun to suspect he already knew of her condition. There was a hard, speculative gleam in his eye when he looked at her these days. He commented on her pallor and the manner in which her new gowns seemed to hang on her shrunken frame. He insisted she eat at the evening buffets at *La Chanceux Maison* and no doubt observed how often she had to excuse herself afterward to allow her stomach to purge. She had managed to keep the subject at bay thus far, but she knew that would not last. She also knew he would turn her out if she did not get the matter under control, and soon.

Madame Laurence had a surprisingly respectable appearance—tall, plump but well corseted, and fashionably dressed. She offered tea and cakes, fetched her wretched pills without a trace of rebuke, and instructed Lizzie as to their use.

"In addition," she said, "you must take a tea made from these tansy leaves twice daily." She handed across another white paper packet. "If you are diligent, you should see your problem resolved within a few days. If not, there are other techniques we can employ. But I warn you, they are not pleasant. Your best hope of a full recovery lies with the medicine I have supplied."

When it came time for payment, Lizzie was relieved to find she had enough funds to satisfy. She tucked her purchases into her handbag and hurried home to begin her treatments.

Her symptoms began the next afternoon—bleeding, slow at first and then in a great rush, accompanied by intense abdominal cramping. She either crouched over the chamber pot or lay curled in a ball next to it, holding her belly, moaning and weeping and wishing she were dead. When the maid came to coif her hair, she sent her away and begged her to inform the gentleman in Room Five that she was unwell and would not be accompanying him that evening. A short time later, Jack knocked on the door to inquire if she needed anything. That he made no further specific inquiry told her he was aware of what she was going through and approved. *Damn his soul to hell!*

By the following morning, she was incredibly weak, but it was over. She spent the remainder of the day and night in bed. Again, Jack did not question her disability and simply told her to sleep as long as she needed. She rose the next morning, did her best to clean up after herself, and gave the chamber servant fifty cents to take away the bloody towels and bring fresh. She went down to the dining hall and ate a hearty breakfast. By the time evening approached, she was ready to resume her duties. It was not much of a life, but it was hers. How long it would last was something she could not, thankfully, know.

Chapter Nine

Lizzie had difficulty dealing with her roiling emotions over the following days. Her relief over having escaped disgrace soon dissipated like a dream on awakening. In its wake came a dragging lethargy and frequent fits of weeping. She felt empty, bereft, as if a part of her had died. She told herself it was an understandable reaction to her ordeal. A potential life may have been snuffed out, but she had done what had to be done. If she had carried the child to birth, both of them would have been societal outcasts, shunned by all, begging for bread on the street corners, perhaps dying in some gutter of disease and malnutrition. Not even God could fault her for preventing such a horrific outcome, could He?

She was surprised to find thoughts of the Almighty worming their way more and more into her daily consciousness. She had always taken His love for granted as taught in Scripture, never dwelling on the other, darker side of the equation—His wrath over sin and disobedience. Indeed, she had never even considered herself a sinful person. She had obeyed all the rules of her culture and been rewarded with a life of ease and security. Now, she had broken convention on so many levels she could not even fathom how He must view her. Would He continue to protect her going forward in light of her recent behavior? Or would she be cast into Satan's clutches to do with as that demonic being pleased?

The uncertainty of what lay ahead nearly drove her mad. Jack would care for her as long as she was useful to him, but if their partnership should ever fail, what would become of her then? Even though she had been happy to postpone it as long as possible, she had always expected to eventually marry, establish a proper, well-bred home, and populate it with children. But what decent gentleman would have her now? She was still confident enough of her feminine wiles to believe she could draw someone's interest, but that was never enough. She had no family to support and vouch for her. No dowry to cinch the deal. Even if she were able to finagle an engagement based on her personage alone, her lack of chastity would become apparent on her wedding night. Could she devise an acceptable story to explain her loss of virginity? Or would her husband put her aside forthwith.

She thought of Celine Pelletier and the arrangement between her family and her paramour. Even if Lizzie were offered the opportunity, would she be content to live a life in the shadows of legitimate society? Would she even be found acceptable for such a role? She was not an unsullied maiden as Celine most likely had been. And she was pure of race, white through and through. Would something she had always taken as a fact of pride be a deterrent even to that type of liaison? What an upside-down world she was living in!

With these confusing thoughts swirling through her mind, she went about her daily routine like an automaton, only minimally aware that the conversation around the faro table dwelt increasingly on the upcoming city election. As far as she was able to determine, current local politics were deeply fractured between those who wished to reform the city's moral climate and those who favored the status quo. The reformers were gaining traction and had thrown their support behind a candidate by the name of John L. Lewis. As a southern traditionalist with lifelong ties to the legal and justice system, he was deeply skeptical of the gambling industry and was ever watchful for evidence of fraud in order to further constrain its practitioners.

Then, three days prior to the election, the candidate paid the house a visit. Play was proceeding as usual in the faro den when a sudden silence in the front room told Lizzie something out of the ordinary had happened. Within moments, the normal din resumed tinged with a new edge of excitement. The punters around the table exchanged puzzled glances and took their earliest opportunity to leave the table and see for themselves what was happening. Jack's eyes flitted back and forth between the dealing box and the swinging doors, but he continued to deal for the three remaining punters until the doors swung open and a tallish, middle-aged man with graying hair, deep-set brown eyes, and a military bearing came in. He was accompanied by the casino's owner, Allan Macdonald, and a small stout gentleman whom Lizzie recognized as one of the regular punters.

"Here is the man himself," said Macdonald. "Our faro banker, A. Jackson O'Rourke. O'Rourke, allow me to introduce Mr. John L. Lewis, very likely our city's next mayor."

Jack bowed, smiled, and came around the table to offer his hand. "I am privileged to make your acquaintance, sir." A magnanimous sweep of his arm. "Welcome to my humble game. Please join our play."

"Mr. Lewis has not come to amuse himself with gaming," said Macdonald. "He has come at the behest of Mr. Maddox, here."

Jack turned his gaze on the smaller man without a flicker of alarm. "Indeed? I believe I have had the good fortune to entertain Mr. Maddox at my table on any number of occasions."

"Good fortune, indeed," said Mr. Maddox in a sour tone. "In fact, much greater good fortune than any man could reasonably expect if he is running an honest game of faro."

Lizzie gasped, causing all eyes to turn on her. Color rushed to her face, and she sent Jack a frantic look of appeal.

He stepped to her side and took her hand. "Your unjust inference, sir, has quite rightly upset my lovely assistant, who has not a dishonest thought in her pretty head. If you are suggesting we run a brace game here, I should like to see what proof you have of it."

"Of course, I have none," the little man sneered. "You are far too accomplished for that. But I have played this game in many cities throughout the nation, and my experience tells me no banker pockets profits such as yours without resorting to subterfuge. If you run a respectable game, then prove it by submitting your equipment for independent analysis!"

Jack bristled with righteous indignation. "Is this how our justice system operates? An innocent man must clear himself before he has even been charged with a crime?"

Mr. Lewis stepped in front of Mr. Maddox with upraised hand. "Gentlemen, please. I have not come here to accuse or condemn. Merely to make the point that if I should have the honor of being elected mayor of this fair city, I intend to keep a sharp eye on all establishments such as this. If there is even the hint of dishonest play being tolerated, I shall close down the offending business without hesitation." A gracious smile. "Not that I begrudge any player or dealer the good fortune of honest winnings. In fact, I shall drink a toast to that very pledge before I take my leave. Will you join me, Mr. Maddox?"

The little man shot daggers of accusation at Jack but eventually turned and went with the candidate back into the main room. The three punters remaining at the table completed the current game but cashed in their checks and left before another could begin. They waited for other men to come through to them, but traffic was sparse, and Jack finally took his sign from the outside wall and began packing up before the clock had even struck midnight.

The following evening's faro attendance was somewhat diminished, but the numbers swelled to normal proportion thereafter, and Lizzie began to think they had dodged the suspicions articulated by Mr. Maddox. Mr. Lewis was indeed elected mayor on the twenty-seventh, and the following day saw a surge of excitement when former President Millard Fillmore paid the city a visit. He was greeted by salvos of artillery and honored with a parade through the streets in an open carriage accompanied by the newly-elected mayor and other dignitaries. Lizzie and Jack were just leaving their rooms to observe the festivities when a stranger came up the courtyard stairs and approached them on the loggia.

Average of build, he had curly black hair, a short-cropped beard and mustache, a high forehead, and a prominent brow over intense dark eyes. His apparel was odd—a long rumpled coat of rough gray worsted, baggy trousers, and a black bowler hat. He stopped in front of Jack, bowed, and said with a pronounced Scottish accent, "Mr. O'Rourke, if I am not mistaken?"

Jack spent several moments looking him over before saying, "Who wants to know?"

"Allow me to introduce myself. Allan Pinkerton, detective. My card..."

He handed across a small white card. Jack studied it. Looked up and said, "What may I do for you, Mr. Pinkerton?"

"A word in private, if you please. On a matter of some urgency."

Jack hesitated with pursed lips, then nodded and said, "Follow me."

Lizzie was not specifically invited to accompany them, but when she turned to follow, Jack did not object, for which she was grateful as her curiosity had been mightily aroused. A detective? She had read the English author Edgar Allan Poe's stories featuring the Parisian detective Dupin as well as Mr. Dickens's recent novel *Bleak House* wherein his Inspector Bucket solves the murder of the lawyer Tulkinghorn. However, she had never known a real-life person who called himself a detective. What did he want with Jack?

When they were seated in Room Five's sitting room, Jack said, "You are a long distance from home, Mr. Pinkerton. Your card places you in Chicago, Illinois, a city I have never had the privilege of visiting. What brings you to New Orleans?"

"I am here on behalf of the estate of an Englishman by the name of Alfred Harley, Sixth Earl of Oxford and Earl Mortimer."

Lizzie was instantly transported back to that stuffy Charleston courtroom. Jack's earnest protestations of innocence, the eventual not-guilty verdict—the incident had been tragic, but it was over and done with. She looked at Jack and was surprised to note a sudden pallor to his complexion. Had this man frightened him? The thought traveled like a jolt to her solar plexis. Her heart seemed to stop as she waited for his reply.

He quickly recovered his composure and settled his features into a mask of sympathy. "Ah, yes, poor man. You may convey my sincere condolences to the bereaved family. I am most grievously sorry the incident ever took place. If it were within my power, I would undo those fateful moments and restore their loved one to them. As it is not... " He spread his hands in a gesture of resignation.

The detective regarded him with cynical amusement. "Very kind of you, I am sure. However, they have not sent me to elicit your regrets. They wish to see you behind bars for the earl's murder, and nothing less will satisfy."

"Murder?" Jack repeated. "Surely you are aware of last month's court proceedings wherein I was exonerated of all such charges. The deceased was the aggressor, not I. When he drew his pistol with intent to shoot, I was forced to defend myself, as any man would do."

"Hm-m, so you say. However, I am in possession of evidence that proves the pistol in question did not belong to the earl as you stated in your courtroom testimony."

Jack narrowed his eyes. "Evidence? And what might that be?"

"I have an affidavit from the estate verifying that Lord Harley did not own a weapon such as was used in his murder. Nor would he ever have purchased such a pistol, which is ineffective in the sport of hunting and suitable only for defending oneself in the type of environs to which he never ventured."

Jack made a scoffing sound. "Such a statement made from halfway around the world is useless. How can it match up to the account of an eyewitness who saw the very weapon in the earl's onboard cabin on many occasions?"

"Ah, yes, the young cabin boy. What would you say if I were to tell you he has recanted his testimony in full? In fact, he now avows that it was your cabin in which he saw the pistol. He further states that you bribed him with a handsome sum to lie under oath at the trial."

"Does he, indeed? And whence comes his proof? If he would lie under one set of circumstances, then he would lie under another. Thus, his recanted testimony is worthless. Furthermore, the verdict has already been read and recorded, and if I am not mistaken, our justice system guarantees that no man may be charged a second time for a crime of which he has been acquitted."

"Perhaps. But you have not been tried for the crime of perjury, and that charge is very much alive. In fact, the City of Charleston is in the process of issuing an indictment as we speak. I am expecting a telegram at any moment, after which I shall return with the sheriff to arrest you."

Jack stood so suddenly it startled both Lizzie and Mr. Pinkerton. In a voice as cold as a glacier, "I must ask you to leave, sir. Your accusations are highly offensive, and I shall not listen to another word. If you do indeed have a legitimate claim against me, you may return at your leisure with the aforementioned authorities. In the meantime, I demand that you leave my lawful premises forthwith!"

Pinkerton nodded and rose, his expression inscrutable. "As you wish." He turned to Lizzie and bowed, said, "Ma'am," and let himself out of the room.

Lizzie sat in stunned silence while Jack paced back and forth, his agitation as uncharacteristic as his florid complexion. At last she said,

"Why would this man come all this way to accuse you of something you have been proven not to have done?"

"Because what he says is true. I did kill the damned fellow."

"Yes, but in self-defense."

"Perhaps, but not in quite the manner I portrayed. He caught me cheating and called me out for a duel on the hurricane deck the following dawn. I had to silence him before I found myself in the same predicament that sent me to England in the beginning."

Lizzie stared at him, too shocked for coherent thought. "But... but... you said..."

An impatient gesture. "I said what I needed to in order to be found not guilty. I was on trial for my life, for God's sake."

"So the pistol was yours?"

"Mine is a dangerous profession. I carry a weapon at all times in order to protect myself. The incident in question was one of the few times I have found it necessary to use it."

"And you paid the boy to lie on your behalf, just as Mr. Pinkerton said?"

"Yes, of course. Come, Lizzie. I should think you would have discarded the last vestiges of your naivete weeks ago. This is the real world we live in, not some fanciful construct of honor and duty and morality such as that with which your deluded southern countrymen cloak themselves."

The words fell on Lizzie like hammer blows. It was the final assurance that life as she had known it was well and truly gone. Her mind still reeling, she decided she might as well hear it all. She said,

"Since you are not the man I thought you were, I would like to know who you really are. Where you came from, how you happened to be on that ship from England—the whole wretched story. If you insist I must live in the real world, then populate it with a true portrait of yourself."

He studied her for some moments. Then nodded and said, "Fair enough. Where would you like me to begin?"

"At the beginning, of course. Not the version you gave my family the first time I met you. The real unvarnished story. I believe you owe me that, at least."

"Very well." He returned to his chair, leaned back, and stretched out his legs. "The beginning—that would be my birth in Ireland. That portion of what I originally told you was true. My parents and I did emigrate to Canada when I was four years old, and my father did die on the voyage over. Mam and I made our way across the border and down to Boston, where she found work as a scullery maid in the household of John Amory Lowell, a businessman and philanthropist renowned throughout the city. I was given small tasks to perform until I grew old enough to take on a full-time position as stableboy.

"Even though we had a roof over our heads and food in our bellies, I could see the great disparity between our lives and those of the Lowell children, a fact that aroused growing resentment. By the Christmas of my seventeenth year, I could no longer contain my outrage. Master John, who was two years my junior, had received a fine saddle and appurtenant tack for a Christmas gift, and he gloated in such an insufferable manner that I was prompted to cut nearly through the girth. The next time he rode out, the thing split apart and he came crashing down onto his aristocratic arse. I enjoyed a laugh at his expense, but I was soon found out, and Mam and I were banished from the estate."

An audible sigh. "That was a bad time for us. We were poorer than poor, and Mam soon died of the typhus. I buried her in a pauper's grave, then shook the dust of Boston's foul streets from my shoes and made my way to New York City. I began to linger about the smaller gambling dens. A master sharper by the name of Devlin Flanagan noticed me and tried to run me off. Being the tenacious sort, I kept coming back until he finally gave up and took me under his wing. He ran a brace room wherein any sucker who entered left without a penny to his name. When I reached maturity, he taught me to be one of his ropers."

"Roper?" Lizzie repeated.

"It was my job to hang about various public places such as hotels, coffeehouses, and billiard rooms and look for gullible, inexperienced out-of-towners who might be susceptible to a skillful swindle. I would ply them with food and drink until I had their confidence, then suggest the two of us go along to a clubhouse where I had made a killing at faro the night before. Bear in mind, Flanagan's game bore only superficial resemblance to the one you and I have been running here in New Orleans. I shan't go into detail, but suffice it to say we used tricks that would never be overlooked by the sophisticated punters we see here. In fact, those ploys were our eventual undoing. I take it as a matter of some pride that the gentleman who eventually alerted the police to our game was not lured there by me but by another roper."

"So you went to prison?"

A smug guffaw. "Hardly. I bolted for the door when the raid began. A hapless policeman tried to stop me. He got his innards sliced open for the effort."

Lizzie's eyes widened. "You killed him?"

"I did not linger to assess the damage. But he probably did die from the wound in the end. As for me, I fled as fast as my feet would carry me and stowed away in the hold of a freighter bound for London."

Lizzie felt her viscera twist with disgust. "So you have killed not just once, but twice. You even sound proud of the fact. Have you no shame?"

She regretted the words even as they left her mouth. No matter how despicable, this man was all that stood between her and destitution. She cringed, waiting for his wrath to descend. Instead, he regarded her with mild amusement.

"Spoken like a true daughter of the South. May I remind you that you had a family to feed and protect you for your entire privileged life, whereas I had none? As the great philosopher Plato once said, necessity is the mother of invention. In the end, survival trumps all morality."

Fascinated in spite of herself, she said, "You quote Plato. From what you have told me of your life, I cannot but wonder how you acquired your fine manners and seeming educational acuity."

He shrugged. "It pleased Mr. Lowell to allow me to sit in on the lessons provided by his children's tutor. I also availed myself of the family's extensive library. I understood early on that gentlemen of means did not attain their wealth by living and speaking like an illiterate immigrant boy."

"You still have not told me how you happened to be on that ship to Charleston. Were you chased out of London as you were out of New York City?"

"Ah, what a jaded attitude you have toward my acumen. No, I did not repeat the mistakes of my benefactor, Devlin Flanagan. I devised the faro system you and I use today. I also refined my sleight-of-hand skills and became proficient at other games of chance as well."

"If you were so successful, why did you leave?"

Another shrug. "Larger profit. English anti-gaming laws and the reserved nature of the populace conspired to limit my income there. That fact juxtaposed against reports of the American West's gaming mania made for an easy choice." He spread his arms. "And here we are. It was a wise decision."

"But what of Mr. Pinkerton? Are you not concerned about him following through with his threat to have you arrested?"

"He was bluffing, a skill I am quite adept at identifying. If he had solid proof of what he claimed, he would not have come to warn me. He would have brought law enforcement to arrest me."

"Then why did he come at all?"

"He could only have hoped to jolt me into incriminating myself. Thankfully, he did not succeed."

"What about the cabin boy recanting his testimony? As Mr. Pinkerton said, could you not be prosecuted for perjury?"

"As could said cabin boy. But would such a minor charge warrant the expense of dragging me back to South Carolina and mounting another trial? No, I do not believe the Charleston authorities are interested in me any longer. This man has been sent by the Englishman's heirs to unsettle me and trick me into some sort of rash action to protect myself. I shall not give them the satisfaction."

"So you intend to ignore what transpired this morning? Pretend it never happened?"

"No. I may not believe myself in imminent danger of incarceration. However, it is true that my credibility has been compromised here. I have no doubt Mr. Pinkerton will spread his pernicious rumors about town. Given the warning we received from the new mayor just days ago, I believe it is time for us to depart New Orleans."

Chapter Ten

They boarded the *Princess* in a light drizzle at six o'clock on the morning of the last day of March. River steamboats such as this were a common sight along the levy, being essential to the disbursement of the myriad goods that came into the city. Lizzie had never expected to sail on one.

The arrangements had been hastily made. Jack had visited a number of vessels before he found a captain agreeable to the terms he presented. Once the bargain was sealed, they had packed their belongings and left the boarding house without so much as a goodbye to Madame Marie. Now here they were about to embark on a new adventure.

This boat was much smaller than the *SS Empire City* on which they had come to New Orleans nearly a month before. It was also much less aesthetically pleasing. The main deck was little more than a large open shed chock full of cargo: wagons, animals, household goods, sacks, bales, boxes, barrels, and massive stacks of cordwood for fueling the roaring fireboxes that would propel the boat. Deck passengers milled in and among these objects vying for the best place to pass their uncomfortable journey upriver. It was with relief that Lizzie followed Jack to the stairs at the rear and up to the cabin deck.

Here was a toned-down version of the luxury she had experienced on the *Empire City*. A central saloon some eighteen feet wide and twelve feet high extended down the length of the boat, a distance she judged to be over two hundred feet. There were a lush carpet underfoot, skylights in the roof to admit the gray morning light, crystal chandeliers for evening lighting, and wall mirrors to reflect the light and add the illusion of greater space. Tables of various sizes, sofas, settees and easy chairs invited passengers to pass the time of day, and several wood-burning stoves provided warmth. Staterooms lined the saloon from front to back, those for the ladies occupying the rear third with the gentlemen's quarters accounting for the remaining two-thirds. A curtain, now pulled back for boarding, separated the two areas.

Boarding cabin passengers and their personal servants searched for their rooms. Jack consulted the tickets he was holding and stopped in front of a door marked with the number five. He opened it and handed her the carpetbag he had been carrying for her.

"Your room. Mine is number forty-two at the far end. I shall see you at breakfast after we are underway."

Lizzie was glad they would be housed in separate rooms, the implied scandal of their arrangement on the *Empire City* still burning like a hot coal in her memory. She murmured agreement and stepped over the threshold into the stateroom.

The interior was considerably darker than the main saloon, which itself was not all that bright on a rainy morning. She had an immediate sense of confinement, the space in which she was to live being, she judged, perhaps eight feet square. A two-tiered bunk occupied the right-hand wall. She could make out a shelf in the far left corner on which rested a basin and pitcher. A single chair rested against the wall beside it. There were two doors into the room, the one through which she had just entered and another directly across from it that she assumed led out onto the promenade guards. There were transoms over each door for ventilation and whatever poor light there was.

She was taking it all in when a high-pitched girlish voice startled her with, "Well, and who might you be?"

She peered up in the direction from which the voice had come and saw a head leaning over the top bunk. The face was a small pale oval surrounded by hair of an astonishing flame-red color.

"I am Miss Hamilton," she answered. "I believe this is my stateroom."

The girl sat up and swung her legs over the side of the bunk. Jumped down and extended her hand. "I am Cora. Apparently we are to be roommates."

Lizzie accepted the hand, which was attached to a petite body barely five feet tall. She was pretty in a pixie-like way and older than Lizzie's initial assessment of eleven or twelve. Her modestly-developed body now suggested an age of fifteen or sixteen.

"I am pleased to meet you, Miss... ?"

It took the girl a moment to understand what she was asking. "Oh, my family name is Fielding, but you may address me as Cora. I do not believe in the silly conventions of modern society. If God is happy to know us by our baptismal names, then who are we mortals to put on airs?"

Lizzie was too taken aback by the girl's forward demeanor to respond.

Taking Lizzie's silence as acquiescence, she continued, "So then, what is *your* Christian name?"

Lizzie recovered herself and said in frosty tones, "My name is Elizabeth. However, Miss Hamilton will do for you. As it happens, I *do* believe in the conventions of polite society, and I feel quite confident our Lord wishes us to address one another with respect and dignity. Especially when discoursing with our *elders*."

If she expected to cow the young lady, she was to be disappointed. Cora simply tossed her head in a dismissive gesture and said, "Why should I be surprised by such sentiments? From your drawling speech, I assume you are from the South. No doubt a product of the misguided, slave-holding plantation culture."

Lizzie had no time to respond to this insult to her heritage before the girl heaved a huge sigh and continued, "But never you mind. We must make the best of it since we are to share this room for some time to come. How far do you travel?"

How far, indeed? A tricky question to which Lizzie had no answer. "Far enough," she said. "And you?"

Her blue eyes sparkled. "Oh, all the way to St. Joseph in the state of Missouri. We are to meet Papa and Carl in St. Louis. Then we shall all take another steamer up the Missouri River to our destination, where we shall begin our long overland journey to California. A more exciting adventure one could not hope to experience!"

Lizzie's inner self groaned. It seemed she was to share this room with a wretched abolitionist, child or no, for the foreseeable future, and she must arm herself to survive it. She turned her back, placed her carpetbag on the foot of the lower bunk and began to unpack it. The task required little effort as the bag contained only her essential toilette articles. All else was in her trunk, which would be stacked with those of the other passengers in an alcove next to the barbershop. She would need to commission the boat's chambermaid to retrieve her gowns as needed since she had no lady's maid, a fact she once again found embarrassing, although she doubted whether this radical-minded young miss would know the difference—or care.

Giving the girl her back proved useless. She continued to chatter as if she had Lizzie's full and rapt attention.

"Mama and Lilly and I have just completed a visit with my older sister, Edith. Her husband owns a dry-goods store on Canal Street in New Orleans, and they have a fine house on Camp Street near Coliseum Place. They have been married just a little over a year and already have a strapping baby boy. Poor Edith. She is quite devastated that we are moving so far away. Mama could not bear to go without one last visit, for who knows if we shall ever see her again?"

She leapt back up to the top bunk and sat with legs swinging. "You might wonder how a girl from Indiana met such a fine fellow as Otto Pickering from New Orleans. It is oh so romantic a story. Otto was traveling up the Ohio River on his way to Cincinnati to buy goods for his store when he took dreadfully ill. Pneumonia of the worst sort. The captain put him off at Evansville, and of course, Papa took him right into our home for treatment. Papa is a wonderful doctor, and sure enough, he recovered. But not before he had stolen our Edith's heart. He continued on to Cincinnati, but on the return trip he stopped again, and before we knew it, he had asked for Edith's hand."

She made a face. "Can you imagine? Asking for her as if she were a prize mare! Of course, Papa was happy to oblige, but it seems sinful for a woman to be bartered away like that. One day we shall have the vote, and then things will change!"

Lizzie sighed. An abolitionist *and* a suffragette. And a loquacious one, at that. She was trying to decide how best to extricate herself from the girl's clutches when she heard the long low bellow of the ship's horn. The deck beneath her feet vibrated with additional power. They were about to leave the dock.

"Oh!" Cora exclaimed. "We are sailing! Come, we must see every last detail." With that, she bounded down, wrenched open the outer door, and ran out onto the guards.

Lizzie waited several minutes, then poked her head out onto the deck. A crush of people stood at the railing, but she did not see Cora's distinctive bright head among them. By the time she had found a place to wedge her way through, the levy with its backdrop of Cathedral Square was slowly slipping away. She stood there until the river made a wide bend and the spire of St. Louis Cathedral disappeared from view.

∞∞∞

Lizzie sat in the stateroom's only chair while Maisie the chambermaid dressed her hair. She considered herself fortunate that Maisie had once been lady's maid to the mistress of a cotton plantation in the state of Arkansas. Her master's death had necessitated the sale of all his property, and Maisie had been bought by the current owner of this and two other river steamboats.

She was a sturdy soul of early middle age dressed in simple gray muslin and the usual white kerchief. She had a complexion the color of fresh-brewed coffee, a round, flat-featured face, and nimble hands. At first, Lizzie had despaired of engaging her long enough to prepare her toilette, but she soon discovered that the highest demand on the maid's services occurred before dinner and supper when those who had no servant at hand sent her scrambling to the baggage pile for the appropriate gown, then availed themselves of her assistance in dressing. At a little before ten o'clock, however, most of the lady passengers were either in bed or lounging in the ladies' cabin. Lizzie alone was preparing for an extended evening.

Young Cora sat cross-legged on her bunk and watched the proceedings with avid interest. She had made every attempt to engage the maid in conversation, having elicited the few details now known about her but failing in her attempt to probe beyond those basic facts. Lizzie suspected it was because of such statements as, "Surely you would rather be free than kowtow to those who are no better in the eyes of God than you," or, "It is not a sin to strain against the yoke of unjust bondage," or, "Have you heard of the Underground Railroad whereby those such as yourself are whisked to freedom? I could make inquiries on your behalf." A slave who engaged in such conversation could find herself in serious trouble. Thus, she had ignored Cora's attempts to draw her out, giving Lizzie perverse satisfaction to see the young abolitionist thwarted by the very person she longed to help.

She had seen no evidence that the remainder of the Fielding family shared this daughter's seditious views when she had sat with them at dinner earlier. The dining tables were placed down the length of the saloon for each meal, and Lizzie had soon seen that the sexes tended to segregate for this activity as they did for onboard leisure-time pursuits. Despite Jack's suggestion that they meet for breakfast, she had not even seen him among those seated at table for that meal. At dinnertime, she had seen him at the far end, but he was surrounded by gentlemen and had not even looked her way. Therefore, she had taken a seat among the ladies and had found herself across from Cora and a plump middle-aged woman whose red hair was several shades darker than her daughter's and shot through with gray. A young girl with mouse-brown hair and a pale complexion sat on the woman's far side, and Lizzie assumed her to be the younger sister.

Cora had grinned up at her and said in an altogether too-loud voice, "Here she is, Mama, the one I have been telling you about. My roommate, Elizabeth." Then, catching Lizzie's frowning stare as well as the sharp look of her mother, "Or rather, Miss Hamilton." To Lizzie, "This is my mama, and beyond her is my little sister, Lilly."

Lizzie acknowledged the introduction and cringed when Cora blasted forth with, "I see you have not brought along your own personal slave as have these other people." A dismissive gesture toward the several ladies whose maids stood behind their chairs waiting on their mistress's pleasure. "But surely you are of the slaveholding class, are you not?"

Lizzie saw Mrs. Fielding give her daughter a discreet nudge in the ribs, hissing, "Cora, mind your manners! And for heaven's sake, lower your voice."

A fake pout. "You needn't be such a grouch, Mama. Are we not entitled to know whence comes this person with whom I am to share lodgings for lo these many days? Unless she is ashamed to admit to her origins."

"Cora! You will control your tongue or retire to your room with no dinner at all." Then to Lizzie with an apologetic smile, "Please forgive my daughter. She has the unfortunate habit of speaking before her brain can filter her words. One can only hope she will learn the finer points of propriety in time."

The woman's tone was warm enough and quite sincere. Lizzie returned the smile and said, "Of all people on this earth, I can best understand her propensity for impetuosity as it was a failing that plagued me as well far into womanhood. As for my background, I am most happy to admit that I grew up on a fine plantation in South Carolina. Adversity propelled me away from my roots, but I cherish every memory to this day." She paused a moment to let her words penetrate the incorrigible Cora's mind. Then, to turn the conversation away from herself, "I understand you and your family are in the process of emigrating to California. From Indiana, I believe?"

"Indeed. My husband and Cora's twin brother Carl have been making their way to St. Louis with our belongings these past few weeks while we visited our eldest daughter in New Orleans. We are on our way to meet them."

Lizzie would like to have known what precipitated such a rash disruption in the family's life, but the conversation was interrupted by the arrival of their food, and there had been no graceful way to return to the subject thereafter. Thinking about it now as she sat beneath Maisie's ministrations, she could only assume it demonstrated a lack of appreciation for their dismal northern culture, a mind-set that would never occur to those of her native land, who held their proud heritage in indisputable regard. Yet had she not, in essence, done the very same thing by fleeing her life in Charleston with nary a backward glance?

The thought came unbidden and caused a strange twisting in her belly. She was glad to be distracted by Maisie handing her the mirror to assess her new coiffure. The candle Mrs. Fielding had thought to provide gave off a poor light, but it was enough to assure her that Maisie was every bit as competent as the maid Jack had hired in New Orleans. She was wearing one of her new gowns, an emerald green silk that picked up the color of her eyes. Satisfied that she looked her best for this debut among the boat's gamblers, she smoothed on her gloves and picked up a handkerchief.

When she rose, Cora blurted, "You still have not told me why you are dressed in such a high and mighty fashion at such a late hour."

Not for lack of your asking, Lizzie thought to herself.

The girl pressed on. "Is there a dance in the cabin tonight? If so, I heard nothing of it from Mama."

"I have an engagement, if you must know," said Lizzie. "But you are right. It *is* late, too late for nosy young girls to be awake." To Maisie, "You may blow out the candle before leaving. It is time for Miss Cora to go to sleep." She swept out of the room and shut the door to blunt any rejoinder the silly child might choose to send after her.

There were still a few ladies lounging in the main cabin. Lizzie did not miss their raised eyebrows and furtive glances. They would no doubt be deep in gossip the moment she slipped around the curtain dividing this from the gentlemen's cabin. She felt her face flame as she passed by.

Jack had caught up with her after supper and whispered that he planned to set up his faro bank in the boat's barbershop at ten o'clock and she should join him then. She was uncertain how this was going to work. They had talked about it as they prepared to depart from New Orleans. It seemed that faro was still a desired game on the steamboats, but no more so than the various other card games such as poker, Mexican monte, and ace-deuce-jack. Her role would be diminished where these games were concerned. Indeed, she got the impression he could well do without her, a suspicion that caused her some inner anxiety.

There had been no time for her to learn the intricacies of these games. He had simply explained the various tricks he had perfected to give himself the advantage. His only request was that she watch for his signal, which might be a discreet cough, a prolonged stroking of his chin, or a shift of his cigar from one hand to the other. At such a time, she was to create a distraction by calling attention away from the table while he accomplished a particularly delicate sleight-of-hand. All the while, she was to play the innocent southern belle that she was. Or had been before she embarked on this foolish adventure.

She walked with careful dignity through the gentlemen's cabin, which was foul with billowing cigar smoke. Many card games were in progress around tables littered with empty drink glasses, each table having its own cuspidor at hand for the disposal of the many chewers' tobacco juice. She dipped her head and offered genteel smiles to those she passed, having learned over the past weeks to disguise her disgust over these ubiquitous male vices. The bow end of the boat held the clerk's office, the bar where spirits as well as decks of cards and checks for gambling could be purchased, and the barbershop. Here gentlemen could sit in a chair that reclined and had an adjustable headrest and footrest to receive a shave or haircut. At the moment, no one was availing himself of this service. Instead, a group of eight or nine gentlemen were seated around a table where Jack had laid out his faro tools. Others stood about with drinks in their hands to observe. When she walked in, all heads turned.

Jack rose and came to meet her. "Here is my charming assistant, Miss Hamilton." He led her to the table and took his place once again, Lizzie at his shoulder. He adjusted the dealing box to his satisfaction, grinned around at one and all, and said, "Let the play begin."

Chapter Eleven

The days that followed soon settled into a mind-numbing routine broken only by the numerous hasty landings to transfer passengers and freight and the occasional grounding of the vessel on a sandbar, requiring mechanical gyrations in order to free it. These minor crises were few due to the high water of spring, and when they did occur, they were easily remedied. Otherwise, Lizzie had little to occupy her during the long monotonous days prior to her required presence at the evening gambling activities. She had experienced the same boredom in New Orleans, but there she had been free to wander about the city during the daytime. Now she had nothing to occupy her time. Add to that the unspoken condemnation of her fellow female passengers, and she was denied even the lady's chief antidote to tedium: idle conversation.

The one exception was the Fielding family. Young Cora had penetrated the veneer of respectability with which Lizzie had tried to cover herself on their second day of travel.

"When you said you had an engagement last night, it was with that fancy gentleman people are calling a professional gambler, was it not? I have even heard it said you assisted him in his activities."

Lizzie sighed. "And how did you hear this?"

"It is all everyone is talking about. Do you deny it?"

Lizzie was tired of pretending to be someone she no longer was. What did it matter, in any case? She would never see any of these people again.

"No, I do not deny it. I aid Mr. O'Rourke in his endeavors in exchange for my keep."

Cora nodded. "I thought as much. These silly proper ladies cannot imagine women having any role but that of wife and mother, obedient to their menfolk. They are quite scandalized by the prospect of someone such as yourself earning her own way by whatever means necessary. As for myself, I admire you. In fact, I hope to live by my own wits one day just as you are doing."

"My dear child, you have no idea what you are saying. It may be admirable to strain against the unpleasant circumstances of one's life, but not all such attempts are successful. I would never counsel you to abandon the principles and boundaries of polite society."

"Fiddlesticks! Your so-called polite society conspires to keep the female gender oppressed. We cannot attend colleges, aspire to the professions, *vote*. I shall fight for those things to my dying breath!"

Lizzie shook her head. It was pointless to argue with this precocious child. She herself had once been a person of strong opinion not averse to sharing those sentiments with any and all who would listen. However, she had never considered breaking the unspoken rules of her culture—until that fateful night in Charleston. She hoped life would tame Cora's spirit without requiring her to submit to such pain as Lizzie had brought on herself.

Meanwhile, she was grateful for the measure of support she took from the girl's ardent words and manner, support that extended to Mrs. Fielding in a slightly less brash but equally benevolent form. Noticing the other ladies' determination to shun Lizzie, this good woman made an effort each day to engage the outcast in conversation or to invite her to dine with her and her daughters. Lizzie accepted these kindnesses sparingly, aware that the other lady passengers were beginning to turn their cold shoulders on her ally as well as herself. Thus the days plodded on, each like the last. Lizzie would look back on them and marvel at her naive ignorance of how soon her life was destined to take another sharp turn.

They were tied up at Cairo, Illinois, the cloudy sky making nighttime sailing dangerous, and were about a day and a half from

St. Louis on the night it happened. The faro tools had long since been put aside, and Jack was engaged in a titan poker battle with a wealthy Californian. A group of spectators, many of whom had dropped out of the game over the past hour, stood watching. As far as Lizzie could tell, Jack had been playing it straight for the most part, cheating only enough to give himself a slight advantage. Now, however, it was his turn to deal, and he had called for a fresh deck of cards from the bartender. She knew this signaled a change in his strategy.

He had cut the captain in on his profits from the very beginning, but he had also paid the barkeep to hold several decks of cards that he had prearranged so he knew which cards would come in which sequence. She had seen him call for these altered decks on only one other occasion, and he had won a substantial amount of money as a result.

He took the deck from the barkeep and shuffled it, having perfected a skill by which the cards ended up in the same order after the shuffle as in the beginning. The ante bet had already been decided and laid on the table between them. He dealt three cards to his opponent, then three to himself. The Californian studied his cards, the gleam in his eye telegraphing that he liked what he saw. He raised the bet by throwing out a one-hundred-dollar check. Jack pursed his lips, glanced again at his cards, and shook his head.

"This deal is yours, my friend," he said as he placed his cards on the bottom of the deck and passed it across for the next deal.

The next hand went for several rounds of raising with each man taking a draw of two additional cards, but in the end, when Jack called the bet, his two pair lost to his opponent's three of a kind. Another pot of several hundred dollars ended up on the Californian's side of the table.

Jack took the deck back and laid it on the table. He stretched his arms and yawned. "You are a worthy opponent," he said, "but the hour is late and I am ready for bed. What do you say to a final hand, winner takes all?"

The Californian studied him. "Are you certain? The luck seems to be going my way at the moment."

Jack shrugged. "I have not wagered more than I can afford to lose."

With a grin, "Nor have I. You are on, Mr. O'Rourke."

Both men piled their evening's checks in the center of the table. Jack dealt three cards to each of them, laid the deck down, and looked at his cards. Lizzie saw his opponent's eyes widen as he looked at his own. With a stiff face no doubt meant to conceal his delight, he said, "I shall take my draw."

Jack dealt him two more cards, then two for himself.

The fellow checked the new cards and said, "I would like to raise you, but as all my evening's earnings are already on the table, I have something else to sweeten the pot." He reached into his breast coat pocket and withdrew a folded packet of paper documents. He handed them to Jack, saying, "I will wager these against the present pot with one addition: the remainder of the night in the company of your lovely assistant."

Lizzie's gasp cut through the sudden silence. She had been aware of the man's lascivious looks during the course of the evening and had even batted his hand away when he attempted to take an unacceptable physical liberty. That he would propose bartering for her body as if she were chattel was beyond the pale. All eyes, including her own, were riveted on Jack. Surely he would put the reprobate in his place forthwith.

He took some moments to study the four identical documents in his hand. He passed one over to Lizzie. It was approximately ten inches wide and six inches deep, had a fancy border, and was engraved in black ink. She had no time to examine it closely, but certain features caught her eye. In large bold letters were the words

BOND OF THE MIDAS MINING COMPANY. And beneath it, ONE THOUSAND DOLLARS.

"Those are bearer bonds," said the Californian. "Payable in gold by the Bank of Rich Bar, California to whomever presents them at the bank on or before January 1, 1855. Four thousand dollars in gold in all. I will risk them for the sum total of your winnings this night and a cozy, private tete-a-tete with the beautiful lady."

Jack's eyes twinkled with amusement as he turned to Lizzie and said, "What do you think, Miss Hamilton? Are you willing to bet your chastity against my luck in order to add four thousand dollars to our winnings?"

"Certainly not!" she cried.

"Ah, you disappoint me. Have you no confidence in my abilities at cards?"

"You are a cad, sir! I shall not listen to another word!"

She whirled and pushed her way through the leering men who now crowded the barbershop. She stumbled and fell against the stove, its heat searing her gown. She managed to keep her tears in check until she reached her room, where she threw herself onto her bunk and succumbed to sobs of misery and hopelessness.

By the time she had regained a modicum of control, she became aware of a light hand resting on her shoulder. She looked up through the semi-gloom and saw Cora's pale face hovering over her.

"Are you quite all right?" the girl asked, her voice heavy with concern.

Something happened to Lizzie's defenses in that moment. She had been attempting to pass herself off as a respectable southern lady even though her circumstances defied all such justification. She could no longer keep up the pretense, especially when she knew this youngster had long since seen through her facade. Honesty was required, chief of all to herself.

Slowly she sat up. "No, I am not all right. In fact, far from it."

"What has happened?"

"My gambling partner, Mr. O'Rourke, has attempted to wager my virtue against a large sum of money. I naturally refused to be used in this manner, but the very suggestion has irretrievably compromised what little remains of my reputation and honor. By morning, every passenger onboard this vessel will regard me as little better than a prostitute. It is not to be borne!"

"Of course it is not. You must leave him posthaste."

She sighed. "Would that it were that simple."

"And why is it not? You are not his slave. He does not own you. He cannot force you to continue your employ if you choose to leave."

"You are young and naive, Cora. I cannot leave because I have no other means of support. I have no money, no family—nothing. Without him I should starve or be forced into just the sort of profession he has insinuated."

"You call yourself his partner in these gambling activities. Has he not shared the winnings with you?"

A bitter laugh. "His concept of partner is no doubt very different from yours. He has given me small amounts of spending money on occasion, but he has kept me dependent on him for all else. I have no cache of savings with which to launch myself on a new life."

"Then you must insist he give you one. Women have a right to be paid for their services, no matter what they are. Most men apply that principle to but one profession, the one to which you just alluded, but that is wrong and immoral. It is akin to slavery, and you know my feelings on that subject."

Lizzie felt as if she were living in a topsy-turvy world. Her present circumstances were being compared to those of an African slave, the very people whose toil and sweat had kept her in a life of privilege and wealth. She thought about the arguments she had heard her former sister-in-law make about the inherent right of the black man to liberty and justice. How she had scoffed at such seditious nonsense! Yet when applied to herself, was there not a certain logic in what Cora said? She had worked hard over the past weeks to facilitate Jack's profits. Why should she not be rewarded as any man would expect to be?

She shook her head, saying, "What is right and what is possible are two different things, Cora. He would never do as you suggest."

"Then you must take it for yourself."

It took a moment for the meaning of her words to sink in. "Take it? You mean, steal it?"

"No. I mean relieve him of what is rightfully yours. No more, no less. It is only fair by the laws of God and nature."

It seemed a rather rash justification. Lizzie's memory of Scripture was of an exhortation to humility and patience. Humans were to accept their lot in life, whether as slave or freeman, whether poor or rich, and look to God for comfort and strength to endure. Still, she was mightily tempted...

She bit a corner of her lip. Then, "How would I accomplish such a thing?"

Cora shrugged. "I have no idea. But I am sure you can come up with the answer if you think on it hard enough. You know the scoundrel better than anyone else. You should be able to find a weak spot and exploit it. I suggest you go to sleep and see where your mind takes you in the morning. Whatever you decide, you will find me a willing accomplice."

Lizzie could not imagine what a slip of a girl could do to advance her cause. But she was grateful for the offer and wrapped her in an impetuous hug.

"Thank you, dear girl. And I shall follow your advice concerning sleep. I am beyond exhaustion."

She rose to undress, her thoughts already probing the possibilities.

∞∞∞

Lizzie wakened with certainty in her heart. Now she went back over her reasoning to probe for any weakness she might have overlooked.

When she accepted Jack's offer to flee from her old life on the night of the St. Cecilia's Ball, she had believed herself to be taking charge of her own destiny. She would forge ahead into a new life that would allow her to throw off the shackles of scandal and reclaim her rightful position in society. What a dreamer she had been! She had completely misread Jack's intentions. Rather than elevating her status by marrying her, he had degraded it beyond repair by robbing her of her virginity, then forcing her into a life of avarice and deceit. Consequently, she was just as dependent on him today as she had been on the largesse of her sister and brother-in-law back in Charleston.

To follow through with Cora's suggestion would be to once again subject herself to the vagaries of fate. This time, however, there would be a difference. She would be relying on herself alone. She had always known herself to be resourceful and strong headed. She would need those attributes as never before. If the God of her youth looked on her efforts with favor, she would thrive. If not, so be it. Either way, she would answer to no one but herself.

But how to accomplish her goal?

A germ of an idea was forming when she heard from the bunk above, "Elizabeth? Are you awake?"

"Yes. And if you must address me by my Christian name, please use Lizzie, the diminutive by which my family has always known me."

The girl's legs appeared over the side of the upper bunk, and she jumped, lithe as a cat, to the deck. She sat on the edge of Lizzie's bunk and grinned.

"There, you see? You are already casting off that insufferable aura of superiority that so many of your class adopt. By doing so, you have taken the first step toward freedom, and no mistake!"

Lizzie pulled a wry face. "You, on the other hand, continue to be the impertinent imp whose radical ideas and behavior virtually preclude her ever attracting an eligible suitor, thus dooming yourself to a life of spinsterhood. And no mistake of that, either!"

"Good. I have no desire to attach myself to some man who will confine and abuse me. But tell me, do you have a plan to accomplish what we discussed last night?"

"More like an idea, the implementation of which escapes me thus far."

"Tell me."

Cora was hugging herself for warmth in the early-morning chill. Lizzie threw back the blanket, inviting her inside. When they were snuggled side by side, she said,

"Jack keeps most of his money in a locked box that he normally stores in his steamer trunk. While onboard the boat, he has transferred the box to the safe in the clerk's office so it is handy when he needs additional funds for gambling. He has sent me to retrieve money and buy checks on several occasions over the past week, and the clerk is accustomed to opening the safe on my request. I believe he would do so again."

"Oh, brilliant!"

"Perhaps, but even if I could retrieve the funds successfully, I would need to get away from the boat before Jack discovered the theft."

She made a tsking sound. "Not theft. Payment for services rendered."

"Yes, yes. But I assure you he will not regard the missing funds in that light. He will know who took them and where to look for them."

"Hm-m. I have an idea about that, but you must let me develop it. Meet me here again before supper. I should have things worked out by then."

"Come anytime you like. I shan't leave this room in the meantime."

A vigorous shake of her head. "Oh, no, you cannot hide away. If we are to prevail, there must be no suggestion of abnormality in your behavior today."

Lizzie knew she was right, but her pride rebelled against the notion of ever showing her face to these people again. In the end, her rational self prevailed.

"I suppose you are right." She threw back the covers. "Then let us prepare for the day. Wretched though it surely will be."

Despite her misgivings, she was amazed at how easily she bore the shocked glances and whispered conversations around her. The Fielding family helped shield her by saving her a spot at table, sitting with her in the ladies' cabin, and inviting her to join them whenever they sought fresh air along the guards. Throughout the day, she noticed Cora flitting in and out of their room, nearly always accompanied by the chambermaid Maisie. She had no inkling what they were up to, but she was increasingly confident that whatever it was would inure to her benefit. A supposition borne out when she and Cora retired to their room to refresh themselves for supper and she learned the details of the very clever ruse the girl had planned.

Chapter Twelve

Lizzie dressed as usual late that evening and sat while Maisie dressed her hair. The slave wore her usual stoic face and obsequious manner, a fact that aroused Lizzie's curiosity until she could no longer be silent.

"Why are you helping me, Maisie?" she said at last. "Surely you know our plan could not be implemented without your assistance, yet you have said nothing about it."

The maid's hands paused, then resumed their duties. "T'ain' nuttin' to say, miss. I done what I could fer a lady who's in a bad fix. Miss Cora tol' me all about it, and I's glad to help."

"Even though I am a person whose family owned servants such as yourself?"

"Don't matter. You's a chile o' God. We's all equal in His eyes."

The statement startled Lizzie. All *equal* in God's eyes? She knew the standard teaching. Slaves were inferior in every way in this world, but in the next, those who believed could expect salvation just as white people could. Nonetheless, she had always assumed that Africans would have their own little corner of heaven, very nice, to be sure, but not anywhere near like the glory reserved for whites on judgment day.

"Well, I... I am grateful," she managed at last. "If all goes well, I plan to demonstrate my gratitude—to you and the young fellow you have recruited on my behalf. If not, then I promise not to breathe a word of your involvement. I would not have you punished in any way for helping me."

"Dat's kind of you, miss. And I'll pray for your safety dis night."

A slave praying for her—it was a novel thought. Still, she could not dismiss it. In fact, it stirred a feeling of warmth that brought tears to her eyes. She cleared her throat and said,

"Thank you."

"You's welcome." She patted the completed coiffure and added, "You's ready now."

Lizzie rose and busied herself with her gloves and handkerchief, too discomfited to meet the slave's eyes. She said, "Well, then... " and went out into the cabin.

Instead of proceeding to the gentlemen's cabin, she sat in a chair that allowed her a clear view of the curtain separating the two cabins, glad of the opportunity to collect herself and focus on the task ahead. Before long, the curtain moved aside and a cabin boy's grinning black face appeared in the aperture, then quickly withdrew.

She rose and walked past the curtain and into the usual miasma of smoke, clink of glasses, and rumble of male voices. The cabin boy, a slender youth of perhaps fourteen whose name she had been told was Jim, stood at the far end where he had a good view into the barbershop. He gave his head an imperceptible nod, and she continued forward, ignoring the furtive grins of the men she passed.

She had sent a message to Jack earlier in the day via the same cabin boy stating that she was ill and would not be joining him that evening. She doubted whether he had given it a second thought. He knew he had humiliated her the previous night and would have expected some small rebellion in return. She had already heard through the gossip mill how his dealings with the Californian had ended. Having been raised in their final hand by the man's bearer bonds, he had gone to the safe in the clerk's office and come back with four thousand dollars of his own so he could call the bet. And sure enough, he had won. There had been no danger of Lizzie being taken away to be prostituted by his opponent, and he had surely known that all along. Yet he had failed to come to her defense, thus allowing her honor to be compromised. He had behaved as a barbarian and deserved all she had planned for him that night.

She crossed over to the port side of the cabin so she would not pass in front of the barbershop where Jack was busy at his craft. She stopped at the half-door that served as a counter into the clerk's office. The officer, a small man with a balding pate and wire-rimmed spectacles, was dozing in his chair and started when she rapped on the doorjamb.

She smiled her prettiest and said, "I do apologize for inconveniencing you. But Mr. O'Rourke has sent me to retrieve funds from his box."

The fellow yawned and hauled himself to his feet. He went to the cast-iron safe, bent, and twirled the dial to put in the combination. The heavy door swung open, and he reached for Jack's wooden box, which he carried to Lizzie. She had no difficulty opening it since Jack relied on the safe's security rather than the key with which he normally locked it. The bearer bonds from the night before lay on top of the usual paper currency. Shielded from the clerk's prying eyes by the open lid, she took out the bonds as well as a few bank notes and a handful of coins, the denominations of which she did not take the time to assess.

"I am told this will do," she said as she handed the box back.

"Do you wish to purchase checks?"

She felt her face flush. "No, thank you. Mr. O'Rourke prefers cash for now."

She felt his speculative gaze for an uncomfortable moment, but he eventually nodded, placed the box back in the safe, and returned to his chair.

She stepped away as if to return to the barbershop. When she was beyond the clerk's sight, she paused and looked to Jim the cabin boy, who could see into both the office and barbershop from where he stood. He nodded the all clear, and she hurried back the way she had come. She pushed through the door to her room and collapsed onto her bunk, her heart pumping like a piston on one of the boat's massive engines.

Cora had been pacing the small room, waiting for her return. Now she plopped down beside her and demanded, "So?"

Lizzie extended a shaking hand to exhibit her pilfered profits.

The girl gave a squeal of delight. "How much is it?"

"The bonds are worth four thousand. As for the rest, I do not know. I just took what I thought would look reasonable and made haste back here."

"Well, count it out now."

Lizzie nodded and licked her lips. She laid the bonds aside and shuffled through the four notes beneath them. They were of varying sizes and designs issued by four different banks. There was a five-hundred-dollar note, two for one hundred, and another for fifty. The coins included two double eagles, three half-eagles, a silver dollar, a two-bit piece, five dimes, and three pennies. She did some mental arithmetic, pulled in a sharp breath, and said,

"Eight hundred six dollars and seventy-eight cents. A virtual fortune!"

"Especially with the bonds added in." A happy grin. "You are a wealthy woman now. And free of your bondage to any man. You can do anything you like with your life from now on."

"But... but it is surely more than I need. It seems wrong to take so much."

"Pooh. It is no such thing. You have been shamelessly exploited and are only taking what is due you. Did you clean him out?"

"Of course not. I took but a small portion of what was in the box."

"There you are, then. Any man who has vast sums of money lying about can well afford to lose this much. Now think no more of it, and let us prepare for the next stage of our plan."

Lizzie pushed her warring feelings aside. She could do little about it now, in any case. Except return the money and admit she had taken it. Which, of course, was out of the question. She had set her course, and she must follow it to the end.

Her first task was to store her new wealth for safekeeping. The bonds represented the largest portion and needed to be especially well hidden. She had already sewn a pocket onto the underside of a clean chemise so it would rest against her flesh, assuming no gentleman would search there in the event she were caught. Now she slid the bonds inside. The remainder of the funds needed to be accessible for her sustenance over the coming days. These she placed in the black velvet handbag she had been carrying since her early days in New Orleans. She engaged the clasp and tucked the handbag into the carpetbag that would be her sole remaining luggage after that night.

Next she packed what she considered to be the bare essentials for the days ahead. Her simplest and most practical day dress of brown gingham with matching undersleeves. A single petticoat and second chemise, similarly fitted with a secret pocket. A clean pair of drawers. Two fresh collars, stockings, day slippers, handkerchiefs, hair grooming supplies, and a nightdress. Last, she folded her lightweight hooded cloak into as small a bundle as possible and crammed it on top. There would be no room for bonnet or parasol, without which she would once have felt naked. As it was, the bag was so full it would barely close and lock.

She laid out what she would need once Maisie arrived, then removed her outer clothing, wrapped herself in a blanket for warmth, and sat on her bunk to wait. All the while, Cora kept up a litany of observations, suggestions and inane chatter that she would once have found irritating but now relished as a distraction from what was to come. The girl eventually ran out of energy, and a soft snore told Lizzie she had fallen asleep. The sounds from the ladies' cabin outside diminished until there was total silence. The dim light coming through the transom disappeared as the cabin lamps were extinguished one by one. Still no Maisie.

Heart pounding with anxiety, she opened the stateroom door and peered outside. Enough moonlight came through the skylights to illumine the deserted cabin. She identified the dark, indistinguishable heap on the far side as the sleeping chambermaid who serviced the staterooms on that side of the boat. Maisie was nowhere to be seen.

She returned to her bunk, wondering in a panic what to do if the maid never came. She had nearly decided she was on her own, after all, when she heard a soft knock at the door. It opened, and Maisie slipped inside carrying a medium-sized canvas bag. Lizzie rose to meet her.

"I thought you were not coming," she whispered, mindful of the still-sleeping Cora.

"I's sorry. The cap'n, he done required me. He does dat from time to time, and I dasn't refuse."

Lizzie was at a loss. "Required you?"

"Yes'm. In his bed."

Lizzie was stunned. Had she heard right? "You mean he... he...?"

"Yes'm. But never you mind. I's used to it."

Lizzie had always known southern white men frequently took intimate privileges with their attractive slave women, and she had never felt particularly scandalized by the practice. Now she was surprised to feel outrage.

"But must you? He does not own you."

"No, but him's friendly wid my massa, and if I refused, word would get back. T'ain't worth da risk. Now here." She thrust the bag forward. "Best get into these."

Lizzie emptied the sack, threw off the blanket, and began pulling on a pair of baggy trousers. She tucked her chemise into the waist, shrugged into a shapeless smock that once might have been white, and tucked it in as well, using a pair of suspenders to keep the trousers in place. There was a pair of well-worn work boots that were several sizes too big, but she laced them as tight as they would go. Next came a large felt hat that she pulled low enough to hide her piles of auburn hair.

Now that the sack was empty, she folded a second day dress made of printed maroon cotton and placed it inside. Next came two additional petticoats and her soft kid side-lace boots. Finally, her packed carpetbag. She spent a moment making sure she had not forgotten anything, then turned to Maisie and said,

"I am ready."

The maid nodded. "Jim's a-comin' any time now. He'll take you da rest o' da way."

Even as she spoke, they heard the whisper of a knock. Before opening the door, Lizzie went to the small washbasin shelf and picked up the two half-eagles she had left out of her handbag. She pressed one into Maisie's hand, saying, "I am truly grateful for your help."

The maid stared at her hand, fingering the coin. Finally she swallowed hard and whispered, "T'ank you. God go wid you."

Lizzie opened the stateroom door and stepped through.

∞∞∞

It was impossible to get comfortable. The cramped space allowed Lizzie to sit, but whether sitting or lying down, the wood-plank flooring was hard, and no matter which position she took, she was soon in pain. She was cold even with her cloak as a covering. The past days of warm sunshine had turned to cloud and rain, and the damp atmosphere only added to her discomfort. Even so, she had escaped detection, and for that she was grateful.

She had heard them searching. Had it not been for this ingenious hiding place and young Jim's knowledge of it, she would have been discovered hours before.

She recalled following him through the darkened ladies' cabin to the stern door and up the stairs to the hurricane deck, where moonlight guided them past the cabin skylights, around the texas where the officers had their quarters, and up another flight of stairs to the deck that supported the pilothouse, which sat between and just behind the two tall flaring chimneys. It was a small, many-windowed structure where whichever pilot was on duty guided the boat. The captain might be the ultimate master, but the pilot was the true boss. It was his knowledge and experience of the river that kept the vessel afloat and out of harm's way.

Jim climbed the few steps to the pilothouse door and knocked. After a few moments of whispered conversation, he returned and led her around to the structure's port face, where he removed a section of wall planks and motioned her into the small space between the deck and the floor of the pilothouse.

She had already been told she would be taken to a place where escaping slaves were often hidden by abolitionist sympathizers. It was a testament to the upside-down nature of her current existence that she had accepted this news without the righteous indignation she would once have felt. How often had she railed against the accursed Underground Railroad that facilitated the escape of property that belonged by law and justice to the people of the South? Now here she was, attempting her own escape and taking advantage of the machinations of those hated enemies. But was she safe... ?

"What about him?" she whispered, gesturing upward toward the pilothouse windows.

"Don' worry," Jim whispered back. "Him's one of us. Not t'other one, though. So take care dependin' on who's at the wheel when we dock."

She nodded and slipped into the dark dank-smelling place, dragging her bag behind her. Jim shoved in another small sack and prepared to seal her inside.

"Wait," she whispered. She grabbed his hand and placed the final half-eagle coin into it. "I am more grateful than you will ever know."

He grinned, his teeth shining white in his dark countenance, then fitted the planks into place, shutting out the last glimmer of moonlight. She had seldom experienced such complete and total darkness. It was also cold, and she fumbled in the sack for her cloak. She threw it over herself, and as she began to warm, she grew drowsy. Exhausted by her long day of emotional turmoil, she lay down and fell into a deep sleep.

A persistent tapping sound roused her some hours later. Disoriented, it took her a moment to remember where she was. The sound was coming from overhead. Soon a deep male voice said, "You all right down there, young fella?"

The pilot. He no doubt thought she was another slave fleeing to freedom. She hesitated, unsure whether to answer.

Another rap, this time louder and more decisive. "Answer me, boy. You okay?"

Having no alternative, she did her best to deepen her voice and said, "Yes, sir."

There was a long silence. Had he recognized the tone of a woman, not an illiterate slave boy? Then,

"We are about to change the watch, so be quiet as can be. I'll be back on in four hours."

Lizzie decided no response was needed. She waited until she heard footsteps climbing the stairs to the pilothouse. There was a short exchange between the two men, its content technical and beyond her understanding. Then she heard the first pilot descend.

She did a quick calculation. It must now be four o'clock, the hour designated for the end of the after watch and the beginning of the dog watch. There would be another rotation at eight o'clock, at which time she would be able to move about more freely. She settled down to pass the interim in much-needed sleep.

As the first faint light of morning filtered between the planks of her little cage, she was roused by the scream of steam escaping through the gauge cocks, which meant they were slowing. Soon she heard the pilot barking orders to his crew through the speaking tube followed by voices rising from below that told her they were stopping along the riverbank to take on wood.

Now that there was a modicum of light, she could see the particulars of her hiding place. The ceiling, which formed the floor of the pilothouse, rose perhaps four feet above the deck. She judged the surrounding walls to be six or seven feet apart with the bow section taken by the lower portion of the massive wooden wheel by which the boat was steered. It swung this way and that as the pilot maneuvered the boat toward the shore. Then came the rumble of the engines reversing in order to effect a stable stop.

Masked by the chaotic sounds coming up from below, she pulled the second, smaller bag onto her lap and opened it to see what Jim had provided. Anxiety had given her a mighty thirst, and she was relieved to see a glass jar filled to the brim with river water. The sediment had largely settled to the bottom, leaving a nearly-clear liquid. She unscrewed the lid and drank deeply. Then she unwrapped a cloth bundle to reveal thick slices of bread, a large red apple, and a slab of roast pork, all of which she decided to save for later. A second jar, this one empty, was a puzzlement until she realized it had been provided for her bodily needs. She vowed to use this convenience only in the direst of need. She had been told they would reach St. Louis by late afternoon or early evening. Holding out that long would be a challenge, but if she drank sparingly, she thought she might be able to do it.

Once they were underway again, she tried to return to sleep but found it impossible. It had started to rain, the water drumming on the pilothouse roof and the deck outside, and the dampness only added to her misery. She shivered, leaned against the side boards, and tucked the cloak closer around her. Time became her enemy as the minutes and hours stretched on.

When the friendly pilot took over from his cohort at eight o'clock, she responded to his brief inquiry as she had done before, then opened her food package to eat, allowing herself only two small sips of water to wash it down. The day dragged by, marked by two more shift changes between the two pilots. By late afternoon, she was sore from sitting or lying on the hard surface, and her bladder was beginning to call attention to itself. The friendly pilot was on duty, and she hoped they would reach St. Louis on his watch.

At last she heard the manifestations of a docking: the piercing shriek of the escaping steam, the pilot's shouted orders, a chorus of ringing bells, the reversal of the paddle wheels. Her mind's eye saw the black smoke pouring from the chimneys and the bustle of activity aboard as well as on the wharf. It was time for her to leave the safety of her hidey-hole and attempt the final leg of her escape.

She put the two jars and the cloth that had contained her food into the smaller of the two bags and pushed it into a far corner where Jim would come to retrieve it in his own good time. Next, she shoved her cloak back into the larger sack and jammed the hat onto her head, feeling with her fingers to make certain all stray strands of hair were out of sight. Satisfied, she pushed against the movable section of planks. It tumbled outward with a crash.

She froze, shoulders hunched in horror. Would some curious soul come to investigate? Agonizing moments later, she forced herself to poke her head outside and look aft along the texas deck. It was deserted. She scrambled out and wedged the makeshift door back into place. She hurried around the pilothouse and nearly collided with a man she assumed to be the pilot as he exited his little lair. His eyes widened as he took in her appearance. Clearly not what he had expected of his hidden passenger. A breathless moment passed. Then he gestured toward the stairway leading down to the hurricane deck, saying, "After you."

She hastened down the stairs, along the hurricane deck to the main stairway in the stern, and from there down to the main deck. The scene before her was one of bedlam. The plank had already been extended off the port bow, and roustabouts were busy offloading freight. Deck passengers were gathering their belongings and vying with the roustabouts for access to the plank. She saw no sign of the cabin passengers, but she suspected they would wait until the way was clear for them to debark in greater dignity. She ducked her head low and wove in and out, holding her sack close to her chest to disguise her female form. She arrived at the plank just as a skinny black man was attempting to coax a recalcitrant mule to cross over. Lizzie grasped the opposite side of the animal's rope halter and pulled. Whether from her additional urging or its own decision to abandon its balk, it moved forward, and Lizzie followed along until she stepped down onto the wharf.

She left the man to deal with the mule and scurried out of sight behind a stack of barrels waiting to be loaded onto the boat. She moved along from obstacle to obstacle until she was far enough away to be certain no one could see her from the deck of the *Princess*. Only then did she stop to catch her breath and take in her surroundings.

It was an astonishing sight. The wide levee stretched in either direction as far as the eye could see. Dozens of steamboats, perhaps a hundred or more, were docked and unloading while many more waited in a second tier for their chance to offload. Untidy stacks of freight and produce sat in haphazard clusters awaiting the roustabouts who would carry them aboard the vessels. Laden wagons made their way to the landing stages. Hoards of rowdies, homeless children, and all manner of disreputable persons prowled among the crowds looking for a chance to fulfill their nefarious purposes. Her ears rang with the cries of vendors hawking their wares and the discordant sound of the organ grinders and musicians playing for tokens of appreciation, all overlaid with the ubiquitous cacophony of steamship bells and whistles. Clouds of black smoke from the steamboats' chimneys as well as the city's foundries, factories, breweries and refineries fouled the atmosphere such that her eyes stung and her chest burned. It was a scene to escape as soon as possible.

She studied the steamers lined up closest to her position, looking for one like the *Princess* that had just landed and was in the throes of off- or on-loading. Some hundred yards upriver, she saw the name *Dubuque* on the paddlebox of a sidewheeler. There was a steady stream of workers loading freight and deck passengers boarding. She pulled her hat down tight, clutched her sack of belongings, and hurried toward the stageplank.

A rapidly-diminishing stack of chicken coops stood at the base of the plank. She grabbed one and hustled aboard, depositing her burden with a growing pile of like coops. No one gave her a second glance in the general chaos. She hastened aft and tried the door to the forward privy located beside the wheelhouse. It opened readily. She stepped inside and dropped the wooden latch into place. She closed her eyes and took a deep breath while her heart settled into a normal rhythm. She was almost there.

She groaned with relief as she emptied her bladder, which was as full as she could ever remember experiencing. She stood and quickly stripped off her disguise. She removed the petticoats from the canvas bag and stepped into them. Next came the maroon day dress, which she pulled over her head, then reached around to fasten the hooks up her back. She stuffed the work clothes and hat back into the sack and dropped it to the privy floor. She took up her carpetbag and velvet handbag and walked out a lady, or as close to one as was possible given her scanty accessories.

Again no one seemed to notice her presence as she wove her way among the growing number of deck passengers and the wagons, animals, and stacks of freight. Somehow she must get herself to California, where she would locate the Bank of Rich Bar and cash the bearer bonds now resting so near to her heart. She had absorbed enough of the Fielding family plans to know what her first step must be.

The sun broke through the clouds just as she stepped off the plank and onto the levee. She turned her face toward its warmth and smiled. It was surely an omen assuring her she would finally, after all these months of grief and humiliation and uncertainty, find the place where she was meant to be. Where she could achieve the contentment and happiness she had always believed she was destined to possess. And contrary to the majority of her gender, she would do so on her own.

Giddy with anticipation, she set off on her search for passage up the Missouri River.

PART TWO—SEEING THE ELEPHANT

Chapter Thirteen

St. Joseph, Missouri
April 19, 1854

The steamboat *Pontiac No. 2* rounded a soaring bluff on the eastern bank of the Missouri River, and the City of St. Joseph came into view. Situated on a broad bend in the river, it spread out along the waterfront before crawling up the valley that split the Blacksnake Hills at its back. Church spires rent the sky, and a majestic temple-like courthouse overlooked it all from a perch on a prominent hill. Farther afield, masses of white tents clung to the base of the bluffs or dotted the sides of lesser hills, the encampments of emigrants waiting to begin their journey westward.

The deep-throated whistle bellowed and the bell clanged as the boat approached the levee, which was thronged with curious customers drawn from the nearby saloons and shops, hotel runners seeking guests, businessmen anticipating the arrival of their cargoes, and townspeople there to meet arriving friends or relatives. Lizzie took it all in from the guards, the bustling scene barely penetrating her melancholy fog.

The prior nine days had been some of the worst of her life, rivaling the desolation she had felt following her brother's death and the family's descent into disgrace. The journey itself had been slow and tedious, the swollen waters of the river they rightly called The Big Muddy having been clogged with floating timber, snags and sand bars that caused countless delays. These were nuisances to be borne, but it was a seminal event in St. Louis that had broken her determined optimism and triggered this black time of soul searching.

It had taken her less than an hour to locate a steamer going upriver to St. Joseph and beyond. The *Pontiac No. 2* was scheduled to depart the following morning, and she had been lucky enough to secure the last vacant berth when she went aboard to purchase her twenty-dollar ticket from the clerk's office. Having the remainder of the day to herself, she had decided to do some shopping to fill out her meager wardrobe.

She made her way across the wharf's wide expanse, ducking around the stacks of freight and produce, avoiding the myriad cargo-laden wagons, and ignoring the street performers looking for a handout as well as the cries and pleadings of vendors and begging urchins. She asked directions of a lady of respectable appearance and after a pleasant walk, entered a dry goods store on Fourth Street.

The place was crowded with last-minute shoppers as closing time loomed. She made two quick purchases using her fifty-dollar note and was exiting onto the sidewalk with her packages, the change from the sale still in her hand, when someone shoved her from behind. She fell to her knees with a cry of surprise, coins and packages scattering. A scrawny figure dressed in tatters snatched her velvet handbag from her wrist and scampered off, immediately disappearing in the surrounding throng.

A heavyset man in day-laborer's clothes stopped and helped her to her feet. He whipped off his slouch hat, gave a little bow of respect, then crouched down to retrieve her packages and coins. He handed them to her, asking, "You all right, miss?"

Lizzie stared after her attacker, her shock leaving her momentarily speechless. At last she blurted, "He robbed me. He took my handbag. All I own in the world... "

She stopped herself and turned to her diffident rescuer, whose broad face exhibited his sympathy.

"Yes, miss," he said. "I'm that sorry, I am. Them scoundrels is like a plague on our city. Great caution must be taken at all times."

Little good that advice does me now, she wanted to say. His obvious concern stopped her. She managed to thank him and start off toward the wharf, so stunned at this sudden reversal of fortune she could scarcely put one foot in front of the other.

By the time she reached her stateroom on the *Pontiac No. 2*, the reality of her new situation had sunk deep into her mind and left her bereft of hope. She was acutely aware of the bearer bonds nestling close to her breast, four thousand dollars whose benefit was as remote as if they were a fantasy. How was she to make her way to California to cash them with less than fifty dollars to her name?

Her untenable position was beyond comprehension. How could she, Elizabeth Jane of the prestigious South Carolina Hamilton family, have been brought so low? Betrayed at every turn, first by her feckless brother, then her fickle beau, and finally by the scoundrel A. Jackson O'Rourke, who rather than save her from her fate had only compounded her fall from grace. How could God have allowed these things to happen? There had been a prolonged Easter service three days before onboard the *Pontiac No. 2* led by a reverend of the Presbyterian persuasion. How eloquently he had proclaimed the love of God as manifested in the death and resurrection of His Son! The irony of the message had cut deep into Lizzie's soul. How did that love apply to her? Where was a sign that He cared a whit for what happened to her?

No, she had been abandoned in the heavenly realms just as she had been on this earth. Utterly alone, she must do her best to soldier on, battered by the winds of fortune, a leaf before a wild hurricane beyond all control.

She sighed as the boat swung in toward the levee. She would simply have to see what she could do to obtain passage with some overland party even though she could afford but a measly fare. She gathered her courage and flagging resolve, gripped her carpetbag, and waited to debark.

∞∞∞

Lizzie's feet hurt and her back ached from trudging along the dusty roads in and about St. Joseph. What had seemed a benign April sun had long since lost its charm. Sweat bathed her face and dripped down her torso, staining her clothes in a most unladylike fashion. She was thankful for the plain bonnet and parasol she had been able to purchase before calamity struck, but she knew they were doing a less-than-adequate job of shielding her face from the sun's rays, which were surely turning her creamy complexion as brown as that of a darkie on her father's plantation. At least the afternoon was finally waning, and a cool breeze occasionally lifted her skirts and slithered along her overheated limbs, bringing renewed hope to her flagging spirits.

Thus far her inquiries had been met with astonishment, curiosity, even occasional sympathy, but no one had been willing to take her on. She had walked the entire length of the long line of wagons waiting to cross the Missouri River into the Kansas territory. Several people had pointed her toward trains camped on the outskirts of town that might be able to help her, but the answer had always been the same. Unless she could pay a fare of at least two hundred dollars to cover her expenses, no one had provisions to spare for an added passenger. Now she was on her way to a train under the leadership of a Mr. Mills that was said to be camped on the height immediately south of town. If this latest destination did not offer a solution to her dilemma, she had no idea what she would do.

She plodded on, huffing for air on the steep road, her carpetbag seeming heavier with every step. She had not even topped the rise before she saw the smoke from the many campfires where people were preparing their evening meal. Her stomach rumbled at the tantalizing mix of odors, reminding her she not eaten since breakfast that morning.

She paused at the top to catch her breath and take in the scene before her. Like other camps she had seen that day, this one had a multitude of white-covered wagons and canvas tents scattered over a wide area as well as the concomitant oxen, cattle, horses, mules, even the occasional family carriage. She had been told this particular train was unusually large with nearly seventy wagons carrying some two hundred fifty emigrants. If there were a party willing to help her, it would be found here or nowhere.

She approached a family group at one of the nearest wagons. The wife was bent over the fire stirring something in an iron pot while three children ran giggling to and fro and the husband worked with his tools on a large wheel balanced on a log.

The wife rose, wiped her forehead with her sleeve, and gave an inquiring smile.

"I wondered whether you might direct me to a Mr. Mills, who I am told is the wagon master of this train."

"He is, indeed. And a very capable one, according to his reputation. If your party thinks to join up with us, you can rest assured you would be in good hands."

She seemed to wait for further enlightenment, but Lizzie simply nodded and prompted, "If you would be so kind as to tell me where I might find him?"

"Of course." She pointed and said, "At the rear of the camp near the drove of cattle."

Lizzie thanked her and continued in the general direction indicated, stopping to make further refining inquiries as she went.

As the wagons thinned out and she reached what appeared to be the farthest reaches of the encampment, she paused in puzzlement. A large herd of cattle grazed on the prairie up ahead. Four rough-looking men lounged around a fire in front of two lean-to tents, a small covered wagon at their backs. Another fire burned some forty feet farther on. A handsome sorrel saddle horse was tethered nearby, its tack piled beside an unoccupied bedroll. A Negro sat cross-legged on the ground holding something flat in his lap. None of these men seemed at all likely to be the person in charge of this massive undertaking.

She started toward the white men. One noticed her approach and nudged the others, a lascivious grin on his face. He was a man of perhaps forty with shaggy dark hair shot with gray, unruly whiskers, and a lean build. His companions were just as unkempt but appeared much younger, one little more than a boy.

She strode forward with her chin set at its most imperious. She stopped in front of the older man and said, "Good day to you, gentlemen. I have been told your wagon master, Mr. Mills, has his headquarters near here. Would you be so kind as to direct me there?"

The man looked her up and down, his impertinent perusal bringing additional color to her cheeks. "Now why would a purty little thing like you be lookin' for the likes o' him? If you don't mind my askin'."

His eyes flicked to the other three men, and they grinned in response.

She put on a frosty look and straightened her shoulders. "It is a private matter of business between the gentleman and myself. Will you point me to him, or must I seek the counsel of someone else?"

He guffawed. "Well, now, little lady, I sure wouldn't want you goin' out o' your way or nothin'. That there camp over there... " He waved in the direction of the black man. "... that's his, all right."

She gave him a curt, "Thank you," and turned on her heel, a rumble of chuckles following as she walked toward the far fire.

As she drew closer, she saw that the object in the Negro's lap was a leather ledger of some sort. He was paying it no heed at the moment, his attention focused on the encounter she had just had with the white men. He had weathered lampblack skin and long black hair tied back with a leather cord. He resembled any one of the hundreds of male slaves who had populated her father's plantation, prompting her to address him as she had such persons from earliest childhood.

"Where is your master, boy? I wish to speak with him."

He gave her a long bland look before saying, "There are no masters hereabouts, young lady."

She waved her hand, having become accustomed to the number of freed slaves who seemed to populate some areas of the country. "Well, then, your employer. Mr. Mills. Where may I find him?"

To her astonishment, he said, "You are looking at him."

She gaped. "I beg your pardon?"

"You heard me well enough." He rose, revealing a tall wiry frame, and gave her an elaborate bow. "Captain Lazarus Mills at your service."

It took her a moment to recover before she was able to blurt, "You are the person in charge of this wagon train?"

"I am. Hired by these good folks straight off my advertisement in the St. Joseph Gazette. And who might you be?"

"Well, I... " She fought through a fog of confusion and humiliation to find the necessary words. Was she truly reduced to begging a favor of a black man? She cleared her throat and forged ahead. "I am Elizabeth Hamilton, and I desire passage across the plains to California."

He folded his arms over his chest and took in her dusty carpetbag and disheveled appearance, sparking indignation. How dare he ogle her in such a way? Yet she could hardly complain. As much as it might gall her, he seemed to be her last best chance. She clamped her lips together and waited for him to speak.

At last he said, "Where is your outfit?"

"My outfit?"

"Yes. Your wagon, oxen, supplies. And your, er, husband, protector, whomever. Why has he sent you to make this request?"

This caused her to bristle. "I make it on my own behalf. Do you question my right to do so?"

"No, no. I merely assumed… I must tell you, Miss Hamilton. This train departs the day after tomorrow, and the charter has been set. It is very late to be adding a wagon."

"But I have no wagon."

"No wagon?"

"I hoped I might find some party in such a vast number who would have room to transport one more person."

His eyes widened. "You expect someone to gift you with a ride to California?"

Here it was again, she thought, remembering the many rebuffs she had already experienced that day. She said, "Well, no, of course not. I could work, help in some way… " Her voice trailed off into futility.

"The charge for such passage would be two hundred dollars for your keep plus another thirty for my services as guide and captain. Are you able to meet this sum?"

She swallowed hard, mortified to feel tears flood her eyes. "No, I am not. I was robbed in St. Louis. I could offer an IOU for the necessary amount as I have prospects of great fortune if I am able to reach California. But I cannot pay it now."

"Mm-m." A long silence. Then, "I am sorry for your misfortune, but I don't see how—"

"Please!" she interrupted, throwing all caution and dignity to the wind in her distress. "You are my last hope! I *must* reach California. That or I will surely die!"

She bowed her head, unable to meet his eyes for fear he would see, despite her grinding will to subdue it, the condescension that had been bred in her since childhood. This moment was unlike any other she had ever experienced. Black or not, this man held her fate, her future in his hands.

He sighed. Rubbed his chin and said, "Can you cook?"

She caught her breath and looked up. "Cook?"

"Yes. As in prepare a meal."

The closest Lizzie had ever come to preparing anything edible had been to pour tea from a silver service placed before her by a servant. She licked her dry lips and said,

"Why do you ask?"

"You have no doubt noticed the large herd of cattle yonder." He nodded in the appropriate direction. "They belong to a Mr. Masters, who is driving them to California to seed his new cattle ranch. The drovers with whom you spoke just now are employed to get them there. There was an additional hand employed as their cook, but he fell ill two weeks ago and died. I might be able to convince Mr. Masters to take you on in his place, although I doubt there would be any payment for the position. Only food and expenses for the journey."

"That is all I require! And of course I can cook. What woman cannot?"

A skeptical expression. "You do not appear to be a lady whose background included such training."

"Well, I grew up surrounded by some of the best cooks in the South. How difficult can it be?"

A wry smile. "You must ask them. As for this situation, I am willing to put you forward since you have such an obvious need. Beyond that, you are on your own."

She clasped her hands at her breast. "I can ask nothing more. Thank you, Mr... " She could not help being aware of the irony of her applying such an appellation to a Negro, even one as well-spoken as he. "... Mr. Mills."

With the twitch of an eyebrow, "Lazarus will do. Shall we go consult with Mr. Masters?"

∞∞∞

As Lizzie would soon learn, the Masters group from Illinois made up the largest contingent in the Mills train, collectively numbering eighteen wagons and sixty-four persons. A wealthy farmer with a large extended family and many friends, all bent on reaching California, Josiah Masters was the one who had seen Lazarus Mills's advertisement in the St. Joseph Gazette and contracted with him to lead the train. Other smaller groups had subsequently joined up, the wagon master's vast knowledge and experience increasing the safety of an otherwise perilous journey.

Selling herself as a cook turned out to be easier than Lizzie would have imagined. Josiah Masters was a large, well-built man with a paternalistic attitude that assumed all females had the skill to cater to mens' needs regardless of their background or training. And so it was that she returned to the four drovers as a fellow employee hired to replace their dead comrade. While Lazarus Mills explained this new state of affairs, Lizzie did not miss the sensual delight that quickly followed their amazement. Lazarus sensed it as well, prompting him to say,

"Miss Hamilton has only one obligation to you fellows, and that is to prepare your meals. Otherwise, you are to respect her privacy. The rules of the train require nothing less, as you well know."

"Why, sure 'nough, cap'n," replied the man she had spoken to earlier. He snatched his hat from his head, held out a horny hand to Lizzie, and said, "Earl Long, Miss Hamilton, and I'm right glad to make your acquaintance. These here cowpokes is Robert Miller what we call Bobby..."

A tall lanky young man with light-blue eyes, sandy hair and a scraggly beard stepped forward, removed his hat, and said, "Ma'am."

"... and this here's Ed Perkins," the man continued.

This one was about the same age as the second, but he had a short stocky build, eyes so dark they were nearly black, and a bushy head of hair of the same color. He stepped up and mimicked his companion's greeting.

"And last but not least, the runt." He ruffled the short brown hair of the youngest of the group, who appeared to be no more than sixteen or seventeen. He had the slight build of a near-man, hazel eyes, and smooth, hairless cheeks. "Meet my nephew, Will Long. Just a whippersnapper from the looks o' him, but he's already a seasoned hand. Right, men?"

The others murmured their agreement, and the awkward introductions came to an end.

Lazarus said, "Right, then. You all get on with your supper..." He gestured toward the chicken roasting on an iron spit over the fire. "... while I rustle up a feather mattress for Miss Hamilton. You will need to rearrange your wagon so she can sleep inside."

A round of shared looks. Then the man named Earl shrugged and said, "Sure thing. We'll get right on it. Meanwhile, you have a seat over yonder, Miss Hamilton, and we'll get to dividing up that there chicken. This chow's on us."

There were several small logs arranged around the fire pit, where the spitted chicken was oozing juices and sending up a marvelous aroma. Lizzie sat on one of them, her carpetbag close beside her, while the others busied themselves with the meal. Lazarus stood watching for a moment, then turned back toward his own camp. His departure left a small knot of panic in Lizzie's stomach. She was essentially on her own with four men whose characters she had no way of knowing. That she had felt more secure with a black man present was a new experience for her.

She waited, her eyes set on the western horizon where the sun was fast sinking. Eventually the one named Earl, the eldest and apparent leader, thrust a tin plate holding a fair-sized chunk of chicken and a slab of dense light-brown bread into one hand and a crude knife and fork into the other. He lifted a tall blackened pot from the edge of the fire, poured coffee into a tin cup, then handed it to her. She looked up into eyes that seemed to be laughing at her and thanked him.

The men arranged themselves around the fire and tore into their own meals, eschewing the use of utensils but using hands that did not appear to have been washed in many days. They periodically wiped their greasy fingers on their pant legs, but Lizzie had no such easy solution for the slime that soon coated her own fingers despite her best effort to eat delicately with her plate balanced on her knees. There was no fine napkin with which to clean herself, so she suffered the discomfort in silence and hoped she would soon have the opportunity to wash.

The men finished eating long before Lizzie. They set their plates aside and rolled cigarettes. Earl took a long drag, plucked some stray tobacco from his tongue, and stretched his legs out, his lazy gaze fixed on her.

"So, darlin'," he said, "looks like we're gonna have the pleasure of your company for some months to come, so we'd best get to know each other. You can start by tellin' us your first name."

Lizzie stared back at him. If she were to keep control of this situation, instinct told her she must begin now. She waited a period of time before saying, "As Mr. Mills has already told you, I am here solely to cook for you. The familiarity you suggest is not only inappropriate but unnecessary. You may address me as Miss Hamilton, and I shall address you as Mr. Long." She shifted her frosty gaze to his nephew. "You as well, young man." Then to the lanky fair-haired man, "Mr. Miller, I believe," and to the dark stocky one, "and Mr. Perkins." Then to them all, "I believe the journey will be more pleasant for everyone if we are respectful and courteous to one another." She stood. "Now, if you will kindly show me where I might find the washing implements, I shall begin my duties at once."

Something dark had crept into Earl Long's expression as she spoke, and she experienced another jolt of doubt as to whether she had made the right decision to embark on this endeavor. He regarded her with narrowed eyes and tightened jaw before saying, "As you wish, *Miss Hamilton*. This way."

He struck out toward the wagon, and she followed, the nape of her neck burning as she sensed the stares of the others with every step she took. From now on, she would need to maintain an implacable will, and she took comfort from the knowledge that, for better or worse, that had always been her strongest trait. Whether it would stand up to the challenge now before her would be decided in the weeks and months to come.

Chapter Fourteen

Lizzie wakened to a loud pounding, the vibrations of which shook the feather mattress on which she lay. It was semi-dark inside the wagon, a faint pearly light barely seeping through the canvas covering. She raised up on one arm, heart thudding against her ribs.

The pounding came again followed by a rough, "Wake up in there! It's past dawn, and you got work to do."

Memory came rushing in: she was responsible for the feeding of four cowboys, and they were no doubt wanting their breakfast. She threw back the blanket and fumbled for the dress she had discarded in exhaustion the night before.

While she was washing their few supper dishes, a man sent by her employer, Mr. Masters, had stumbled into camp with a mattress slung over one shoulder and a bundle of bedding in the crook of the other arm. Earl and Bobby had climbed into the wagon box and, after much banging and scraping and cursing, had beckoned the man to heave his burden inside. Later, as dusk settled over the camp, she had climbed into a space barely eight feet by four into which had been crammed so many barrels and boxes, canvas bundles and odd-shaped lengths of wood—even several spare wagon wheels—she could move about only by crawling on said mattress. A blanket had been supplied, but there were no sheets or pillowcase for the thin excuse of an item meant for that purpose. She had not even bothered to put on her nightdress but had simply slipped out of her dress and petticoats and lain down in chemise and drawers. Her hands were clean from having dealt with the supper things, but her face still bore the grime of the day and her hair, though loosened from its pins, did not get its usual nightly brushing or braiding. She had fallen straight asleep and not twitched a muscle until rudely wakened by that fist on the side of the wagon box.

She fastened the hooks of her dress and did up her hair as best she could. The rear side of the wagon box could be dropped by removing two iron pins. She pulled them out and let the section fall with a thud so she could climb out. It was a little past dawn, and fires already burned in other camps within her view. Not, however, in this one. Earl Long stood before her with his fists on his hips, his scowl just visible in the nascent light.

"Well, if it ain't the sleepin' princess. Did her highness decide to wake up and join us?"

She gritted her teeth and said, "I am sorry. It will not happen again."

"I reckon time will tell 'bout that. Any chance you could get the fire goin' so's we could have our coffee?"

She was glad it was too dark for him to see her blush. "Well, I, uh…"

"Let me guess. Don't know how to unbank a fire. Or start one, for that matter. Right?"

Her silence was his answer.

He sighed. "Okay. I'll show you what's what, but it'll be the last time, so take heed. I got enough work to do without doin' yours, too."

"I do not expect you to do my work. If you will instruct me concerning things with which I have no experience, you will only have to do so once."

He turned away with a skeptical grunt, and she followed him over to the fire pit, which was in a slight depression that had been bordered with stones. She saw that the previous day's ashes had been piled up against the stones in one spot. He took a piece of the dismantled iron apparatus they had used to spit the chicken and gently pulled the ashes away to expose a dull red center. He knelt down and blew on the coals while he fed them with a small twig. Flame rose instantly. He added more twigs and branches from a pile that lay to one side of the pit, and a sizable fire soon leapt upward.

"This here's the last of the wood," he said. "After we leave, you'll have to go over yonder to the woods… " He swept his arm out into the darkness. "… and gather more."

She gaped at him. "You are leaving?"

"You think we got nothin' better to do than lollygag around camp? We're workin' men. Today we'll be movin' the herd to better pasture so's they get their fill 'fore the drive begins tomorrow. So how 'bout rustlin' us up some grub?"

Here it was, her first test as a cook—a position she knew nothing about. She tamped down her panic and said, "What would you like?"

With heavy sarcasm, "Lemme see. How's about we start with a bowl of strawberries and cream followed by some eggs, a mess o' fried potatoes, and a big juicy steak?"

He was going to make this as difficult as possible for her. She stood silent until he continued with, "No? Well, then, I guess we'll have to settle for bacon and the rest o' that bakery bread since you're gettin' such a late start. And coffee. Don't forget the coffee."

"All right. I can manage if you will show me where to find the needed foodstuffs. I shall familiarize myself with the wagon and its contents after you are gone, but for now, it seems a jumble to me."

He shook his head, muttered something unintelligible, and went back to the wagon, where he thumped his hand on a medium-sized barrel and said, "Bacon." He opened the hinged front of the large square pine box into which she had put the washed plates and cups the night before. This time he pulled out a heavy black skillet, a long iron fork, and a strange wooden apparatus topped by an iron cup from which protruded a long handle. He thrust it at her, saying, "You know what this is, right?"

"Well, I—" She caught a familiar odor rising up. "—of course. A coffee grinder."

"Thank the lord, she ain't a complete ninny. Now get crackin'. We gotta get goin.'"

"Where are the others?"

"Bringin' in the horses." Even as he spoke, she heard muffled voices approaching as well as the distinct sound of horses' hooves striking the ground. He turned without a word and headed in that direction.

She took a deep breath and let it out slowly. All right, then. Where to begin?

Her eye fell on the blackened coffee pot that had been pulled from the fire the night before. She picked it up, carried it several steps away, and dumped out the remaining dregs. She carried it back to the ten-gallon water barrel attached to the side of the wagon and used the dipper hanging there to rinse it out. Then she filled it nearly to the brim and set it down while she investigated the intricacies of the coffee mill.

The wood base was some six inches square and four inches in height with a drawer taking up most of that space. She pulled it out and saw that it was filled with rich-colored ground coffee. She understood the mechanism immediately. Beans, which were found in a large burlap bag marked in green paint with the single word *coffee,* were placed in the iron bowl atop the apparatus and ground via the wooden handle so that the usable product collected in the drawer below. Ingenious, she thought, more than a little proud that she had conquered at least one aspect of her new job. She scooped some of the grounds in the drawer into the pot and took it back to the fire, resting it in the hottest place.

She went back to the rear of the wagon, climbed up, and raised the lid of the barrel Earl had identified as containing bacon. A smoky odor floated up, sending her mind on a poignant journey back to the smokehouse at Rocklands. If the meat in this barrel had even half the flavor of the wonderful hams and pork shoulders that had emerged from that magical place, they were all in for a treat.

A flaky brown substance covered the barrel's contents. She plunged her hand down and felt around until her fingers came into contact with a cool slimy object. She pulled it out, a large chunk of smoke-browned meat that must have weighed close to five pounds. She could see that portions had been cut from one end. She rummaged in the pine cook box for a flat cutting board and a wicked-looking butcher knife. She sliced off what she considered to be an adequate-sized amount and returned the remainder to the barrel, shoving it deep beneath whatever it was that covered it.

As she replaced the lid, she heard a sizzling sound coming from the direction of the fire. She jumped down and ran over, horrified to see coffee and grounds spewing from the spout of the coffeepot and cascading down onto the fire. She started to reach for the handle but stopped just in time. How would she do her work if she burned her hands? Her eye fell on a stout stick among the few remaining pieces of wood beside the pit. She grabbed it and slipped it through the handle. By the time she had dragged the pot out of the center of the fire, more had spilled out, and she had no idea how much remained for their breakfast. Things were not going well.

∞∞∞

Lizzie watched the four cowboys ride off with a sigh of relief. They had filled their canteens with water, taken some hardtack and jerky, and told her they would return for supper late in the day. She had been instructed to go into town after she completed her morning chores in order to buy whatever she needed to prepare a hearty evening meal, which would be their last before setting out for California on the morrow. She was told Mr. Masters had credit at all the stores in town, so she could be generous in her purchases. She had never in her life shopped for foodstuffs, but how difficult could it be? That aside, a trip to town would serve as a pleasant reward for having gotten through her first meal as a cook unscathed.

She had managed to fry the meat without burning it too badly. They had made faces over the coffee, which she had to agree had a disagreeable bitter taste, but they had eaten the meat with obvious relish and dipped the remainder of the bakery bread in the grease from the skillet, seeming satisfied in the end. Now she was free of them for the entire day, which would give her time to slow the juggernaut of the past day's happenings and acclimate herself to her new role.

She decided her first task was to heat some water. She had washed the previous night's dishes in cold water, the harsh lye soap sudsing eventually but still leaving a thin film of grease on the tin plates. She found an iron kettle in the cook box and filled it with water from the barrel. At the fire pit, she threw what remained of the wood pile onto the faltering fire. While it took hold, she studied the device they had used for spitting the chicken: two iron rods of equal length with a point at one end and a ring at the other plus a stout iron bar with two hooks attached in the center. She pushed the pointed end of each iron post into the ground on either side of the pit and slid the bar through the rings. She lifted the water kettle and settled the handle onto one of the hooks so it was suspended over the fire.

When the water was hot, she dipped some into a tin washbasin and washed the breakfast dishes. After putting them away, she spent some time exploring the contents of the barrels and sacks of food in the wagon. In addition to the bacon and coffee, she found beans, rice, flour, hardtack, lard, sugar, molasses, cornmeal, salt, and something called saleratus, the use of which was a mystery to her. It struck her once again that she was adrift in a sea of ignorance where the getting and preparing of food was concerned. Yet her ability to get to California and redeem the bearer bonds depended entirely on performing that very service to the satisfaction of four skeptical, disrespectful men. What if she failed?

She shoved the thought and the anxiety that came with it to the back of her mind. She had managed thus far, and she would continue to do so no matter what the odds. She clenched her jaw in determination, tied on her sunbonnet, and set out to accomplish her next duty, that of collecting wood for the fire.

A forested ravine lay perhaps an eighth of a mile distant where Black Snake Creek descended to the Missouri River. She kept her eyes on the ground as she moved in that direction, but the prairie where the wagons were camped had already been picked clean of burnable fuel. Once she entered the woods, she saw other women and their children embarked on the same mission. She wandered farther and farther afield, bending to pick up any dry branches she encountered. Arms finally loaded with as much as she could carry, she headed back.

It was another fine day with a cloudless sky of blue and temperatures much warmer than was usual for the season. By the time she had dumped her load beside the fire pit, she was flushed and perspiring.

She decided it was time to do whatever she could to enhance what she knew was a most disheveled appearance. Although the fire had died out, the water in the kettle was still warm. She dipped some into the washbasin, carried it to the rear of the wagon, and climbed up, securing the gate behind herself. She pulled the rear canvas cover as tight as possible and crawled onto the mattress. She untied her sunbonnet, which was never off her head when she was out in the damaging sun. She still wore the clothing into which she had changed after discarding her disguise when she escaped from the *Princess*. She wrinkled her nose at their sad condition and pulled her extra dress and underthings from her carpetbag.

Sitting Indian fashion, she placed the washbasin in front of her and took up the bar of mild soap she was glad she had thought to keep with her. She washed her face and dried it on the hem of her skirt. Next she stripped to the waist and washed her torso, once again using her clothing as a towel. She removed the bearer bonds from their hiding place in the soiled chemise and tucked them into the clean garment's pocket, then pulled it over her head. She finished washing her lower regions. Finally, dressed in fresh drawers and petticoats, she put on her clean though somewhat wrinkled brown gingham dress.

She pulled out her brush, loosened her auburn hair, and brushed it with long steady strokes. After she had pinned it up again, she pulled out her hand mirror to study the result. She felt nearly as clean as if she had been attended by her personal maid Polly as in the old days, but she acknowledged, as she often had since leaving South Carolina, that her hair-dressing skills did not begin to match those of her former slave. Nonetheless, she decided she was presentable enough for her jaunt into town.

Before leaving, she used the remaining water in the kettle to wash her discarded dress and undergarments. She draped them over some nearby bushes to dry, took up her parasol, and set out toward town.

She took her time, curious to study the particulars of her various fellow travelers' camps. She was passing some wagons somewhere near the center of the company when she stopped cold, a gasp of surprised recognition sending her hand to her mouth. Slight frame, flaming red hair—it could be no one else.

"Cora!" she cried.

The girl turned and cocked her head, shading her eyes from the morning sun. It took only a moment for her to grin and call back, "Lizzie? Is it really you?"

They closed the distance between them in the blink of an eye and embraced, Lizzie's joy at seeing a familiar face so intense she could barely contain herself.

Cora pulled back and gushed, "I was so sad to wake up that morning and realize you were gone without me even saying goodbye. I knew the plan worked because all the passengers were abuzz about it. That Mr. O'Rourke raised such a stink as you would not believe. Carrying on about how you had robbed him when he was the one who had held you practically in servitude all that time. It did my heart good to see him fume and squirm. But you—I never thought I would see you again. It is like a miracle. Still, what are you doing here? I thought you would return to New Orleans and take sea passage to California. You certainly have the means to do so. So why—"

"Give the poor lady a chance to speak, Cora," said Mrs. Fielding , who had come up behind her daughter with a look of indulgent exasperation. She turned a friendly face to Lizzie. "What a lovely surprise, Miss Hamilton. I apologize for my daughter's forward chatter, although I am sure you became well used to it on our journey up the Mississippi. Please, come over to our fire and let me offer you a cup of tea. We are so pleased to see you again."

Lizzie smiled in turn. "I was on my way to town, but I would be delighted to break my journey and accept your invitation. Such a coincidence as our finding each other surely deserves more than a hasty greeting and farewell."

They led her into a camp where three wagons were angled around the ubiquitous fire pit, this one rather larger than the one at the four drovers' camp. A number of wooden chairs, barrels and milking stools sat scattered about, only two of which were occupied at the moment. A bonneted lady who was heavy with child sat on a sturdy rocking chair in the shade of the near wagon, her nimble fingers busy with needle and thread on what appeared to be an infant's gown. A tall bespectacled man sat on a low-slung ladder-back chair a short distance away, his long arms and legs canting in all directions, an open book suspended between his knees.

Cora grabbed Lizzie's hand and rushed toward them, crying, "Aunt Sarah, Uncle Jonathan, you will never believe it! This is the very lady I told you about. The one who was so badly used by that gambling scoundrel on the *Princess* riverboat. Lizzie—no, we must do it properly." She pulled herself up and put on a serious expression. "May I introduce Miss Elizabeth Hamilton?" To Lizzie, "Lizzie, meet my aunt and uncle, Mr. and Mrs. Jonathan Collins."

The man stood, cradling his book in one arm. He swept off his spectacles and pushed a shock of light-brown hair away from his high brow. He gave a slow, easy smile that brought dimples to his chiseled, sharp-featured face and a warm light to his hazel eyes.

"We are most happy to meet you, Miss Hamilton. Our niece has regaled us with the story of your courageous escape, the particulars of which seemed so fantastical we wondered whether she had made them up out of her rich but sometimes overactive imagination."

Lizzie blushed. "She no doubt embellished what happened, but the fact remains that I would not be here were it not for her encouragement and aid, and for that she has my eternal gratitude."

Mrs. Collins had struggled to her feet and was also smiling. Lizzie saw she was rather tall for a woman, towering over her by at least half a foot, but pretty with delicate features, cornflower-blue eyes, and golden hair now hidden beneath her bonnet. She offered her hand. "My dear, we are so glad you are safe."

"Please do not stand on my account," said Lizzie. "I see you are near to your confinement, and I know from my elder sister's experiences that such a time is not pleasant."

"I have no reason to complain. But I shall take your advice and sit."

"As shall we all," said Maude, taking Lizzie's elbow and leading her to another chair. "It will take me but a moment to make a pot of tea in celebration of this lovely reunion. Unless you would prefer coffee?"

Lizzie made a face. "I think I have gone off coffee after the disgusting brew I concocted this morning. The four cowboys whom I am responsible for feeding could barely choke it down."

"Cowboys!?" Cora exclaimed. "Feeding? What on earth... ?"

"Give the poor lady a chance to catch her bearings," her mother chided. "The tea will be ready before we know it. Time enough for explanations then."

She bustled over to the fire, removed the kettle simmering there, and carried it around the middle wagon and out of sight.

Cora pouted but pulled up a stool, fisted her hands in her lap, and scuffed her feet in the sandy soil. Lizzie smiled at her, then sent her gaze about the camp. A lad with bright red hair whom she assumed to be Cora's twin brother Carl straddled the wagon tree of one of the wagons as he whittled a piece of wood. A group of children were playing some sort of running game just beyond the wagons, their high-pitched laughter wafting in on a light breeze. She recognized Cora's little sister Lilly among them.

"Lilly has not wasted time in making friends," she commented.

"No credit to her," said a sour Cora. "They all belong to our party, and they have known each other for ages. There are twenty of us traveling from Evansville."

Lizzie's eyes widened. "In three wagons?"

"No, silly. These three are ours. Or two of them, anyway." She canted her head toward her aunt and uncle. "Uncle Jonathan, Aunt Sarah and Missy have the other one, making eight people in this camp. Our minister Reverend Jamison and his family have seven wagons and twelve more people. All of us plus the people in six independent wagons form the Jamison group. Lazarus gave us that name because Jamisons are the largest family, but that did not stop the men from electing my papa as captain of the group when they got together last night."

Lizzie smiled at the girl's obvious pride over this apparent distinction bestowed on her father.

"Now, of course," she continued, "you must belong to our group as well. What fun we shall have!"

Lizzie shook her head. "A nice thought, but I cannot be part of this group. I have a job I must fulfill."

"Job? Why on earth would a wealthy lady such as yourself need a job?"

Her mother, who had come around the wagon carrying a wooden tray laden with tin cups and a teapot, frowned a rebuke, but Lizzie intervened with,

"I understand Cora's curiosity, Mrs. Fielding. It is a fair question, and one I am happy to answer."

As Mrs. Fielding settled into a chair, tray on her lap, and began pouring out the tea, Lizzie launched into her tale of robbery and her subsequent desperate search for a pathway to California.

"And so," she concluded, "Lazarus appealed to Mr. Masters on my behalf, and I was hired on to replace the cook that died."

Cora was wide eyed. "But do you know how to cook?"

A wry grimace. "Although I pretended otherwise out of desperation, I admit I am a novice at the culinary arts. Not even a novice, I fear. Witness the horrible coffee I prepared this morning."

"Did you let it boil over?" asked Mrs. Collins, her pretty face predicting the answer she expected.

"Why, yes. It made a terrible mess and almost put out the fire."

"Then there is your solution. Coffee becomes bitter when it is boiled. It is best to let it simmer just below a boil. If you do so next time, you will find a quite tasty brew, I assure you."

"Such a simple thing. Thank you for the advice."

"It was my pleasure. You must be certain to ask if you have other questions. My sister-in-law Maude and I have been cooking for many years and would be happy to share our knowledge with you at any time."

Her husband looked up from his book with a fond smile. "You could ask for no finer teachers than these two, Miss Hamilton."

"Then I shall take advantage of their kind offer," Lizzie replied, a measure of anxiety slipping from her shoulders.

The sound of approaching hoofbeats led Maude Fielding to say, "That must be Richard." To Lizzie, "My husband went into town this morning for some last-minute supplies. The thought of a months-long journey out of reach of all but the scantiest of stores is a new experience for a man who has spent his entire life in town."

They rose as a man rode into camp on a sturdy-looking chestnut gelding. He wore work clothes and a floppy felt hat, hardly what Lizzie would have expected of the successful physician his daughter had described. He dismounted and pulled bulging saddlebags from the horse's back. Maude stepped up to receive a kiss on her cheek, then turned to Lizzie and said,

"Here is my husband, Dr. Fielding. Richard, this is the Miss Hamilton with whom the girls and I shared the journey up the Mississippi. To our great surprise and pleasure, we find that she is attached to this train as well."

The doctor came forward, a medium-sized man with jet black hair, kind brown eyes, and a sunburned face above a full moustache.

He took Lizzie's hand and bowed over it. "Another intrepid traveler who wishes to see the elephant. Welcome to our camp, Miss Hamilton."

Lizzie was puzzling over his words—see the elephant?—when two little girls broke away from their peers and ran into camp.

The older, whom she knew to be ten-year-old Lilly Fielding, skidded to a stop in front of her father and cried, "Did you bring it?"

The other was a yellow-haired moppet of perhaps five years whose resemblance to Mrs. Collins left no doubt as to her identity. She pulled up a step behind Lilly, her face wreathed in a hopeful smile. "Yes, Uncle Richard. We are ever so hungry!"

He looked down on them with mock severity. "Hungry, are you? After such a hearty breakfast but a few hours ago? Surely you have no room for... " He rummaged in his trouser pockets and brought forth a small paper bag. "... these pieces of rock candy."

Lilly giggled and snatched the bag from her father's hand, saying, "Silly Papa."

She was turning away when her mother reached out a hand to stop her. "And what do you say to your kind papa for bringing you such a fine treat?"

A sheepish smile. "Thank you, Papa"

Her little cousin parroted the sentiment. She had been eying Lizzie with curiosity. Now her mother pulled her to her side and said, "This lady is our new friend, Miss Hamilton. She has just joined the train, and we are sure to see much of her in the days and weeks to come." To Lizzie, "This is our daughter, Missy."

The child shook her golden curls. "No. I am Sarah Collins, just like my mama. They call me Missy. But it is not my true name. I am *Sarah*."

Lizzie hid her smile and put on a grave face. "And a fine name it is, Sarah. A favorite of mine since I have an older sister of the same name."

"Well, then," the child said, "you may call me Missy like everyone else. So long as you *know*."

"Missy it is, then. But you may be sure I shall never forget your real name."

Appeased, she ran off to join her cousin, who was already investigating the contents of the paper bag.

"Well, now you have met us all," said Mrs. Fielding. "Except for Cora's twin brother." She looked over to the young carver and called, "Carl? Come and meet Miss Hamilton."

The boy hesitated, his slight frown revealing his pique at having his handiwork interrupted. Eventually he laid down his tools, kicked his leg over the wagon tongue, and slouched forward. He might have been Cora's twin, but they looked nothing alike except for the bright red hair and blue eyes. Whereas Cora was short with a slight body just beginning to bloom into womanhood, Carl was nearly as tall as his father with broad shoulders, burgeoning arm muscles, and a face marred by the spots that often plagued boys of his age. He muttered his greeting, then returned to his whittling at a nod of dismissal from his mother.

Dr. Fielding took his saddlebags to one of the wagons to unpack their contents, Mrs. Collins returned to her sewing, and Mr. Collins fiddled with his book, obviously anxious to continue his reading. Lizzie decided it was time to stop intruding on their private time.

She handed her tea cup to Mrs. Fielding and said, "I shan't keep you from your business any longer. It has been such a pleasure conversing with you."

"Oh, you cannot leave yet!" cried Cora. "You have barely arrived. And it is such a boring day with nothing to do but wait for the morrow when we shall be off on our adventure."

"But I must get on with my chores," said Lizzie. "I am to have a hearty supper ready by the time my charges return from whatever they are doing with the cattle, and I have not a clue what I must buy in order to provide it."

"Why not take your noon meal with us?" said Mrs. Fielding. "Perhaps we can help you decide what might be needed for your supper. Besides, Cora is right. There is little to occupy us today. In fact, I might join you in a walk into town. Richard has found the things he needed at the hardware store, but I should like the exercise of a trip for myself. We must all strengthen ourselves for the journey since even we women must traverse most of it on foot."

This was startling news to Lizzie. Walk to California?

"Please stay," pleaded Cora.

And so she was persuaded to spend the following hours with the Fielding and Collins families. By the time she and Maude Fielding set off for town in the early afternoon, she had received needed instruction on the basics of outdoor cooking and had promised to come back often in the days ahead. It was an easy promise to make. This boisterous but kind family seemed to accept her as one of their own, allowing her to believe for the first time since the days before disaster befell her family that life might have good things in store for her, after all. The path ahead would not be easy. Of this she was certain. But she might not be as alone in facing it as she had feared.

Chapter Fifteen

The great journey to California began before dawn on a cold, drizzly morning. Despite the inclement weather, a buzz of excitement permeated the surrounding camps, and Lizzie used it to fortify her spirits as she went about her morning chores. Following Maude's advice, she had gathered more wood the night before and stored some of it in the wagon against the possibility of rain. Thus, she was able to start a small fire to brew coffee and warm the remains of the beef roast purchased in town the day before. She enjoyed watching the faces of her charges as they took their first sip of coffee, their initial suspicion turning to amazed pleasure at its robust, smooth flavor. Earl Long gave her a grudging nod of approval before rising with the others to prepare the herd for travel.

Lizzie had been surprised to learn that the wagon train would operate under a careful set of organizational and legal principles. Wagon master Lazarus Mills had held a general meeting of the various captains and their assistants the night before to review what had already been agreed to in writing by all adult male travelers. The meeting was held around a fire at Lazarus's nearby camp, and she had walked over to see what she could learn.

It seemed there were five sub-groups within this large train: her boss's Masters group with its eighteen wagons and sixty-four people, her new friends' Jamison group with their thirteen wagons and forty-two people, the Faraday group of twelve wagons and forty people, the Eastman group of thirteen wagons and forty-nine people, and finally, the Stafford group of fourteen wagons and fifty-three people for a total of two hundred and forty-eight souls. All groups had sent their elected representatives to the meeting. These along with other interested persons created a large complement of chattering, excited individuals. The moment

Lazarus Mills stepped into their midst, however, silence fell and his clear resonant voice carried to one and all.

He began by reiterating the rules of the upcoming journey. There would be no drinking of alcoholic beverages except for medicinal purposes, no gambling, no fighting, and no swearing in the presence of women. Any infractions, be they minor or major, would be brought before the group captains with Lazarus himself acting as judge and disciplinarian. Any major crime would be adjudicated in the same manner absent a government-sanctioned officer of the law.

As for the particulars of daily trail life, a rifle would be discharged at four o'clock in the morning as a signal to rise. All parties would be ready to travel by seven o'clock, which hour would be marked by another rifle discharge. How far the train traveled each day and when it would stop depended on the wagon master's judgment alone. However, any group captains who so desired could ride out with him in the mid-afternoon and participate in the choice of a spot to pitch camp for the night, providing it was understood that his judgment would take precedence if there were any disagreement among the others. Whenever possible, the train would not travel on Sunday mornings in order to accommodate any planned religious services. Again, this decision would be his alone depending on their location and any difficulties anticipated ahead. He would also be the ultimate arbiter as to interruptions of travel for reasons of illness, equipment repair, or needed domestic tasks such as washing of clothes and other maintenance needs. Finally, each group would be responsible for guard duty one night out of five between the hours of eight o'clock p.m. and four o'clock a.m. unless circumstances dictated such duty to be unnecessary. In the same manner, each group would provide herders in rotating sequence who would be responsible for letting the oxen and other animals out to pasture at night and driving them in for hitching in the morning unless security required these animals to be corralled within the nightly circle of wagons. He then went on to describe how each group would form up at the end of the day's travel.

The final piece of business was to call out the order in which the sub-groups would travel, the Masters group at the forefront of the train and the Jamison group at the rear, a fact that pleased Lizzie in that she would be close to her friends given that the Masters cattle herd would travel last so as not to engulf the other wagons in the dust cloud it would surely create. After a short period allowed for questions, of which there were very few and none of which challenged his authority in any way, Lazarus dismissed the meeting, and the participants began to disperse.

As Lizzie made her way the short distance through the darkness to her own camp, she had contemplated the respect and power these white men were willing to afford a black man. They were not only willing to submit to his authority, but they had even signed legal documents verifying their acquiescence. How had he come to hold such an unlikely position, not to mention his cultured command of the English language? Where was he from? And what had he done to earn the trust of these people?

Her questions had remained unanswered, however, since the rush to prepare for travel had taken every single moment from the meeting's dismissal until the following morning when Will Long, Earl's young nephew, hitched two yoke of oxen to the wagon and waited for the train to move out ahead of them. Even though she had been warned she would be expected to walk much of the way, Will, who had been the most respectful of the cowboys, suggested she sit on the forward driver's box. He gave her a hand up, then took his place to the left side of the lead oxen. When it was finally their turn to fall into line, he snapped his long whip with a loud crack, and the animals lumbered forward.

The thrill Lizzie experienced over finally being on her way to California soon leaked away like water from a holey bucket. They had barely started down the hill toward town when they came to a halt behind what looked like hundreds of wagons snaking down to the ferry landing at the end of Francis Street. It was a scene of ordered chaos: hordes of milling, complaining animals flanking a sea of white-covered wagons, the drivers and passengers lounging against their wagons or gathered in groups to while away the time, the road beneath their feet a swamp of mud from the previous night's rainfall. She rightly assumed it would take most if not all of the day just to work their way to the riverbank and board one of the several flat boats or the steam ferry plying the river's muddy waters from bank to bank. Even then, the congestion would not end, for the far bank looked like a vast camping ground for those who had stopped to regroup after making it across. How this great wash of humanity would ever sort itself out was beyond her.

She settled in to wait, but tranquility was impossible to achieve given her growing impatience. The morning hours crept by at a pace commensurate with their snail-like progress forward. Toward mid-day, the heavy cloud cover lightened and broke up, allowing thin watery sunshine to dry and warm the air. She thought about getting down and taking some exercise, but the realization of what the mud would do to her fine kid boots sent the idea fleeing. Then her eyes fell on a familiar figure walking toward her along the side of the road, and her mood brightened.

"Mr. Collins!" she called.

Jonathan Collins looked up, saw her, and removed his felt hat in recognition. He came closer, smiling and saying, "Good day to you, Miss Hamilton. How goes it?"

"Too slowly for my taste. And you? You seem to be going in the opposite direction from everyone else. Did you leave something behind?"

"Not at all. Sarah and Missy are napping in the wagon, so I took the opportunity for a little walk. Our oxen are happy to inch along behind Richard's team and need little direction at the moment."

She patted the board seat beside her. "Then come up for a time and help me pass this interminable day."

He glanced over his shoulder. Hesitated only a moment before saying, "Why not?"

He placed a muddy boot on a wheel spoke, hauled his long frame up into the box and sat down.

"Today may, as you say, seem interminable," he said, "but the elephant's tracks stretch for a very long distance. I fear our patience will be sorely tried many times between now and the happy day we reach our destination."

"*Elephant's tracks*? Whatever do you mean? Such a beast hardly seems likely to be found in the wilds of Western America."

He laughed. "On that score, you are correct. Buffalo, antelope, coyote, even bear—these we are sure to encounter. But absent the stray circus or two, no elephants."

His grin was infectious, his eyes crinkling with warmth, his dimples deep and charming. She smiled back and said, "Then why, pray tell, do I hear people, including your own Dr. Fielding, make reference to seeing the elephant?"

"I admit it is an odd turn of phrase. Current use has little to do with its rather mundane origins during the early years when circuses first used elephants in their parades. As the story goes, a farmer heard there was a circus in town. He had never seen an elephant and very much desired to do so. So he loaded his wagon with vegetables to sell at market and set out for town. On the way, he encountered the circus parade, which was being led by the elephant. His frightened horses bolted, overturning the wagon and ruining his load of vegetables. According to the legend, the farmer was not angry over this turn of events. Rather, he responded with, 'I don't give a hang, for I have seen the elephant.'

"The phrase was picked up and popularized by the gold rushers of the last decade. For them, the elephant symbolized two things: the perils involved in their overland journey to California and the overarching, unequaled experience of living the adventure of a lifetime. Thus, even emigrants of today use this phrase to describe the sum total of their experiences in traveling to California."

"What an interesting story. You are a fount of information, Mr. Collins."

"Merely a fool for the printed word. I cannot help myself. If I am curious about a matter, I must dig until I find the answer."

"That is an admirable trait, not a foolish one."

"An opinion not always shared by my family, I fear."

She raised her eyebrows. "Oh?"

"My father was a man of industry. A chair and cabinetmaker who believed that working with one's hands is akin to Godliness. He would point to St. Paul, whom Scripture says made his living as a tentmaker, for affirmation as to the nobility of his profession. Alas, I was a hopeless carpenter, preferring to read a book over learning that trade. Fortunately for us all, my younger brother inherited my father's skill and has now taken over his business."

"Freeing you to pursue your own interests?"

"Would that it had been that simple. My father's next aspiration was for me to enter the ministry. My religious faith would have been up to the task, but I have no affinity for public speaking. Nor do I especially care for the strictures and limitations of the organized church. He was forced to search for yet another honorable profession. He decided on medicine and sent me to the Louisville Medical Institute. The poor man was to be disappointed once again. I had much more interest in reading Plato than in learning my anatomy. At last, he listened to my pleadings and agreed that I might transfer to Louisville College and finally attain the classical education I craved."

A soft smile. "The one benefit to accrue from my academic wanderings was finding my Sarah. Her brother Richard and I took rooms together during our first year in medicine. He continued on to be the brilliant physician he is while I turned my mind to the arts, but we maintained our living arrangements and became the best of friends. I traveled home with him to Evansville one Christmastide and met my dear girl." He spread his hands. "You have seen for yourself the result of that fortuitous holiday junket."

Lizzie could see the light of love on his face as surely as if it were a bright beacon guiding a ship to shore. Her mind flashed back to the days when she had imagined herself to be in love with Jack O'Rourke. She had not discerned even a vestige of such devotion in his visage or behavior. How could she have been so misguided as to trust him?

She knew the answer. It was naivete. And panic. She had expected someone else—Jack, even God Himself—to solve her problems. The result had been absolute failure. Now she was left with nothing but her own cunning to see her through. Perhaps one day she would be loved by a man such as this, but she would not allow her well-being to depend on it. She must never forget that her destiny lay in her hands alone.

Which was exactly what Jonathan Collins had done by refusing to allow his father to deter him from what his heart desired. Intrigued, she asked,

"Did it anger your father when you failed to follow his wishes?"

"Anger? No. Disappoint, as I have said? Definitely. He would rather have had a preacher or a medical doctor for a son than a lowly teacher. But he adjusted."

"A teacher. Where... ?"

"I operated a private school for boys in New Harmony, Indiana." Seeing the name meant nothing to her, he added, "New Harmony is a community on the Wabash River some forty miles northwest of Evansville. Close enough to Sarah's family for frequent visits but a place that prizes education above all else."

"It sounds ideal. Why did you leave it all to emigrate to California?"

"That young state has great need of the civilizing attributes of education. But to be perfectly candid, it was Richard who convinced me to join him. He was active in the Underground Railroad—"

Her sharp intake of breath cut him off. With raised eyebrows, "You have experience of this movement?"

"Indeed I do! It was instrumental in my family's downfall!"

Now it was her turn to relate her painful family history. As she spoke, she saw his innate compassion morph into barely-concealed distaste. Yet his voice was gentle as he said,

"I am sorry for the great pain your family endured. However, I firmly believe the institution of slavery to be an abomination in the eyes of God and man. No human being has the right to own another."

Once Lizzie would have mounted a full-throated rebuttal as she had done so often when her northern sister-in-law had challenged the moral underpinnings of the southern way of life. Now, rather than self-righteous indignation, she was astounded to feel what could only be described as shame. She looked down as he continued,

"Nonetheless, I am cognizant of the deep divide this issue has rent in our great nation. Meanwhile, the State of California has been admitted to the union as a free state, which was a large factor in my brother-in-law's decision to emigrate. That and concern for his family's safety."

"Safety?"

"Indeed. The southern portion of Indiana is a prime destination for slaves fleeing their masters. As a result, large numbers of slave catchers have inundated our area. These vile men make their living by hunting and capturing the fugitives, then returning them for the offered bounty. To increase the odds of success, they are known to wreak reprisals on any and all whom they suspect of aiding the escapees. Thus far Richard's family has avoided notice, but he was unwilling to risk the possibility of future discovery and decided it was time to leave. He convinced Sarah and I to join them. And here we are."

He looked about him, blinking as if waking from a dream. "Well, Miss Hamilton, your stated goal of whiling away the time has been accomplished. Look how far we have come."

Lizzie saw that they had indeed crept down to the very heart of town.

He rose, saying, "I must return to our wagon. We should be able to cross soon, and Sarah will be fretting over my absence."

Lizzie could see his thoughts were no longer with her but with his family. With a pang of regret, she said, "I apologize if I have kept you too long. Please give them all my regards."

He flashed his dimpled smile. "You have nothing for which to apologize. It was a delight passing the time with you, and I encourage you to visit our camp as soon as we are all settled on the far side of the Missouri."

Lizzie watched him go, then craned her neck toward the riverbank. The great pilgrimage was about to begin.

∞∞∞

Two days later, Lizzie wakened to a clear, cold dawn. The day before had been their first of real travel, and they had covered nineteen miles of flat, fertile Kansas prairie before stopping beside a small creek where there was plenty of wood for fires and copious grazing for the animals. Since it was Sunday, the train would remain in camp until religious services were completed at mid-morning. Absent the early wake-up signal, Lizzie had slept until the first rays of sun shone onto her face through the wagon cover. She stretched and allowed herself the luxury of a few moments of reflection before beginning her duties.

The river crossing had been a memorable spectacle. Given the vast numbers of people waiting, every man with an entrepreneurial spirit and a boat, raft or scow was offering his services. Since Lazarus had already registered their party with one of the larger ferries, a steamboat with a single stack and a stubby bow, they proceeded with a minimum of confusion. However, the river was high and muddy, and the sight of it thrashing and slapping against the ferry's wooden side gave Lizzie considerable misgivings. She witnessed a group of frightened, braying mules press up against one roped side of a flat boat, tip it over, and leap into the roiling waters. After much shouting and cursing, it seemed their handlers had the situation under control. Later, however, she was not surprised to learn that two of Mr. Masters' herd had drowned when the four cowboys swam them across. It was a milestone she was glad to have put behind them.

The far side was as flat and featureless as the eastern side was rugged with bluffs. They had camped there among hundreds of other wagons and started out the following morning on a trail that was nearly a quarter of a mile wide. A choking dust cloud had enveloped the trains on all sides, a vast parade of flapping wagon covers and plodding animals that caused Lizzie to wonder whether they would be in the midst of this churning throng the entire way to California. By the time they stopped in the late afternoon, however, the trains had sorted themselves out, and Lazarus had found the quiet, relatively unpopulated spot where they were now camped.

She had been more than ready for the day to end. The supposed springs beneath the driver's box did little to mitigate the effects of the rough, uneven ground, and within an hour of starting out, her bones had been shaken until she ached all over. In desperation, she had called out to young Will Long, who continued to walk with his whip beside the lead yoke of oxen, and asked him to stop the team long enough for her to climb down. He had obliged at once, coming to offer her assistance from her high perch. They had walked side by side much of the remainder of the day, talking to while away the time.

She found his story to be an interesting one. He had been raised on an Ohio farm that bought cattle driven up from Texas in order to fatten them and sell them at market. At the age of fourteen, he had signed on to participate in one of these cattle drives, gaining experience that suited him well for his present occupation. His ambition, however, went far beyond the realm of cowboying. Once he got to California, he hoped to strike it rich in the gold fields.

Lizzie thought him a daydreamer whom life would soon bring back to reality, but she kept her opinion to herself out of gratitude for his polite, respectful demeanor, which she appreciated all the more given the testy relationship that existed between her and his companions. Their lack of patience with her cooking skills seemed to crackle in the air whenever they were around her, raising a prickle of unease. Thus, she was working hard at learning from her mistakes and gaining whatever knowledge she could from Maude Fielding and Sarah Collins.

The first crisis had occurred the previous morning. Having used the last of the ground coffee the morning before, she had scooped beans out of the burlap bag marked "coffee." Even though she thought they had a rather strange greenish color, she ground them up and made the brew as she had been taught. She learned of her error when Earl spat his first mouthful onto the ground and bellowed, "Stupid wench, you didn't roast the beans!" A quick consult with Maude over the nooning stop had resulted in properly roasted beans for the evening meal. However, her troubles had not ended there. Thinking to appease the drovers, she had followed Sarah's suggestion that she make bread dough in the morning, knead and shape it, then place it in the Dutch oven to rise as the day progressed. When she baked it over the fire that evening, however, it had been as hard as a stone and inedible.

Another consult with her willing teachers had quickly pinpointed the problem. She had not added saleratus, a leavening substance that caused the dough to rise and become light. This morning she would try again and hope to appease the men with a more pleasing product when they stopped for the night. Now, however, they were doubtless looking for their breakfast. She sighed and threw back her blanket, shivered into her clothes, and climbed down from the wagon.

Their camp was behind and somewhat distant from the main parties, which had divided into their official groups with each one forming into a large circle. She had watched the nearest group, that of her friends, as the lead wagon stopped to allow the one behind to pass inside and slightly ahead, then stop so the next wagon could do likewise until the first and last wagons were tongue to back. The result was a large corral into which the valuable saddle horses and milk cows could be driven to keep them safe from marauding Indians. This was also the place where Reverend Jamison would conduct the morning's church service.

She went about her morning duties as quickly as possible, made a fresh batch of bread dough, tucked it into the Dutch oven with crossed fingers that it would rise as expected, and left to join the ragtag congregation gathering at the Jamison camp. All wagons in the group had put out whatever chairs or stools or barrels they had, but these did not begin to accommodate the large crowd. She edged around to where Cora stood with her family and the Collinses. She shook her head when offered a seat and stood beside Sarah's rocking chair as the reverend, a tall barrel-chested man with black hair shot through with silver and a thick beard, intoned the opening prayer in a deep, sonorous voice that rolled like thunder over the crowd.

Lizzie was there less from religious fervor than from a need for the companionship of these two families. Now that she was safely on her way to California, she was willing to give God the benefit of the doubt and see what He might have in store for her, but she remained skeptical of His overarching love and care. She would take a neutral stance, attending services when offered and refraining from any disparaging rhetoric where the Supreme Being was concerned but not counting on any assistance outside of her own good capabilities. Time would tell how He intended to deal with her.

It was as if the Reverend Jamison had read her mind, for he preached a sermon on the Parable of the Lost Sheep, a story she remembered her mother referencing in her daily devotions for the gathered house slaves of Rockland. Her mother had utilized the parable to emphasize a slave's moral duty not to stray from his or her master's sheepfold, assuring them that in such an instance the stray would be hunted until it was found and brought home. The Reverend Jamison's take on the passage was entirely different. He maintained that the lost sheep refers to the person who wanders in the wilderness of temptation and sin, relying on his own desires and ambitions rather than trusting in Jesus to guide him on his life's pathway. The Good Shepherd does not give up on such a soul but sends His angels to seek him out and bring him back into the fold, at which time there is great rejoicing in heaven over the repentance of one sinner who is thus saved to all eternity.

Lizzie found herself applying the lesson to her own situation. True, she had not consciously sought God's direction these past months. Or ever, for that matter. But what of *His* responsibility toward *her*? She was but a poor weak woman thrown unprotected into a cruel world that seemed intent on ruining her. Could He not extend a measure of His vaunted mercy to her for a change? Give her some sort of outward sign that He cared?

She had no time to pursue her thoughts. Cora and her mother were herding her through the dispersing crowd to the Jamison wagons, where they introduced her to the minister's wife Eliza, his newly-wed daughter Harriet and her husband, Stephan Lockwood, and their son Henry, a young man who appeared to be close to Lizzie in age. He was large like his father, handsome in a meaty sort of way, and most pleased to meet her. She knew her current appearance was dowdy at best, but the intense gleam in his deep brown eyes told her he liked what he saw. She could not help preening just a bit. How commonplace such looks had been in her former life! Young men swarmed about her and shouldered others out of their way in their eagerness to engage her in conversation. She had taken it all for granted back then. What a pleasant surprise it was to experience such a thing in her current circumstances. For the first time since she had allowed Jack O'Rourke to seduce her, she felt admired and appreciated.

The moment did not last long. Reverend Jamison disengaged himself from those who wished to congratulate him on his message and came over to join his family. He acknowledged Lizzie when introduced, exchanged some brief but polite rhetoric with her, then turned to his son and said, "We had best get the teams yoked up. Lazarus is eager for us to move out so we can make the most of the remainder of the day."

Henry gave Lizzie one last lingering look, then left to do his father's bidding. The others turned to business as well, and Lizzie returned to finish packing up her own wagon. Within the half hour, the train was on its way again.

Chapter Sixteen

Another failure. How could she have done it? The bread was perfect. Or at least passable. The rest was a disaster.

Thinking to offer a little variety to the evening meal, she had rummaged among the sacks and barrels that constituted their food supply and decided on a mixture of beans and rice to complement the bread that had risen as promised and been baked in the Dutch oven to a nice golden brown. Her knowledge of beans and rice amounted to the simple fact that they were boiled in water. Thus she placed a scoop of each into a large kettle, added some water, and suspended it all over the fire. The result an hour later was an inedible mess of crunchy beans and mushy rice mixed in with a few tiny pebbles and sticks that had apparently been in the barrel with the raw products.

Earl Long's diatribe on testing the contents of his plate included words she had never even heard and hoped never to hear again. She attempted to appease him and the others by quickly slicing off a piece of bacon and frying it, but as she did so, he retreated to one of the bottles of whiskey he had purchased in St. Joseph against train regulations. He and the two older men passed it around and were already partially drunk by the time she handed them their reconstituted supper.

She quickly cleaned up the remains of the meal and left them to their mutterings while she went to the Fielding/Collins camp to relate her latest culinary debacle. At first she was annoyed by her friends' amusement over her story, but she soon recognized the absurdity of the situation and joined in their laughter. Sarah and Maude soon put her straight on the preparation of beans and rice, which were never cooked together because each required different techniques. By the time she left them, she had absorbed the lesson that she must never attempt to prepare a type of food until she was fully educated about its properties and correct cooking procedures.

As she reentered her own camp, she found Earl and Will Long sprawled by the fire, the other two men having gone out to take their turn at guarding the herd now that they were in Indian country. A nearly-empty whiskey bottle dangled from Earl's hand, his stare surly, his lips curled in a contemptuous scowl. Young Will avoided her eyes as she walked past them, prepared a small basin of water for washing her face and hands, and climbed up into the wagon.

She had difficulty falling asleep. The Longs remained at the fire, Earl's rantings more and more belligerent with frequent references to her cooking. She was greatly relieved when she finally heard them stumble off to their tent. She drifted off, only to be wakened an indeterminate amount of time later by sounds just outside the wagon.

Loud whispers, the staccato cadence of a serious argument. The scuff of boots circling the wagon and stopping just beyond the canvas opening. Her blood turned to ice, panic rendering her immobile. The sensation of the wagon box dipping under the weight of a foot on the undercarriage finally broke her trance. She gathered breath to scream, but she was too late. A hard dry hand clamped over her mouth as Earl Long heaved himself up into the wagon.

She began to struggle, whipping her head from side to side, hands clawing at the offending hand. In response, a pair of fingers clamped down on her nose, cutting off her air supply. A face close to her ear hissed, "Lessen you want to die, you'd best lie still."

She continued to fight until she felt herself grow faint. Her starved lungs were heavy stones in her chest. Lights began to flash behind her eyes. Out of desperation, she allowed her body to go limp.

He muttered, "That's better," his fetid, alcohol-laced breath making her gag. He scooted farther into the wagon and threw a leg over her, plopping down hard on her solar plexis. "Now then, *Miss Hamilton*," the words filled with sarcasm, "since you can't cook worth piss, I figure you can earn your passage on your back. If you're good to us boys, could be we won't tell the boss you can't perform the job he hired you to do. Now you just spread your legs and lie back and enjoy it."

She arched her back and began kicking and clawing. She gnawed with her teeth in an attempt to catch a piece of the leathery flesh covering her mouth. Strained to scream, the sound coming out as little more than a moan. His fingers returned to her nose. Defeated, she fell still again.

Will Long's whispered voice came from just outside the wagon. "Leave her be, Uncle Earl. You done made your point."

"I ain't made it by half," his uncle growled. "Git yourself up here and hold her for me. You can have her next."

"Jeez, Uncle, this ain't right. Come on down 'fore we get ourselves in a world of trouble."

The unmistakable click of a revolver being cocked cut through the night air. "You're the one's gonna be in a world o' trouble, boy, if you don't get your cowardly ass up here and do like I say!"

"Aw, don't do this. Ma'd have a fit if she knew."

"Your ma ain't here, now is she? She told me to make a man o' you, and that's what I figure to do. Now don't make me ask again. *Git...up...here!*"

A guttural whimper. Then the scrape of a boot as the young cowboy placed it on the wagon frame. Lizzie saw his shadow loom in the front opening. Then, suddenly, he was gone. In his place another figure appeared, this one pointing the long snout of a rifle into the wagon.

Earl did not see this new development until impatience pulled his gaze around with the words, "I said—"

He froze.

Lazarus Mills climbed into the wagon, rifle cocked and aimed at Earl Long's chest. He grabbed a handful of the man's shirt and pulled him off Lizzie.

She scrambled back and huddled as far away from them as the small confines of the wagon allowed, arms hugging herself in the night chill.

"You all right, ma'am?" Lazarus asked.

Hand covering her mouth, heart hammering, she managed a strangled, "Yes."

"You go back to sleep, then. These two will not be bothering you again."

He jerked the now-cowering Earl Long to the canvas opening and pushed him out of the wagon ahead of himself. She heard,

"All right, you two, you are under arrest and will be restrained until I can call a meeting to deal with you."

"Aw, cap'n, we didn't mean no harm," whined Earl. "Just scarin' her a little. You wouldn't believe the crap she serves us to eat. She needed to learn we won't stand for it no more."

"Save it for the proceedings, Long. You were fixing to rape that young lady. My nose also tells me you have infringed on the train rules by drinking in excess."

"We was just makin' up for her lousy cookin'. Come on, cap'n, be reasonable… "

Their voices retreated into the night. Lizzie crawled back under her blanket, allowing herself the luxury of tears now that the danger had passed. Sleep was a long time in coming.

The following morning began in the same manner as the previous two except that she had only two mouths besides her own to feed. The two remaining drovers, Bobby Miller and Ed Perkins, were subdued, refusing to meet her eyes and hurrying off to round up the herd for travel. As she was cleaning up and re-packing the wagon, she noticed a man approaching from the direction of the Jamison group's camp. As he drew nearer, she recognized Henry Jamison, son of the previous day's preacher. He snatched his hat from his head and said,

"Good morning, Miss Hamilton. I understand there were some, uh, difficulties in this camp last night. Lazarus asked me to come and drive this wagon until things get sorted out."

His crimson face told Lizzie he knew exactly what had happened. The entire train probably knew, she realized with chagrin. Beyond that, it had not occurred to her that she could not possibly handle the wagon while the two remaining cowboys drove the herd. That Lazarus had provided for this deficiency impressed her. Black man or no, he had rescued her from certain violation—if not even greater bodily harm—and was continuing to help her even today. Given the condescension with which she had treated him the day of her arrival, she would not have blamed him for turning a blind eye to what had nearly happened. For the first time in her life, she felt a genuine gratitude and respect for a person of his race that went beyond the inbred conviction that the natural order of things required Negroes to serve those of her superior status. He was a man who had behaved in the same protective manner as any white man would have done. What did that say about the validity of southern attitudes toward those whom they had enslaved?

She stirred herself from these startling thoughts to smile at Henry. "I appreciate your willingness to help. I have no idea how to hitch the oxen, much less drive them along the trail."

A wide grin. "No man worth his salt would expect you to perform such tasks. I am honored to fill the void."

"Well, then... " She pointed to a group of six animals grazing nearby. "... I believe those are our oxen over there."

He gave a little bow, put on his hat, and headed for the oxen. By the time he had them yoked up, all was in readiness. The long train unwound itself camp by camp and was soon on its way.

Lizzie saw nothing of Earl and Will Long as the day progressed and assumed they were confined in one of the wagons. She walked along beside Henry, enjoying his obvious attraction to her. He went back to his own wagon for the nooning time while Lizzie offered cold bacon, hardtack and warmed-up coffee to Ed and Bobby. Lazarus rode by several times during the day to make sure everything was in order, not stopping to talk but merely raising his hat and nodding at her. She smiled and gave him a little wave, hoping by doing so to communicate her new regard.

They stopped in the late afternoon on the bank of Grasshopper Creek. Word was passed that the two miscreants would be tried before the group captains at a court of sorts after supper. The gathering would take place within the wagon corral of the Masters group since theirs was the largest group, not to mention the fact that Mr. Masters was the men's employer.

Lizzie could think of little else as she fetched water, gathered wood, made a fire, and went through the motions of preparing an evening meal: the bread she had mixed that morning, fried bacon, coffee. Bobby and Ed ate without comment, thanked her—a courtesy not offered her by any of the men before—and scurried off to check on the herd. They did not mention their fellow cowboys or the upcoming gathering, but she suspected they would be there to see how things played out.

As soon as she could, she went to the Fielding/Collins camp, where she was greeted with great concern by all. A wide-eyed Cora rushed to meet her and pull her into the family circle, gushing,

"Oh, Lizzie, what a terrible thing! We could scarce believe it when we heard. Tell us all about it."

Although Lizzie wanted nothing more than to forget what had happened, she warmed to the worried faces all around. Even little Missy Collins regarded her with round, sympathetic eyes, although she surely did not understand the full nature of the assault. In response, she told the story from beginning to end, taking comfort from the many expressions of support and outrage.

"I suppose I should have expected it, or something like it," she finished. "It is no secret that I cannot cook. I even understand their frustration, which is not to say they acted rightly. But I should have been forewarned since they made their feelings abundantly clear on many occasions." She sighed. "Truth be told, I am partly to blame. I accepted this position out of desperation in my need to get to California, knowing I would be unable to fulfill my responsibilities as might have been expected."

"That is no excuse for what they did," said Sarah Collins from her ever-present rocking chair. "I do not accept that any blame whatsoever resides with you. You were learning fast, and they only needed to exercise some patience and Christian charity."

Murmurs of agreement from a group that now included not only the Fielding and Collins families but many from the Jamison contingent as well.

"What will you do now?" asked Cora. "Surely you cannot stay in that camp after what they did to you."

This was something Lizzie had not considered until now. She had been functioning automatically, trying her best to ignore the hovering cloud of the previous night's horror. Now she focused on Cora's words, and new anxiety twisted her stomach. What *would* she do now? Cora was right that she could not remain in camp with these men who so despised her, even if they were to behave as gentlemen from then on. But what other option did she have? Turn around and go back to St. Joseph? How was that even possible?

Maude took in her distress and said, "Now is not the time, Cora. Miss Hamilton has enough to trouble her without adding worries about the future."

"I cannot agree," said Jonathan Collins. "After having nearly experienced the worst violation a woman could face, I believe Miss Hamilton deserves to know her future on this journey is secure. And I am prepared to offer such an assurance here and now."

Startled silence. Lizzie held her breath, waiting for him to go on.

"You all know of my concern for Sarah. Her time is still some weeks off, but her life becomes more difficult with every passing day. Therefore, I propose that Miss Hamilton join our family group to help with the chores Sarah is unable to perform. I believe our stores will accommodate one more person." A warm smile in Lizzie's direction. "And a rather small person at that. So if Miss Hamilton agrees... ?"

Tears welled in Lizzie eyes. Emotion constricting her throat, she said, "I more than agree. I accept with heartfelt gratitude. And I believe I can promise the meals I prepare will be those to which you are accustomed since Sarah will be able to guide my every move until I am more proficient on my own."

"Then the issue is settled. Shall we make our way to the Masters camp to see what fate these two scoundrels face?"

Sarah and Isabelle Jamison, wife of the reverend's nephew Walter, remained behind with Missy Collins, Lilly Fielding, and the five Jamison children. Everyone else walked to the head of the train where the Masters contingent was camped. A sizable group was already gathered around Lazarus and the two Longs, who were bound with rope and looked haggard after a night and day in confinement. Earl's expression was defiant while Will's reflected shame and fear. Despite what had happened, the sight of the young man's distress pierced Lizzie's heart.

Lazarus held up a hand for silence and began to speak, his voice pitched to carry in the crisp air of the dying day. "It is no doubt already common knowledge what transpired at the drovers' camp last night. Were we in a town of any size, these men would be brought before a court of law to answer for their actions. In the absence of a formal legal remedy, the documents signed by all dictate that any infractions on this train be judged as fairly as possible by the group captains."

Josiah Masters came forward, an ugly bullwhip in his hand. "Not necessary in this instance! These men are my employees. They have committed a most grievous act, and I shall deal with them as I see fit." He turned to a small contingent of men who had stepped up with him. "Seize them and tie them to the wheels of my wagon. They shall be whipped as a warning to any others in my employ who might be tempted to similar brutish actions."

The crowd stirred, voices raised in consternation as the men moved to seize Earl and Will. The loud retort of a pistol brought immediate silence. Lazarus pointed his weapon at Masters' men and said in steely tones, "Stand down, or I will shoot."

They froze, glanced back at their employer, exchanged uncertain looks among themselves, and finally stepped back.

"Now, then," said Lazarus, "as I have already stated, we will proceed with the business at hand. It will be dark soon, and we are all eager to put this behind us and return to our camps. Miss Hamilton has been traumatized enough without being required to give a firsthand account of what happened. I can attest to what I saw and heard while making my rounds. This man... " He pointed to Will. "... was climbing up into the wagon where Miss Hamilton was sleeping. I pulled him back and took his place only to see this man... " Pointing at Earl. "... pinning Miss Hamilton to her bed while gagging her with his hand and demanding the other come up and restrain her so he could force himself on her."

Even though everyone already knew the basics of the story, his words elicited a murmur of outrage.

"A lesser but still significant charge lies in the fact that the men were drunk against the very clear rules of this train. Now, having heard the charges against them and in the interest of fairness, these two will be given a chance to mount a defense of their behavior."

Earl Long raised his head and growled, "'Bout time! This here—" He seemed to struggle for the right word and finally settled on, "*person* was 'sposed to feed us hardworkin' hands. That was her job. You wouldn't believe the garbage she put in front of us. She's the one oughtta be judged for hirin' on under false pretenses. She ain't no cook, that's for sure. As for t'other night, we wasn't tryin' to hurt her. We was just scarin' her a little so she'd know she had to do better with the cookin'. That's all it was. Weren't no rape like they're sayin'. I admit we'd had a bit too much whiskey. But if any o' you'd had to eat what she gave us for supper, you woulda had a little nip yourselves to make up for it. An' that's all I got to say."

A buzz of reaction. Then Lazarus turned to Will, saying, "Son?"

The boy hung his head and shook it.

"Well, then—"

"Wait!!"

Heads turned to look at Lizzie, who was pushing her way through the crowd. She was unsure what had prompted her outburst, but a deep urge was propelling her forward. She came out into the center space and stopped in front of Lazarus.

"I would like to speak, if I may."

His black face scrunched in surprise, but he nodded, saying, "Of course, if you wish."

Her mind went blank for a moment. Then the words began to tumble out.

"This young boy does not deserve to be punished for what happened. He tried to stop it time and again until his uncle pulled a pistol, cocked it, and threatened to shoot him if he refused to cooperate. Who could blame him for his reluctant compliance under threat of bodily harm? As for his consumption of alcohol, I observed him take only one small swallow at the insistence of his uncle, and I do not believe he was drunk at the time of this event. Therefore, as the injured party, I beg those who will judge him to be lenient."

She could see from the expressions of those nearest her that her point had been well taken.

Lazarus said, "Duly noted. The captains and I will now withdraw to deliberate."

The men left to gather outside the circle of wagons. Lizzie waited, fretting about the fate of Will given that his employer, Josiah Masters, was included in the impromptu jury as captain of his group. The fact that Richard Fielding was also a member gave her room for hope. All she had learned of Dr. Fielding told her he was a reasonable, level-headed person who would judge fairly. She decided to put her trust in him as well as in Lazarus to see that justice was truly done.

Time dragged on, the crowd growing more restive with every passing minute. At last the men returned, and Lazarus announced they had voted five to five in favor of a guilty verdict for Earl Long and four to one for an acquittal of the charges against his nephew. Lizzie rejoiced that the boy had been vindicated. However, there was more to come.

After releasing Will, Lazarus addressed the crowd once more. "As to Earl Long's punishment, there was a spirited disagreement. Mr. Masters has already made his feelings known. One other captain agreed with him. The remainder and I settled on what we believe is a reasonable sentence. We believe this man's violent, belligerent behavior has proven him to be a danger to this company. Therefore, he will be expelled from the train. He will remain confined until first light, at which time he will be sent on his way with his horse and two days' provisions. That should be sufficient for him to return to St. Joseph, if that is what he chooses to do. Regardless, he is forbidden from having any further contact with this train or anyone in it."

The crowd seemed satisfied and showed signs of preparing to disperse when Josiah Masters stepped up and called out, "One moment, if you please. This matter is not settled by a long shot!"

He gestured at Lazarus and addressed the group at large, saying, "I do not recognize this man's jurisdiction over this proceeding! He is infringing on my right of control over my own property. Earl and Will Long are *my* employees driving *my* herd to *my* property in California. The matter of their punishment is, therefore, *my* responsibility, not his. "

Lazarus said in a voice cold as ice, "Are you suggesting, sir, that you own these two men? That they are your slaves with all the onerous power that implies?"

The man's color deepened, visible even in the waning light. Voice quivering with indignation, "Of course not! I come from the free state of Ohio and abhor the institution of slavery. I even hired you, a former slave, to lead this train. But in doing so, I did not abdicate my entrepreneurial rights. I have already agreed that young Will is blameless in this affair. But the elder Long is as guilty as the day is long. If you are allowed to expel him from the train, I will be one drover short in handling a very large herd over a perilous journey, putting my property at great risk. If he is merely flogged, then sent back to work, my interests are preserved even as justice is done. It seems a perfectly reasonable solution."

"To you, perhaps, but not to the person who would receive those lashes. I have observed firsthand what such punishment does to a man, or woman—" An audible gasp. "—and I assure you it is a life-threatening event. Nowhere is it written that an employer has the power of life and death over his employees. That privilege lies only with the institution you claim to abhor. More pertinent to this matter, you and every other man present signed a copy of this train's governing constitution. And that document specifically designates me as the final arbiter of disputes. I have made my judgment along with the majority of the group captains. And it will stand."

Josiah Masters's expression revealed he had been backed into a corner. Having publicly challenged Lazarus's authority, he could not simply capitulate. On the other hand, he had no legal ground on which to stand. With dogged determination,

"Then we are at an impasse. I see only one way to settle this matter. The entire train must decide."

Lazarus lifted his brow. Considered and finally said, "Perhaps you are right. I am either master of this train, or I am not. If a majority wish me to withdraw and return to St. Joseph, I shall do so. This is how the matter will be decided. I shall walk away from camp in a northeasterly direction. You do the same to the southeast. Those who agree with you will follow you. Likewise for those who wish me to remain in charge. We shall see who has the greatest number of followers."

"Very well," Masters agreed. "The majority will decide whether we continue under thrall to a dictator—or in a manner in which each man controls his own destiny."

Lizzie was appalled at the turn of events. How had her unpleasant ordeal turned into a political confrontation over freedom versus tyranny? Her fellow travelers seemed as confused as she, standing inert as the two men left camp in opposite directions.

Murmurs of discussion arose, but still no one moved. Lizzie looked about her, then set her jaw and started off toward Lazarus. She heard others following but did not know how many until she stopped in front of Lazarus and looked back. The vast majority of the gathered company were headed in their direction. She looked to the south and saw only a smattering of people moving toward Josiah Masters. Lazarus had won.

Chapter Seventeen

Having put his influence to the test, Josiah Masters felt obliged to leave the train, taking with him the eighteen wagons and sixty-four people in his party. Their departure was of little consequence to the remaining travelers. It even made the train smaller and easier to manage. The greatest benefit, however, was the absence of his large herd of cattle, which had served only to stir up clouds of dust that drifted over the entire train. It was assumed the splinter group would take the same basic trail. Indeed, over the coming days, the lumbering herd could be observed in the distance from the breast of the occasional rise. However, there was no further direct contact, for which Lizzie was grateful.

She could hardly believe her good fortune in being attached to the Collins family for the remainder of the journey. Everyone, including the Fieldings, took her to the bosom of their family, and soon they were all on first-name terms. She quickly came to appreciate Sarah's gentle, loving nature and shared the others' concern for her deteriorating health. Although she did not complain, she would admit, when pressed, to a nagging pain beneath her right ribs. Her feet were so swollen she could barely force them into her shoes, and the swelling now seemed to be creeping into her hands and even her face. She spent her days riding in the front driver's seat. Even though Jonathan did his best to steer the team onto the most level ground, Lizzie could see her grimace when the wagon lurched over a rock or unavoidable deep rut. In camp, she sat in her rocking chair and guided Lizzie through whatever meal preparations were needed. The results brought no complaints. Even the occasional compliment, although whether genuine or merely meant as encouragement to keep trying was impossible to tell.

She found little Missy to be a delightful child with a vivid imagination that saw animals in the clouds and magical forests in the occasional copse of trees. Most of the landscape, however, was flat, which made for faster travel but offered little to interest the mind. Jonathan helped the time pass as they walked along by weaving fanciful stories, tales that gave nearly as much pleasure to Lizzie as to the child for whom they were intended. The remainder of the time, he either held a book in his hand and read or made conversation with Lizzie, his vast knowledge of things about which she had never even thought opening new vistas to her mind.

She was particularly interested to learn about the background of their wagon master, especially after Josiah Masters's revelation that he had once been a slave. Jonathan seemed to know the particulars since he had been there from the beginning of the train's formation, prompting her to observe,

"He seems to be better educated than any Negro I have ever encountered. How can that be if he was a slave?"

"His story differs markedly from any you might know of, coming as you do from South Carolina, which is the strictest of all the states over the issue of slavery." He pretended not to notice the dark look these words provoked, continuing, "He was born in northern Maryland into the household of a shopkeeper by the name of Mills. This person owned Lazarus's parents, whom he employed in his home and shop. When Lazarus came along, he appeared particularly bright, and Mills soon realized what an asset he would be in the business. Since he and his wife were childless, she took it upon herself to school him as she would one of her own. He was such an apt pupil that he took over keeping the shop's books when he was but fifteen and eventually managed it altogether when his owner's health failed. When Mills died, his will granted Lazarus and his parents their freedom. Lazarus kept the shop going as Mrs. Mills's employee until her death, at which time he moved to the free State of Pennsylvania and obtained employment as an accountant for a black business in the Eighth Ward of Philadelphia. He was on an errand for his employer when he was captured by a slave catcher, who confiscated his free papers and planned to sell him back into slavery. Lazarus was able to bide his time and eventually overpower his captor, but the incident taught him he was not safe anywhere in the east. So he headed west."

"How did a bookkeeper transform himself into a—what?"

"Mountain man. Fur trapper. Hunter. Explorer. Trailblazer. Take your pick. I do not know the whole story, but I do know he spent time with various Indian tribes and can speak many of their dialects, especially the Snake language. He knows the West, including all the pitfalls and dangers of the trail from here to California. We are lucky to have him."

Lizzie could not yet vouch for his overall expertise, but she had already experienced his benevolence and strong leadership and could not help but hold him in higher regard than she would ever have thought possible. Given all she knew of him, she was more than happy to trust his ability to guide the train safely to California.

Four days after parting company with the Masters group, they arrived at the Big Blue River, where they found the immediate vicinity packed with wagon camps. The riverbanks were so steep that crossing required each wagon to be lowered by rope on one side and then hauled up by the same means on the other. Instead, Lazarus decided they would cross by means of Marshall's Ferry some seven miles north of the main trail. He took the upper trail branch and settled the train at a wooded spot on a small tributary some distance to the east.

The mood of the emigrants was unusually light now that they had reached the first major milestone on the trail. That evening after supper, great campfires flared into the sky. Reverend Jamison's son-in-law Stephen Lockwood got out his violin, prompting someone else in their group to produce a melodian, and music soon filled the camp. Some took up dancing around the fire, and Henry Jamison appeared before Lizzie and asked her to join him in a round. She accepted, feeling for one brief moment as if she were a desirable belle attending a ball surrounded by admiring beaus. Before long, however, exhaustion from five days of walking sent her to her bed in the second Fielding wagon, which she had been sharing with Cora and Lilly.

They wakened the next morning to heavy rain that was fast turning the campground into a sea of mud. Lazarus rode from camp to camp encouraging all to get packed and hitched as quickly as possible. Breakfast was a hasty affair, the Collins and Fielding families sharing a small, hard-won fire to prepare coffee to be drunk with cold beans and dry pilot bread. They completed the morning chores with as much efficiency as possible. Jonathan milked Blue Bell, the cow that had been trailing along attached to the wagon all the way from Indiana, then went out to bring in and yoke the oxen. Lizzie gave a cup of the warm milk to Missy and encouraged another on Sarah, who had eaten next to nothing for breakfast. Then she retrieved the small bucket containing the previous night's milking from beneath the wagon, removed the thick cream on top, and put it into the churn attached to the wagon side, ensuring the day's bouncing would produce fresh butter for the evening meal. Instead of making the day's bread dough as usual, she decided to wait until they were moving, at which time she would mix it in the back of the wagon out of the rain. She rinsed and put away the few breakfast dishes, rolled the Collins's bedding into a tidy bundle for travel, then went to help Cora and Lilly stow that bedding. By the time they heard the signal to roll, they were ready.

The rain had let up some by then, making easier footing for the animals, and they arrived at the ferry within the hour. Again they had to wait their turn and did not reach the far side until mid-afternoon. They pushed on another five miles before stopping for the night. Some of the men went out hunting and came back with an antelope, which they skinned, butchered and divided among the families. Wary of scurvy, Sarah suggested dried apples stewed with a spoonful of citric acid to accompany their fresh meat for supper. She was able to instruct Lizzie on the preparation of this dish, but she did so from her bed in the wagon, hands pressed to her temples to alleviate a vicious headache. By the time the meal was ready, she refused to eat, her low moans a distressing accompaniment as Jonathan, Missy and Lizzie ate in silence. Afterward, Jonathan asked Richard to come and examine Sarah, but he could offer no suggestion as to how to alleviate her pain since it was too dangerous to administer laudanum so late in her pregnancy.

Lizzie tidied up after the meal as quietly as possible and sat by the fire with a subdued Missy until the child's yawns told her it was time for her to be put to bed. She did her best to settle the girl on her side of the wagon, but the little thing sensed something was wrong and would have nothing but to snuggle next to her mother in her parents' bed. Sarah opened her arms and waved Lizzie away with a wan smile. She tiptoed back to the Fielding camp and crawled into bed beside Cora and Lilly, exhaustion and a full stomach superceding her concerns for Sarah and driving her to instant sleep.

She was wakened sometime during the night by a sudden piercing cry. Moments later, Jonathan appeared outside the wagon bonnet carrying a sleeping Missy.

"Sarah's time has come," he whispered. "Will you take Missy in with you?"

"Of course. But is it not too early?"

Grim silence was her answer. She held out her arms to take the sleeping child, after which he turned and disappeared. As she was tucking Missy in beside her, Cora raised her head and whispered,

"What is happening?"

"Sarah's birthing has begun."

"So soon?"

"I know. Not good."

There was nothing more to say. They heard Cora's father and Jonathan pass by, their voices low but intense. They exchanged grim looks in the darkness, then clasped hands and lay back, worry overshadowing all other thought, ears strained for any indication of what was happening in the adjacent camp. Over the next hours, muffled sounds of anguish drifted into their wagon, robbing them of all sleep. Finally, just before daybreak, they heard the thin wail of newborn life.

They exchanged satisfied smiles, then Cora turned over and nestled in with the intent of catching some sleep before the signal sounded. Lizzie was wide awake. She made certain Missy was still asleep, pulled on her clothes, and climbed down. Through the gathering light, she saw Richard Fielding cross from the Collins wagon carrying his black bag.

"How are they?" Lizzie asked.

A tired smile. "As well as might be expected. The child is early and very small, but he appears to be sound enough. Sarah is resting comfortably. Her headache has gone, and she should recover without ill effect."

Lizzie's heart lightened. Her friend was out of danger, and there would be a new little being to bring delight to the camp. It was as she was building up the fire that it hit her. When Sarah returned to full health, they would have no further need of her. She doubted they would turn her out, but she could no longer justify the burden she represented if she were not pulling her weight in the workload. She pushed the uncomfortable thought from her mind, picked up the water bucket, and went to fill it from the small stream by which they were camped.

When she returned, Jonathan was standing by the fire, his face haggard but peaceful. He gave her a weary smile, saying, "You heard?"

"Yes. Is Sarah all right?"

"She seems to be, thank God. Still sleeping."

"And the little one? A boy, I believe."

A beam of joy amidst his exhaustion. "Yes. Caleb Joseph. We had hoped for a boy, although health was, of course, first and foremost in our minds. Our baby Robert died of cholera in fifty-two. Not that we could ever replace him, but this little guy helps ease the pain."

She reached out and squeezed his arm. "I am very happy for you. I look forward to meeting him."

A tiny bleat came from the wagon. "And so you shall. In fact, come along with me now. I expect he is hungry, and Sarah must be wakened."

She went with him to the rear of the wagon, where the back panel had been lowered and a homemade two-step stool placed beneath the opening for easy access to the interior. The wagon box had been arranged so that the food and cooking supplies were closest to the rear, the trunks containing their clothing and the remainder of their tools and supplies to the front. A narrow passage led to the middle section where the bedding was laid out during the night.

Lizzie could see Sarah's form beneath the quilts and the squirming bundle beside her. The baby's initial fussing had become unremitting protest, but his mother seemed oblivious to it. Jonathan climbed up, took a kerosene lantern from where it sat on top of the cook box, struck a match, and hung the lantern from a hook attached to one of the hickory bows that supported the canvas covering. He gave Sarah's shoulder a gentle shake. She started, exclaimed, "Oh!" and sat up.

It was not until she had scooped the baby into her arms and begun to shush him that she saw Lizzie standing outside the wagon. Her face melted into a beatific smile.

"Come," she said. "You must see our dear little Caleb."

Lizzie was somewhat uncomfortable intruding on this intimate family scene, but she read genuine invitation in her friend's eyes. She climbed up and picked her way past the barrels, sacks and boxes. Sarah's face was pale, her golden hair a tangled mass where it had escaped from its night braid during her ordeal. All other traces had been replaced by the utter joy of new motherhood. She held up the tightly-wrapped baby for Lizzie to take.

She held the warm little bundle and parted the soft flannel to see the tiny face. She had seen her nephews when they were but weeks old, but never a newborn with its scrunched features and slightly misshapen head. As she watched, the baby turned his head from side to side, mouth open and seeking. Then his face reddened and screwed up in displeasure as he emitted a lusty cry. Sarah was unbuttoning her nightdress even as Lizzie handed him back. She decided it was time for her to leave.

News of the birth had spread, and the camp was fast filling with well-wishers. It occurred to Lizzie that it was well past dawn and there had still been no wake-up signal from Lazarus. When she inquired of Maude, her friend said,

"Richard went to him last night and requested a late start. He was more than happy to oblige."

And so the early-morning hours passed. Missy wakened to the news of her little brother's arrival and bounced from wagon to wagon, dancing barefoot in her nightdress and singing hallelujahs at the top of her voice. Lizzie prepared a special breakfast of johnnycakes slathered with butter and molasses. Sarah insisted on coming out to join them and was helped from the wagon in a weakened but determined state. Everyone agreed that Caleb was the most beautiful baby ever born, and he was tucked into his cradle for his first day as a California emigrant.

They stopped to noon seven miles later at the Little Blue River, a lovely clear stream with a bluish tint and a pebbly bottom. Rich foliage graced both banks with open countryside stretching to either side, providing charming vistas in every direction. It was sunny and unusually warm for the last day of April. Lizzie took Missy to the stream bank after the meal, where they sat on a rock, removed their shoes and stockings, and bathed their feet in the cold water, laughingly splashing each other more than was altogether necessary. When it was time to go, she knelt before the child, dried her feet with her own skirt hem, and began to replace her stockings.

She had never enjoyed the company of her nephews, who were rowdy, undisciplined and a general nuisance. By contrast, this little girl plucked at her heart strings with her gregarious, spontaneous ways. It made her think that she might, after all, have the instinct toward motherhood that she had often felt lacking in herself.

This thought led to the darker one that she had done all in her power to suppress since leaving New Orleans. She had willfully destroyed a child of her own body, no matter how shamefully it had been conceived. In a powerful flash of insight, her mind's eye transformed Caleb's little face into the delicate features of a little girl with reddish-brown hair and her own green eyes. Would she ever be allowed to welcome such a being into this world? Tears sprang to her eyes as a wave of loss so powerful she nearly groaned aloud swept over her.

A small soft hand on her cheek drew her eyes upward. Missy's face was puckered with concern. "Do not be sad, Lizzie," she said. "I am sorry I splashed you."

She grasped the hand and drew it to her lips for a quick kiss. Forcing a bright smile, "I am not sad, silly. And you may recall that I am the one who started the splashing, which was welcome on such a beautiful day as this. Now we had better get back before they send a scouting party to look for us."

Missy's tinkling laugh accompanied them as they returned to the nooning camp.

Once underway again, they continued along the river's northwest course, making good time over the rolling prairie, slowed only by the crossing of an occasional ravine. Happily, Sarah seemed fully recovered from her pre-birth ailments. She rode in the driver's box with the baby in his cradle just inside the wagon and Missy either snuggled beside her or skipping along beside Lizzie or her father. They were passing through Pawnee Indian territory, necessitating a doubling of the nighttime guard, but they had encountered no difficulties thus far. Lizzie was even a trifle disappointed not to catch at least a glimpse of these supposed savages. As for other new sights, she had seen an abundance, among them antelope, a wolf or two, and many rattlesnakes. What caused her blood to chill, however, were the graves they passed here and there, testament to the perils of the journey. She could not imagine such a fate befalling any of her new friends and did her best to pray that God would protect them all.

They traveled another eleven miles that day and an impressive twenty-four miles on the following day, putting them some hundred and fifty miles from St. Joseph and well into the Nebraska Territory. It was around suppertime on that day, the first day of May, that Sarah first showed signs of illness. They were eating a meal of bacon, beans, and buttered bread when she began to shiver and shake so severely her plate fell from her lap and her body went rigid.

"C-c-c-cold," she stammered through clenched teeth.

Jonathan hurried to her side, placed a hand on her brow, and said, "Dear Sarah, you are burning with fever. Are you in pain?"

She nodded, her hand hovering over her lower midriff.

He put his arm around her and helped her up. "You must lie down. Then we must ask Richard to come and examine you."

She did not protest but allowed him to half lead, half carry her to the wagon.

Lizzie put her own plate aside and said, "Shall I go for Richard?"

He cast a grateful look over his shoulder and said, "Please."

Just then, Caleb's cry came from the wagon, and Lizzie wondered if Sarah would be able to feed him properly. Fear gripped her heart. They had made it through one crisis without lasting harm. Now here was another. What was happening?

Missy looked from her departing parents to Lizzie, eyes wide and troubled. "What is wrong with Mama?"

Pushing her anxiety aside, she forced a smile and said, "She is tired and needs to rest. Would you like to come with me to Aunt Maude's camp? Perhaps your Cousins Cora and Lilly will play a game with you before bedtime."

Somewhat mollified, she took Lizzie's offered hand and walked with her across the wagon corral to where the Fieldings were in the midst of their meal. They looked up in surprise as the two approached.

Lizzie gave them an abstracted greeting, then went to Richard, leaned close and whispered, "Sarah has taken ill. Will you come?" To Cora, "Missy hopes you and Lilly will play a game with her before she goes to bed."

Cora gave her a probing look. Reading the silent message there, she said, "Certainly. Come here, little one. We shall play as soon as Lilly and I finish eating. How about Follow My Leader?"

Missy's enthusiastic agreement told Lizzie the child would be occupied for awhile. She returned to the Collins camp, washed the supper plates, and kept the fire going until Richard Fielding climbed down from the wagon. Her heart nearly stopped when she saw his face.

In a weak voice, "Is it so bad?"

He heaved a sigh. Stared into the fire before answering, "I am afraid so. The chills, a rapid pulse, the abdominal distress—it is childbed fever."

Lizzie gasped. She had heard of this horrible ailment that sometimes followed childbirth. It was a death sentence.

"Are you sure?"

"There is no doubt."

"How long?"

A weary shrug. "Three, four days at the most."

"And there is nothing you can do?"

His silence was her answer.

"Does Jonathan know?"

"I did not voice a diagnosis, but he reads widely and is brilliant in the bargain. His eyes tell me he has it figured out."

He lumbered off, defeat in every line of his body, reminding Lizzie he was losing not only a patient but a beloved sister. She remained by the fire, uncertain what, if anything, she should do. She heard Missy's squeals as she and the Fielding girls played the imitation game. Eventually, Jonathan came down from the wagon with his daughter's nightdress and handed it to Lizzie.

"Do you mind taking Missy to sleep with you again? Tonight and..."

The pain in his voice broke Lizzie's heart. She finished his sentence by saying, "... for as long as is necessary. Her daily care as well."

"She will need to see her mother as much as possible, but all will depend on how Sarah fares over the next days."

"I understand." Then, surprising herself, "I shall pray for Sarah."

"Thank you."

This in little above a whisper. He turned back toward the wagon, his shoulders rounded, his gait that of an old man. Lizzie waited until he disappeared into the wagon before returning to the Fielding camp. She passed the next hour in quiet conversation with Maude and Richard, then corralled Missy when it was full dark and helped her wash her face and get ready for bed. The child asked for her mother several times, but Lizzie was able to convince her it was a special privilege to sleep with the big girls, and she went into the wagon without further complaint.

Over the following two days, Sarah's condition seemed to stabilize somewhat, although the swelling and pain in her abdomen grew progressively worse. She rode supine in her bed, not rising for meals but feeding Caleb when he cried and snuggling with Missy for much of the day. Meanwhile, they traveled nearly fifty miles along the general northwest course of the Little Blue River, crossing and re-crossing the stream several times when it made errant loops. On the evening of May third, they stopped by the river for the last time, its course turning south at that point, the trail continuing northwest toward Fort Kearny more than thirty miles ahead. Lazarus announced that the train would remain in camp for the next day to rest the animals and allow the women to wash clothes and the men to make any necessary repairs.

Immediately after breakfast the next morning, Jonathan pulled a large washtub from the wagon, and Lizzie began heating kettles of water over the fire. She had been rinsing out her own and the

Collinses' undergarments every few evenings, but a general laundry was long overdue. It no longer bothered her that she must now be responsible for tasks that an army of slaves had worked night and day to perform in her former life. Those days were gone, never to return, and she could accept that fact and move on or drive herself mad with regret and longing.

She climbed up into the Collins wagon to collect the dirty clothes for washing, moving as quietly as possible, but Sarah sensed her presence, opened her eyes, and reached out her hand with a wan smile. Lizzie took it, forced herself not to recoil at its fevered heat, and knelt down beside her friend. What to say to a woman who was dying? In the event, Sarah saved her the trouble. She said,

"You know I shall not live to finish this journey. My thoughts lie only with my dear Jonathan and Missy. And C—" Her voice caught. She cleared her throat and finished, "Caleb."

"You must not give up," Lizzie heard herself say. "You may conquer this wretched illness yet."

She shook her head. "It is not to be. I am in such agony that I cannot bear even the lightest touch to my... " She glanced down toward her enormous belly. "So you must not wish for the end to be prolonged. But I know my Jonathan, and when the time comes, he will not want to continue on. If he gives up, it will all have been for naught. He is a stubborn man and will take convincing. To that end, you may tell him of our conversation and convey these my heartfelt wishes. The future for our family lies in California. We decided this together, and my death changes nothing. Promise me you will do all within your power to keep his face turned westward."

"Of course I shall."

A quiet sigh. "Thank you. I can only believe it is God's hand that has brought you to us. I did not expect to rest the entire burden of my family's welfare on your young shoulders. I thought

I would be able to resume my duties, and we would continue as friends, helping each other through the certain rigors to come."

"I am able to do this, Sarah. I admit I am young, and I know my privileged background does not inspire confidence that I am up to this task. But I pledge to take care of your family as if it were my own until we reach the safety of California. On this you can depend!"

"I know you will do your best, Lizzie. But I am particularly worried for our little Caleb." She stopped speaking and swallowed hard, tears forming in her eyes. "How will he survive without his mother to provide the nourishment his tiny body needs? And if he cannot, it is an even further torture to know he will not be laid to rest beside his loving mother."

Lizzie took Sarah's face in her hands and looked through her eyes and into the depths of her soul. "That will not happen! I pledge to you that he will survive. And when he is old enough, he will be told of the love and courage of his mother. He will live to remember you, Sarah. You have my solemn oath!"

"Thank you." This little more than a sigh as she closed her eyes and drifted off to sleep.

Lizzie kept their conversation to herself, pondering the huge responsibility she had taken upon herself and wondering whether she was, indeed, up to the task. She had never given much thought to the travails of other people. Instead, she had been consumed with her own pleasure, always assuming her favored status in life was her right and prerogative as a lady of the South. Now, for the first time, she had not only focused her heart on the well-being of a family whom she had known but a few short weeks, but she had pledged to protect them from all future harm. Who was she to make such a promise? And where would she find the stamina and sheer force of will to fulfill it?

She threw herself into the washing as an antidote to her troubled thoughts. She filled the washtub with hot water, scrubbed the pile of dirty clothes until her hands were raw, and spread them out on any available surface to dry. The weather had been unusually mild and dry for the past days, and by evening the garments were dry enough to collect and pack away. There was no iron to remove the wrinkles, but simply having a clean dress to put on was reward enough for her sore back and chapped hands.

She and Jonathan took turns at entertaining Missy throughout the day, Lizzie allowing the girl to splash her hands in the washtub even though she ended up with as much water on herself as she left in the tub, Jonathan reading aloud from one of the collections of children's stories they had brought along. Both agreed that she be kept away from her mother as much as possible lest an inadvertent poke cause the poor lady more discomfort than she already suffered.

The felicitous weather lasted only long enough for people to settle in their wagons for the night. A deluge ensued accompanied by lightning and thunder and high winds that threatened to overturn the wagons. When the wake-up signal sounded before dawn, a light rain still fell, and Lizzie donned her cloak, threw an India-rubber blanket around her shoulders, and climbed down from the Fielding wagon.

Maude was already struggling to start a fire with the small amount of wood she always kept dry in the wagon. They greeted each other, and Lizzie proceeded to the Collins camp, where she was astonished to see Sarah seated by the fire pit while Jonathan worked to ignite a pile of twigs for their own fire.

She looked up at Lizzie and beamed. "It is a miracle! I feel so much better today. The pain is nearly gone. I do believe I may get well after all."

Overjoyed, Lizzie stooped to hug her, failing to notice that Jonathan's expression did not match the relief of his wife's. She removed the blanket from her shoulders and held it over the nascent blaze taking hold in the fire pit, then draped it around Sarah. By the time she had the bacon sizzling in the fry pan, the intermittent drizzle had stopped altogether.

She was about to go wake Missy when the child came running and threw herself into her mother's arms.

"Are you not sick anymore, Mama? Shall I be able to ride with you today?"

"Yes, my pet. You shall not leave my side. I promise!"

Pleased, the child turned to take her breakfast plate from Lizzie. When she saw the ubiquitous bacon floating in its own grease, her smile faded into a pout.

"Must we have bacon every day? Why can we not have johnnycakes instead?"

Lizzie smiled down at her. "There is no time for johnnycakes today, little one. But we shall have them one day soon."

"With butter and molasses?"

"Of course. Now eat your breakfast."

They had barely begun to eat when Caleb's cry drew Sarah up from her meal. There was enough light now that Lizzie could see the concern etched on her face. "My, but he is a hungry boy today. I fed him barely an hour ago, and here he is calling again. As he has all night. It is almost as if my milk is not sufficient to satisfy him."

Jonathan's eyes followed her to the wagon, and Lizzie was surprised to see them fill with tears. She turned her back to Missy and pitched her voice low, saying, "You do not credit this miraculous recovery?"

He merely shook his head, his expression as bleak a one as Lizzie had ever seen. Thus she was not altogether surprised to see Sarah abandon her post on the driver's box after they had been underway for less than an hour and crawl into the bed of the wagon, Missy following close behind. Jonathan pulled the wagon out of line and brought the oxen to a halt. He untied the dapple-gray saddle horse tethered with Blue Bell to the rear of the wagon box and waved Carl Fielding over.

"Will you ride forward and tell Lazarus we must stop? We shall try to catch up when... when this is over."

The lad took the reins and mounted without a word, his eyes telling Lizzie he understood the grave peril of Sarah's condition. The two Fielding wagons pulled out of line as well, flanking theirs as if their considerable bulk could ward off the effects of the illness wracking Sarah's body. Richard climbed up into the wagon box with Jonathan, who lifted a protesting Missy over the side and into Lizzie's arms.

"No!" the squirming child screamed. "I want my mama!!"

"You must be a big brave girl, Missy," said Lizzie, her voice so strained with emotion she could barely get the words out. "Mama is ill, and she needs to be with your papa and Uncle Richard right now."

"But she said she was better! I want to see her! Mama!! Help me!"

Lizzie carried her over to where Maude and Cora were standing helplessly by. The three women did their best to distract and entertain Missy, but the little girl's instinctive fear for her mother was too strong to overcome.

Carl rode back to report that Lazarus had ordered the entire train to stop out of respect for the health crisis now unfolding in the Collins camp. The Jamison family gathered round, and they all bowed their heads as the reverend petitioned the Almighty to spare their sister in faith. It appeared the Godhead was not inclined to listen, however, and within the hour, they heard Jonathan's deep, uncontrolled sobs. The end had come.

Chapter Eighteen

Word spread like lightning up and down the train. Men with shovels gathered and set out across the prairie toward a small copse of trees, where they found a suitable spot and began to dig.

Richard Fielding came down from the wagon and went to stand between his wife and oldest daughter, an arm around each while Lilly clung to her mother's skirts and Carl hovered nearby. Except for the sound of quiet weeping, the earth might have stopped spinning altogether given the utter silence. Even nature seemed to have paused. Not a breeze stirred. Not a bird flew. Not a chirp of cricket or thrum of a grasshopper could be heard. Then, like a clarion call, little Caleb's howl rent the air from the confines of the wagon. His cries grew to fever pitch, and Lizzie decided action was required.

She went over to the wagon and looked in. Jonathan knelt beside his wife's body, his expression trance-like, the swaddled infant tight in his arms.

"Give him to me, Jonathan," she said. "You must go to Missy. She needs to hear what has happened from you."

Her words seemed to jolt him out of his fugue. He looked down at the baby, back at her, and nodded. He rose and made his way to the rear opening. Handed Caleb out and said, "Will you send her in to me?"

"Of course." She took the squalling infant over to where Missy stood with Maude and Cora. She reached out for Missy's hand, saying, "Your papa wants to speak with you."

The little girl fixed wide frightened eyes on the bundle that was her little brother and said, "Is he sick, too?"

"No, dear. Your papa will explain everything. Come."

At first she refused to move. Then she began to shuffle forward. Lizzie guided her up the steps to the wagon box and saw her fling herself forward and into her father's arms.

Lizzie had never felt as useless as she did in that moment. Then she looked down at Caleb's red, angry face and knew what she had to do. She set off down the train, stopping to inquire here and there until she came to the Faraday group and the wagons belonging to a family from Iowa by the name of Saunders.

Like everyone else in the train, this family stood in respectful idleness, whispering among themselves and waiting for further news. Lizzie approached a heavyset woman surrounded by children of various ages whom she assumed to be the brood's mother.

"Mrs. Saunders?" she asked.

"That I am. And you must be the Miss Hamilton who has been helping that unfortunate family."

Her words confirmed that even among such a large collection of emigrants, little escaped the general knowledge. Before Lizzie could respond, she continued,

"And this," reaching for the still-bellowing Caleb, "would be the poor orphaned infant who is in dire need of his breakfast." And without another word, she unhooked the front of her dress and began to suckle the little boy.

Lizzie was speechless. It was an age-old practice in the South for the newborns of the planter class to be turned over for feeding to a wet nurse, usually a slave who had recently given birth to her own child. But for this northern white woman to be so spontaneous and generous in offering her breast was stunning.

Mrs. Saunders read her amazed expression and smiled. "As you can see, I have plenty of milk for two. My little Ella… " She nodded toward a chubby baby in the arms of a girl of perhaps thirteen. "… will be happy to share her mama. This little fellow is very small, but we shall soon remedy that."

Lizzie could not stop herself from asking, "Why would you so readily agree to do this?"

"God has blessed me with eight children and the ability to nurture them. Why would I not share that blessing with a helpless soul who would surely die without my help? The world is cruel enough without its inhabitants rejecting the chance to alleviate the suffering of another. And I have no doubt that those left behind by this tragic affair will suffer enough without the added burden of another loss."

Her clear eyes and convicted tone sent a shiver down Lizzie's spine. She murmured her thanks, and they went on to arrange the details of Caleb's care. Mrs. Saunders would keep him overnight as long as he required nighttime feedings. Lizzie would bring him forward as needed during the day. All assuming Jonathan agreed to continue on to California.

This latter thought brought a frisson of unease. She remembered Sarah's prediction that her husband would want to turn back after her death. Would Lizzie be required to intervene as she had promised? If so, would she be successful?

She waited with growing impatience until Caleb had drunk his fill and fallen asleep before taking him in her arms and turning back up the train. When she arrived at the Collins wagon, she found that the grave had been dug, and Maude was in the wagon preparing the body for burial. Jonathan and Missy were seated on the ground some distance away, the little girl wrapped in her father's arms, his head bent to hers as she wept. A gathering crowd stood in deferential silence, waiting to participate in whatever final formalities would be performed.

In the event, it was a simple affair. People stood around the open grave as Richard and Carl Fielding lowered Sarah into the earth. Reverend Jamison read the Methodist service for the dead and said the appropriate prayers. A stone-faced Jonathan picked up a handful of loose soil and threw it into the grave while a stunned Missy clung to his pant leg and hid her eyes from the sight of her mother's body being thus defiled. Other mourners repeated the ritual, then turned away as the self-appointed grave diggers got busy with their shovels.

Lizzie took Missy back to the wagon with the others, allowing Jonathan time alone for his private farewell. As they walked, Missy turned her tear-stained face up and said, "Will you be my mama now, Lizzie?"

She crouched down, shifted Caleb to her other arm, and folded the child close. "Not your mama, little one. But I shall be your dearest friend until we reach California. And that is a promise."

In a fretful voice, "But I need a mama. All little girls have a mama. What shall I do without one?"

"Your mama will always be with you in here." She pressed a finger against the little chest.

"But Papa said she is in heaven. If she is in heaven, how can she be... " She looked down and placed her own finger on top of Lizzie's. "... here."

Such theological issues were far beyond Lizzie's ability to understand, much less explain to a five-year-old. "Well, it is like a miracle, I suppose. You know what a miracle is?"

A vigorous nod. "Like when Jesus raised his friend Lazarus from the dead."

Lizzie knew the story, of course, but she had not thought of it in years. That their wagon master bore the same name came as a jarring coincidence.

Missy went on to say in a bright, hopeful tone, "Do you mean Jesus might raise my mama from the dead, too?"

Horrified that she had given even the smallest false hope to this poor child, she said, "No, Missy. I merely meant that when people die, their soul leaves their body and is no longer confined. It can be anywhere. Maybe even in two places at once. One in heaven. The other in your heart."

She was in dangerous territory best left to Jonathan. She hurried on to say, "Besides, you have many ladies who will be like a mama to you. Aunt Maude, me, even Cora. Now come along."

She stood and tugged on the child's arm, but she resisted, frowning up in defiance.

"Missy… " This in a sterner tone.

"No, I am not Missy. My name is Sarah. I want you to call me Sarah."

Lizzie stared down at her as understanding dawned. The need to hold on to anything connected with her mother, even her name, was overwhelming to this confused, grieving little girl. Finally she smiled and said,

"Of course, Sarah. Come along, now."

Her small face lost its rebellious cast, and she resumed walking without further protest.

Back at the train, preparations were already being made to continue the journey. Lazarus rode up to Richard Fielding and said, "My sympathies on the loss of your sister. But we have already lost considerable time, and I feel compelled to order the train forward."

Richard looked across to where Jonathan still knelt by the grave. "Can we not give him time to grieve?"

"Do you think another half hour, or even another day will accomplish that? A broken heart takes much more time to heal than we could possibly give. I must think of the good of the whole."

A reluctant nod. "Of course you must. Give me a moment to speak with him."

He set out across the prairie. Lizzie watched as they spoke and saw Jonathan's adamant head shake. Richard returned with troubled countenance.

"He refuses to go on. Says he and the children will turn back."

"May I try?" asked Lizzie.

Taken aback, Richard said, "Do you really believe you can succeed where I have failed?"

"Sarah anticipated this and left a message for him, a message I hoped never to deliver."

"Then by all means, go to him." To Lazarus, who still sat atop his horse listening to the exchange, "If the others must go on, we shall remain to the side and catch up later."

Lazarus took a moment to consider. Then he said, "We can wait another short while." To Lizzie, "See what you can do."

Heart in her throat, Lizzie handed Caleb to Maude and walked toward Jonathan. When she reached his side, she placed a gentle hand on his shoulder and said, "She knew you to the core. She warned me this would happen."

He raised startled eyes to hers. "What do you mean?"

"Sarah spoke to me yesterday. She knew she was going to die."

"Not today. She was so—" His voice broke with emotion. "—so happy this morning when the pain was gone. She thought she would get well."

"I saw that as well. But I also saw that you knew otherwise."

A bleak nod. "Richard told me what to expect. When the mortification finally takes hold, there is often a brief period of revival. I knew it would not last. But I did not have the heart to tell her."

"Nor would it have served any purpose for you to do so. In fact, it would have been cruel to rob her of that last glimmer of hope. But prior to that, she had accepted her fate and pondered the consequences of her mortality. Her greatest concern was for you and the children. She made me promise I would do all in my power to prevent you from turning back. She believed her family's future lay in California."

He shook his head. "What future is there for us without her?"

"I cannot answer that. But I do know she wanted with all her heart for you to continue on. If you do so, you will honor her wishes and prove that the decision you made together was the right one." She paused a moment, then continued in a flat, heartless tone, "Besides, turning back would be a death sentence for your son."

His head snapped up as she continued, "He is but days old and needs the nourishment only a mother can give. I have already found a wonderful woman with a baby of her own who is willing to share her milk with Caleb. With her help, he will grow and thrive and live to hear about his dear mother from the lips of the one who knew her and loved her best. You, Jonathan. But if you turn back, who will meet his needs? He will surely perish. Which was Sarah's greatest fear."

He sank back, shoulders and head bowed. She saw his lips move as if in prayer. Then he straightened and stood. Without another word, he started back toward the wagon train. Lizzie watched him go with a sad heart. She might have convinced him to continue on, but it was only the first step in what would surely be a difficult climb out of the valley of grief. She vowed to do all in her power to help him. For the first time in her life, she had a mission that would focus her thoughts and actions on someone besides herself. A fact that sent a surprising wave of peace rolling over her as she followed in his footsteps.

∞∞∞

The road ahead was more level with fewer of the ravines that had slowed their travel over the more undulating landscape behind them. They covered another ten miles under cloudy skies before stopping on the open plain beside a small stream with little surrounding vegetation. They made a small fire from dry grasses and some wood stored in the wagon, but it was sufficient only to brew coffee and fry some bacon, which they ate with hardtack softened in their coffee. Partway through the meal, the wind came up, the temperature dropped, and it started to rain.

They took their plates into the wagon to finish. Caleb was fretful and needed feeding, so Lizzie pulled on her cloak and draped the waterproof blanket over her head before splashing through the puddles to Mrs. Saunders' wagon, where she left him for the night. When she returned, Jonathan had lit the kerosene lantern and was reading a story to Missy. By the time he finished, the little girl's eyes were heavy, her head nodding, but when it came time to help her into her nightdress, she began to whimper for her mother.

Jonathan gave Lizzie a despairing look, shook his head, and climbed down from the wagon, the steady rain notwithstanding. Lizzie cuddled Missy, rocking back and forth as she hummed the little tune she had heard Sarah use to comfort her daughter. When the child finally succumbed to her exhaustion, she tucked her into her bedroll and crawled to the back opening to see what had become of Jonathan.

He stood just outside, rain soaking his coat and running in rivulets from his broad felt hat.

"She is asleep," she said. "Please come inside before you catch your death of cold."

"I had best turn in. I could use that blanket—"

"You cannot possibly sleep outside tonight," she interrupted.

They had already discussed their sleeping arrangements for the remainder of the journey. Missy was adamant that Lizzie not leave her for a moment, and Jonathan had agreed it would be best for her to remain in the wagon overnight rather than go to the Fielding wagon as she had done until now. Since it would be inappropriate for them to share the wagon overnight, no matter how innocently, he would make his bed on the ground beneath it henceforth.

"You are already soaked to the skin," Lizzie continued. "You can sleep where you normally do, and I can lie on the far side with Missy between us."

Even as she spoke, a sharp wind gust shook the wagon, and hail began to patter overhead. A bright stab of lightning followed by a deafening clap of thunder helped him make up his mind. He climbed up just as the hail began in earnest.

Despite her belief that the arrangement was best, his presence so nearby kept her from sound sleep that night. His soft shallow breathing told her he was wakeful as well. The occasional smothered sob spoke to the weight of his grief over spending his first night without his beloved Sarah. She longed to comfort him but knew it was beyond her power. When the rain stopped near morning, she finally drifted into a deep, heavy sleep from which she wakened at the sound of Lazarus's rifle shot to find him gone.

She had slept fully dressed. She reached for her cloak and climbed down, careful not to disturb Missy. Jonathan was leading Blue Bell back from the central corral where she had pastured with the other animals. He nodded as he passed, tied the animal to the wagon, collected the milking stool and proceeded with his morning chores.

Lizzie trudged through the mud to the Saunders wagon to collect Caleb. When she returned, she realized a campfire was impossible. She tucked the sleeping Caleb into his cradle, roused and dressed Missy, and put together a breakfast of dried fruit and hardtack washed down with Blue Bell's warm milk. Maude waved at her from across the camp, but she did not come over. Everyone else, including the Jamison clan, kept their eyes and faces turned elsewhere, whether out of respect for Jonathan's loss or disapproval over the two of them having shared a wagon she could not tell. She doubted the latter simply because it had been dark and stormy when Jonathan came back into the wagon, and she thought it unlikely anyone had seen him. Besides, did she really care? She had given up worrying about her reputation months before. She was being sensible and compassionate in light of difficult circumstances, and that was all that mattered.

The skies cleared by the time they stopped to noon, giving people a chance to lay out bedding or other storm-dampened items to dry in the sun. Again the way was level and not too muddy given the absorbent nature of the soil over which they traveled, and they were able to cover a total of twenty-three miles to camp in the Platte River's bottom near Fort Kearny.

For the first time in days, the sparse trees scattered along the riverbank provided enough fuel for a wood-fed fire, allowing for a more substantial supper of beans, reconstituted vegetables, and fresh-baked bread. Some groups gathered around their fires to sing or play musical instruments. The merry sounds drifted over them as a cruel reminder that life must go on. Missy went to play with her cousins and the younger Jamison children, a welcome respite from the oppressive sadness that had crushed her sprightly spirit over the past days. Jonathan lit the kerosene lantern and retreated to the wagon, telling Lizzie he planned to write letters to his relatives in Kentucky to tell them of Sarah's death, letters he would take to Fort Kearny in the morning to post.

Lizzie sat by the fire holding Caleb and pondering her growing fondness for this family. She wanted with all her heart to care for them and ease their grief over the coming weeks and months. But when all was said and done, they were but a transient means to an end, that end being her transport to California. There would come an inevitable time of parting, and the less she allowed herself to care, the easier that parting would be. Would she be able to control her feelings and keep them in proper perspective in the meantime? Only time would tell.

Caleb began to wiggle and whimper, signaling it was almost time to pass him off to Mrs. Saunders, who had made a temporary nest for him in her washtub and would be waiting for his bedtime feeding. She jiggled and shushed him, nuzzling his little face and planting kisses on his downy cheek, hoping for a few more moments of serenity before she must go to the wagon, change his napkin, add his nighttime pilcher, and make the trek to the Saunders wagon. It was not to be. He was working up to a gusty wail that would crescendo to a full-throated howl if she did not act soon.

"All right, you little tyrant," she laughed. "You win." She rose with a sigh and headed for the wagon.

The following day was Sunday, which meant there would be a late start. After Reverend Jamison's service, there was general interest in going to the nearby fort, a request to which Lazarus acceded, having judged they were making adequate progress despite the delays of the past few days. Every saddle horse and light wagon was pressed into service to accommodate the large number of those who wished to make the excursion. Jonathan rode his dappled horse Shadow while Missy and Lizzie, with Caleb in her arms, accepted Harold Jamison's offer to ride in their light spring wagon along with his wife Isabelle and their brood of five.

Many people, including Jonathan, were bringing letters to mail via the once-monthly stagecoach between Independence, Missouri and Salt Lake City in the Utah Territory, but Lizzie knew no one who cared to hear news of her travels. This thought brought with it a melancholy that surprised her and which she worked hard to ignore. Instead, she looked about her while listening to Missy's excited chatter over this new adventure.

The trail followed the Platte River, which was very wide and populated by numerous timbered islands. They passed many other encampments, attesting to the popularity of the fort as a stopover place. Lizzie was studying the various outfits when she heard the sound of a horse cantering in their direction from behind. She turned to see Henry Jamison draw up alongside.

He lifted his hat. "Good day, Miss Hamilton." Then, to his relatives in the wagon's driving seat, "Harold, Isabelle." Back to Lizzie, "May I be so bold as to compliment you on how lovely you look today?"

Lizzie laughed. "You are either delusional from the hardships of the journey, or you have been so long away from polite society that you fail to remember what constitutes true loveliness. In either case, reality proves you wrong. I am covered with dust and wearing a dress much abused by the rigors of camp life."

"I assure you your natural beauty transcends all the minor incommodious details you mention. But perhaps you will find a new dress to suit you when we arrive at the fort. I am told the stores there are quite amazing given the remoteness of this place."

"I have neither the inclination nor resources for such a shopping expedition, Mr. Jamison."

"Then you will continue to delight just as you are." Eyes on Caleb, "And how is your little charge? I must say, you look most natural with a babe in your arms."

The comment made Lizzie uncomfortable. "He fares as well as might be expected after losing his mother. Meanwhile, we must not keep you from your ride any longer. I have no doubt you will reach the fort well ahead of us given your fine mount there."

He gave her a long look before accepting her words as the dismissal they were intended to be. He raised his hat again, said, "Until later, then," and rode on ahead.

Lizzie caught Isabelle's sideways glance and felt her face flame. She had allowed herself some minor flirting with Henry, whether out of habit or boredom she could not say, but she had given it no more credence than she had during her days as a desirable belle.

Had her saucy behavior been interpreted otherwise by the young man? Was she, despite her current circumstances, being courted?

Appalled by the thought, she looked down at Missy, who had taken in the exchange with a confused expression. She gave the child a reassuring smile and turned her attention back to the countryside.

Soon they branched off the main road and followed the trail to Fort Kearny, which stood on a slight elevation a few miles from the river. Built as a military post whose purpose was to protect the travelers on the California and Oregon Trail, it seemed to Lizzie a poor excuse for an establishment of such purpose. To begin with, it had no walled fortifications but stood open and vulnerable in the morning sun. Five unpainted wooden structures stood around a large open parade ground with two dozen long, low sod buildings extending in haphazard fashion from the roads running along the square. Young trees bordered the parade ground. Scattered among them were the blockhouse guns, field pieces, and two giant howitzers for defending against Indian attack.

The fort's soldier population was even less impressive than the unkempt buildings. They were an unshaven, long-haired lot with patched uniforms and the bearing more of drunken louts than members of the United States military. Regardless, the goods available for purchase were extensive, and large crowds milled about the sutler's store and blacksmith's shop or stood in groups conversing and sharing their experiences.

Jonathan came looking for them and took Missy away with the offer of whatever treat might be available. Lizzie joined Maude, Cora and Lilly for a leisurely walk around the square. The largest structure was the commanding officer's house, which had piazzas extending along the front facade of each of its two stories. A two-story building directly opposite served as a barracks for the soldiers. The remaining five wooden buildings housed the officer's quarters, the hospital, and the sutler's store where emigrants jostled for access to its commodities. Although poor compared to the buildings to be found in more civilized places, these wooden buildings appeared quite fine when contrasted with the tumbledown mud structures that completed the fort's installations.

The women chatted in desultory fashion, passing Caleb among themselves to rest Lizzie's arms, until Missy came racing up with a handful of penny candy. Jonathan followed, an awkward package under his arm that turned out to be a tent and poles that he would pitch at night rather than sleep under the wagon as he had done the night before. Lizzie thought he looked somewhat restored. He had kept to himself over the past two days, saying little, often walking with his Bible in his hand, his expression unfailingly morose. Now he seemed to enjoy the change of scene from the monotony of the trail, taking special delight in little Missy's excitement over her sweet treasure. He even reached for Caleb and rocked the sleeping babe in his arms, his expression one of tenderness and awe. Lizzie knew it was but a tiny nudge forward on his path to healing, but she was pleased to see him make a beginning.

They stood talking for a time until they saw Lazarus going from group to group, presumably with the message that the train needed to be on its way. They were preparing to join the others when Lizzie happened to look to her left and notice a figure standing apart from the general bustle. The sun was behind him and she could not make out his features, but there was something familiar about his slouching posture and the forward thrust of his head.

He seemed to be focused on their particular party, causing her skin to prickle. She turned to her friends and said, "Who do you suppose that is?"

"Where?" asked Cora.

Lizzie looked back only to see that he was gone. She pointed. "Over there. He looked familiar somehow..."

"Your eyes must be playing tricks. But I see Carl beckoning for us to come."

Lizzie stared for a moment at the place where the man had stood, then shrugged, took Caleb from Jonathan, and went to find the Jamisons.

Chapter Nineteen

The train set out on the Great Platte River Road after the noon meal. The trail was broad and flat between a string of high sand-colored bluffs to the left and the south bank of the river, which was wide and muddy but shallow and strewn with many islands. The scenery changed little over the next five days. Lazarus and the group captains would ride ahead in the middle of the afternoon to find a place to halt for the night, not always an easy task given the dozens of other trains vying for the best spots. Thanks to Lazarus's experience and knowledge of the trail, however, they always managed to find a suitable location either near the river or beneath the bluffs. The sparse vegetation often made it difficult to find enough wood for a decent fire, but they learned to substitute the low silver-green scrub called sagebrush along with buffalo chips, a form of fuel that disgusted Lizzie even as she acknowledged its necessity.

    She tried to stay as close to Missy as possible, sometimes riding and cuddling in the wagon, sometimes walking hand in hand along the road. For the first day or two, the child clung to her as if she expected her to evaporate into thin air. It was during this time that Missy rummaged in the clothes trunk and pulled out her mother's dresses, which she presented to Lizzie with the words,

    "You can have these now."

    Lizzie found the thought of wearing a dead woman's clothes decidedly unattractive. In addition, she thought seeing Sarah's clothes worn by another would be painful to both the child and her father. Then it occurred to her that just as Missy demanded on occasion to be addressed as Sarah, this might be another attempt to keep her mother's memory alive in a tangible way. She discussed it with Jonathan and was surprised to hear him agree with her assessment. So she spent several days' evening hours with needle and thread taking up the hems to accommodate her shorter stature. The first day she wore one of the dresses, Missy's anxiety began to lessen. She would let go of Lizzie's hand and wander off to play with her cousins and the Jamison children, or she would pester her father for a story as had been her habit prior to Sarah's death, requests he would most often dismiss with a gentle but firm,

"Not now, little one."

He would walk alongside the oxen in brooding silence, speaking only when spoken to, often as not carrying his Bible and reading to himself. Finally on the fourth day, Lizzie could stand it no longer.

She took a deep breath and said, "I understand you are in pain, Jonathan, but I fear it consumes you to the detriment of your daughter."

He looked up from his Bible with a surprised expression. "I beg your pardon?"

"You are distant and inaccessible to her. Would it not be possible for you to tell one of your stories to help her pass the time? She needs to feel a semblance of normalcy return to her life."

Anger flashed in his eyes. "Normalcy? There is not one aspect of our present life that is normal. You wish me to pretend a contentment I do not feel?"

She lifted her chin. "I wish exactly that. Your wife is dead, but your children are very much alive. And they need you."

"Who are you to lecture me? A young woman who has never borne a child? Who is little more than a child herself? And a pampered one, at that."

Lizzie's temper rose. "Since when did this become about me? I may be young and childless, but far from pampering me, my recent life experience has brought me through the harshest of trials. Trials you are not qualified to judge. As for the current situation, I care about your children and am doing my best to help Missy through the loss of her mother. It hardly seems fair for her to have to deal with the virtual loss of her father as well. So I suggest you direct your anger where it belongs. Instead of searching the Scriptures for comfort, perhaps you should ask God why He has allowed this to happen!"

He stared at her for some moments, then spread his hands in surrender. "You are right, of course. I had no reason to berate you as I did. Your presence during this time is a gift from above, and I am more grateful than you could ever know. As for God, I do not blame Him for Sarah's death. None of us is promised a life free from strife and grief. I merely seek the strength to endure what I must."

His words banished her anger but piqued her curiosity. "And have you found it?"

For Lizzie, it was more than an idle question. She had railed at God from the moment her former life collapsed, first blaming Him, then deciding He did not care what happened to her. Instead, she had turned to her own grit and determination to see her through. Did Jonathan know of another way?

"I do not pretend to have put my sorrow to rest," he answered. "But the Bible addresses the emotions that taunt the bereaved. Emotions such as doubt, fear, loneliness, guilt."

"Guilt? Surely you do not hold yourself responsible for what happened!"

"Perhaps not in my head, but in my heart, I wonder whether she would have fallen ill if she had been home in her own bed for Caleb's birth. When I am tempted to such thoughts, the Bible tells me I do not have the power to judge even myself, for that authority belongs to God alone. And His mercy is infinite as well as His power to turn the evil happenings in this world into ultimate good."

"You sound like a preacher. Perhaps you should have followed that calling, after all."

"No. I am a simple man who loves the written word, whether it emanates from the heart of man or of God. And for the moment, I take solace in the words, '*And we know that all things work together for good to them that love God.*' I am trying to trust that the good will become apparent once we reach California. Meanwhile, I pray that my faith will stand up to this test."

"You believe God took Sarah from you as a test of your faith?"

"No. God is infinitely good and would never will pain and suffering for His children. But when such times come, as they inevitably will in this sinful world, and we survive them with our faith intact, we are purified just as gold is purified when it is refined by passing through fire. Purified and strengthened. And that is the condition I wish to attain for myself."

Lizzie certainly agreed that hardship and privation changed people. As far as she could tell, her own trials had transformed a silly, idealistic, naive girl into a woman who understood the self-centered nature of the human character and had learned to control and harness it for her long-term benefit. She was not sure where God fit into what had happened to her, if at all, but she could feel the power of Jonathan's faith emanating from him like steam from a boiling kettle, and a small new part of her envied his certainty in the face of his grief.

He smiled and said, "Now enough of theological discourse. I appreciate your bringing my neglect of Missy to my attention. I shall rectify my behavior to the best of my ability."

And he did. The fantastical stories of dragons and the handsome knights who slay them or brave princes and the maidens in distress whom they rescue continued as before. He hoisted the little girl onto his shoulders for occasional "pony rides." Held her on his lap around the fire in the evenings and read to her at bedtime. The salutary effects on the child's demeanor were a source of great satisfaction to Lizzie.

After they had camped that afternoon and she had hauled water and collected enough fuel for a small fire, she decided she had time before supper to do a bit of exploring. She took Missy's hand, and they set out toward the bluffs, which lay in a continuous line split by deep ravines. She approached the nearest one and saw that it was constructed mostly of compacted sand devoid of solid rocks or debris. They passed a perpendicular slab that had a number of names carved into the soft face, evidence of the hundreds, even thousands of people who had passed this way before them. They found a relatively easy slope and a vague path that led to the top, where they paused to take in the spectacular view. The river stretched like slivered strands of ribbon for miles in either direction. They could see the numerous campsites on both sides of the river as well as the plodding progress of trains that had yet to stop for the night. Lizzie's eyes were drawn to the far side, where she saw a large mass of cattle foraging for edible grass on the broad plain. Some dozen wagons were circled nearer to the river. It gave her a start to realize it was the Masters group.

She shaded her eyes and squinted in an attempt to make out any of the people she had known, if only briefly. Two men sat on horseback on either side of the herd, but she could not tell which of the three remaining cowboys they were. She gave a little shiver as she remembered the feel of Earl Long's weight crushing her, his hands clawing at her body. He was gone, but the very sight of the herd brought the memories back in a flood.

She felt a tug on her hand and looked down to see Missy watching her in consternation. "Why are you scared, Lizzie?"

It was not the first time the little girl's uncanny instincts had caught her up short. She shook her head and smiled. "I was simply remembering how late it is and how I must get back to camp. Come along. I shall race you back."

They flew down the path, Missy's shrieks of delight leading the way.

The following day they camped near the place where they would ford the South Fork of the Platte. The river was very wide at that point—some said more than a mile— and somewhat deeper than normal due to recent rains. Lazarus went from camp to camp advising that wagon boxes be raised prior to crossing. In addition, he suggested that all extra oxen be utilized as the riverbed was sandy and might contain pockets of quicksand, which meant that once entering the water, all wagons, men and animals must move steadily forward so as not to bog down.

All that evening in accordance with the comity and camaraderie that had developed among the forty-some members of the Jamison group, the men worked in concert to raise each wagon box off its undercarriage using the blocks of wood brought along for that purpose and to apportion any extra oxen among those who had only their original team. Some heavier wagons would require at least ten yoke, and all agreed that once their wagons were safely across, their oxen would be available to assist with others that had yet to cross.

Early the next morning, they drove the short distance to the river and pulled up behind the scores of others waiting to cross. When their turn came, Lizzie climbed into the wagon with Missy and Caleb and braced herself for what would surely be a rough ride. She watched through the front opening, heart in her throat, as Jonathan urged the animals into the river. Their bawls of protest blended with the swish of the water as it passed around them. The wagon swayed and lurched while the water rose from Jonathan's ankles and knees to above his waist. She feared it might swallow him altogether, but it finally leveled out at chest height, and he plodded onward until they climbed up onto the far riverbank. He unyoked the oxen and led them back into the water for the use of others. By the time all in the train had crossed, it was mid-afternoon, and they drove but another five miles before stopping to camp so that the wagon boxes could be lowered and any articles that were damp from the crossing could be aired out.

They followed the North Platte for the next two days, camping the first night in the midst of a prairie dog village. Lizzie was as enchanted as Missy by the lively little creatures, which resembled squirrels far more than they did dogs, although their bark was quite reminiscent of a puppy. They lived beneath the earth, the mounds of soil from their digging dotting the landscape in various heights and sizes more numerous than it was possible to count. Entire families sat up outside their burrows watching the activities of the interlopers with bright eyes and no hint of fear. Missy wanted to try befriending them, but Lizzie was as stern as she had ever been in her refusal. An inadvertent bite might breed any number of health problems for her little charge, and she was not willing to take that risk. Missy pouted but accepted the edict and contented herself with simple observation.

The second night, a storm of wind, rain and hail passed through similar to the one they had experienced the night after Sarah died. Again, Lizzie urged Jonathan to come into the wagon and he complied, a decision that was to bring consequences they could not imagine in the midst of the storm's fury.

It happened the following evening. The train had left the river bottom after the nooning and taken a track that climbed a gentle slope some three miles toward the tablelands above, ending at a delightful glen called Ash Hollow, so named for the numerous trees of that variety found there. There were a clear sweet spring and massive limestone rocks jutting as many as two hundred feet upward, as beautiful a spot as Lizzie had seen thus far on the journey. There were many other encampments scattered about as well as evidence of countless others before them. But the grass, wood and water were plentiful, and some members of the Stafford group had killed a bull buffalo that morning and had shared its bounty among all groups of the train. The Jamison group's portion had been enough for every family to have a supper of fresh meat, and the general feeling was one of good cheer.

After the meal, they were surprised to see Reverend Jamison approaching their camp. He removed his hat and nodded in an uncharacteristically formal manner.

"Good evening," he began. "I have come to invite you to a convocation of the members of our group. There is a matter of some concern that people wish to address with you."

Jonathan stood, frowning. "What matter would that be?"

His severe expression faltered. "I would rather elaborate once we are among the others. Cora Fielding is waiting to take charge of your children while we talk."

A strange prescient feeling flitted through Lizzie's mind. Something unpleasant was about to happen. Nonetheless, she stood, set her jaw and said to Jonathan,

"I have no objection to finding out what this is about."

He gave a grudging nod and went to find Missy. They found the company gathered in a clearing around a large fire a short distance away. Lizzie took some comfort in the fact it was not a train-wide affair and Lazarus was not there. Cora's eyes were bright with curiosity as she came to take Caleb and Missy to another fire where the other children were already playing. Maude and Richard looked uncomfortable, refusing to meet their eyes when they slid in beside them.

The firelight fell on Henry Jamison's face where he stood a short distance away. He was watching Lizzie with an intent expression, lips curved in an incipient smile. She ignored him and focused on the reverend, who seemed to be in charge of the meeting.

The churchman stood with his hands behind his back, a common posture when he was preaching, and addressed Jonathan. "Everyone present knows you are still suffering greatly over the loss of your beloved Sarah, and we have no wish to cause you further distress. However, it has come to the attention of various of our number that your present situation falls short of the accepted bounds of propriety. I refer, of course, to your close association with Miss Hamilton."

Jonathan's face flushed with sudden anger. He stepped forward, fists clenched. "How dare you—"

Reverend Jamison held up his hand and interrupted, "Please do not think I am accusing you of any impure act. I have known you for many years as an honorable man of impeccable morals, and I have no doubt you are conducting yourself in like manner with regard to Miss Hamilton. However, the outward appearance of a man sharing a wagon with a woman who is not his wife not only offends the delicate sensibilities of the ladies of our company, but it is a bad example for the children."

"And what of *my* children?" he shot back. "They have lost their mother and need the tender care only a woman can give. God was merciful in sending Miss Hamilton to us, even though we did not appreciate how very much she would be needed in the end. For anyone to suggest that I would take carnal advantage of her mere weeks after my wife's death is obscene!"

"As I have already told you, no one is accusing you of impropriety. It is the appearance that concerns us. We acknowledge that she is a great benefit to you and your family in your present time of need, but her sleeping arrangements are not acceptable. Especially given that you have joined her in the wagon on more than one occasion."

Jonathan shook his head, speechless over this man's interpretation of a perfectly innocent situation. At last he said, "And what would you suggest? That she sleep outside in the tent while I enjoy the comfort of the wagon?"

"No, no. But I believe there is room for her in one of the Fielding wagons. In fact, that is where she slept prior to Sarah's passing."

Lizzie had heard enough. She stepped forward and said, "It is not this company's place to decide what is best for Missy and Caleb. If Missy takes special comfort in having me close by when she wakens during the night, then that is where I plan to be. Indeed, I have promised her, and nothing will make me break that promise!"

"Have you no concern for your reputation, young lady? What would your mother say were she to find you in such unchaperoned contact with a man not your husband?"

Lizzie wanted to laugh. Whatever reputation she had once enjoyed had been destroyed many months before. Thus her mother, were she still alive, would have much more egregious conduct to condemn than the innocent sharing of an emigrant's wagon.

She was composing a response when Henry stepped out from the crowd and came toward her, hat in hand.

"I have a solution to this impasse," he said, his eyes burning into hers. "Miss Hamilton is no doubt aware of my growing feelings for her. I would be most honored if she would accept me as her husband. Lazarus has already decided the train will remain in this charming place tomorrow for a washing and repair day. My esteemed father could perform the wedding ceremony in the morning, and we could enjoy one another for that day and night, after which she could return to the Collins wagon without any vestige of shame. Whenever little Missy is ready to be alone during the night, she would share our wagon while still cooking and caring for the Collins family during the daytime. Thus insuring that the lady's honor remains intact... " A large grin. "... while granting my heart's desire for a wife whom I shall adore until my dying day."

Stunned silence greeted the young man's declaration. Once her shock had passed, Lizzie recognized the deep irony of her situation. On the night of her escape from Charleston, she had assumed a proposal of marriage was but a formality to be delivered once she and Jack were safely away. She had even sacrificed her virginity in her certainty. Now here was the longed-for declaration from a man whom she knew even less than she had Jack. And he was offering the respectability she had thought forever beyond her reach.

She could feel dozens of eyes directed her way, but the ones she cared most about were Jonathan's. His skin had grown pale. His lips were parted as if he wished to speak but did not dare, and his deep eyes projected a confused plea.

She took a deep breath and said to Henry, "I am flattered and honored by your proposal. But marriage is a serious matter not to be decided based on rumor and innuendo."

"That is only the precipitating factor," he argued. "I love you most dearly and would have asked for your hand before journey's end, in any case."

Dismayed, she countered, "But you barely know me or my circumstances. I have my own plans once I reach California, and they do not include marriage, no matter how earnestly proposed." She spread her arms to include the entire company. "I do understand your concerns. Indeed, I come from the South where they would surely be echoed. However, I have begun a new life made possible by the Collinses. I made a pledge to a dying friend to see her family safely to California. And I intend to keep it. But I also pledge to all of you that nothing inappropriate will ever pass between Jonathan and me. Beyond that, I must ask you to treat us as the temporary family we have become and leave us in peace."

With that, she turned her back on the company and proceeded with determined steps toward the children's fire. It was time for Caleb's nighttime feeding.

∞∞∞

The next day, Lizzie went about her washing chores with intense concentration, not allowing herself to notice how others in the camp were reacting toward her and her unconditional refusal to bow to their concerns. Jonathan was busy with various repairs, and although he did not engage her in any but the most necessary conversation, she felt his eyes on her as she worked. She had carried a bucket to the spring for fresh water when she felt his hand on her shoulder.

His face was troubled, his brow showing deep furrows. "May I have a word with you?"

"Of course."

"There is a little glade behind that rock formation," he said, pointing.

She nodded, and he took the bucket from her hand and waited for her to lead the way. They found a low flat rock on which to sit. He fixed her with earnest eyes that held something indefinable she had not seen before, something that sent a rush of blood to her cheeks.

"You know how much I appreciate all you do for us," he said. "I have been selfish in exploiting you as I have without a thought to your own feelings."

"You have not exploited me! You are providing me passage to California, and I merely return your kindness to the best of my ability."

"Did it never occur to you that you had opened yourself up to cruel taunts such as you heard last night? In my grief, it certainly did not occur to me."

She shrugged. "I admit the meeting took me by surprise. But I should have seen it coming. For one raised in the hidebound culture of the planter class, I was abysmally naive."

"Yet you did not take the escape Henry offered you."

She shook her head. "I do not love Henry Jamison. Nor do I believe marriage is in my future."

A quizzical tilt of his head. "Whyever not? You are a... " He paused long enough for an embarrassed flush to creep up his face. "... a beautiful woman. Any man would be fortunate to have you for a wife."

Her tone was more bleak than she intended. "There are things you do not know about me. Do not want to know. You must simply accept my assurance that I will never marry."

"Then that will be a pity. You are very good with Missy, and your tenderness toward Caleb is obvious. You would make a wonderful mother."

His words brought an inordinate rush of pleasure. Even if it were never to be, she was gratified to hear him judge her so.

"As it happens," he continued, "that is the reason I asked to speak with you. I admit to being stunned when Henry spoke last night. And I have thought of little else since. You know how dearly I loved Sarah and how bereft I am without her. However, I am realistic enough to know that I will no doubt marry again someday. For my own sake as well as that of my children. Given that near certainty, I am the one who should have thought enough of your honor to offer marriage."

She rocked back in surprise. "But I could never take Sarah's place."

"No," he admitted. "But you have your own sterling qualities that would endear you to any man. Have already done so to me. I am not ready to love again. But I could easily imagine myself entertaining those feelings for you one day. Given that, why not proceed now when your moral character has been called into question?" A boyish grin. "Assuming you would have me."

Emotion flooded Lizzie's heart to the extent she was forced to rise and pace about the narrow space in which they sat. Two marriage proposals in two days? It was beyond comprehension. She had had little trouble refusing Henry the night before. But Jonathan? He was the exact sort of man she had always dreamed of marrying. Honorable. Settled in a profession and capable of supporting a family. Easy to talk to. Sincere in his opinions and attitudes toward life. And rather handsome in a scarecrow sort of way. Her breath came in short gasps as she contemplated agreeing to what he was suggesting.

Then reality came crashing down on her. He believed her to be a chaste maiden who deserved to have her honor restored. She could not marry him without telling him everything. The cavalier manner in which she had abandoned her family. The shameful loss of her virginity. The life she had snuffed out with little thought of the nascent human being growing inside her body. Why would he want her then?

Besides, she had already decided her future lay in her own hands. She would cash in the bearer bonds and establish herself in a comfortable but independent life in California. She would be beholden to no one. Would never depend on another soul for her welfare. Then, and only then would she decide whether to seek out the companionship of a man to finish out her days. One thing was certain, however. If it happened, it would be on her terms. Or it would not happen at all.

She stopped pacing and knelt on the grass before him. "Thank you for your offer, Jonathan. You are a kind, generous man and will find someone to love you properly one day. But I am not the woman for you. That said, I shall fight for your welfare and that of your children to my dying breath. And when we part in California, it will be as dear friends who will always be grateful for the time we have spent together on this journey. Please do not trouble yourself about my reputation. I care not a whit for it. Nor do I care what people think of me."

She rose. "Now help me carry some water back to camp. I still have a mountain of clothing to wash."

Chapter Twenty

Lizzie was grateful for the backbreaking work that remained, her red, swollen arms and hands a distraction from what had transpired between herself and Jonathan. It was late afternoon before she had scrubbed, wrung out, and laid the last article of clothing on the surrounding shrubs and rocks to dry. Supper was a quiet affair, Missy picking up on the awkwardness between the two adults as she moved her wide-eyed gaze from one to the other. After cleaning and storing the plates and cups, Lizzie made the rounds to check the laundry and bring in whatever was dry. Now that it was the middle of May, the days were getting longer, which allowed her to leave the last-washed articles until the final dim light of dusk. It was not until the next morning as they prepared to pack up and leave that she realized her brown gingham dress was missing.

She told Jonathan, who was hitching the oxen, "I neglected to bring in one of my dresses last night. I must have overlooked it in the dark."

"I can help," said Missy, glad of a final opportunity to scamper about the pleasant glen where they were camped.

Jonathan nodded and went back to his task while Lizzie patrolled the immediate vicinity for the missing dress. Finding nothing, she was about to conclude someone had either stolen it or picked it up by mistake when she heard Missy crashing toward her through the underbrush.

The little girl's eyes were sparkling with excitement. "A dragon tried to eat it! Come and see!"

Lizzie followed her to a large boulder and around to the uphill side, where she pointed to a shredded heap of brown cloth lying in plain sight. Lizzie picked it up. It was indeed the missing dress, and it had been slashed to ribbons by a very sharp knife. Stunned, she went back to the wagon to show Jonathan with Missy skipping beside her and chanting, "The dragon did it. The dragon did it."

Jonathan shushed his daughter, fingered the fabric, and shook his head. "This is the vicious act of a deranged person. We must show it to Lazarus."

The wagon master was making his rounds to verify that all was in readiness for the journey. They found him mounted on his horse in the Eastman camp. He listened to their story with obvious concern.

"You saw nothing out of the ordinary yesterday?" he asked. "No strangers, no one who did not belong to our party?"

They both shook their heads, but Missy piped up with, "I saw Mr. Weehoe. But he is my friend. He gave me a candy stick."

The adults fixed her with startled eyes. Her father said, "This is no time for you to make up stories, Missy." To Lazarus, "My daughter has a vivid imagination. Perhaps encouraged by me. I conjure up tales to help pass the time as we walk along."

"But I did not make it up, papa. Mr. Weehoe told me a story, too. A wonderful story about the sun and how it had a pair of magic pants." A giggle. "That is so silly. How could the sun have a pair of pants? But in the story, a naughty boy stole the pants and ran away. But no matter how fast and far he ran, he could not get away from the sun. So the sun used his magic to set the pants on fire and teach the boy a lesson that it is bad to steal."

She beamed up at them, pleased that she had remembered so much of the story. Their disapproving expressions took the smile from her face. Her father knelt down, cupped her shoulders, and said,

"Missy, how many times have we told you never to talk to people you do not know?"

She hung her head and scuffed her toe in the dirt.

He blew out his cheeks. Took a moment to calm himself, then said, "Where did you see this man? This Mr... Weehoe, was it?"

"By the spring. We went for a walk. And he gave me candy."

"You must *never*... " A gentle shake to make his point. "... go *anywhere* with a man you do not know. Or accept any gift, including candy. Instead, you must run away as fast as you can and find me. Do you understand me?"

Her lip quivered as she nodded, adding, "But he was so nice."

"Nice is not enough. Bad people can pretend to be nice. That does not make them nice." A pause to allow his words to sink in. Then, "Was this the first time you had seen him?"

A barely audible, "Yes."

"What did he look like?"

Puzzlement. Then a shrug.

"Was he tall?" her father persisted. "Or short? Clean shaven or bearded?"

"Oh, very tall. With a fuzzy beard. He let me touch it."

Jonathan looked up at the others and shook his head. She could have been describing any one of a hundred men attached to the train.

To Missy, "Do you promise never to talk to this man again? To come and tell me if you even see him?"

A chastened nod.

"Very well. Go back to the wagon and make sure your brother is still asleep. We shall join you shortly."

He turned to Lazarus. "What do you make of this?"

His troubled expression said it all. "Nothing good. Cheyenne Indian mythology tells of a spider trickster by the name of Wihio. The story she just related is similar to one of their legends. Someone was sending you a not-so-subtle message. Through the child as well as the dress vandalism."

"You think the two incidents are related?"

"Two odd occurrences in one day? It seems a stretch to consider them a coincidence. Can you think of anyone who harbors ill will toward you?" To Lizzie, "Or you, Miss Hamilton?"

Lizzie could think of one, but he was no doubt far away fleecing as many unsuspecting gamblers as possible. She shook her head.

Jonathan was equally baffled.

"Then we have no choice but to move on with heightened security. I shall caution people to keep an eye out for this elusive Mr. Weehoe. I shall also order the night watch to be doubled. Needless to say, I advise you folks, as well as your entire group, to increase your vigilance and come to me at the first sign of anything untoward."

And thus it was that the train returned to the trail. Lizzie's anxiety over the destruction of her dress—a dress she had worn so often she was sick to death of it—dissipated as the days passed. Thoughts of Jonathan and their discussion at Ash Hollow rushed in to fill the void.

She still believed marriage to him was impossible for all the reasons she had already acknowledged. Nevertheless, she could not deny that her attitude toward him had changed. Once she had regarded him as a capable but older man whose physical attributes were inconsequential to her. Now certain sights caused her innards to reverberate. His muscled torso when he shaved shirtless in the mornings. His dimples when he smiled. The way his glasses slid down his narrow nose when he read. The easy swing of his long legs as he walked. He was a constant presence in her consciousness that disturbed and confused her.

As for Jonathan, his demeanor seemed more introspective and contemplative than before their discussion, but the cause was impossible to know. Her refusal of his proposal might have been a factor, of course. More likely, his grief had been renewed by the thought that his circumstances would one day force him to find a new mother for his children. Whatever his inner thoughts, by the time they had traveled far enough along the south side of the North Platte to come within sight of the phenomenon known as Courthouse Rock, the interactions between them had returned to a semblance of normalcy.

The guide books described Courthouse Rock as a massive pile of rock that jutted abruptly out of the prairie, a smaller formation known as Jail Rock poking up nearby. The closer they came to it, the greater Missy's excitement. When they drew even, she begged to mount an excursion to its base to see whether they could climb it. The strange formation was still some four miles distant from the road, however, and the train moved inexorably on, leaving the child with nothing but her imaginings over what fantastical things she might have found at its summit.

Soon after passing Courthouse Rock, they came near a Sioux village containing some two dozen lodges constructed of buffalo hides wrapped around a cone of sapling poles. They had already seen the occasional Indian here or there along the way, but this was the first settlement they had encountered. The inhabitants stopped their various chores or came out from their homes to watch them pass, the women in buckskin dresses, the men wearing nothing but a small apron around their waists. Missy took it all in from the safety of her father's arms, but she soon wiggled down as another curiosity beckoned on the horizon, the now-visible spire of Chimney Rock.

They had made slow progress since leaving Ash Hollow, averaging but fifteen miles per day at best. Sandy roads had often required a snail's pace as the oxen strained to move the wagon wheels through the yielding surface. A string of rainy days had not helped matters. Now, however, the road was better, the day sunny and warm, and they managed another twenty miles before stopping on the river two miles from the single sand-and-stone pillar with its wide steep base aptly named Chimney Rock.

Missy could speak of nothing but her desire to see the strange obelisk-like formation up close. Having already walked many miles that day, Lizzie was less than keen about another two-mile jaunt, but to her surprise, Jonathan came up with a solution.

"We can all three go on Shadow."

"On one horse?" said Lizzie.

"Certainly. I can hold Missy in front and you can ride behind."

Lizzie considered herself an accomplished horsewoman, but she had always ridden in a smart riding habit atop a lady's sidesaddle.

With skepticism, "You mean astride?"

"How else? Sitting sideways would not be safe without the support of a saddle designed for that purpose."

"Well..."

"Oh, do come, Lizzie!" cried Missy, jumping up and down in her excitement.

Unable to resist, she smiled and said, "Why not? Cora will no doubt watch Caleb while we are gone."

Jonathan saddled the dappled gelding, a massive animal whose height she judged to be close to seventeen hands. He mounted and reached down to take Missy from Lizzie's extended arms. Then it was her turn. At Rocklands, a slave boy had always been at hand to bring the mounting block whenever she wanted to ride. Having no such implement, she was at a loss.

Jonathan kicked his boot out of its stirrup and instructed, "Left foot there. Right hand on the canticle."

It was a very long stretch, but she managed to get a toe onto the stirrup's metal rung and take hold of the saddle's back. He reached for her arm, said, "Up you come," and pulled as she pushed off.

She ended up face down across the animal's rump, her legs dangling unceremoniously in the air.

Red-faced, she wiggled around and pulled herself upright. She did her best to arrange her skirt and petticoat to cover her exposed legs, but in the end, she was forced to accept that a scandalous amount of flesh would of necessity remain on display for the world to see. She wrapped her arms around Jonathan's waist and felt the animal's muscles bunch as he leapt forward in response to Jonathan's urging.

Despite the oddity of riding astride, she felt a surge of joy at the familiar sensation of a fine animal beneath her. Or was it her sudden close proximity to Jonathan? The solid feel of his chest against her hands. The warmth emanating from his back. The male odor clinging to his shirt. Giddy with pleasure, she turned her face into the wind and watched the ground fly by beneath the animal's hooves.

Jonathan pulled up at the base of Chimney Rock, gave Lizzie a hand down, and lowered Missy to her before dismounting. The formation looked quite different up close. Rather than the smooth surfaces perceived from a distance, the rock was rife with cracks and crevices around which scrub vegetation clung wherever nature allowed. The wide base made a massive cone from which the spire protruded like a pole stuck in a giant's haystack. Missy scampered up with Jonathan and Lizzie close behind, but the grade was very steep, and they soon slowed to a near crawl. They noticed that many names had been either painted with axle grease or carved into the exposed surfaces.

"We must write our names as well," said Missy. "Then all the world will know we were here."

"I have nothing with which to carve," said Jonathan, adding when her face clouded, "But there will be other opportunities, I promise. Now have you seen enough?"

"Oh, no. I want to go higher!"

Jonathan glanced at Lizzie, saw the sweat glistening on her face, and said, "You may go a short distance more while we wait here."

The little girl clawed her way upward as Jonathan gestured to an elevated rock shelf and offered his hand to ease Lizzie down onto it. He squatted beside her and waved his arm in a wide arc.

"Now there is a sight we will not likely experience again."

Indeed, their perspective was one of exceptional beauty. The lowering sun cast a golden glow across the lush undulating prairie and glinted like fire off the surface of the distant river. The endless mass of emigrant wagons appeared like children's toys where they were circled for the night or still plodding along the road. Lizzie remembered a similar scene when she and Missy were standing atop the river bluff some weeks before. She also remembered identifying the Masters group on the far side of the river and scanned the horizon to see whether they were visible now. It was, of course, a futile exercise. She put them out of her mind and brought her attention back to the moment.

A peaceful camaraderie shimmered in the cool, clear air. She studied Jonathan's hands where they rested on his bent knees. Long, aesthetic fingers rising from a broad base. Strong yet gentle hands. Hands she had a sudden urge to touch.

He caught her glance, cleared his throat, and stood, turning to call Missy back to them. Confused by her rebellious feelings, Lizzie stood as well. When Missy had scrambled down to their level, they picked their way down the steep incline to where Shadow waited to take them back to camp.

∞∞∞

Missy's chance to leave her name for posterity came when they stopped to noon opposite Scotts Bluff the following day. Here a collection of bluffs rose some eight hundred feet above the prairie, reminding the fanciful eye of fortifications that might have been built in ancient times to protect a castle from marauders. It was also the place, according to the emigrant guide books, where the traveler left the Great Plains behind and entered the foothills of the Rocky Mountains.

While Lizzie prepared the noon meal, Jonathan rummaged in his tool box for a gimlet, then led his little daughter up the steep incline to the perpendicular face where people recorded their names and the date of their passing. When they returned, Missy could speak of nothing else.

"We put your name in the rock, too, Lizzie. And mine and papa's and Caleb's. Now everyone who comes this way will know we were here and we are a family."

Lizzie gave her a startled look and decided it would be best to change the subject. "I wonder how the name Scotts Bluff came to be?"

It was no surprise when Jonathan spoke up. Was there any limit to the man's knowledge?

"The story goes that many years ago, a group of fur traders were returning from the Oregon Territory when one of them, a Mr. Hiram Scott, was wounded in a skirmish with the Indians. He made it here but was unable to travel farther. His companions remained with him as long as possible, but their supplies were running low, and he insisted they leave him and go on in order to save their own lives. Later his bones were discovered near the bluffs, prompting folks to name the place after him." He shrugged. "Who can tell how much is truth and how much fabrication? Regardless, that is the story told in the guide."

It was difficult to imagine such hardship on a mild sunny day with nary an Indian in sight, but the story captured Missy's imagination and diverted any further talk of them being a family. Lizzie cleaned and packed the few utensils they had needed for the simple meal and went to fetch Caleb from Mrs. Saunders, who had given him his midday feeding.

They moved on another six miles to camp in a lovely, tree-shaded spot near a spring brook. Lizzie was preparing the day's bread dough for baking when Cora came into camp, her eyes glowing with excitement.

"You would not believe what we found!" she cried. "Just up that ravine." She pointed to a cleft in two moderately-sized bluffs. "We were looking for the head of the spring when we saw it."

"What?" Lizzie asked.

"I shan't spoil the surprise. Come and see for yourself."

Jonathan and Missy's interest had been piqued as well, so Lizzie took up Caleb, who was beginning to fuss in any case, and followed them up an overgrown path winding along the clear little stream. She was about to think it a fool's errand when the trees widened into a small clearing containing several deserted, dilapidated log buildings, one of which had been a blacksmith shop, the forge still intact. Scattered within and among these structures were the miscellaneous castoffs of any emigrant's outfit, items such as wagon remnants, rusted barrel bands, and the odd ox yoke or broken wheel spoke. Anything of use had long since been pilfered by others who had stumbled onto the abandoned place. What remained was mere junk.

They were not the only adventurers wandering amongst the detritus. General opinion held that this had once been a small independent trading post much like others they had encountered along the way. It gave Lizzie an eerie feeling to be standing where others had conducted their lives. Where and why had they gone? Had it been of their own free will, or had they been driven out by Indians or other miscreants?

The walk up had lulled Caleb, but now he was squirming with impatience and whimpering preparatory to a full-fledged protest.

She looked down at his reddening little face and felt a rush of warmth sweep over her. He was now three-and-a-half weeks old and had lost his wrinkled newborn look. Despite his early beginning, he had already grown enough to flesh out his cheeks, arms and legs. His eyes were a very dark blue with a hint of brown, suggesting they would turn hazel like his father's. His downy hair was dark, and his limbs seemed longer than what she remembered of her three nephews. Whereas Missy was a replica of her mother, she suspected this little guy would favor his tall, lanky father. Which, she thought, was as it should be.

He began to cry in earnest, and she turned back down the way they had come. Interesting distractions aside, it was time to get on with the nightly ritual of a traveler's life.

The following three days took them across Horse Creek and along the south bank of the North Platte, a flat monotonous landscape without wood or fresh water beyond the river itself. The distant sight of snow-capped Laramie Peak, however, portended the change that was coming. They passed a number of temporary trading posts as well as many Sioux Indian villages, once observing a group of hunters chase a herd of some fifty buffalo, several of which they managed to kill. They rode without benefit of saddle, guiding their ponies with nothing but a simple halter, their sole weapon a bow and quiver of arrows. Savages or no, they rode as one with their mounts, exhibiting a rudimentary grace that was worthy, in Lizzie's opinion, of great admiration.

When they arrived at the Laramie River, their progress was interrupted for a day while they waited for the many wagons ahead of them—possibly a hundred and fifty or more—to ferry across. Lizzie spent the day baking and mending and washing those articles they had dirtied since Ash Hollow. There was a general feeling of exuberance among her friends in the group. The women gathered between chores to gossip and exchange ideas about streamlining their routines or to share their dreams of the future. The men either went out to hunt, worked at various repairs, or stood in groups to smoke their cigars and opine about the train's progress and the various complaints and grumblings that were inevitable when such a large gathering of disparate people were thrown together in intimate circumstances for such a long period of time. After supper, they gathered around a huge bonfire in the center of the circle, musical instruments came out, and the evening passed in dancing and singing.

Lizzie noticed that Henry Jamison was absent from the festivities. She had seen him but a few times since his failed marriage proposal and then only in passing. On those occasions, he had avoided her eyes, mumbled an embarrassed greeting, and hurried on. She knew his male confidence had suffered a humiliating blow, and the realization pained her. She could only hope time would heal his wound and allow him to return to his former charming self.

She retired to the wagon long before the youngest and hardiest of the group were willing to give up. She crawled in beside the sleeping Missy and was asleep moments after her head touched the pillow.

Missy's piercing scream wrenched her from a deep slumber in the wee hours of the morning. These late-night wakenings, frequent in the days following Sarah's death but gradually dwindling until they were all but nonexistent, had always begun with quiet but heart-wrenching sobs. Never with a primal cry such as this.

Lizzie reached out and drew the little girl to her breast, rocking back and forth and making shushing noises even as Jonathan's frantic voice cried from outside, "What is wrong?"

He climbed up and crawled toward his daughter, whose cries had been reduced to gulping sobs. She pulled away from Lizzie and threw herself into his arms.

"Th–the dra–gon. He wants to e–eat me. I heard his cl–claws on th–the wall. He wants t—to come in."

He stroked her hair, murmuring, "You have had a bad dream, dear one. There is no dragon. They only exist in make-believe."

"But I heard him," she insisted. "Right there." She reached out and touched the canvas covering to her left.

"Then I shall chase him away."

He crawled to the back of the wagon box and climbed down. Moments later, he returned.

"Not a dragon in sight. And if one should dare to appear, I shall jump on my trusty steed and slay him with my magic sword."

A tentative giggle.

"Now, then, you know my tent is right outside. I will not allow any beast, regardless of shape or form, to come anywhere near this wagon. And that is a promise you can rely on."

She gave a shuddering sigh and nodded. He kissed her and returned to his tent. She allowed Lizzie to tuck her back into bed, although she insisted they clasp hands as they lay there. Within but a few minutes, her small hand went slack as she slipped back into sleep.

They had been informed the evening before that the train would not have its turn at the ferry until mid-morning. Thus, Lizzie allowed herself the luxury of sleeping past dawn until the sun's first rays hit the wagon canvas. She had pulled on her clothes, edged past the still-sleeping Missy, and crawled to the wagon's end when Maude Fielding's concerned face appeared just outside.

Both women gasped in surprise. Lizzie pressed a hand to her chest, then laughed and said, "Gracious, you gave me a start. Did you think I was going to sleep all day?"

Maude returned the smile, but the dark underpinnings of her deportment remained. "You are going to need that extra sleep when you see what has happened."

She beckoned Lizzie down and led her around to the outward side of the wagon. Pointing at the bonnet's canvas side, "I saw it when I went for water."

Erratic black slashes marred the dusty white surface. It took a moment for Lizzie to perceive that they were intended to form letters. She made out an H, then an O, and finally an R. Her hand flew to her mouth. The letters formed an unschooled person's version of the word whore.

Maude's expression told her she had come to the same conclusion. She asked, "Where is Jonathan? Has he seen this?"

"I—I have no idea."

They went back around the wagon. Jonathan's tent had already been struck preparatory for travel, but he was nowhere to be seen.

"Who would do such a thing?" asked Maude.

"I wish I knew. There was another incident... " She went on to tell Maude about the ruined dress, ending with, "Someone wishes me to know I am disliked. But who?"

A moment for pondering. Then, in near perfect unison, "Henry?"

The two women had spoken of the young man's proposal only once, at which time Maude had squeezed Lizzie's hand and said, "You did the right thing." Now Lizzie said,

"I know I humiliated him in front of the entire group, but I have detected no malice in him since. Having expressed such passion for me, misplaced though it may have been, I find it difficult to believe he would wish me harm now. Not to mention that his spelling skills are surely superior to—" A nod toward the lettering. "—this."

"I expect you are right, but who else... ?" Her voice trailed off as a grim-faced Jonathan strode into camp with Lazarus at his side.

They all went around to the offending side of the wagon. Lazarus studied the hideous desecration. Searched the area until he found the offending instruments, the bucket of axle grease normally suspended from the rear axle and a broken tree branch, the end of which was black with grease. The obvious writing instrument.

"This explains Missy's nightmare," said Lizzie. For the benefit of Maude and Lazarus, she explained, "She wakened screaming during the night and insisted she had heard a dragon clawing at the wagon canvas and trying to get in."

"I looked around," Jonathan added, "but I saw no one. Her screams obviously chased him away."

"Him—or her," said Lazarus. "Neither this incident nor the destruction of the dress would preclude a woman being the culprit."

Lizzie conceded the possibility, but her deepest instincts told her this enemy was not another woman. She heard rustling sounds coming from within the wagon. Missy was waking up.

She straightened her shoulders and put steel in her voice. "Whoever it is, I refuse to be intimidated. We must go on as if nothing has happened. Most important, we must keep any anxiety from affecting Missy, whose imagination is active enough as it is. I shall help her get dressed and then fetch Caleb and prepare our breakfast. We must not keep the ferry waiting."

Chapter Twenty-One

The train ferried across the river without incident and soon arrived at Fort Laramie, a military post situated near where the Laramie River emptied into the North Platte. Like Fort Kearny, it lacked secure fortifications, its one old adobe wall abutted by a collection of wood and adobe buildings around a parade ground. An abundance of Indian tepees dotted the surrounding plain, their inhabitants coming and going from the fort or trading with the other emigrants stopped there.

Most from their group went to the fort after the noon meal, but Lizzie stayed behind with Caleb. Their wagon's vandalism was still fresh in her mind, and she was reluctant to leave their camp unattended lest the perpetrator take advantage of the opportunity to create more mischief. She used the time to tidy the wagon, including Jonathan's collection of books. He had returned to his former habit of reading during any free time or as he walked along beside the oxen. The books he had chosen to bring with him, no doubt a small portion of those he would have wished to bring, represented a broad spectrum of literature: classics such as Dante Alighieri's *Divine Comedy*, philosophy such as Plato's *The Republic*, adventures such as Herman Melville's *Moby-Dick*, popular fiction such as Charles Dickens's *David Copperfield*, even the controversial *Uncle Tom's Cabin* by the southern heretic Harriet Beecher Stowe. And, of course, a number of children's storybooks. That he was determined to pass his love of reading on to his children was obvious.

When he returned from the fort, he brought with him a container of whitewash and several letters from home. While Missy chattered on about the fort and the Indians they had seen, he smeared the whitewash over the vile black marks on the bonnet's side, not completely obliterating them but turning them to a light gray visible only up close. Then he walked some distance away to read the letters, which were addressed to both him and Sarah since they had been posted before news of her death arrived back in Indiana and Kentucky. Reading them plunged him into a quiet gloom from which he would not emerge for days to come.

The train left Fort Laramie to begin the steady climb up the high plains to the very edge of the Rocky Mountains. First came the Black Hills, wild country where cedar and pine forests blanketed slopes riven by innumerable sandstone ledges and clear streams cascaded in waterfalls with Mt. Laramie's snowy crest soaring above it all. The road was rougher and rockier than any they had experienced thus far, causing several breakdowns to slow their progress. The second night they camped on the Platte near the gorge where it passed through a seven-hundred-foot fissure in the earth. The following day was a Sunday, when allowance was made for a late start due to the usual religious service. Many used the time to climb to the top of the gorge and survey the river below with its twists and turns as well as the many teams and camps in both directions along the road. The next day brought a different landscape, barren sand hills covered with stunted grass and no water until they reached the LaBonte River near nightfall. High winds, blowing sand, and several periods of rain made for two more long difficult days until finally, on the first of June, they were through the Black Hills.

The prairie grass was now so poor it was necessary to drive the livestock to islands in the middle of the Platte where the vegetation was of better quality and abundance. This necessitated an increase of the night watch in order to guard against poaching by the Indians who sometimes trailed the train and attempted to barter with the emigrants. It was desolate country where prickly pear dominated the riverside and wolves could be heard howling during the night. Despite the inauspicious countryside, they were surprised to find a number of enterprising souls who had established makeshift groceries along the way, once even coming upon a blacksmith plying his trade.

On the afternoon of the second day after leaving the Black Hills, they passed a large procession of Sioux Indians traveling in the opposite direction. They counted four hundred or more men, women and children along with their ponies and dogs. They packed their provisions on their backs or suspended between tent poles attached to either side of the ponies, which were festooned with feathers and beaded leather coverings or straps. The emigrants speculated that the village was either moving to more auspicious hunting grounds or was on its way to wage war against another tribe. Neither explanation quelled Lizzie's uneasiness, and she was glad to see the last of them.

Eight days after leaving Fort Laramie, they came to the toll bridge across the North Platte. Prior river or stream crossings had involved either a precarious ford or a time-consuming wait for ferry passage. This sturdy thousand-foot-long railed span allowed both wagons and stock to cross in record time. The proprietor had established a number of business enterprises on the far side, including a coal mine to fuel everything from his home to his blacksmith shop. They moved on a few miles to camp beside the Platte, the last time they would do so since they would now leave this river they had been following for the past weeks.

The first real desert crossing lay ahead, twenty-five miles of arid prairie where alkali water dangerous to both man and beast would prevail until they reached the fresh water of Willow Springs. In anticipation of the rigors ahead, they remained in camp another day to allow for Sunday services and an afternoon of washing clothes and filling water barrels for the long dry stretch ahead.

They made an early start the next day. The road ascended westward along a ridge, then turned south through a gap to descend past what was known as the Avenue of the Rocks, a crest of jagged sandstone boulders that rose to the west of the road. They stopped to noon at the rocks before continuing on through a narrow passage with room for only one wagon at a time. They soon came to a miry, foul-smelling slough of alkali water where extra attention was given to the stock lest they attempt to drink of the water. The sight of several animal carcasses stressed the importance of this added vigilance. They pushed on through a dry, dusty, hot afternoon to Willow Springs, a welcome oasis of green grass and clear cold water.

This being the best resting place between the Platte and Sweetwater Rivers, there were many other encampments scattered about the sizable draw. Lizzie's eyes were especially drawn to a large drove of cattle occupying a nearby slope beyond a small group of wagons. She wondered whether it might be the Masters group, a speculation that was confirmed that evening when Richard Fielding returned from a group captain meeting to inform them they would be taking an even earlier start in the morning. Lazarus had spoken to Josiah Masters, and he had agreed to hold up until their train had passed by so they would not be forced to endure the added dust stirred up by hundreds of animals as they plodded along.

Lizzie wondered about Will Long and how he was faring now that his uncle was gone. She had no doubt he was better off absent the older man's immoral tutelage, and she hoped he bore her no grudge for being the cause of his present circumstances.

They started out when it was barely light. The road climbed a long ridge known as Prospect Hill, then began the descent into the Sweetwater River valley. A grueling sixteen miles later they passed a fair-sized lake whose shores were crusted white with saleratus, which some in the train scooped up to replenish their depleted supplies brought from home. A mile and a half farther on, they reached the Sweetwater River, a swift clear stream of refreshingly cool water. Independence Rock rose on the prairie ahead, a vast oval hump of rock that looked to Lizzie for all the world like a giant turtle's shell.

The emigrant guide books stressed the importance of reaching this landmark by July Fourth, thus anointing it with the name by which all knew it. This timing would insure the travelers' arrival in Oregon or California before the winter snows made the mountains impassable. The Mills train had beaten this goal by nearly a month, for which most members credited the fine leadership of Lazarus.

They made camp a short distance from the Rock to allow those who wished to do so a chance to add their names to the hundreds already emblazoned there. Missy would have nothing but to join the others of their group who were determined to once again leave their mark. Jonathan agreed, but Lizzie insisted on staying behind with Caleb, who was due for a late-afternoon feeding. She waved the two of them off, then went in search of the Faraday group's camp, banking on the probability that Mrs. Saunders had also stayed back with the youngest of her children.

She found the older woman sitting in the shade of a wagon against the lowering but still fierce sun, her fingers busy with needle and thread as she mended a child's smock. She stood in welcome, a warm smile lighting her face.

She said, "And here is my precious little bundle come for his supper. I sent all mine along to the rock with their father. I have little enough peace with that noisy brood always clamoring for one thing and another."

She laid her mending aside, reached for Caleb, and sat back down. She indicated an empty upturned barrel. "Sit a spell. I expect it will be some time before the thundering herd returns. And I have a suggestion to make concerning our little fellow here."

Lizzie complied, saying, "I would welcome any advice you care to give. I am woefully inexperienced where babies are concerned."

"You must not discount your own abilities, my dear. I have watched you with the babe, and your instincts guide you admirably. But it has been my experience that infants reach a certain milestone at around the sixth week of life, which is but a few days away if my calculations are correct. You have surely noticed how he has grown and filled out. And he is beginning to be responsive to those around him."

Lizzie nodded. She had indeed noticed how much more focused Caleb's eyes seemed to be of late. When she spoke to him, his little face took on a more intense expression as if he were trying to understand her words. He had offered a sweet smile on a number of occasions when she was being playful with him, once even emitting what could only be described as a gurgling guffaw. At such times, she had felt a tug on her heart as if she were tethered to him in some mysterious way.

"You know I am happy to supply a mother's milk as we move along," Mrs. Saunders continued, "but he will need to be largely self-sufficient by the time we part in California. We must prepare him as best we can."

"But how?" Lizzie could not keep the despair from her voice, eliciting a tsking sound from her friend.

"It is not so difficult as you might think. The first step is to introduce him to a nutritious pap to supplement my milk." She rose, still cradling the babe to her breast, and went around to the rear of her wagon, returning with a small bowl that resembled a gravy saucer. It was made of white porcelain etched in blue and had a round closed spout at one end.

"My little Ella is beyond this, and given my advanced age, I do not expect to need it again. It is my gift to you and little Caleb."

"But... ?"

"Begin with bread or flour. Add fresh milk and butter. Boil the whole together until you have a thick broth. When it cools, pour it into the pap boat, cover the snout with a clean cloth, and offer it to him. He may object at first, but he will soon learn to suckle from it."

Lizzie repeated, "Bread or flour, milk, butter. Boiled to a thick broth."

"Later, probably not for another couple of months, you can begin offering other foods. Rice, fruits, vegetables, all smashed to a soft pulp and fed from the tip of a spoon. I have raised all my children on such a regimen. I continued to suckle them until they were ready to be weaned, of course, and this little fellow will have no such luxury. But he will thrive. Of that I am convinced."

When Caleb had had his fill, Lizzie carried the sleeping babe and the pap boat back to the campsite, her mind busy with what she had learned. She was so preoccupied she failed to acknowledge Maude's wave from where she was building her evening fire. She pulled Caleb's cradle into the shade and laid him down. It was as she was standing up again that her eyes fell on the damp soil beneath the wagon's water barrel. Frowning, she went over to investigate.

She sucked in a sharp breath. The barrel's slats had been slashed clean through. The instrument of this rupture stood upright against the wagon box where Jonathan had last left it—his long-handled ax. Most of the barrel's water had been used on the long dry haul from the Platte, and the small remaining amount was no loss now that they had access to an endless supply of fresh water. But the barrel...

As a rule, it was left empty when they traveled in order to spare the oxen the added weight. However, they would need it again when they reached another desert crossing. Their very lives could depend on it. What would they do now?

She called to Maude across the central corral and waved her over.

"It has happened again. Look!" She pointed at the ruined barrel.

Maude examined the damage and shook her head. "I cannot imagine who would do such a thing."

"It happened while I was gone for Caleb's feeding. You were here. Surely you saw or heard something."

In a somewhat defensive tone, "Do you think if I had, I would not have stopped it?"

Lizzie's face flamed. "Oh, Maude, of course you would. I did not mean to imply... Perhaps you did not realize... "

Maude laid a hand on her arm. "This has been a shock, and you are rightly upset. Anyone would be. As it happens, I went out to collect sagebrush for the fire. I wish that were not the case. I wish I had been here to catch whoever is perpetrating these hateful things. I can only believe he will slip up one of these times. And when that happens, you can be sure Lazarus will see he is punished as he should be. Meanwhile, I fault Jonathan for leaving you here alone."

"Oh, please, he is not to blame! I encouraged him to take Missy to the rock, and I am glad they were gone. She is so attuned to the moods of others that my reaction would have caused her great anxiety. She has enough to deal with without my burdening her further."

A soft smile. "Far from burdening her, you are the primary reason she is doing as well as she is. I hope I do not speak out of turn when I tell you it is my fondest hope that you and Jonathan will someday seal the bond that already ties you together. I miss Sarah more than I can say, but she lives with her Savior now, and I should like nothing more than for you to take her place in our family."

Lizzie was stunned. Her mind clawed through a rush of conflicting feelings for a response, but before she could speak Maude laid a finger on her lips and said,

"Shush, now. Please disregard the ramblings of an old fool who should have learned by now when to hold her tongue. Time and prayer will sort out what is best for you and Jonathan. For us all, for that matter. Meanwhile, we must redouble our vigilance against this villain who plagues you so. As for the barrel, perhaps one of the small trading posts we have seen will be able to supply a new one. If not, I am certain all within our group will be glad to share. Now I must get back to my fire. The others will be back soon expecting their supper."

Lizzie watched her walk away, uncertain which now troubled her more, the vandalized barrel or her friend's comments about her future. Time and prayer would sort it out, she had said. Except for a few awkward attempts at the time of Sarah's death, Lizzie had not consciously addressed the Almighty since the days of her childhood, and then only through the simple rote prayers taught her by her mother. What would she say were she to attempt such communication now? It was one thing to petition on behalf of someone else, but quite another to ask favors for oneself, especially from a Being Who seemed to have abandoned her long ago. She had already assured her own future by obtaining the bonds. What need did she have for the intervention of One Whose whims she did not understand? The only thing that threatened her current circumstance was some misguided enemy. And she would defeat him as she had every other obstacle on her road to future security.

She squared her shoulders and turned her mind to supper.

∞∞∞

Jonathan received the news of the damaged water barrel with as deep a scowl as Lizzie had ever seen him wear. As Maude had suggested, the item itself was easily replaced when they camped the following night near a blacksmith who had a suitable barrel to sell. The acquisition did little, however, to assuage the uneasiness they both found heavy on their minds as they moved forward.

They passed the famed Devil's Gate, a four-hundred-foot slash in the surrounding rock through which the Sweetwater River had somehow managed to carve a path, and continued up the river for five difficult days. The river meandered between a line of low hills on the south and the snow-capped Wind River Mountains on the north. Its tortuous course made numerous crossings necessary, once requiring three crossings within but two miles. The road was often deep with sand, and the weather took an ugly turn, punishing them with rain, sleet, and cold. On the day they left the Sweetwater and continued due west up a gradually-ascending plateau toward South Pass, however, the sun had returned and everyone's spirits lifted.

As they climbed, they passed isolated banks of snow as well as fields of colorful, fragrant wild flowers. The cool, clear, rarified air was exhilarating even as it increased the exertion necessary to put one foot before the other. After a trek of some seven miles, they reached the summit, a broad sage-and-grass-covered saddle with low ridges and hills on both sides. This was the halfway point of the journey, the crest of the Continental Divide where the waters flowed either west to the Pacific or east to the Mississippi River. It also marked the train's passage into the Oregon Territory, and someone had planted a flag as a marker of this important milestone.

It had been a dry climb, but three miles on the far side brought them to Pacific Springs, where they stopped to noon. From there, the gradual descent took them along Pacific Creek and then west across another long stretch of flat, waterless sagebrush prairie to Dry Sandy Creek, so named because its water level varied according to the time of year, full-flowing in spring, dry in the late summer and early autumn. They were fortunate to be early enough that the creek bed offered enough flow to sustain their needs, although nearby pools of alkali water posed a danger to livestock to which they needed to be diligent. Dark was closing in when they arrived, giving them time only to unpack, prepare and eat supper, and crawl into bed.

    Lazarus called a meeting early the next morning to decide which of two options the emigrants wished to take. A short distance from Dry Sandy, the trail would fork. The left-hand fork would take the traveler along the main trail to Fort Bridger. The fork to the right would take them straight west across a forty-five mile desert to the Green River and then across a series of mountain ridges to reconnect with the main trail at the Bear River. This cutoff would save nearly fifty miles and up to three days of travel. However, it would be a grueling crossing and would require commitment and a willingness to risk any stock unable to endure the hardships of no water and little grass for an around-the-clock day of travel.

    The majority of the company favored the shorter but more rigorous route. The large extended Faraday family was the exception. Of their group of twelve wagons, they made up eight carrying twenty-five people, many of whom were low on supplies and felt they must reach Fort Bridger in order to restock. Lazarus distributed the group's remaining four miscellaneous families among the Jamison, Eastman and Stafford groups for the remainder of the journey. It pleased Lizzie when Mr. and Mrs. Saunders and their lively brood were assigned to the Jamison group. She not only enjoyed the motherly Mrs. Saunders's company but the passing back and forth of Caleb would now be much easier.

    Lazarus announced they would remain at Dry Sandy until noon so the men could fan the stock out in search of better forage before moving on. The day was promising to be one of the hottest they had encountered thus far, the thermometer in the Fielding wagon reading ninety degrees by mid-morning. Rather than wait in camp while Jonathan attended to the animals, Lizzie decided to take a red-faced Missy and cranky Caleb for a walk along the river to the shade of a lone cottonwood tree visible some distance away.

They were just starting out when she noticed a great cloud of dust approaching from the east—the Masters group and their large drove of cattle. She had seen them in the distance ever since leaving Willow Springs where they had graciously allowed the train to precede them out of the pass. She wondered whether they would risk the dangerous desert crossing or continue on the longer route, in which case this would be the last they would see of them.

They reached the tree and found a measure of relief in its shade, aided by a light dry breeze. Lizzie removed hers and Missy's shoes and stockings so they could wade in the water, which was cool but muddy and stagnant. Missy splashed happily, the hem of her dress soon soaked, and Lizzie lowered little Caleb so his feet drifted in the water, eliciting a delightful little chuckle. She heard the approach of a horse's hooves and looked up to see a familiar figure riding toward them.

Will Long pulled up, hopped down, and snatched off his hat, a wide grin on his face.

"I was hopin' to find you. They said you'd struck out this way."

Lizzie blinked away her surprise and smiled back. "How nice to see you, Will. I noticed the herd coming this way earlier, but I assumed you would be too busy with your duties to break away."

"Mr. Masters kindly gave me leave. I never had the chance to properly thank you for comin' to my rescue back... you know. I figure this is my last chance."

"So your train will go on to Fort Bridger from here?"

"Yes'm. It's way too dangerous to cross that there desert with so many cows. They say the other way has plenty of good water and at least adequate grass for feed. We aim to take a few days to restock at the fort, so you folks'll be far ahead of us when all's said and done. So I figured this was it."

"Well, you need not bother yourself on my account. I simply told the truth about what happened. It was none of your doing."

He scuffed his toe in the sandy soil. "I shoulda... coulda... "

"Nonsense. You were being threatened with a gun and had no choice. Now tell me how you have been these past weeks. Are you getting enough to eat... " A wry face. "... absent my horrible cooking?"

He laughed. "T'warn't so bad as Uncle made out. And not a bad trade given the refinement you brought to us uncouth cowpokes."

"Well, you certainly look hale and healthy now, so I suppose it all turned out as it should have."

"Yes, ma'am, it sure did."

On impulse, she extended her hand. "I wish you all good fortune on the remainder of your journey, Will. I have no doubt you will find your pot of gold in California."

He took her hand and kissed it, murmuring his gratitude once more. Then he settled his hat on his head, sprang onto his horse, and disappeared from her life. Or so she thought.

Chapter Twenty-Two

The following days turned out to be every bit as difficult as Lazarus had promised. They took the cutoff a short distance from Dry Sandy, crossed Little Sandy Creek three miles later and went another six to ford Big Sandy Creek and camp. They spent the next day preparing for the desert crossing. The men drove the stock out in search of good grass so they could eat their fill before the deprivations to come. The women baked and cooked in order to provide meals for a twenty-four-hour trek during which they would not stop. Every available barrel and container was filled with water. At two-thirty the next morning, Lazarus sounded the alert, and they were on the trail by three.

The night cold soon gave way to unbearable heat after the sun rose. There was no question of seeking respite in the wagons. Every able-bodied person was required to walk to ease the burden on the oxen. Lest their determination flag, they saw ample evidence of those who had gone before and failed. Abandoned wagons and other detritus lined the trail. A sickening stench rose from the bloated bodies of those animals who had succumbed. The emigrants turned their faces away and plodded on.

Night fell, and the coats and cloaks and blankets came back out. Well past midnight, they had their first inkling that the end might be near. The stock, nearly crazed with hunger and thirst, smelled the Green River and began to bawl and whinny and bray, requiring a strong hand to prevent them from stampeding ahead. At last, footsore and weary, they left the trail and began the process of setting up camp along the river's bank.

They spent the next day recovering and waiting in line to ferry across the river. Once across, they ascended a high bluff on which hundreds of their predecessors had engraved their names. The road henceforth was rough and hilly, but they found adequate grass and water to sustain them for two days until they reached one of the prettiest spots they had seen since leaving the Sweetwater. A pool of clear cold water lay in a lush hollow beneath a rugged cliff from the base of which flowed the spring that fed it. That this was a favored stopping place was evident from the many wagon camps surrounding the hollow, their numbers enhanced because a second cutoff from father south came in here to join theirs. Lazarus led them some distance away to camp near a grove of fir and aspen trees. For the first time in many days, their group gathered around a blazing fire for an evening of singing and dancing and camaraderie. Lizzie noticed that Jonathan entered into the fun with more enthusiasm than she had seen from him since Sarah's death. It pleased her to know the raw wound of his grief had scabbed over and was beginning to heal.

They were to remain there an extra day, and Lizzie wakened in unusually light spirits. She prepared a leisurely breakfast of cornmeal mush and Missy's favorite, johnnycakes. Afterward, she and Jonathan sat by the fire enjoying the sunny morning and watching Missy play with her dolly, a hand-me-down from Cora's younger sister Lillian. At present she was feeding it a pretend breakfast of mud cakes, which she had formed by mixing the loamy soil with water, resulting in mud spatters from her face to the hem of her blue gingham dress.

Jonathan gave a wry grimace. "Should you indulge her so? What a grimy spectacle she makes!"

Lizzie had Caleb lying in her lap, a tiny fist wrapped around each of her thumbs. She clucked at him and gave him a little bounce, eliciting a contented coo. Without looking up, "Soap and water will remedy her person. As for the dress, I plan to do a small washing this afternoon. Let her enjoy herself."

He turned to her, a soft smile dimpling his cheeks.

"You always seem to know what is best for her. And the results are plain to see. The nightmares have stopped, and she seldom even mentions Sarah. Part of me is saddened to think her mother's memory is fading so quickly, but I know it is as it should be."

"For now, perhaps, but as time goes by, we—" She caught herself, color creeping into her cheeks. "I mean, *you*. *You* will keep Sarah alive by telling stories of their shared time together and reminding her how much she was loved."

"Meanwhile, you have slipped into that place as easily as a hand into a glove. And I am grateful."

It was the right thing to say, and he sounded sincere. But why did it leave her with such a sudden empty feeling inside? What else did she want from him?

She said, "In any event, I am happy to be a substitute until you decide on someone to be her new mother. Then all thought of me will disappear."

He was silent long enough that she was forced to look up at him. His eyes were intense, penetrating, seeming to look into the farthest corner of her mind.

"Are you so very eager to see me wed?"

The question brought her up short. She had recognized from the beginning that theirs was a temporary liaison. Despite the easiness that had developed between them since Sarah's death, despite the genuine love she felt for his children, she had known it would end once they all reached California. He would find someone to marry. Someone who would hear Missy's fanciful ramblings and receive her good-night kisses. Someone who would see sweet little Caleb take his first steps, hear him speak his first words. And none of them would ever think of her again. Why did that reality send such a barb into the pit of her stomach?

She stammered, "I— I— You said yourself—"

"Look!"

Missy's cry saved her from the awkward moment. The child was standing at the edge of the mud hole she had created and pointing to the open space between their wagon and the next. A mule deer doe was feeding in the meadow beyond while her twin fawns frolicked nearby.

"Oh, I want to pet them!" She whirled to Lizzie. "Come with me!"

"It is probably useless," said Jonathan, "but why not?"

He reached for Caleb, and Lizzie handed him over. "Very well. But first… " She led Missy to the water bucket and poured a dipperful over her mud-caked hands. The child ignored the towel she offered and skipped off toward the meadow.

Lizzie hurried after her, calling, "Slow down or you will frighten them away."

Missy skidded to a halt even as the doe raised her head. She sniffed the air, haunches quivering as she assessed the danger they might pose. Interminable seconds passed before she lowered her head and nosed toward a new grazing spot. One of the fawns scampered to its mother and began feeding. The other looked their way with cocked head and curious eyes.

Missy stretched out her hand and inched forward. The fawn watched with interest, then took a tentative step toward them. The distance between them narrowed, and Lizzie was beginning to believe Missy might actually be successful in her quest to touch the little thing when a loud report sent all three animals bounding toward the grove of trees.

She whirled around and saw Harold Jamison, the reverend's nephew, standing near one of their group's wagons, a rifle aimed in their direction. She snatched Missy to her breast and threw them both to the ground.

"Hey!" Jonathan had come from behind their wagon and was charging in the offender's direction. "Are you crazy? That is my family!!"

He collided with the rifleman, knocked him to the ground, and began to pummel him with his fists. Several men came to pull him off, and by the time Lizzie had righted herself and Missy, he was running full bore in their direction, yelling, "Are you all right?"

His face was a mask of horror as he pulled up in front of them and repeated his frantic query.

Lizzie took a shaky breath and answered, "We are fine. But why did he shoot at us?"

"Not at you. The idiot had his eye on that doe for his supper! Says he shoots so well you were never in any danger."

"So well he missed his target," she pointed out, raising a small smile.

"Lazarus will deal with him. It is enough to know neither of you was hurt."

Missy's lip was quivering, but it was not from fear over the danger they had just escaped. She looked up at Lizzie and wailed, "The fawns are gone. Can we go find them?"

She knelt down to the child's level. "They run very fast, dear. I doubt if we could catch them."

"But we could try. Please?"

Her pleading tone was more than Lizzie could bear. She looked up at Jonathan, who nodded his agreement. She rose, took the child's hand, and started for the trees.

She knew the deer were gone. Even if they were still nearby, she and Missy were making enough noise as they advanced through the underbrush to send them off again. She decided it was something Missy would have to discover for herself, and they kept going for some time before the child's footsteps began to drag. She was about to suggest they turn back when they heard a rustling sound off to their right.

"I knew it!" cried Missy as she sped off in that direction. Within moments she was out of sight.

"Missy! Wait for me!"

No response. She started after her, the sound of the little girl's running feet growing more distant by the moment.

"Missy, come back!"

Sudden silence. Then a high-pitched scream.

Dread sent Lizzie into a dead run. The trees seemed to close in around her, robbing her of all sense of direction.

"Lizzie! Help me!!"

She reoriented herself and ran on. Soon she saw a glimpse of blue through the trees ahead. When she finally cleared the last tree, she pulled up in stunned disbelief.

The little girl stood sobbing in front of a sturdy aspen tree to which she was bound by rope. Before she could fully take it in, a familiar figure stepped from behind the tree.

"Well, lookee who's here. If it ain't the high and mighty Miss Hamilton."

Earl Long.

Lizzie stared at him as at an apparition.

"Cat got your tongue, whore? Ain't you gonna say howdy?"

"How did you get here?" she finally managed. "I thought..."

"That I went on back to St. Joe with my tail between my legs? No, ma'am. Weren't about to let you and that nigger cap'n keep me from gettin' to Californy. Went back to the boss and took my licks." He raised his shirt and turned so she could see the welts on his bare back. "He was in a fix, bein' shorthanded and all. I knew he'd take me back."

Understanding rushed in. "So it was you. The dress, the water barrel, the... the paint on the wagon."

Even as he grinned his agreement, Missy hiccuped through her weeping, "He—he— Mr. Weehoe—bad—man."

Lizzie rushed to her, knelt down and plucked at the rope attaching her to the tree.

"Let her go this instant!"

"She ain't goin' nowhere 'til we have this out."

In a near scream, "What are you talking about? What do you want from me?"

An unmistakable leer. "What I always wanted. Leave her be and get yourself down on the ground. I aim to finish what I started that night."

Blinded by fury, she shot to her feet and launched herself at him. In one fluid motion he whipped his pistol from his holster and aimed it at her forehead.

"I don't think so, little lady. Now you do like I say or I swear I'll blow your pretty head off."

Lizzie's anger was beyond reason. "Go ahead! Shoot me! Then you can hang for murder and get what you deserve!"

"Tough lady, eh? Well, what about this?" He swung the gun toward Missy. "You willin' to sacrifice your little charge just to deny me? Or better yet... " He reached out to stroke Missy's hair, eliciting a scream of terror. "... here's a nice fresh piece of female vir-gin-i-ty. Maybe I prefer her to you."

"No!" cried Lizzie. "All right. I will do it. Just leave her alone."

"That's better. Now get down on—"

"This has gone far enough." A new voice came from among the trees to Lizzie's back. She whirled around to see Will Long moving toward them. "You've had your fun, Uncle. It's time to end it and come back with me to Fort Bridger."

Earl gave his nephew a hard look. "How'd you find me?"

"Pure luck, I reckon. Me and the boss figured you took the Slate Creek cutoff. Saw your horse tethered at the edge of this here grove, heard the commotion, and here I am."

"Well, you can just take yourself on back the same way. I'll come when I'm danged well ready."

"What if the boss finds another cowpoke willin' to take your place before you get back? You're lucky he's of a mind to overlook another one of your crazy shenanigans, as it is."

"A few more minutes won't make no never mind. I got business to attend to first."

The boy shook his head in frustration. "Jeez, Uncle. You gotta give this up."

Earl turned the gun on his nephew and bellowed, "You deaf, boy? I said I'm stayin' 'til I get done what I gotta do. You can either turn tail, or you can stay and help me. What's it gonna be?"

Will eyed the gun and licked his dry lips. "What about the little girl? You gonna do this while she's watching?"

His words seemed to ignite a new idea. "Naw. Wouldn't be right, now would it? There's somebody else needs to see this."

He returned his pistol to its holster and pulled a wicked-looking knife from a sheath on his belt. He bent to the coil of rope that fell from Missy to the base of the tree and sliced through it. He found the place where the rope passed through an eye to form a lariat loop, measured out a length of some four feet, and cut it off from the rest. He slipped the loop over Lizzie's head and pulled until it rested loosely around her neck. Then he hoisted the remainder of the rope onto his shoulder.

To Will, "Since you're still here, you can get on over here and make yourself useful."

"Aw, Uncle—"

"Do as I say! Or maybe you'd rather I gave a jerk on this here rope and broke the whore's neck."

The boy's face went ashen. He shuffled forward.

"Now untie the whelp and hang onto her. We're goin' for a little walk."

Missy whimpered as Will obeyed his uncle's instructions. When she was free, she sprinted toward Lizzie and threw her arms around her legs. Earl jerked her away and all but threw her in Will's direction.

He took her hand and leaned down to whisper in her ear. Her eyes grew round as she stared first at him, then at Lizzie and Earl.

"What'd you tell her?" barked Earl.

"That she should do as she was told, and everything would work out fine. You want her to cooperate, right?"

A grunt of acknowledgment. Then, "Now no more jawin'. Let's move."

Lizzie had no idea where they were going, but Earl seemed to have a destination in mind. He held tight to the end of the rope that lead to the noose around her neck, and it tightened and slackened with every step. She was careful to place her feet on firm ground and stay close lest an unintended stumble brought calamity. After what seemed hours but was in fact only a matter of minutes, she saw campfire smoke hanging in the air and the white of wagon canvas through the trees. Earl took out his pistol, aimed it at Missy, and led them all out into the meadow beyond the trees. They stood there a moment during which no one seemed to notice them. Earl raised his gun and fired it into the air.

First one, then another of their group came out to the perimeter of the wagon corral. As they comprehended the situation, shouting and general pandemonium ensued. Jonathan pushed through the growing crowd until he broke free.

"No!" he bellowed. "Missy! Lizzie!"

He started to charge forward, but Earl discharged his gun again and shouted, "Stop right there, Collins, if you know what's good for these two. I'm here to make a trade. Your daughter for that black son of a bitch Mills. Get him out here before my trigger finger gets itchy!"

Jonathan's head swung from side to side, his face red with impotent rage. "Harm them, and you are a dead man!"

"Nobody's gonna die here lessen you ignore me," Earl called back. "This is about justice. And I'll have mine. When the score's even, you can continue on to Californy with your whelps and your whore without any bother from me."

Lazarus came thundering around the perimeter of the Jamison camp astride his sorrel gelding. He reined in several hundred feet in front of Earl Long. His hand went reflexively to his gun holster, but Earl yelled,

"Don't even think it, Mills. Not lessen you want me to pump a bullet into this little girl's head."

Lazarus stared at him for a long moment, then returned his hand to a nonthreatening position. "What do you want, Long?"

"Glad you asked, you uppity nigger. I want you to come along with me. In exchange, I'll let the little girl go."

Lazarus's eyes narrowed, but he nodded and began to dismount.

"Keep those hands where I can see 'em," Earl cautioned. To Will, "Go relieve him of his pistol. Lay it down nice and slow. Same with that there Bowie knife he always carries. Then bring him over here."

Will hesitated until he heard his uncle cock his pistol. Then he did as ordered. When Lazarus had been disarmed, the two men walked to Earl, who gave Missy a shove and said, "Scat."

She ran as if the hounds of hell were pursuing her until her father swept her up into his arms. Even as he hugged her to him, he called, "Now Miss Hamilton."

"She ain't part of the bargain," Earl called back. "She'll be along 'fore long, but first I got use of her. The nigger'll be my witness. We're goin' back in the woods now, and I warn you and anybody else who's of a mind to be a hero. You see this here noose? I'll choke the life outta her the minute I hear anybody followin' us. You understand me?"

Lizzie saw the helpless anguish on Jonathan's face, but he nodded.

"All right, then. Let's go."

This time they did not go as deep into the grove. When Earl called a stop, he handed the coiled rope and his knife to Will, saying, "Tie the black bastard up. And remember, I got a good hold on this noose. One false move and—"

"I get it," Will interrupted, his voice tight with loathing. He took the rope over to Lazarus and cut off a sufficient length. He dropped the knife on the ground and said, "Sorry about this. Hands behind your back."

He took several moments to tie the wagon master's wrists together, then stepped away.

Earl licked his lips. "All right, then." He holstered his weapon. Turned to Lizzie, snugged the noose tight around her neck, and reached for her breast with his free hand. She saw the vengeful lust on his face and recoiled, but the rope held her close to him. "Now let's see what you got under all those petticoats."

He was pulling up on her skirts when there was a loud crack. His eyes widened and he staggered a step backward, the rope falling from his grasp. Lizzie ran free as he whirled to face the other two men, a red stain blooming on his right shoulder, his arm dangling limp at his side.

Will stood some ten feet away holding his pistol in a shaking hand.

"What'd you do, boy? Shoot your own flesh and blood?"

The boy dropped the gun as if it were on fire. Tears streamed down his face. "I had to stop you. It ain't right. Ma'd never forgive me if she knew I let you do such a thing."

The older man made a snarling sound very like that of a cornered animal. "I got news for you, you no-good whippersnapper. Your ma's got more to worry about than me. 'Cause her son's about to come home in a box."

He reached for his own pistol, but without the use of his shooting arm, his movements were awkward. He did not even have it fully out of its holster when Lazarus pulled his hands from behind his back, lunged in one smooth motion for the discarded knife, and threw it. It penetrated Earl's chest to the hilt with a sickening thud. He collapsed, dead before he hit the ground.

∞∞∞

Lizzie would always look back on that terrifying experience as the defining moment of her journey to California. She was gratified to have found her faith in Will Long vindicated. Not only had he gone against the bonds of family to shoot his uncle, but he had calmed Missy by promising her Lizzie would not be harmed, and he had bound Lazarus such that he could easily free himself and execute the final blow. When he returned to Josiah Masters, she sent a letter explaining what had happened, extolling his bravery, and exonerating him of any blame. She never heard from him or of him again, but she knew in her heart he prospered. How could one so young but of such staunch integrity not do so?

The biggest ramification of that afternoon's events, however, was her changing interaction with Jonathan Collins. His response to her safe release rivaled the passion and relief he had exhibited when Missy was returned to him. He had clutched her to him, then held her at arm's length to verify that she was indeed unharmed, letting her go only when he noticed the curious stares of the relatives and friends who stood about them. From that moment on, he was different in his dealings with her. The comfortable camaraderie continued, but it contained a depth and warmth that was entirely new. A more intimate timbre undergirded his voice when they spoke. His eyes followed her as she went about her duties, and when they met hers, their intensity made her inner parts quiver. As did his occasional random touch, which nearly always seemed to linger a fraction longer than was necessary.

Their conversation took on more substance. He told her about his books, his philosophies both secular and religious, his dream of opening a school of classical learning when he arrived in California. He pressed her to tell him about her childhood, her schooling first at her mother's knee and then at Miss Datty's Boarding School, her family. He seemed to crave any and all knowledge about her, which led her to take particular care when divulging such information.

After being taken in by the Collins family, she had expanded on her initial story by claiming that Jack was a distant relative who had taken pity on her after her family and home were destroyed by her brother's ruinous decisions. In this version, there were no sister and brother-in-law willing to provide for her. Only a gambler who offered to supply room and board if she would learn to be his assistant. A chaste and proper offer that had done nothing to compromise her virtue.

Jonathan had never seemed to question this version of her background. Nor did he blame her for taking the bearer bonds and escaping from a person who took undue advantage of her helpless circumstances. Thus she was able to maintain the fiction as they proceeded on toward California.

The most taxing portion of the journey lay ahead. Several high mountain ridges had to be crossed before they reached the Bear River. Up that body of water lay one of the more peculiar sights they had seen, Soda Springs, where water foamed and bubbled up out of hollow cones and a phenomenon known as Steamboat

Springs rumbled and roared so loudly it could be heard all over the valley. Then came a mountainous cutoff that ended in a stretch of waterless desert. Beyond lay the Raft River, which they followed southwest to the City of Rocks, a place where huge rocks and boulders canted out of the ground to resemble a stone village complete with cottages, church steeples, and domes. From there they crossed two rugged passes to Goose Creek, which they followed to its end. Another dry, barren stretch took them to Thousand Springs Creek, a lovely oasis where they stopped to celebrate Independence Day.

American flags came out, and each family prepared a dish to share with the entire train for the evening meal. The singing and dancing and games went on well into the night, and Lizzie was pleased to see Henry Jamison lavish his attentions on a pretty young girl from the Eastman group. She was drawn into the festivities as well when Jonathan took her hand and led her onto the makeshift dance floor, an area cleared of brush earlier in the day. She had not taken him for much of a dancer, but she discovered he was rather graceful despite his gangly frame. The feel of his arm around her waist produced a pleasant tingling in her midsection, but she could not look into his eyes for fear of what she might read there. His growing attachment to her did not fit into her plans any more than did her own affection for him and his children. The time of parting was drawing closer by the day, and she could not even think of it without a flood of intense regret and loss.

The next day took them to the headwaters of the Humboldt River, which they followed south and west for two weeks to the Humboldt Sink, where the river disappeared into a marshy alkali lake. From there, they faced one of the biggest challenges of the journey—the Forty-Mile Desert, an uninviting, barren wasteland that would test their resolve and resources to the maximum. Again they must endure an overnight trek over loose salt-covered sands and baked alkali clay without fresh water, relying once again on animals who had already been weakened by the long journey. Although several households lost some stock, they reached the Truckee River largely intact and spent the next day, a Sunday, recovering and thanking the Almighty for safe passage.

From there, Lazarus would guide the majority of the train along the Truckee and over the Sierra Nevada through Donner Pass, named in memory of the unfortunate party that was stranded there in the winter of 1846. They would then proceed to Sacramento where the Collins, Fielding and Jamison families intended to settle. However, a contingent of some dozen wagons planned to split off in two days' time along what was known as the Beckwourth Trail, which would take them north and west through Beckwourth Pass and along Grizzly Creek to American Valley, then south to Marysville.

This was the trail Lizzie needed to take, and she had already made arrangements to travel with a young couple for the sum of fifty cents per day. Her resources were largely intact since Mr. Masters and then Jonathan had borne the majority of her expenses in exchange for her services. Going forward, however, she would need to husband her remaining cash so it lasted long enough for her to reach the Bank of Rich Bar and redeem the bonds. According to Lazarus, Spanish Ranch, the settlement from which she would be able to access Rich Bar, lay some four or five days beyond the cutoff, which meant her cost would be two dollars, two-fifty at most. A necessary expense that could not be avoided.

These logistics decided, the question of how she could separate from the Collins family with a minimum of pain dominated her thoughts. Various scenarios looped through her mind as they followed the river through a long, narrow, rocky canyon, across a difficult slough, and out into Truckee Meadows, a verdant area of good forage and abundant water. They set up camp near the ford where the Beckwourth Trail split off, and Lizzie knew the time had come even though she was no more ready for it than she had been two days before.

She fed Caleb his pap for the last time and tucked a forlorn Missy into bed.

"Why must you go?" she wailed. "I promise to be good if only you will stay."

Lizzie choked back her own tears and said, "You are not the cause of my leaving, dear one. And I shall always carry you in my heart. But I must follow my own path, as must you and Caleb and your father. It is not as if I have not warned you this day would come."

"I thought you would change your mind. I know papa would like it if you did. Then you could be our mama."

The little girl's pleading tone was like a knife in her heart. She forced herself to put on a stern countenance. "I have told you many times that is not possible. Perhaps you will have a new mama someday. But that is up to your papa. Meanwhile, you must accept that it will not be me. Now it is time for you to go to sleep. Goodnight, Missy."

She leaned down to give her a kiss, but she jerked away, declared, "My name is not Missy! It is Sarah!" and turned her back.

Lizzie knew there was nothing more she could say that would ease the child's heartache. Missy perceived her leaving as an abandonment similar to the death of her mother, and nothing would change that until Jonathan chose a new wife. Meanwhile, she would suffer the grief of another loss. And Lizzie was helpless to prevent it.

Caleb had been sound asleep in his cradle since his feeding, but as she looked down on him, she could not stop herself from lifting him into her arms and carrying him to the fire, where Jonathan was waiting for her. She knew she faced another even more difficult conversation, and she hoped the warmth of the sleeping little body would give her the courage to get her through it.

After she was seated, he wasted no time in saying, "I could not help overhearing. She loves you very much."

A deep sigh. "I know. I love her, too."

"And what of me, Lizzie? What are your feelings for me?"

She watched the fire as a fresh branch flared up. At last she said, "You know I have deep affection for you. As well as gratitude for all you have done for me."

"Affection... gratitude..." A moment of silence. Then, "I know you plan to go to Rich Bar and redeem your bonds. But what then? What do you desire out of life?"

She thought it over and shrugged. "What I have always said I wanted. Independence. Self-sufficiency. A life of my own choosing."

He, too, stared into the fire. Then, "A very wise man once said, 'Beware lest you lose the substance by grasping at the shadow.' Do you understand what that means?"

"Is that from Plato again?" He had once told her about the philosopher's allegory wherein captives in a cave are forced to sit facing a wall. A fire burns behind them, and behind the fire people are moving about and casting their shadows onto the wall. Since the captives see only the shadows and not the people making them, they believe the shadows to be actual beings rather than inanimate manifestations.

"It is the same idea, I suppose. But this comes from Aesop, the ancient Greek storyteller. One of his fables was 'The Dog and the Shadow.' Do you know it?"

"I may have read it at Miss Datty's, but I cannot recall the particulars."

"Then allow me to summarize. There once was a dog who had found a piece of meat and was carrying it home to eat at his leisure.

His path took him over a bridge, and he looked down into the water below and saw his reflection. Thinking it was another dog who also carried a piece of meat, he determined to have that one as well. So he opened his mouth to snatch it, lost the piece he already had, and ended with nothing. Do you think it possible that, like the dog in the fable, you are eschewing what is yours for the taking to pursue a dream that may have no substance whatsoever?"

Before she could answer, he came over and knelt before her, reaching beyond the sleeping baby to place a hand on either side of her face.

"Lizzie, dearest, you have surely seen how my feelings for you have grown over the past months. My first thought on waking is of you, as is the last before I sleep. I feel peace and contentment when I am in your presence. A vague unease when we are apart. I once asked you to marry me out of obligation. Now I ask out of love and devotion. Please remain with us. Help me establish a new life for both of us. For all four of us. Please consent to be my wife."

She barely had time to absorb his words before he leaned forward and drew her face to his. Their lips met in a gentle, soft caress such as she had never experienced. Jack's kisses at the time of her seduction had been insistent, demanding, even harsh. This warm, respectful act nearly took her breath away even as it ignited a fire in her body that threatened to melt all resistance.

He pulled back and smiled deeply into her eyes. "I know I am asking you to rethink your future. Only you can weigh the consequences of the two paths before you. I shall await your decision in the morning."

He rose, walked over to his tent, and crawled inside, leaving Lizzie to ponder his words. How was she to think in a rational manner when her roiling emotions were pulling her in so many different directions?

How easy it would be to succumb to his proposal. As a young girl, she had always assumed she would marry a well-placed gentleman, have his children, and take her rightful place in polite society. She had destroyed that dream by running off with Jack O'Rourke. Now Jonathan was offering her another chance. She did not doubt his expressed love. Nor did she deny her own feelings, not to mention the pleasant warmth that flooded her body when she contemplated the physical intimacy that would follow their marriage.

One insurmountable obstacle remained. Accepting him would require a complete airing of her past. Could she endure the sight of his face contorting with revulsion when he learned the truth about her? To see his love draining away before her eyes?

No, it was impossible. Besides, what of her vow to be independent of any man? Even if, unlikely as it was, he married her despite her past, she would never know what she might have achieved on her own. Such doubts would plague her to her dying day.

She closed her eyes and willed her errant feelings to flee before the logic of the only decision open to her. All that remained was to make things right with him. Allowing herself the shroud of cowardice, she devised a plan.

PART THREE—CHASING THE SHADOWS

Chapter Twenty-Three

Spanish Ranch, California
July 29, 1854

Lizzie bade her companions goodbye, lifted her carpetbag, and started up the dirt track to Spanish Ranch, a small mining town in the forested mountains of northern California south of American Valley. She was truly on her own for the first time in over three months, and she could not decide whether to feel liberated or frightened out of her wits.

It was a pleasant day, sunny and warm with a light breeze. She had still not grown used to the loveliness of her surroundings, the gurgling mountain streams, the lofty fir trees that gave off such spicy fragrance, the snow-crowned granite mountaintops that lifted their heads to the very heavens. The contrast with the barren, dusty roads she had traveled over the past weeks could not have been more stark.

Lazarus had told her this small but busy hub was a distribution center for goods flowing out to the surrounding mining camps. Therefore, it was a place where she might be able to purchase passage to Rich Bar, which was located on the east branch of the north fork of the Feather River some twelve miles to the northwest.

The town lay a short distance off the Beckwourth Trail and consisted of a number of log cabins clustered around a handful of split-plank buildings housing a blacksmith shop, a general store, and a two-story hotel. She entered the latter and approached the crude board that served as a reception counter.

The grizzled old man who sat behind it rose and looked her over, then shoved the wad of tobacco he was chewing into his cheek and said, "What kin I do fer ya, little lady?"

Lizzie put on her most imperious face. "I have been told it might be possible to book passage on a supply train from here to Rich Bar. Would you be so kind as to tell me to whom I should direct my inquiries?"

"Yer inquiries, is it? Wal now, I was you, I'd go on down the street and talk to Mr. Rodgers. Might be he could help you out."

She thanked him and went back out into the street, at the end of which she saw a group of weathered, unpainted buildings, the largest of which bore fading whitewash letters that read *Richard Rodgers Freight Company Warehouse.* Next to it was what appeared to be a barn with a dozen or more mules and burros fenced into a corral to the side. She took the small structure in front to be the company's business office.

She stepped inside and found it empty. She went across the dirt forecourt to the barn and peered inside. A middle-aged man in rough clothes sat on a tall stool in front of a workbench where he appeared to be repairing harness. She cleared her throat, and he looked up.

"I am looking for Mr. Rodgers," she said.

He smiled, stepped down from the stool, and came forward. "Then you have found him. How may I help you?"

He had a well-trimmed beard, mild brown eyes, and a pleasant face. She returned the smile and said, "I am Miss Hamilton. I have just left the Mills train from Missouri and am on my way to Rich Bar. Mr. Mills informed me there is no stage route there, but he suggested I ask about attaching myself to a supply train out of Spanish Ranch. I am able to pay a reasonable fare."

His expression registered his surprise. "Would you be traveling alone?"

"Yes. Is that a problem?"

"No, no. It's just... What do you know about Rich Bar?"

"Only that important business takes me there. Why do you ask?"

"I wondered whether you were aware of the declining fortunes of Rich Bar. The big gold strikes have played out, and very little is extracted there nowadays. Many of the shops and saloons are now out of business. I would not like for you to make that long tedious trip if its end result proved to be futile."

His words were unwelcome. Given all she had heard about the legendary gold fields of California, she had imagined the mining company that had issued the bonds to be a thriving entity. That it might be in a less-than-robust state was something she had not considered. Yet he had not said the gold business there was extinct. Only that it did not match its former grandeur. She took firm hold of her remaining conviction and said,

"You have not told me whether you are able to accommodate my request for passage."

He pursed his lips, brow furrowed, but nodded. "Would you require one-way or round-trip transportation?"

"Round trip, but I would need at least an hour to conduct my business before returning. If the train's turnaround time were less than that, I would need to stay overnight, assuming there is a hostelry in town."

"There is the Empire Hotel where my skinner takes his dinner before heading back. I would guess it takes him an hour and a half to unload the freight and eat. If your... " A skeptical pause. "... *business* were completed in that length of time, you could return with him. Otherwise, you would need to wait for the next train seven days hence."

"That sounds ideal for my purposes. When is the next train scheduled to depart?"

"Day after tomorrow. Would you like to accompany it?"

"Please."

"Have you any experience of riding a mule?"

She suppressed a laugh. She had ridden a fine horse nearly every day from childhood. A mere mule was unlikely to give her difficulty. "I assure you I am an accomplished rider."

"We have no ladies' side saddle. You must ride astride."

"That will not be a problem."

She reached for her carpetbag and the coin purse she had acquired along the way. She paid him the required two dollars and was turning away when he said,

"You must be here no later than four-thirty that morning."

She nodded and continued on. Except for that brief ride with Jonathan and Missy on his horse Shadow, she had never ridden astride. She felt her confidence dip a measure as she contemplated doing so on a rough mule for however many hours it would take to get to Rich Bar. She soon brushed the thought aside. Of all the barriers she had conquered in order to get where she was, this would surely be the least consequential. She stepped up into the hotel to make arrangements for spending the next two nights.

Her financial resources were dwindling at an alarming rate. Nonetheless, if she were to spend a day riding astride, modesty demanded she make one necessary purchase. She went to the general store and bought the smallest pair of men's trousers she could find to wear under her petticoats. She would cover them with her best dress and hope they were not visible when she arrived at the bank. If they were, it would be but one more of the degradations she had been forced to endure in order to establish a new, respectable life for herself.

She returned to the hotel and spent the afternoon in her room, a tiny windowless place furnished with a narrow bed and a crate for a washstand. She propped herself on the bed with her back against the wall, the straw mattress crackling beneath her, to wait out the long dull hours ahead.

She could not stop her mind from returning to the cowardly manner in which she had departed from the Collins family. She had known Jonathan would accept her decision to leave only if he knew the truth about her past. Telling him in person would have been the honorable path. Instead, she had taken paper and pen with her when she carried Caleb to Mrs. Saunders for his last nightly feeding. By the light of their lantern, she had written it all out.

First, the truth about her family connections, namely that she had a sister and brother-in-law who had rescued her and her mother after the family's downfall and were pledged to provide for her for as long as necessary. Jack O'Rourke was not a distant cousin but a scoundrel who had used his considerable charms to convince her life with him would be preferable to the one she was living. He had seduced her and taken her away to New Orleans with the implied promise of marriage, a promise he then refused to honor. Their one shameful night together had left her with child. Rather than accept her fallen state and see the pregnancy through to fruition, she had elected to snuff out that poor innocent life. She had murdered her own child, an act for which God would surely never forgive her. And neither should he.

After returning Caleb to his cradle in the Collins wagon, she had placed the letter on the pillow where she had rested her head for the past three months. She had gathered what she could in her carpetbag and walked a distance down the Truckee River to hide in a hardwood copse along its bank. When the train came by the following morning, she had flagged down the young couple who had agreed to take her with them over the Beckwourth Trail. She had not even said goodbye to Jonathan.

The memory of his love-filled visage brought tears to her eyes. What did he think of her now? She tried to imagine his expression as he read her letter, but her experience of him did not allow her to visualize the loathing he must have felt. Her only solace lay in the fact that she had not been witness to it.

She slept fitfully that night and wakened in the wee hours from a dream so disturbing it would remain with her for days. In it, she saw herself going through the routines of her former life at Rocklands. Her pride, her self-indulgence, her callous disregard for her servants, her airheaded refusal to think about anything except what she would wear for the next gown change of the day or what pleasures and diversions she could devise to amuse herself. She saw a disagreeable, spoiled creature whom she did not even like, much less admire.

Was this the life she had so often looked back on with nostalgia? The life she regretted leaving and to which she had often wished to be restored?

She felt a strange calm settle over her. It was not too late for her to make a difference in the world. To become the gold Jonathan had once spoken of, gold that had been purified by passing through the refiner's fire. He had emerged from his own time of testing unscathed, and she sent what could only be described as a prayer heavenward that she would be given the strength to do so as well.

∞∞∞

By the time she reached the mining camp of Rich Bar, Lizzie's body was in a crippled state from which she doubted she would ever recover. Straddling the broad back of a plodding mule for six hours over steep, rugged mountain ridges had caused every muscle and joint to scream in protest. When she finally dismounted, her legs nearly refused to support her. Were it not for the saddle's stirrup close at hand, she would have fallen without ceremony into the dusty street. The mule skinner, a short, wiry, ferret-faced individual named Billy who had not been keen on having her along in the first place, watched her awkward dismount with superior amusement. He shook his head and led the eight-mule train off to make his deliveries, leaving her to attend to herself without so much as a backward glance.

She took several feeble steps and stopped to assess her surroundings. What she saw was not encouraging.

The camp's setting could not have been more beautiful, located as it was along a bend in the Feather River's east branch where forested slopes rose thousands of feet along the steep canyon's walls. The mining camp itself, however, did not echo the majesty of its physical environs. The primary street was lined on both sides with dozens of motley structures, some constructed of logs or rough planks, some mere frames over which fraying canvas had been stretched. She set out to walk the length of the street in the hope she could locate the bank.

Most of the buildings she passed were closed and abandoned, and none showed signs they were or had been a bank. A few small stores were in business, one a general store, another a bakery, a third a tobacco shop where Billy the mule skinner had stopped to unload a portion of his freight. The hotel Mr. Rodgers had mentioned was a peculiar-looking establishment, two stories covered in unfinished planks with a canvas roof and canvas over its front facade where large capital letters announced "THE EMPIRE" in fading black paint. A couple of rough-dressed men loitered in front of it. Otherwise, the street was deserted.

She entered the hotel and found a large room, part of which was fitted as a barroom with fluted red calico framing a large mirror and a table covered in green felt whose purpose she knew all too well. The remainder of the room served as a shop where various articles of clothing and foodstuffs were offered for sale. At the moment, there were no buyers to be seen. She took the four stairs leading from the barroom into the parlor, a straw-carpeted space where red calico again prevailed by way of the window curtains and the covering for a long, narrow sofa. Another green-topped table and six cane-backed chairs awaited whatever card players remained in the camp. A plump, middle-aged woman sat in a rocking chair before a cook stove that was doing its best to dispel the chilly mountain air.

She rose at sight of Lizzie, brows arched in apparent surprise. "Gracious me, where have you come from, my dear?"

"I rode up with the pack train. I have urgent business with the Bank of Rich Bar. Would you kindly direct me to it?"

The woman stared at her as if she were from an alien planet. "The Bank... Oh, I fear you have been misinformed. We have no bank here."

"But—" She reached into the pocket of her dress and withdrew one of the bonds. "—this clearly states it is payable at the Bank of Rich Bar."

The woman examined the bond, eyes squinting in the poor light. She shook her head. "There might have been such a place in Rich Bar's heyday, but I assure you it is no longer here. Not since my husband and I purchased the hotel last summer."

Lizzie was so stunned she could not speak.

"I can see this comes as a shock," the woman said. She took Lizzie's arm and led her to the chair. "Sit here while I prepare a cup of tea for you. I am Mrs. Caldwell, by the by."

She gave Lizzie an expectant look, to which she replied in rote fashion, "Miss Hamilton. And I would greatly appreciate a cup of tea."

She sat, numbed beyond thinking, while Mrs. Caldwell bustled about fetching a cup from a nearby cupboard, placing a strainer over its lip, and adding tea from a tin. She lifted the kettle simmering on the stove and poured the steaming water over the tea leaves, allowing the brew to steep for several minutes before handing it to Lizzie. She offered a teaspoon and bowl of sugar, but Lizzie gave her head an absent-minded shake. She returned the sugar bowl to the cupboard, pulled over one of the cane-backed chairs, and sat down facing Lizzie, her pasty round face pinched with concern.

"If it would be of any help, I would be happy to ask around about the bank. There are a few old-timers remaining. Perhaps... "

Lizzie shrugged. "It would be a kindness were you to do so, but I am not optimistic. Banks do not close their doors and disappear if any funds remain within their coffers."

"It does no harm to inquire, nonetheless." A sympathetic pause. Then, "What will you do now?"

A sigh. "Return to Spanish Ranch with the mule train, I suppose."

"Well, you must have a hearty meal before you go. The dining room offers simple but substantial fare, of which your mule skinner will no doubt avail himself after he has unloaded our order of supplies."

Lizzie thanked her and went to find the dining room, where several people were already seated. She was nearly finished with her boiled beef, potatoes and onions when Billie came in to take his own meal. A short time later, Mrs. Caldwell came to inform her that the bank had indeed operated from the summer of 1850 until the spring of 1853, after which it had gone bankrupt. It was what she had expected to hear, but it came as a blow nonetheless. She sat wallowing in her despair while Billy finished his meal, then followed him out to the street where the dreaded mule waited to take her back to a future that had never been more uncertain.

It was after dark by the time they returned to Spanish Ranch. Lizzie took a light supper and fell into bed in the same poor room she had occupied for the prior two nights. Despite the aches and pains wracking her body after the day's torturous ride, she willed herself into the oblivion of sleep and wakened in a repaired physical state but in such a low mental bog that she could hardly will herself to rise.

Rise she must, however, and after breakfast, she gathered her sparse belongings and started back up the Beckwourth Trail. She had exhausted nearly all her financial resources and knew she must find employment if she were to keep starvation at bay. It was beyond her frazzled imagination to picture what type of work she might be capable of performing, but some tentative inquiries had assured her no such opportunities were available in Spanish Ranch. She recalled their small group of wagons camping near a haphazard collection of buildings known as Quincy in the American Valley some seven or eight miles back. While there, she had heard talk of a booming mining town named Elizabethtown located not far from Quincy. Perhaps she could find something there.

She trudged along beneath a sun that seemed to burn straight through her clothing. A succession of wagon trains passed her heading south. She garnered many curious glances and a smattering of greetings, but she knew these folks were depleted from their long overland journey and had no time or resources to devote to a nearly penniless vagabond. So she averted her eyes and stepped aside until the train's last wagon had passed by, then walked on.

After an hour or so, she heard the familiar sound of moving vehicles, but this time they were approaching from the rear. She turned and saw a great cloud of dust surrounding a hodgepodge of freight wagons, carts and pack mules led by a horse-drawn buggy. The driver was an imposing lady who wore a voluminous pink satin dress with purple ruffles and a wide purple hat decorated with silk roses. Large in stature, she had an ample bosom, corseted mid-section, and a face dominated by high, wide cheekbones, a full sensuous mouth, and deep-set brown eyes beneath thick, dark eyebrows. She pulled her horse to a halt, held up her hand to signal the retinue behind her to stop, and peered down at Lizzie.

"What's a pretty little thing like you doing out here all alone? Don't you know you're ripe fodder for the first scoundrel who comes along?"

Lizzie had not thought of herself as being in danger. Now the lady's words sent a frisson of unease up her spine. She said, "I am traveling to Elizabethtown and have no other means of getting there."

"Well, now you do. Come around here and hop up."

Lizzie was not in the habit of *hopping* anywhere, but the woman's less-than-refined speech was no reason not to take her up on her offer. She circled around in front of the horse, a beautiful black mare with a perfect star on her face, and stepped up into the buggy. The woman slapped the reins against the animal's rump, and they rolled forward.

"I am most grateful, Mrs., uh... " She glanced at the plump hands holding the reins and saw no wedding ring. "... Miss... ?"

Her implied question produced a snort. "No Mrs. No Miss. Just plain Lucy Mae will do. If your surname was Crabb like mine, you wouldn't want to advertise it either. Now, what about you?"

"Miss Hamilton." A raised brow and impatient gesture prompted her to add, "Elizabeth. My familiars call me Lizzie."

Her lips twitched. "Ah, yes. Your familiars. Well, since we are to share this buggy for the next few hours, I'll count myself as one of those and call you Lizzie. Now tell me why you are headed to Elizabethtown."

Lizzie decided it was no use attempting to maintain her dignity with this person. "I am in need of employment. Elizabethtown is the closest community of any size where I might find it."

"What kind of work do you want?"

"Anything that will maintain my honor while providing for my needs. I am in... rather straitened circumstances."

"Indeed? And how did that happen? Your speech tells me you come from a well-bred southern background. Why are you here thousands of miles from the bosom of your family?"

In Lizzie's world of old, no one would press such intimate questions on a person they had met but moments before. Indeed, they would not ask them at all absent a close personal relationship developed over a long period of time. However, it was not the first time she had been reminded that she no longer lived in that world and must adjust accordingly.

She surprised herself by not only laying out the basics of her situation but going into rather exhaustive detail as the buggy navigated the steep ridges that lay ahead. When she had finished, Lucy Mae nodded, pursed her lips, and fell into a reverie of thought. At last she said, "If I might make a suggestion, Elizabethtown's star is falling. The gold is playing out, and the tide has turned toward the new town of Quincy, which is just now being laid out and built on land owned by Mr. Hugh Bradley."

Lizzie gave her a skeptical look. "We camped near there four nights ago. I did not find it particularly impressive."

"Not now, perhaps, but trust me when I tell you that is rapidly changing. Quincy is the temporary county seat of the newly-created Plumas County. A referendum will decide the seat's permanent location later this fall, and Elizabethtown will no doubt compete vigorously. But its canyon location puts it at a disadvantage over the broader American Valley where Quincy is located. Add to that the temporary courthouse Mr. Bradley has built behind his hotel at no cost to the county until a permanent building site is chosen, and you have strong incentives for Quincy to prevail. Which is why I now live there. If you want to be on the side of destiny, I suggest you do the same."

"But if the town is not yet fully built, how would I find an established business at which to apply for employment?"

She chuckled. "I do love to hear you talk. A real lady, that's what you are. Now listen up. You will have noticed the wagons and such following us. I am bringing them up from the town of Marysville loaded with the building materials necessary to put up the fine saloon I intend to run in Quincy. How would you like to work for me?"

Lizzie felt her jaw drop. A saloon? She thought back to her weeks in New Orleans. The only females she had ever seen there besides herself had been plying a disgraceful trade with which she could never associate herself.

"But... but what sort of work could I possibly do for you?"

An assessing gaze. "Well, you are a most handsome specimen. I don't suppose... ?"

"Certainly not! I shall starve before I degrade myself so."

"Well, then... " Another reverie. Then, her eyes sparked and she said, "I have it. Surely you know how to dance."

Lizzie frowned. "As at a ball?"

"Yes. The waltz, the schottische."

"Well, the waltz certainly. The schot— What is that?"

"The shottische. A new dance that's all the rage these days. You would learn it easily enough. Here is what I propose. You need to earn a living. I need an angle to distinguish my place from the others. You with me so far?"

Lizzie nodded.

"All mining towns have any number of saloons and dance halls, and I doubt Quincy will be any different. What I need is a hook to distinguish mine from the others. The big city saloons and gambling hells offer French girls as an enticement to the men. What if you became my enticement? Suppose I named the place The Southern Belle and offered you, the authentic article, as a hostess? You could charm them with your refined ways, dance with them, lead them to the bar for drinks, stand at their shoulders as they played their faro or monte or poker. Those vices are where the money is. That, and certain other activities that need not concern you. I would pay you a living wage, say ten dollars a week as well as a ten-percent commission on all drinks sold due to your influence. What do you say?"

Lizzie's mind was reeling with the possibility being offered her. She had certainly had enough experience in saloons and knew the mind-set of the men who frequented them. She had not been above conspiring with Jack to fleece the unwary of their earnings. Was this any different?

"But look at me." Her hand moved from her poorly-dressed hair to her dusty plain frock. She knew her face was sun-browned despite her best efforts, the creamy complexion expected of any southern lady long gone. "I hardly look the part you would have me play."

"Oh, my, easily solved, dearie. These wagons carry not only building supplies but bolts of silk and satin and all the necessary folderol we ladies need to make ourselves appealing to the opposite gender. We'll have some gowns made up in no time. Certainly by the time the building is complete. With a little pampering, your former beauty will return. Now I repeat, are you in?"

Lizzie's last vestige of pride fell away. She sighed and said, "Yes. God help me, I am in."

Chapter Twenty-Four

American Valley was a broad expanse seven miles long and four miles wide where meandering streams and marshes supported lush farmlands in all their summer fullness. The town of Quincy was fast rising on its southern edge from land previously known as American Rancho. The town's magnificent backdrop of timber-clad hillsides and snow-capped mountain peaks captivated Lizzie from the moment she stepped down from Lucy Mae's buggy in front of Bradley's American Hotel late that afternoon.

On closer inspection than she had given the town earlier, she saw that it was bustling with activity. Buildings were being erected up and down the street. Sandwiched in between were the businesses necessary to a thriving community, most housed in crude log structures or makeshift temporary abodes of planks and canvas. Horses and mules, either individually saddled or hitched to buckboard wagons, stood tethered to the posts provided along the street. Pedestrians went in and out among the shops. Most were men, but she saw a few women with the sun-browned faces of emigrants or the more settled appearance of settlers from the surrounding ranchos. Several groups of men dressed in miners' rough garb stood about talking, smoking, and chewing tobacco. The air was filled with the pounding of hammers and the pungent aromas of fresh-cut timber and animal dung.

Lucy Mae's caravan continued down the street and stopped before a vacant lot where several temporary shelters had been erected. She gestured in that direction and said, "There lies the future Southern Belle. You'll be surprised how quickly it'll rise from the dust. We'll be in business within the month. Meanwhile... " She took Lizzie's arm and led her up to the hotel.

It was a fine two-story building constructed of sawed lumber, the only such one in town, although it was clear others were in progress and would soon rival its preeminence. Lizzie was surprised by the attempt at opulence she observed on entering. Like the Empire at Rich Bar, the large lower room was divided into a barroom on the left, a general store on the right, a parlor and dining area to the rear. The front windows were draped in red calico, the apparent decorating choice of Californians, and a slightly-worn red carpet covered the parlor portion's board floor. The barroom's prime feature was a magnificent mirror framed in gold leaf before which sat the usual array of spirits. In addition, there were a pine bar, a wall of bunks for accommodating single male guests, and the ubiquitous gaming tables and chairs found in all such establishments.

Lucy Mae had already offered to share her hotel room with Lizzie until such time as the saloon was built, another gesture for which she was grateful since the fourteen-dollars per week fee for board was beyond her reach. They climbed to the second floor, and the older woman extracted a key from her bosom and let them into the space they would occupy for the coming weeks.

It was an improvement over her room at Spanish Ranch. Although not much larger, there was a window to let in the light. The bed was wider but still rather narrow for two people, especially when one was of Lucy Mae's girth. There was a single straight-back chair and a small chest of drawers that doubled as a washstand. The wall pegs already overflowed with an array of colorful dresses, which mattered not since Lizzie had but one frock besides the one she was wearing.

She looked out the window, which was on the back of the building, and saw another structure of rude shake shingles on the same lot. In response to her inquiry, Lucy Mae explained that it was the temporary courthouse she had spoken of earlier.

"The courtroom is on the lower level, the offices of various county officials on the upper. Town meetings, political gatherings, even a dance or two have been held there." A satisfied smile. "Those won't draw much support once The Southern Belle is up, though. Ours will be the finest dance hall in Quincy once I'm through with it. You just wait and see."

Waiting seemed to be exactly what Lizzie was destined to do over the coming days. She accompanied her employer to view the workmen's progress on the new saloon daily. Otherwise, she had time on her hands that was difficult to fill. She explored the town, including the businesses of Main Street such as the much less grand log-built Plumas House, two or three other saloons, an emporium selling foodstuffs, another selling dry goods, several eating houses, and the Bullard Building, a substantial structure being raised on the corner of Main and Harbison Streets. The cross streets radiating out from the business district revealed boarding houses and private residences, many of which were log cabins being replaced by more ambitious homes of cedar plank or, in a few instances, of the finer sawn lumber. She ventured out into the countryside where the various emigrant encampments lay. Watching these people go about their daily chores bit deep into her memory, and she found herself thinking more and more of the Collins family.

Had they reached their destination of Sacramento by now? Their crossing of the Sierra Nevada would have been much more difficult than hers, for the Beckwourth Pass was known as the lowest and easiest access to the valley beyond, whereas the Donner Pass was steep and treacherous and required the fiercest resolve of man and beast. If they were, pray God, safely across, had they found a place of their own? Had Jonathan begun his inquiries as to schools of classical learning?

These wonderings would have been appropriate for anyone who had shared a journey such as theirs. Her thoughts, however, went far beyond the expected. Had Jonathan recovered from whatever feelings he had experienced on reading her letter? Did he ever think of her now? Or was she but a fading memory as he began casting his eye about for a suitable mother for his children. Had Missy already forgotten her in the manner of a child's unformed mind? Or did she still bear resentment at having been so precipitously abandoned. As for Caleb, the image of his dear sweet face brought a physical ache she could scarcely tolerate.

She tried hard to push such thoughts from her mind for they brought only misery and regret. Instead, she focused on the amazing rapidity with which The Southern Belle was rising from the California dust.

Two weeks after she arrived in Quincy, Lucy Mae made another trip to Marysville and beyond. Further building materials were needed due to some changes to her original plan. In addition, there were furnishings to buy and a staff to be hired. Lizzie could not fathom where this woman had acquired the wealth to finance this huge endeavor, but Lucy Mae had never broached the subject, and Lizzie was too schooled in proper manners to ask. Nor did she particularly want to know since she suspected the means would not have met with her approval. She was simply grateful to have money in her pocket, for Lucy Mae paid her wages each week even though she had done little to earn them. Her employer might not have the highest of moral integrity, but her generosity was unquestioned.

During Lucy Mae's absence, Lizzie remained in their shared room, the fee for which had been paid forward. She slept better than she had since her arrival now that she had the bed to herself absent the robust snores that normally kept her awake much of the night. She walked for daily fittings to the Blackwell Rancho a half mile distant where the proprietress, an accomplished seamstress, was constructing several gowns for her. Lucy Mae had chosen the fabrics, which were somewhat more gaudy than Lizzie would have selected, but she had allowed Lizzie to direct the styling since the goal was to replicate the costumes a traditional southern lady might wear.

Lucy Mae returned with a new caravan of materials, and the construction process continued at an even more rapid pace. Lizzie resumed her daily visits to the site with her employer. The Southern Belle might not be as fine in architecture and workmanship as the homes and businesses of Charleston, but it was certainly remarkable when compared with the other buildings in Quincy, including the vaunted American Hotel. The large pine-board central hall had a raised dias where Lucy Mae's new piano, which had come around the horn on a sailing ship and whose price Lizzie could not even attempt to guess, would stand in all its glory. The musicians would ply their trades on the same dais while the customers danced before them. Dozens of tables where people could drink, gamble, and socialize as they pleased surrounded the dance floor. The lucrative business of dispensing spirits would take place at a massive bar backed by the requisite mirror. The rear portion had been sectioned off to accommodate the long narrow tables where diners would be served a simple but hearty fare. A small office where Lucy Mae would manage the entire affair had been boarded off in the far northeast corner.

The building's second story had a long corridor off of which were eight rooms, four on each side with an iron heating stove at the far end. A large sign to be posted on the saloon's front facade had been painted in Sacramento and offered a romanticized version of a comely maiden dressed in the finery of a southern lady—bonnet, parasol, and gloves included—beneath the words *THE SOUTHERN BELLE* in large block letters. By the time it had been nailed in place and the furnishings moved to their appointed places, the small retinue of previously-hired staff had arrived.

They were a disparate lot. Big Joe Bell, the bartender, was a barrel-chested, black-haired hulk whose size was no doubt meant as a deterrent to trouble. The piano player, Timothy Peters, was his opposite, a small, fine-boned man with sandy hair and beard and long, agile fingers that could make the instrument bellow forth with lusty vigor or whisper the most moving of love songs. The fiddle player, who was to double as cook, had a swarthy Spanish look and a name to match, Jose Martinez. The four giggling, high-spirited girls whose purpose and vocation were unspoken but apparent varied in looks from coarse to tolerably pretty. Their trunks were immediately transported to four of the upstairs rooms. Lucy Mae had another to herself as did the bartender. The piano and fiddle players shared the seventh. Lizzie and the vocalist were to share the final room.

Rachel Barnes was a slip of a girl who had a wispy frame barely reaching five feet and smooth nut-brown skin. She had a pretty face with elliptical brown eyes, prominent cheekbones, a small rounded nose, and a mouth with a Cupid's bow upper lip, reminding Lizzie of a slave whose charms had been the precipitating factor in her brother's downfall. The singer seemed not in the least discomfited by the prospect of living with a white woman. Lizzie, however, had some adjusting to do.

She had come to modify her opinions of the Negro race, influenced to a significant degree by her experience of the people who had helped her escape *The Princess* and most especially, of Lazarus Mills. Not only had she found the wagon master to be intelligent, wise and compassionate in his use of authority, but he had rescued her on two occasions when she would not have blamed him had he not bothered given her condescending, dismissive attitude at the beginning of their journey. Now, however, she was expected to stretch her tolerance to a level she never would have thought possible a year ago.

Black house servants had been an integral part of her daily life for as far back as she could remember. She was accustomed to sharing the most intimate activities with her personal maid Polly. The girl had often slept on the floor at the foot of her bed. All interactions, however, had been governed by a time-tested hierarchy in which each participant knew where the power lay. Now she was to share her living space, even a bed with this girl on an equal basis. She could not stop herself from raising the issue with Lucy Mae.

The older woman gave her a jaundiced look. "You want your own room like the other girls? Well, fine. But they need their privacy when they entertain the gentlemen. You willing to do that, too?"

Lizzie felt her face drain of color. "Of course not. You know that already."

"Exactly. That's why you and Rachel are sharing a room."

"But why... why *her*?"

"You haven't heard her sing yet. As soon as you do, you'll understand."

And understand she did when Rachel took the stage that night for The Southern Belle's grand opening. The rich contralto voice that proceeded from the girl's small frame was worthy of awe. The onlookers' initial racial taunts quickly disappeared, and the entire establishment fell silent as she gave her rendition of Jenny Lind's "I've Left the Snow-Clad Hills" followed by Stephen Foster's "Old Folks at Home" and Henry Bishop and John Howard Payne's "Home! Sweet Home!" Wild applause begged for more, but Lucy Mae had decided to space the girl's offerings throughout the evening interspersed with rousing dance music. More and more customers came in as the sounds of the festivities carried out through the open door. By the toll of midnight, the place was packed, its success assured.

As for relations between Lizzie and Rachel, what began as a frosty acceptance on Lizzie's part soon gave way to grudging admiration. The girl's unassuming yet self-confident demeanor did not lend itself to discord. Any slight she might have perceived coming from Lizzie did not prompt a like response. Indeed, she lived as though insulated from all that surrounded her, concentrating only on her artistry. Lizzie attempted to explore her background, but Rachel would admit only to having sailed around Cape Horn from Virginia six months before to make her musical way in California. Despite various appearances at the theaters of San Francisco and Sacramento, she had not settled on a permanent location until Lucy Mae heard her and offered her employment here in Quincy. Lizzie thought it odd that someone of her talent would want to hide away in this remote region, but her questions elicited only a placid smile and the inane comment, "It suits me." Lizzie's curiosity continued unabated, however, and she looked for an opportunity to satisfy it.

The two women were in the habit of rising late given that their duties in the saloon kept them up early into the morning. This was a pattern that Lizzie had already mastered during her days as Jack's assistant, but Rachel had more difficulty adapting to it, often waking early and plodding through the day with sleep-deprived lethargy. As the days went on, however, she acclimated. They would take a late breakfast, then Rachel would remain at the piano to vocalize with Timothy, the pianist. It was while she was thus occupied that Lizzie undertook her explorations in their room.

In the end, it was even easier than it had been to find Jack's money box. At the bottom of Rachel's unlocked trunk she found a leather folder. Inside were a series of news clippings dating back three years. They were from such organs as the *Alexandria Gazette*, the *Fredericksburg News* and the *Richmond Daily Dispatch*, and they all extolled the extraordinary voice of "The Black

Nightingale," Rachel Barnes, a slave owned by John Horace Barnes, Sr. of Hope Park Plantation located five miles southwest of Fairfax Court, Virginia. The girl had studied under the most reputable vocal coach in the state from the age of twelve and had begun her concert career at age sixteen. She had since performed at the state's best concert halls and even at New York City's Metropolitan Hall in early 1853. Her proud owner gloried in her accomplishments, not to mention the considerable financial benefit he accrued thanks to her talent and fame.

Lizzie read the accounts with utter fascination. What was this remarkable girl doing in California? Had she escaped her bondage and fled? Then she picked up the final item, a legal document smudged with the occasional ink spot but still legible.

Commonwealth of Virginia SS.
City of Fairfax Court
Know all men by these presents that I John Horace Barnes, Sr. of Fairfax County in the State of Virginia from Motives of benevolence & humanity have Manumitted and do hereby manumit & set free from Slavery my Negro Girl Rachel Barnes aged nineteen years said Rachel being about five feet and very slight Built of medium brown complexion and I do hereby give grant and release unto the said Rachel Barnes All my right and title & claim of in and to her person, labour and service and of in & to the estate and property which she may hereafter acquire or obtain. In Witness whereof I have hereunto set my hand and affixed my seal the 12th day of January in the year of our Lord 1854.

J. H. Barnes, Sr. (beside which name appeared his seal)

Recorded January 21st 1854

The document brought Lizzie no closer to the answers she sought. Indeed, it raised new questions. If the girl had been freed by her master—an act that was illegal in the State of South Carolina but not in many of her sister states—and had already achieved professional acclaim, why would she leave her home to start over in a state that no doubt had much to learn about the finer points of culture? And why, as Lizzie had wondered initially, would she abandon the large cities where she was most likely to gain recognition for this backwater place?

She could not pursue the matter without revealing that she had pried into her roommate's private possessions. Probing around the edges gained her nothing, and she finally gave up. Meanwhile, there were many day-to-day happenings to occupy her mind.

Her duties at the saloon were not taxing. She dredged up the habits of a lifetime to greet the customers with a combination of gracious charm, vivacious banter, and mild coquetry. She accepted their invitations to dance. The remainder of the time, she made certain they were well supplied with drink and steered them to the gaming tables, where she stood by as they played while offering admiring encouragement. Whenever a man displayed untoward interest in moving to a more intimate plane, she maneuvered him toward one of the girls provided for that purpose.

These women, who ranged in age from late teens to early thirties, had quickly formed an unholy bond that excluded all others, including Lizzie and Rachel. They were quick to use mimicry and vulgarity to poke fun at any pretense of dignity. One in particular, a hefty, big-bosomed tart by the name of Mariah, took a particular dislike to Lizzie and did everything within her power to foment trouble. As for Rachel, all four exercised their contempt for her race with impunity, their hurtful comments raining on the poor singer's head whenever Lucy Mae was not around to stop them. Lizzie could not help herself from rising to her dusky roommate's defense, which only served to aggravate the abuse. In the end, both women learned to avoid the agitators, which in turn drove them closer together.

As the weeks went by, Lizzie relied more and more on Rachel to assuage her loneliness. She remembered the close friendship her former sister-in-law had established with her lady's maid, a friendship that had seemed scandalous to Lizzie at the time. Now it was her turn to know a bright, kind, good-natured girl who was different from herself only in the color of her skin. In every other respect, they were equals. Admitting this forced her to acknowledge the vast injustice perpetrated by the slave-holding culture of which she had been such an integral part and to feel the collective shame her family shared with all others of their acquaintance.

Such ruminations led her to ponder the larger question of her personal future. Working for a weekly wage as the hostess of a dance and gaming establishment was a far cry from what she had anticipated her new life would be. She had entertained a vague notion that once she attained the wealth offered by the bearer bonds, she would find a worthwhile endeavor to champion, something that would make meaningful sense of her life. Instead, she seemed to be stuck in a dull, day-to-day existence that profited no one, least of all herself.

She could discern no such doubts in Rachel, who spoke openly of her firm belief that God would not only guide her to whatever place He wished her to occupy but would also give her the strength and will to thrive wherever that place might be. Such sentiments reminded Lizzie most painfully of Jonathan and his similar belief that God would provide for him and his family.

She began encouraging Rachel to read aloud during her daily perusal of her well-worn Bible. Unlike the days of old when she had suffered through her mother's daily devotions, she listened as she never had before. Disturbing thoughts roiled her mind whenever it was unoccupied by immediate concerns. Was she here in Quincy by the will of God—or the will of Lizzie? She had made what amounted to a religion out of her determination to make her own way in the world independent of any man. Had she been so obsessed with this resolve that she had missed her one viable opportunity for happiness? Had she, as suggested by Jonathan, rejected the substance of his marriage offer to chase after the wispy shadow of independence?

Lucy Mae had certainly prospered on her own in a world that denied positions of power and influence to women. But at what cost to her honor and self-respect? She had exalted herself at the expense of vulnerable men and women, as well as her own moral turpitude. Was this a course Lizzie was willing to emulate?

No matter how convoluted her thinking, it always returned to one irrefutable fact: Jonathan would surely have retracted his offer when he discovered the truth about her past. So why did she torture herself with a possibility that would have evaporated like smoke were she to have seized it? A possibility that was now irretrievably lost? She tried with all her might to vanquish these circuitous musings—an effort that became easier as the summer waned into autumn and autumn into winter.

The weather turned increasingly cold and wet, with the mountain snows occasionally making it down into the valley. Mining operations slowed, and idle miners flocked into town to spend their earnings, a circumstance that greatly benefitted The Southern Belle and, by extension, Lucy Mae's fortunes. As that woman's spirits soared, Lizzie's fell into a persistent slump, especially as the Christmas holiday season approached. She could not help recalling the happy times at Rocklands when big house and slave quarter alike had made merry as at no other time of the year. Even remembering her last Christmas in the Townsend household brought a degree of nostalgia that she experienced as a physical ache. What type of celebration would there be in this rough-and-tumble town in the middle of nowhere? It was certainly not a prospect she anticipated with even the slightest degree of optimism.

One bright spot occurred on the eighteenth of December when one of Lucy Mae's supply caravans arrived with a copy of the *Sacramento Daily Union* that contained a piece about The Southern Belle and its amazing black vocalist, whose ability had been extolled by a recent traveler to that bustling small town. The last paragraph also mentioned the unusual hostess who, from all appearances, embodied all of the attributes implied by the saloon's name despite her presence in a common public house.

Lizzie showed the pertinent page to Rachel so she could see how her fame had spread. The singer read the piece with a surprising look of dismay.

Lizzie said, "You should be delighted to have your talent extolled by such a prominent newspaper."

Rachel bit her lip and shook her head. "I have no wish for fame. It is one of the reasons I accepted Lucy Mae's offer of employment. I wish to exercise my craft in anonymity."

"But why? You have acknowledged that your incredible talent comes from God. Surely He would wish for you to share it with the maximum number of people."

She took a moment to answer, her brow furrowed with an anxiety belied by her calm voice when she finally said, "*'Pride goeth before destruction, and an haughty spirit before a fall.'* Proverbs 16. And in the Gospel of Luke, *'he that humbleth himself shall be exalted.'* I am content with whatever small notoriety I have achieved right here in Quincy and have no wish for it to stretch beyond the town's confines."

In a light, mildly-teasing tone, "Well, it seems you have no say in the matter, so you may as well accustom yourself to the fact. As for me, I shall allow myself enough pride on your behalf for both of us."

Rachel did not smile in response. Instead, she shook her head and turned away, the subject closed. Lizzie puzzled over her strange reaction over the coming days, but no explanation presented itself until two days before Christmas when a stranger's arrival changed everything.

Chapter Twenty-Five

To Lizzie, the only remarkable thing about the young man was the manner in which he stood out from everyone else in the town. His fine broadcloth frock coat, silk cravat, embroidered waistcoat, kid boots and gloves and tall hat identified him as a gentleman of the type she had not seen since leaving South Carolina. His southern roots were confirmed the moment she heard him speak in the refined drawl with which she had been surrounded from childhood. What she could not have anticipated was Rachel's extreme reaction to his sudden appearance among them.

The singer had just stepped up onto the dias and was waiting while Timothy Peters played the introduction to her first song when she suddenly froze in place, her eyes riveted on the doorway where the newcomer had just entered. When she did not begin to sing at the appropriate time, Timothy replayed the introduction, then stopped altogether when again she did not respond.

The customers began to murmur, then to jeer, their growing agitation finally breaking her seeming trance. "I fear I am unwell," she called above the cacaphony. "I apologize, but I am not able to sing at present."

She stepped down and made a hasty retreat to the stairway leading to the second story, the men's boos and catcalls following her. The commotion soon drew Lucy Mae from her office. She caught Lizzie's eye and stormed toward her.

"What is the meaning of this? Where is Rachel?"

"She claims to have taken ill."

A skeptical frown. "She was fine earlier. Shall I send for the doctor?"

"Allow me to inquire after her first. Perhaps it is but a passing spasm."

"Very well." She turned to Timothy and barked, "Play, you fool!"

He launched into one of his livelier dance tunes, immediately joined by Jose, the fiddle player. Lucy Mae gestured to the three girls who were available, and they fanned out to find and pull a willing man onto the dance floor. Mariah gave the stranger whose appearance had caused Rachel's odd behavior a calculating look before heading in his direction. Lizzie saw her thrust her body up against his, pull his head down to whisper in his ear, then hook her arm through his and urge him toward the dance floor. He complied, but his gaze followed Lizzie with a half smile and hooded eyes as she made her way up the stairway and out of sight.

The room she shared with Rachel was the last one on the right at the front of the building. The bawdy sounds coming from the room next to theirs explained why the fourth girl was not downstairs with the others. Lizzie had grown used to the giggles, squeals and grunts that often emanated from the four women's rooms, and now she barely noticed. She opened the door to their darkened room and found Rachel curled in a tight ball on the bed.

She lit a candle, sat beside her, and waited. When nothing happened, she said, "Who is he?"

Rachel lay unmoving, her breathing barely audible. At last she heaved a great sigh, straightened her body, and said, "My former master's youngest son, Horace Barnes. He is the reason I left Virginia."

Lizzie's position was somewhat delicate. To cover up her ignoble spying, she must pose her questions as if she knew nothing of Rachel's past. After a moment's thought, she said, "If he is your *former* master's son, then surely he has no power over you now. Why does his appearance here distress you so?"

"Because he has never accepted his father's decision to set me free. Master Barnes was near to death when he did so, and Horace has always maintained that I exercised undue influence on a man who was not in his right mind. He was preparing to take the matter to court when I fled with nothing but the clothes on my back."

Rachel's story reminded Lizzie of her own flight from home. She asked, "How did you manage it?"

"I hired on as a chambermaid on a vessel bound for California. When I arrived, my voice saved me from starvation. Now—" She closed her eyes and shuddered. "—he has found me, no doubt thanks to that article in the *Sacramento Daily Union*. You wondered why I was not pleased to be singled out and praised. Now you know."

"But—" *Be careful*, she counseled herself. "—you are in California now. Surely he cannot prove you to be his slave."

"No. More to the point, I can prove I am not. I carry my freedom paper with me wherever I go."

Lizzie breathed an inner sigh of relief. It was out now, and she need not worry about being found out. "There you have it, then. He cannot touch you."

"No? On the day he stormed off to the Virginia authorities to have me arrested, his parting words were, 'You will be my slave, or you will die. It is your choice, bitch.'"

The crude appellation did not shock Lizzie. She had heard white men of the South use far worse language when addressing those of the Negro race. She also knew that such men could kill a black person, especially one of their own property, with impunity and get away with it nine times out of ten.

"This is not Virginia, Rachel. This is a free state."

"Perhaps in law. But you have heard the taunts that follow me despite admiration for my voice. People of my race are no more respected here than in other parts of the nation. In fact, reason tells me you are from an ardently pro-slavery state and I am a fool to trust you with my tale of woe. What is to prevent you from conspiring with this foul man to whisk me back into slavery?"

Lizzie recognized the sensibility of such doubts even as she felt a stab of shame, for there was no doubt she would have acted in just such a manner not that long ago.

"Nothing but my honor," she answered. "The past year has taken me as far from my former sentiments as it has from my physical home. I now believe you have the same right to be free as do I, and I pledge to do all within my power to see that you remain so."

A soft smile. "Lizzie, my white champion. I confess I had no substantive doubt as to your loyalty and friendship. Forgive me for such cynical talk. You have done nothing to deserve it."

"Have you forgotten my initial resistance when I was required to share this room with you? But that is all in the past. Now we must consider what must be done to assure your safety and freedom."

"It is the latter that concerns me most. Despite his threats, I doubt Horace would resort to murder. Such an act would 'kill the goose that lays the golden egg,' as the saying goes. He wants me as his property so the fees my concerts engender will revert to him, as was the case before I was freed."

Lizzie arched her brows. "So he pursued you for the sake of greed?"

"He is a young man of great resentment. His father's sizable estate was divided eight ways, with the house and grounds going to his mother, the mill and mill house to his eldest brother, and the remainder to his four sisters, another brother, and himself. His portion was too poor to provide for the comfortable life to which he was formerly accustomed. He wishes to correct that disparity by means of my voice."

"Then we must make certain he cannot. Is the paper proving your freedom in a safe place?"

"Well... "

"Where is it?"

"In a leather case in the bottom of my trunk."

She frowned as if hearing it for the first time. "That does not seem a particularly safe place. What if the folder were stolen? Or destroyed in a fire?"

"I admit there is an element of risk. I have always intended to file with the county authorities when I settled in a permanent place. I felt no urgency because I thought I was well beyond Horace's reach."

"That must be put right first thing in the morning. The county offices are in the building behind the American Hotel. I urge you to take your proof there immediately on waking tomorrow."

"I shall certainly do so."

"Meanwhile, I suggest we find a less obvious place for your document."

"Excellent idea. I doubt I will sleep a wink tonight if we do not."

She retrieved the folder, removed the document, and they put their minds to finding a secure hiding place. It was a difficult proposition. The wall and floorboards, being of new construction, were all tight. They considered hiding it among the clothing hanging on the wall hooks, but there were no pockets to keep it from falling out. The idea of folding it and placing it beneath the rather sizable ceramic washbowl seemed a good solution until they realized having it anywhere near water ran the risk that some would splash out, smudging the ink and rendering it unreadable.

Finally Rachel cried, "I know!" She returned the document to the folder, pulled up the bed mattress, and slipped it between the mattress and cross slats.

She grinned. "*Now* I shall sleep well."

"Meanwhile, you must come downstairs and continue your song schedule as if nothing were amiss. Let the scoundrel preen and gawk, but it will be of no use."

Rachel patted her hair into place as Lizzie extinguished the candle. They stepped into the hall and saw Mariah scurrying ahead of them toward the stairs.

Lizzie frowned, murmuring, "That hussy is no friend to either of us. I wonder why she is in such a hurry?"

The question was beyond answering, and they continued on.

∞∞∞

In her dream, Lizzie was walking along beside the Collins wagon in bright sunshine carrying baby Caleb. His little arms were free and flailing as he made happy, gurgling sounds. Suddenly, one hand shot up and covered her mouth so she could not breathe properly. Her eyes flew open to the black of night and the realization that a hand was indeed pressing against her lower face. She began to thrash about even as Rachel struggled beside her, muffled whimpers leaking into the night air.

"Both of you lie still and listen," came a raspy whisper. "If you value your lives, you will be silent. I have a pistol and am prepared to use it if I must. I prefer to proceed in a civilized manner. It is up to the two of you which it will be."

Lizzie willed herself to slacken her body even as she reached out to grasp Rachel's hand.

"Much better," said the voice. Then in a different direction, "Give me some light here."

She heard the rasp of a match followed by the dim glow of a candle. It was enough for her to make out the man Rachel had identified as Horace Barnes hovering over the bed. He pulled his hands from their faces, backed away, and picked up a small but deadly-looking firearm. Beyond him, the harlot Mariah held the candlestick aloft and smirked down on therm.

"Ain't so high and mighty now, is you, *Miss Hamilton*?" using the title Lucy Mae had directed the entire staff to use in front of the customers. "And you, little nigger girl. Never saw nobody put on airs like you. Just like you was sumpin' special instead of a common slave."

"Shut up," Horace barked in her direction, "and let me get on with this." He turned back to Rachel and softened his tone. "Understand I mean you no harm. You were well treated in my father's house, and so you shall be in mine. But you belong to me by rights, and I intend to take you home where you belong."

Rachel regarded him for some time, her level gaze showing no fear. Then, "You know very well your father intended for me to be free. So strong was his conviction that he rose from his sickbed to see to it. You besmirch his memory by behaving as you are."

Anger flashed in his eyes, and he raised a hand as if to strike her. She did not shrink away but kept her gaze steady and sure. He hesitated, then lowered his hand and said in a lower but venomous voice,

"How dare you call my devotion to my father's memory into question! As you well know, he was sick of body as well as mind when he set you free. He would never have taken such action in his right mind."

"You are mistaken, Horace. He—"

"You will not address me by my Christian name!" he bellowed, startling them all.

"Hey, keep it down," whined Mariah. "You want the whole place in here? I got a job to protect, remember."

"It matters not what I call you," Rachel continued with steadfast calm. "Your father, whom I deeply respected, promised me many years ago that I would be free one day. In fact, he prepared me for that role from my earliest years, providing me with education and vocal training. Because of that, I did not resent his taking my earnings for the good of the family. I considered it due payment for his expense on my behalf. But that debt has been paid in full. I owe you nothing."

"Say what you will, I intend to convince the Plumas County court that you fled to California to escape slavery. You crossed state lines, thus invalidating any claim you might otherwise have. By state and federal law, you entered the state an escaped slave, and I may take you in transit back to Virginia."

"Are you mad?" said Lizzie, finding her voice for the first time. "Rachel can prove she was free when she came here. You have no case, as any judge would agree."

"Ah, yes. The freedom document." He pressed the pistol hard against Rachel's forehead. "Where is it?"

She set her chin. "In a safe place."

"So you say. But I happen to know it is somewhere in this room. I intend to have it."

"Then find it."

He gave Mariah a questioning look.

She shook her head, saying, "Like I already told you, they never said. Just that they found a good place."

Now Lizzie understood why they had seen Mariah hurrying away from their room the prior evening. She had been listening outside their door and overheard them discuss a possible hiding place.

"Then start looking," he snapped.

The woman stared at him for a long moment, then shrugged, put the candle on the washstand, and crossed to the trunk, where both women kept their petticoats, under things and stockings. She pulled everything out onto the floor, then straightened and looked around the room. She took the gowns from their wall pegs and patted them down. Looked behind the washstand and under the bed.

She shook her head. "T'ain't here."

Horace Barnes had had enough. He climbed onto the bed, pushing Lizzie aside and straddling Rachel's slight body, the gun held fast against her forehead.

With deadly calm, "I do not want to kill you, Rachel. But as I told you back in Virginia, I will do so if I must. You may live as my slave or die in your precious freedom. The choice is yours."

Lizzie stumbled out of the bed and whirled on him, her anger compensating for the cold air her flannel nightdress did little to repulse. "This is insanity! How can you possibly believe you could get away with murder with two witnesses to the event?"

"I ain't gonna be no witness," came Mariah's snarling voice as she grabbed Lizzie from behind and held her in a vicelike grip. "In fact, him and me'll make it look like *you* did it. How about that, Miss Southern Belle?"

"Not a bad idea," said Barnes.

"Who would believe such an accusation? Everyone here knows Rachel and I have a most cordial relationship. I would have no reason on this earth to harm her."

He smiled, a gesture that held more malice than geniality. "A return to your roots, perhaps? You did not approve of a Negro rising above her proper station. Or perhaps a quarrel, the intensity of which Mariah and I will relate."

"What nonsense! I have no gun. How would you explain that?"

"With difficulty, I admit." He set the pistol aside and placed his hands around Rachel's throat. "These are weapons possessed by everyone." Exerting pressure, "Now where is the document?"

Rachel stared back at him, her chest heaving with the sudden restriction of her airway.

"I would rather die than tell you," she croaked.

"Very well." He rose up and put more of his weight onto his hands.

"Stop!" cried Lizzie. "I will tell you. The document is in a folder beneath the mattress."

A huge grin. "Good decision, Miss Hamilton." He hauled Rachel, coughing and rasping, out of bed, then handed the pistol to Mariah, lifted the mattress, and picked up the folder. He spilled its contents onto the bed, riffling through the news clippings until he came to the legal document.

He snatched it up with a triumphant, "We are done here."

Lizzie and Rachel stood as if made of stone while the two intruders went out into the hall and closed the door behind them. They heard their footsteps retreat to Mariah's room followed by the sound of that door closing. Rachel gave a deep moan and sank to the floor, her face in her hands as she wept.

Lizzie knelt beside her and took her in her arms, rocking back and forth and saying, "Sh-h-h-h. All is not lost. They will not get away with doing this."

"They—already—have. You are so—so good, but you—cannot help—me."

"I do not accept that!"

Lizzie rose and stormed into the cold dark hall and down to Lucy Mae's room. It was very late, perhaps even near dawn, and she heard her employer's sonorous snores through the door, but she was in no mood to be considerate. She pounded on the door and waited. By the time a groggy, scowling Lucy Mae opened it, other doors along the hall had opened, the curious occupants staring in their direction.

Lucy Mae raised her candle and growled, "What is going on here?"

"Rachel and I have just been assaulted by a certain Horace Barnes assisted by your very own Mariah! I demand that you intervene on the side of justice!"

The proprietress's eyes widened, then narrowed. She glanced down the hall and commanded, "Back in your rooms, all of you." Grabbing Lizzie's arm and pulling, "Get in here and explain yourself."

Lizzie closed the door behind her and said, "This scoundrel, Horace Barnes, has come for the sole purpose of taking Rachel back to Virginia as his slave. He forced her to surrender her freedom document at gun point. He took it to Mariah's room with the sure intent of destroying it so that Rachel will have no legal claim to her freedom. If you do not act quickly, you will lose your top entertainer, and she will be returned to slavery."

It took a moment for Lucy Mae to digest what she had heard. She snatched up a wrapper to cover her voluminous nightdress and stormed down the hall to Mariah's room. She burst in and came up short at the scene before her. Mariah and Horace Barnes were in the bed, he atop her and thrusting gustily. He finished his task and rolled off, a smug grin on his face.

"Well, what do we have here?" he said. "Voyeurs? I admit I have never had the privilege of performing my manly pursuits before an audience."

"What have you done with the document?" Lizzie demanded.

"And what document would that be?"

"The one you stole from our room but a short time ago."

A smirk. "My dear lady, you are delusional. As you can see, I am well occupied right here and have been for the past hours. For which, I might add, I have paid dearly."

Lizzie appealed to Lucy Mae, saying, "He is lying. He and Mariah came to our room and forced us to surrender Rachel's freedom papers on pain of death."

"She is the liar," said Mariah, sitting up in bed without bothering to cover her nakedness. "Ain't no such thing happened. We been here for hours, just like Horace here says."

Out of frustration, Lizzie glanced around the room. Discarded clothing, but no sign of the document. A slight whiff of smoke plus a black glob floating in the spittoon told her all she needed to know.

"You burned it! Have you no honor to treat this acclaimed singer so?"

"Acclaimed singer or no, she is my property. She escaped some months ago, but now she is found and will return to her rightful place forthwith."

Lucy Mae had finally had enough. "Now hold on here. Rachel is my employee and is going nowhere against her will. And as for you... " She pointed at Mariah. "... you have been baiting Lizzie and Rachel from the beginning, and if I discover you have conspired against them in this, I will kick your fat ass out onto the street."

An angry pout. "You got no call to talk to me like that. I been entertaining this here gentleman just like he said. We didn't do nothing like what she says." A venomous glare at Lizzie.

"We'll see about that in the morning. I intend to have the sheriff in here first thing to sort this out."

"Excellent," said Barnes. "My suggestion precisely, because I intend to have him arrest Rachel Barnes—her very name proves she is my property—and hold her until I can obtain a hearing before a judge. Meanwhile, I shall post myself outside her door until morning lest she attempt to escape again."

He jumped from the bed stark naked, his defiant expression challenging them to stop him.

Chapter Twenty-Six

By the time Lizzie returned to their room, Rachel was back in bed and had exchanged her prior despair for calm acceptance. On reflection, she had realized that her music was her life, and if returning to slavery were the only way she could continue to sing, then she would submit.

"He will not mistreat me," she said as Lizzie crawled in beside her. "He receives my fees only as long as I sing well. Remember the golden goose analogy. He will pamper me so I continue to lay his golden eggs."

"But that happens only if the court accepts his claim. He may have destroyed your document, but I shall testify to its existence."

"How can you do so without perjuring yourself? You did not even see it up close."

It was time to come clean. "But I did. I am ashamed to admit that I pried into your belongings and found the folder with the news clippings and the document. I read every word and can remember enough to repeat before the court."

A quick intake of breath. "You are willing to do that for me?"

"Of course. My only concern is your reduced opinion of me now that you know of my unconscionable invasion of your privacy."

"It is a small offense when weighed against your loyalty and friendship. I am, after all, a person whose privacy was never acknowledged or respected as a slave, even by my beloved master. I would have shown you the document myself had it not been for the news clippings in the same folder. Showing those would have been the height of pride."

"Oh, Rachel. You who has every reason to swell with pride over your amazing voice shuns such feelings and replaces them with humility. It is a lesson I could have learned to my edification and improvement long ago."

In a drowsy voice, "Life is a journey of discovery, my friend. And one in which we can rely on our Creator to safely guide us if we but surrender the reins to Him. Now, I believe I shall sleep awhile."

Lizzie thought about her friend's words long after her soft regular breathing signified she was fast asleep. It sounded so easy. As if all one had to do was ask God to provide a map for one's life and then follow it point by point. But it seemed to Lizzie the map was far from knowable. The days came and went and with them choices made in the moment that had possible ramifications for a lifetime. It all seemed so arbitrary, so subject to whimsy and the individual's random mood. How could God possibly work with such a frail, self-centered being to achieve His goals?

Too roiled in her thoughts to sleep, she watched dawn's light seep through the window and finally rose to dress. It was another in a series of dreary, rainy days that served only to deepen the melancholy that had gripped her for weeks. She felt a sudden need for fresh air despite the weather. She threw a wool shawl around her shoulders and picked up the umbrella and India-rubber boots that were essential possessions in a town turned to mud by torrential winter rains.

She walked along the cold, silent hall and down the stairs in stockinged feet. In the unforgiving light of early morning, the deserted saloon looked what it was, a crude playground for men with too much time on their hands and too little virtue in their character. A place that carried the taint of tobacco smoke, alcoholic spirits and rank bodies even in its emptiness. A place to which she had attached herself for as far into the future as she was able to see.

She stopped to pull on her boots, greeting Joseph, the black man with a game leg whom Lucy Mae had hired to come each morning to chop wood, fire up the stoves, and sweep and mop up the prior night's tobacco juice and vomitus. He nodded and tipped his hat. Outside, the rain had diminished to a steady drizzle. She raised the umbrella and set off down the street. When she passed the American Hotel, she glanced into the corral with its hay lean-to where guests were allowed keep their mounts for a small daily fee. There were six or seven mules and two horses, one a large dapple-gray that reminded her of Jonathan's horse Shadow. She caught her breath at the sudden wave of nostalgia that washed over her. Would she never be able to put it behind her?

She walked well out into the country, the fields where the emigrants had camped during the summer now deserted. She returned to The Southern Belle later to find that Sheriff George W. Sharpe had arrived to conduct his inquiries.

The sheriff was a man of medium height but uncommon girth with a protruding belly and a round moon face featuring a bulbous nose, small brown eyes, and a bushy moustache. After listening to the five people arrayed around him tell both sides of the issue, he blew out his cheeks, shook his head, and said,

"What a pretty kettle of fish we have here. You, sir," pointing at Barnes, "claim this woman is your escaped slave. And you," turning to Rachel, "claim to be a free black. But neither of you has proof. And I happen to be a fellow who likes to see some evidence before I arrest someone."

"She bears my family name," Barnes protested. "That alone is proof."

"Nonsense," said Lizzie. "It proves only that she once belonged to your family. It is true she has no legal document. But I saw and read that document and can attest to its validity. That she cannot present it now supports our claim that it was stolen last night and destroyed. For which Mr. Barnes himself should be arrested and prosecuted."

"Again, I have only your allegation of the supposed break-in and assault. This gentleman and, uh... " He glanced at Mariah. "...his companion claim otherwise. That makes it two against one."

Lizzie drew herself up. "No, it is two against two. Rachel was there as well as I and can swear that it happened."

He shook his head. "A person of color is not allowed to give testimony in legal matters in the State of California. Without the witness of another white person, the charge cannot be proved."

"I am very much a white person," Lucy Mae interjected, "and I saw Miss Hamilton's agitated state when she appeared at my door last night. She was not play acting."

"We was in bed," Mariah insisted, her malignant gaze not wavering from Lizzie. "She's making it all up on account of she don't like me."

The sheriff raised his hands palms out and said, "Enough talk. This can only be sorted out by Judge Ward. Trouble is, he's off to visit family in Indian Valley where he hails from. Won't be back until day after Christmas. Probably won't be available to hold a hearing until day after that."

"Then you must arrest my property until he arrives back," said Horace Barnes. "If you do not, she will likely flee just as she did when she left Virginia."

Lucy Mae stepped forward with a steely glare. "Don't you dare do any such thing, George Sharpe! It is Christmas Eve and I expect one of the biggest crowds ever tonight and tomorrow."

Lucy Mae had ordered all sorts of delicacies for her Christmas celebrations to be brought up from Marysville and Sacramento. She had printed flyers and posted them throughout the town to advertise the event.

She continued, "I have promised my customers that Rachel will sing all their favorite Christmas songs and carols. And I intend to keep my promise. I give you my personal guarantee she will not leave town. That should be enough."

"I object—"

"Enough, I said!" bellowed Sheriff Sharpe. "In honor of the holiday and out of respect for one of the town's leading businesswomen, I am accepting Lucy Mae's word."

Lucy Mae nodded with satisfaction. Horace Barnes huffed his indignation. Mariah slunk away from her employer's disapproving countenance. And Rachel remained as stone-faced as she had been throughout the interview. The meeting scattered, and the two friends took their breakfast, after which Rachel and Timothy rehearsed while Lizzie went to their room to rest. The emotion of a trying morning soon overwhelmed her, and she fell sound asleep.

A gentle shake of her shoulder wakened her some hours later. She opened her eyes to find Rachel bending over her.

"A gentleman is here to see you," she said.

Lizzie knitted her brow. "A gentleman? Not that wretched Horace Barnes."

"No. This one seems quite genial."

"Who is he?"

"He would not say." A sly smile. "However, he is very tall."

Lizzie's heart lurched. First a dapple-gray horse, now a tall gentleman. Her hand flew to her mouth. "Could it be...?"

Rachel pulled on her hand. "I suggest you go see for yourself."

She barely felt the floor beneath her feet as she walked down the hall. When she reached the stairs, she took a deep breath and stepped onto the landing.

It was a very different Jonathan she saw looking up at her. Gone were the emigrant's rough work clothes, replaced by a professional man's suit. His light-brown hair was combed, his jowls freshly shaved. His smile, however, cratered his cheeks with the same appealing dimples, and his eyes blazed with the same passion they had displayed the last evening she saw him.

Too filled with wonder to speak, she descended the stairs and walked into his embrace. He held her for several moments, then pulled away to look down on her.

"You are every bit as beautiful as I remembered. How have you fared since last I saw you?"

She ignored the question to stammer, "But—but what are you doing here?"

"To see you, of course."

"How did you find me?"

"*The Sacramento Daily Union* wrote of this place a week or so ago. The primary focus was the accomplished vocalist who sings here, but the final paragraph described the charming hostess as well. I knew in an instant it was you."

"I—I cannot think what to say."

A grin. "How about, 'Hello, Jonathan?'"

She laughed and led him to a table in the farthest corner of the saloon. She could not wait another moment to say, "Tell me about Missy. And Caleb." A note of anxiety. "Is he well?"

"Very well. Quite chubby, as a matter of fact. He eats appropriate table foods and drinks from a cup. Crawls all over the house and has begun pulling himself up to his feet. He will be walking soon, I suspect."

"And Missy?"

"Well. But she misses you still. Hardly a day goes by that she does not speak of you."

Lizzie felt a lump rise to her throat and tears to her eyes. She fought them back and proceeded to less emotional ground. "So you are settled in Sacramento as you had hoped. Have you established your dream school?"

"No, but I have found the next best thing. The professor of classics at the Sacramento Academy fell ill and was unable to start the present term. The principal offered the position to me."

"It sounds perfect for you. But how did you manage to get away to make this trip?'

"It is the Christmas break."

"Of course." The day's happenings had nearly driven the upcoming holiday from Lizzie's mind. "I am flattered you would take this time to come, but should you not be at home with the children? Surely they would want their papa there on such a day."

"To the contrary. I have come to fulfill Missy's fondest Christmas wish." He took her hand. "I realize you have made a new life for yourself here, and perhaps it is everything you wished for. But throughout these past months, we have not been able to strike you from our minds and hearts. We need you, Lizzie. More to the point, we love you. *I* love you. Please come home with me and be my wife."

Lizzie could barely breathe for the rapid beating of her heart. He still wanted her. But how could he?

"Did you read the letter I left for you?"

"I did. And it broke my heart."

"So you know I am a liar, a fallen woman, a murderer. Add to those my current employ in a house of drink, gambling and prostitution, and surely you can see I am no proper candidate to be your wife."

He shook his head. "Our fallen humanity requires all of us to face stark choices from time to time. We make mistakes. We also accept degrading circumstances in order to survive. You are no exception. I assume you were unable to cash your bearer bonds, requiring you to seek employment. I cannot fault you for accepting whatever opportunity presented itself."

"And you have no doubts about my behavior here?"

"None whatsoever. I know you. Your goodness and decency. Your high moral character. You are the helpmate I desire. The only question is whether you are willing to accept me."

"I—I am overwhelmed."

"As you have every right to be. I would be irresponsible if I allowed the emotion of this moment to sway you into a rash decision. I must begin my journey home by the middle of next week. If that is not enough time, I am willing to wait until you are ready. All I hope for is your pledge that you will take my proposal seriously."

Her eyes searched his for any sign of insincerity and found none. He had gone to great trouble and expense to find her. He was willing, even eager to take her as his wife despite her past. And what possible reason did she have for refusing him?

She had given independence and self-sufficiency a chance. Rather than a grand adventure, she had found it lonely and lacking in the type of fulfillment she had discovered while traveling west with the Collins family. Before meeting them, her life had been focused entirely on herself. Suddenly she had been needed, which required her to subjugate her own personal welfare to that of others. Far from experiencing that as a burden, she had discovered a new richness, depth and significance to her life. Now she had the opportunity to regain that.

She smiled at him. "I shall not only take it seriously, I shall accept it with all my heart. I love you, Jonathan. I love Missy and Caleb. And I am honored to be invited into your wonderful family."

She felt as if she would drown in the loving depths of his eyes. He rose, pulled her to her feet and kissed her. As remembered, his lips were soft and yielding yet infused with a controlled power that swept through her like fire through dry brush. He pressed her to him so that she felt every inch of his body, including the unmistakable bulge that told her, if any doubt could remain, that he desired her. It was not the shameful, profligate desire she had experienced with Jack, but the sincere, honorable, respectful longing of a man whose goal was not immediate gratification but a lifetime of love within the institution of marriage.

They remained thus until approaching footsteps drove them apart.

"Well, what have we here?" came Lucy Mae's voice.

Lizzie's face was rosy with happiness, not embarrassment, as she introduced Jonathan to her employer. She made no reference to their new attachment. That difficult discussion would need to wait for another time.

"My pleasure," said Lucy Mae. Then, with eyebrow cocked in unquenched curiosity, "I hate to interrupt such pleasant activities, but… " She gestured at the customers who had begun coming in. "… as you can see, it's time for you to be on duty. I'm sure Mr. Collins will excuse you."

Jonathan smiled down on her. "Go. I shall be right here all evening."

As Lizzie changed into her evening gown, every ounce of her being quivered with happiness. She thought back over the previous year. No matter how hard she had tried to guide her destiny, she had been foiled at every turn, blaming God for not being the magic genie Who would grant her every wish. Perhaps Jonathan and Rachel had it right. In the midst of life's uncertainties, the only sure thing came from trusting Someone larger than oneself to provide the wherewithal to navigate whatever challenges arose. The result, as in her case, might be more than one could even dream on one's own.

With gratitude in her heart, she went downstairs to the gathering throng. It being Christmas Eve, the crowd was larger than normal in response to Lucy Mae's promise of a fine feast to be served late in the evening. Lizzie felt Jonathan's eyes follow her every moment and could not keep her unfettered joy from showing. She also paid uneasy notice of Horace Barnes, who had taken up with two rather scruffy individuals dressed in what she had come to recognize as the miner's costume: dark-blue flannel shirts, pants with boots drawn up over them, and a low-crowned, broad-brimmed felt hat. Mariah was giving a great deal of attention to these men—sitting on their laps and taking them upstairs one by one after stuffing the cash Horace handed her into her bosom. Why he would be indulging these men was beyond knowing.

Jonathan left for his bed at the American Hotel after the last drunken customer had been shooed out into the night, promising to return by eight o'clock the following morning. When Lizzie and Rachel were alone in their room, Rachel whirled on her with a wide smile and said,

"It is settled, then?"

"Was it that obvious?"

"Absolutely." Then, exhibiting not the slightest hint of regret over losing the one person who cared for her in this place, "When will you be leaving?"

"The details have not been worked out. But of this you can be certain. I shall remain until I am able to testify before the judge. Horace Barnes will not prevail!"

Rachel reached out to hug her. "Bless you, I know you will do your best. As I have already said, the rest is in God's hands."

She began to undress, saying, "Have you told Lucy Mae she will be losing you?"

"Not yet. I am uncertain how she will take it."

Despite her employer's generosity at the beginning of their relationship, the two women had never forged a bond that could be described as friendship. Business was Lucy Mae's one and only motivating interest, and she had never treated Lizzie as anything but an employee. Would she greet this news with a businesswoman's dispassion? Or would she see it as a betrayal since her entire rationale for The Southern Belle was built on Lizzie.

Rachel said, "Waste no anxiety on her part. Have you ever seen a cat fall from a height? They always manage to land on their feet."

Lizzie laughed at the comparison, the levity reminding her that any small inconveniences standing between her and her new life paled before the power of the love she felt for Jonathan.

The weather cleared overnight, and Christmas Day dawned with but a few stray wispy clouds scattered here and there across a pearly sky. Jonathan came as promised, and Lizzie greeted him with undiminished wonder, still barely believing he had actually sought her out and wanted her for his wife. He insisted they take their breakfast at the American Hotel where they would have more anonymity and privacy, after which they would walk and talk. They had much to plan.

The hotel's dining room was crowded and afforded little opportunity to delve into substantive issues. Instead, they exchanged details of what had happened in each of their lives since parting. Jonathan told her about their new home in Sacramento, the kindly woman he had hired to care for the children when he was away, and the students whose curiosity and appreciation of classic literature was not always what it should have been. He brought her up to date on the Fielding family and Cora's new passion to become a physician like her father despite the fact that that profession had yet to welcome women into its ranks. She told him about Horace Barnes and the threat he posed to her friend, whose voice Jonathan had heard and greatly admired the night before.

"Whatever we decide, I must be here to prove her freedom document existed," she warned.

"Of course you must. I would expect nothing less of you."

When they were finished, they put on their outerwear and went out into the brightening morning. The sun had just crested the mountains to the east and begun to warm the chilly air. Jonathan stopped and drew her into a kiss.

"Happy Christmas, my dearest Lizzie. May this be but the first of many with you by my side."

He took her hand, and they walked up the street, failing to notice the two figures who slipped out from behind the far side of the hotel and followed behind.

∞∞∞

Lizzie was stunned by the rapidity with which pure happiness could devolve into terror. One moment, she and Jonathan were walking along hand in hand and making plans for their future. The next, a cloth sack whooshed over her head and a strong arm held her fast. Within moments, she felt rope wind around her body, pinning her arms to her sides. From the muffled shouts and scuffling noises to her right, she knew something similar was happening to Jonathan.

"Settle down, now," said a gruff voice. "We ain't gonna hurt you. Just taking you for a little ride."

Lizzie felt herself being tugged off the road as the voice said, "Go get them mules. I'll wait here with these two."

It was impossible to know how much time elapsed before they heard the plodding of hooves and the squeak of saddle leather.

"Up you go," said the gruff voice, and Lizzie felt herself hoisted into the air and planted astride the broad back of a mule. With a grunt, her assailant mounted behind her and kicked the animal forward.

She heard a second animal following behind. Then came Jonathan's calm, steady voice. "I have some money back at the hotel. You are welcome to it if you will let us go."

"Keep yer money, mister," came another voice, this one thin and high-pitched. "You cain't begin to match what our employer already paid us, so save yer breath."

"Where are you taking us?"

"Now that'd be tellin', wouldn't it? Not far, though. Just far enough so's you cain't get back to town a'fore that there trial takes place. Soon's it's over, you'll be free to go on about yer business."

Even though she already knew the answer, Lizzie asked, "Horace Barnes is behind this, is he not?"

"So what if he is? You cain't prove nothin.'"

"We saw the three of you together last night. We also saw the favors Mr. Barnes was providing you by way of Mariah."

"We ain't been nowhere near The Southern Belle today," said Gruff Voice. "Fact is, we got half a dozen miners who'll swear we was workin' the long-tom like sons o' bitches all day long."

"On Christmas Day?"

"Sure 'nuf. The gold don't pay no attention to what day it is."

"Nonetheless," Lizzie persisted, "I will identify you and see that you are punished unless you turn these animals around and let us go."

A guffaw from High Voice that was more squeal than laugh. "Gotta find us first. There's hundreds of us up in these here hills. Give it up, missy. We got the upper hand here, and t'ain't nothin' you kin do to change that."

Lizzie realized it was pointless to argue further. She concentrated on leaning as far forward as she could so as to limit physical contact with the smelly chest behind her.

Whatever path they were on, it was rough and went up and down numerous steep slopes. She could see nothing through the fabric covering her face, but she was aware of passing from shadow to light and back again, as well as the occasional warmth of a direct ray of sun, telling her they were moving through a forest. After what must have been the better part of an hour, they plodded down yet another steep incline and pulled to a stop. Her captor swung down and lifted her to the ground. She heard Jonathan and his kidnapper also dismount.

They were pushed forward over irregular ground for a short distance. The rasp of a rusty hinge. Then High Voice giggled, gave her a final shove, and said, "Step right in, yer royal highness. Yer palace awaits."

She stumbled forward, managing just barely to keep her balance. She could tell from the sudden cool air and earthy odor that they had entered some sort of structure.

"Now lookee here," said Gruff Voice. "You're gonna be here for a couple 'o days, and we got no call to make you any more uncomfortable than needs be. We're gonna untie you and take these here bags off your heads. Just so you know, we've got weapons, and we won't mind usin' 'em. Behave yourselves, and you'll be okay here. There's food and water. Even a bed, which you two oughta like seein' as how you're such lovebirds. We'll be back to let you out after that hearing's over and our boss is off on his way. You got that?"

"Yes," said Jonathan.

"Then stand still and don't turn 'round 'til we're gone."

Lizzie felt the ropes fall from around her, freeing her arms. She sighed with relief when the stuffy bag came off and she was able to take a deep breath of fresh air. She heard the door close behind the two men and turned to Jonathan, who reached to embrace her.

"Thank God you're all right," he murmured.

She nestled against him, his solid presence a comfort. Then the enormity of what had happened crashed in on her, and she felt tears prick her eyes.

"How could I not have guessed he would try something like this? We should never have left the hotel."

"I admit you have a knack for landing yourself in uncompromising situations." The words would have been harsh were it not for his teasing, indulgent tone.

A little hiccup of a laugh. "I do, do I not? I would not blame you if you were to retract your marriage proposal and hurry home as fast as Shadow could take you. Assuming we ever get out of this... this... place."

He pulled back and smiled down at her, wiping a stray tear from her cheek.

"No chance, Miss Hamilton. You are stuck with me." To emphasize the point, he kissed her. Then, "Now let us see what we can do to get ourselves out of this predicament."

They spent a moment studying their surroundings. The rudimentary cabin was constructed of logs chinked with mud. It had a rough-shingled roof over a sloping dirt floor still muddy in places where the rain had leaked in. There was a stone and mud fireplace and a large enough stack of chopped wood to see them through for a day or two.

The furnishings included two low milking stools close to the fireplace, a homemade table that canted at a crazy angle, two overturned barrels to serve as chairs, and the aforementioned bed—a reasonably thick straw mattress lying on an India-rubber blanket and covered with two far-from-clean red wool blankets. There were a number of boxes and sacks of food, a water barrel, and a few crates stacked lengthwise to form a work space for food preparation. A blackened cast-iron pot and skillet sat on the dirt beside the fireplace, and a small shelf offered various mismatched cooking and eating utensils. There were no windows and but one door, which had no inner hardware and opened outward.

Jonathan pushed against it with all his might, but it would not budge. "Must be barricaded from the outside."

He crossed to the woodpile and looked around it. Shook his head. "No ax. No mining tools. Nothing we can use." He went to the fireplace and bent to look up the chimney. Straightened and came back to Lizzie. "Come and sit."

They went to the table and each took a seat on a barrel. She gripped his hands and said in desperation, "What are we going to do? I must be present at that hearing tomorrow."

He shook his head in defeat. "I see no way we can escape. We have no tools with which to smash our way out. The chimney is too narrow to climb. I am so sorry, dearest. I have let you down."

"No! Never!" A deep sigh. "My friend Rachel is convinced that our lives follow a plan designed by God Himself, and we must believe He knows what is best. I have tried to believe it, too, but I admit this situation strains my ability to do so."

They fell silent, aware that the sun was now high in the sky given the chinks of yellow light slicing through the gaps in the roof. Jonathan worked his heel back and forth on the dirt floor, mesmerized by the widening groove produced.

Suddenly he fell still. Gave a hoot of discovery. "This is it! Our way out!"

Chapter Twenty-Seven

They studied the baseline of the cabin's walls and chose a place at the lowest elevation where light already spilled in over a small washout. They gathered whatever utensils they could find—a wooden spoon, a flapjack turner, two tin spoons—and began to dig in the packed, rocky soil. It was laborious work. By the time an hour had passed, they were drenched with sweat and covered with dirt. But they had opened a hole approximately two feet wide and six inches deep.

They took a short break to drink and rest. Then they got back to work. The necessity of kneeling without respite caused those joints to scream with pain. Lizzie's back ached from constant bowing, and their inadequate tools formed blisters on her hands. She gritted her teeth against these discomforts and redoubled her efforts, determined not to allow Horace Barnes to prevail.

By the time they had opened a space they judged to be adequate, the light coming in told them it was mid- to late afternoon. They had already decided to make the hole only large enough to allow Lizzie with her smaller frame to slither through. She removed her gown and petticoats until she stood in chemise, drawers and stockings, blushing despite Jonathan's gallant effort to avert his eyes. She stretched out face up on the dirt floor and tilted her head back into the hole. She bent her knees, dug her heels into the dirt, and inched backward. By the time her shoulders had dropped into the hole, her eyes and nose had emerged into fresh air.

She experienced a moment of panic as she realized the precariousness of her position. If some danger were to present itself, she would be helpless to defend herself. She looked from side to side and saw only trees and sky. She set her jaw and bent her legs to gain another purchase. Gave herself another push and felt her shoulders clear the cabin wall. Next came her torso, and she bit her lip as the wall's rough underside scraped across her breasts. She raised onto her elbows and pulled the remainder of her body through the opening.

She sprang up, shivering in the cool air, and looked around to make certain she was alone. She picked her way over the hard, stony ground to the front of the cabin, grimacing as she imagined the damage being done to her stockings. She saw that Jonathan had guessed right. A sturdy log had been angled up against the door, effectively barricading them inside. She wrestled it aside and entered the cabin.

She looked down at herself and grimaced. She had never been so thoroughly grimy, not even when she played outside with the slave children as a little girl. Jonathan had the good graces not to laugh as she did her best to brush off the worst of the dirt and pine needles before stepping back into her cast-off clothing. They dipped water from the barrel to wash their faces and dirt-caked hands. Lizzie did her best to tuck away stray stands of hair and adjust her disheveled plaits. Jonathan donned his creased but still-serviceable hat, and they went outside to orient themselves.

The cabin was located on the flattest portion of a rather steep slope. Some distance downhill, they saw a simple cemetery surrounded by a stone fence. Farther down through the trees, they saw the buildings of a not insubstantial town beyond which ran a rushing stream with the paraphernalia of mining such as sluices and cradles of every size visible even from this distance.

"This must be Elizabethtown," said Lizzie.

Jonathan cocked an eyebrow. "How do you know?"

"This was my original destination after my fruitless trip to Rich Bar. I had heard it described as a bustling boom town, and I thought it might be the best place to find employment. But then Lucy Mae came along and convinced me the future lay in Quincy.

Since then, I have heard a great deal about Elizabethtown. Over two thousand mining residents and dozens of businesses reside here. I also learned it lies but two miles into the mountains from Quincy. Close enough that any miners who tire of the amusements here often come to explore those in Quincy. As witnessed by the presence of our two abductors at The Southern Belle last night." A wry face. "I can also say as a veteran of mule riding, the amount of time we spent in transit fits with that two-mile distance."

"But in which direction? We cannot simply set out and hope for the best. We could get hopelessly lost and risk our very lives."

"I have been told there is a fair amount of commerce between here and Quincy. There must be a connecting trail."

"Finding it is the challenge. We cannot risk asking for directions in town given that our captors are no doubt still thereabouts."

Lizzie could not have agreed more. The two men had been hired to do a job, and their pay no doubt depended on them bringing it to a satisfactory conclusion. Which meant she and Jonathan must avoid them at all costs.

"If we go somewhat closer under cover of these trees," she suggested, "perhaps we can find someone on the periphery to ask."

They moved downhill, the sounds of music and merriment from the town's saloons drifting up to their ears. When they were within a stone's throw of the small cemetery, they saw a lone black-clad woman kneeling before a fresh grave. At their approach, she lifted a tear-streaked face and struggled to her feet. Her rounded mid-section made it apparent she was with child.

Jonathan stepped forward, removed his hat, and said, "Please forgive our intrusion on your grief. We have only a brief inquiry."

She sniffed and dashed the tears from her eyes. "What is it?"

"We are bound for Quincy. Can you direct us to the correct path?"

She pointed without hesitation to the southwest. "Go down past the Masonic Hall. Should be marked well enough."

Jonathan thanked her and said, "May Christmas blessings comfort you in your time of loss," which brought fresh tears to her eyes. He bowed and retreated.

The closer they came to town, the more cabins and tent homes they passed, most laid out in haphazard fashion. The business district seemed to pass straight through town, and they were able to stay well behind the buildings, which ranged from solid one- and two-story structures to those constructed of planks and canvas. They eventually came to a well-worn mule track that proceeded south and east from the main street. Although they saw no identifying sign, they felt confident enough that it was the correct trail that they decided not to press their luck by venturing closer to town for confirmation. Dark clouds had rolled in over the western hills, obliterating the setting sun and any warmth it had offered, and rain again threatened. Lizzie pulled her shawl close, took Jonathan's offered hand, and started down the trail.

It was a miserable trek. A steady rain fell, and the temperature dropped close to the freezing point. Through chattering teeth, they discussed how to proceed. They needed to keep out of sight until the judge's hearing, which would not occur until the day after tomorrow at the earliest, according to the sheriff's reckoning. But where to go in the meantime?

They could, of course, go straight to the sheriff and beg asylum, but would he believe their improbable tale? Even if he did, where could he put them that would be totally beyond Barnes's reach? He had already demonstrated his resourcefulness and determination to stop Lizzie from testifying. Her shared room at The Southern Belle was no less risky. Rachel would not give them away, but it seemed likely that Barnes would camp out there in order to keep an eye on Rachel rather than spend much time in his own room. Which left

Jonathan's room at the American Hotel as the safest option. Even though Barnes also had a room at the hotel, he no doubt spent little time there. If they could sneak inside without being seen, there was a good chance Barnes would not know they had escaped his nefarious plot until Lizzie appeared at the hearing.

It was well into the evening when they finally trudged into town. They kept to the backside of the buildings on Main Street and stopped in the shadows of the American Hotel. They could hear music and sounds of festivity drifting down the street from the various places of entertainment. Jonathan tucked her behind a tall wood bin and pointed to a window in the back corner of the hotel's second story.

"Watch for a light there. That is my room."

Hugging herself for warmth, "I believe I shared that very room with Lucy Mae when I first arrived."

"Good. Then you know the hotel's layout. I shall go in alone. If no one sees me, especially Barnes, I shall hold a candle in the window. If you see it, come up and knock three times on the door. If no light appears, you must run back along the road, and I shall come for you later. But I suspect the place is deserted. From what I can hear, the town is embroiled in Christmas revelry and is nowhere near ready to give it up."

He held her shivering body for a moment, then left. She huddled where she was, so cold and wet she thought she could not survive another moment. After what seemed hours but was in fact only minutes, she saw wavering candlelight in the window above. With a sob of relief, she scurried to the front door and entered the hotel.

She removed her mud-caked boots, picked them up, and crept forward, meeting not a soul as she passed by the parlor and tiptoed up the stairs. Jonathan opened to her knock, his sodden coat and shirt already in a heap at his feet. They embraced, the bare skin of his chest cold where she laid her cheek against it. He released her, saying,

"You are trembling." He snatched a blue wool blanket from the bed and wrapped it around her. "Take off those wet clothes."

Shielded by the blanket, she stripped off her dress and petticoats. He took up another blanket for himself, and they sat side by side on the bed as they warmed.

When some semblance of comfort had returned, he said, "What shall we do about your clothes? They would surely dry in time, but... "

She looked down at the bedraggled mess that had been one of her best new day dresses. It was so covered with mud the green color had all but disappeared. Laundering it was out of the question. She considered. Then an idea came to her.

"There is a lame black man named Joseph who comes in to clean The Southern Belle every morning. If we got a message to him, he could pass it along to Rachel... " A wide yawn. "... who would find a way to get some clothes to me."

"Hm-m. Allow me to think on it. Meanwhile, I insist you lie down and sleep. You are beyond exhaustion."

"But what of you?"

With a fond smile, "We have slept side by side in innocence several times before. Are you willing to trust your virtue to my honor once again?"

She reached up to stroke his cheek. "How could I not trust you? You are my lifeblood and will be until my dying day. Of course you must lie here with me!"

He bent his head to kiss her. "I love you, Lizzie."

He eased her down onto the bed and lay beside her, spooning her body with his. And so they slept.

∞∞∞

Jonathan rightly assumed the Christmas revelers would be late to rise the following morning. As soon as it was light, he made his way to the hotel's kitchen and arranged for the cook's young son to take Lizzie's message to the man Joseph at The Southern Belle. The youth accepted his twenty-five-cent piece with shining eyes and earnestly promised to fulfill his mission. Scarcely half an hour later, there was a light knock on their door.

Lizzie stood out of sight while Jonathan opened it far enough to peer out. He grinned and opened it wide to a rather bulky-looking Rachel. She swept in and into Lizzie's embrace.

"I have been so worried about you," the singer said with more emotion than Lizzie had ever heard her display. "When you did not appear for your hostess duties and not even to sleep, I feared you had met with disaster."

"I very nearly did, " said Lizzie, after which she pulled Rachel to sit beside her on the bed and told her the entire sorry tale.

Rachel nodded, her face grim. "I feared something of the like. He has not let me out of his sight for two days. Meanwhile, he gives the appearance of great smugness. And supreme confidence of prevailing in his quest for me."

"Does he know you are here?"

"No. He was sprawled outside the door snoring like a steam engine when I stepped around him moments ago. If he wakens, he will have no way of knowing I am not still in my room."

"I am so grateful you came. But the clothes... ?"

She gave a sly smile and rose. To Jonathan, "If you would be so kind?" gesturing for him to turn his back.

She unfastened her dress and stepped out of it. Beneath it was one of Lizzie's own dresses and beneath that several extra petticoats. She removed those as Lizzie let the blanket she had been using to cover herself fall away. They dressed themselves, and when they were both decent, Lizzie told Jonathan he could turn back.

Rachel had also brought a small bag in which were a brush and hairpins. There being no looking glass, an amenity provided by Lucy Mae in their own room, Rachel sat Lizzie down and loosened her much-matted coiffure. She brushed the tangles out, then plaited and pinned it in respectable fashion.

While she worked, Lizzie asked, "How has Lucy Mae taken my absence?"

"With annoyance at first. But as last evening progressed, I believe she grew as worried as I. She knows Horace is determined to keep you from testifying at the hearing. Which, of course, is not in her best interests as she depends on keeping me here to bring in the custom."

Lizzie had often wondered whether Rachel would remain at The Southern Belle if they were able to confirm her status as a free woman. She could not imagine a person of her talent agreeing to squander it in this remote place after the fear of being returned to slavery was gone. Now, however, was not the time to address long-term issues.

"What about the hearing?" asked Jonathan. "Is there any news?"

"Not yet. I am told the judge will return late today. You can be certain Horace will press him to hold it tomorrow. Whether he will comply is not yet known."

"It is important that no one knows we are back in town, but if it were possible, it would be helpful to know what arrangements are made."

"Of course. I shall send word through Joseph. He is no admirer of Horace Barnes and would like nothing more than to see him defeated in this."

She slipped the final hairpin into Lizzie's plaits and said, "There. I am no hairdresser, but I believe you are quite presentable."

Lizzie rose. "Thank you. But now you must go back before he misses you. How will you avoid him?"

A wicked grin. "I am not sure I shall. I would enjoy watching his expression when he discovers I have been out without him. Let him wonder where I was. He certainly will not find out from me!"

She said a final farewell and slipped out the door.

Lizzie and Jonathan spent the remainder of the day in quiet companionship. Jonathan had made arrangements with the cook for her son to carry meals up to them, a task the lad was happy to perform for a generous gratuity. They tried to keep as much physical distance between them as possible because their mutual carnal attraction began to cause problems. Lizzie never doubted Jonathan's resolve to wait for intimacy until they were wed, but she could see it was increasingly difficult for him to adhere to his promises, especially when they lay down to sleep for a second night.

At half past eight the following morning, they heard a soft knock at the door. Jonathan looked out and motioned Joseph into the room. He stood favoring his good leg, his hat in his hand.

"Just came from Miss Barnes," he said. "She says to tell you that there hearing's gonna be this mornin' at ten o'clock."

"Good man," said Jonathan. "Did anyone see you come?"

"No, sir. That there white slaver don't give no never mind to a feller like me. May he rot in hell."

"My fervent wish as well," said Jonathan as he dug in his trouser pocket for a coin. When he offered it, Joseph shook his head.

"Thanks all the same, but I don't need no money to do what's right."

"Then God's blessing to you."

He nodded, put on his hat, and left.

The next hour and a half passed slowly. They stood at the room's window, which looked down on the temporary courthouse building behind the hotel, and watched various functionaries arrive for their duties. They tried to distinguish which one might be the judge, but it was impossible to tell. When Jonathan's pocket watch read a few minutes before ten, they saw Horace Barnes stride past the hotel and into the courthouse. Within moments, Sheriff Coates appeared shepherding Rachel.

"Come along, then, my dearest," said Jonathan. "It is time to put this matter to rest once and for all."

They went out into the hall, down the stairs, and out the back door. The courthouse door opened into a large hall with pine-board flooring and walls. A large table flanked by an American flag sat near the rear with several smaller tables nearby. Two parallel rows of straight-back chairs ran perpendicular to the table, and a dozen or so crude benches sat before the whole to accommodate spectators. The place was deserted.

They went upstairs and found the small group in a room that served as the judge's chambers. Judge William T. Ward sat behind a polished mahogany desk. He was a man of middle age and stature whose thin brown hair framed a gaunt face featuring a hawk-like nose and deep-set eyes magnified by a pair of thick-lensed spectacles. Rachel stood to one side with Sheriff Coates's restraining hand on her arm. Horace Barnes stood before the judge, shoulders back, head high, hands clasped behind his back.

He was saying, "... simply disappeared despite the honor and privilege she was afforded in our household, even to one of her race. I was able to determine she had taken passage to California and finally discovered her exact whereabouts here in Quincy. She broke both federal and state statutes by fleeing across state lines to obtain a freedom to which she is not entitled. I merely request the authority to take her back to Virginia as my rightful property."

"A fact I dispute with all vigor!" said Lizzie as she marched into the room ahead of Jonathan, her voice ripe with conviction.

Barnes whirled around, his face registering first astonishment, then loathing. "You!" He turned back to the judge, saying, "This woman has done everything in her power to interfere with my rights in this matter. She has nothing of substance to contribute to this hearing and is wasting the court's time with her shameful outburst!"

The judge rose and gave Lizzie a stern look. "And who might you be, young woman?"

"I am Miss Elizabeth Hamilton, late of Charleston, South Carolina, and I am a friend and confidante of Miss Barnes. I am also an employee of The Southern Belle. I would like to give testimony in this matter because I have information vital to its just conclusion. I beg you to allow me to speak."

"Your Honor—" Horace began, but the judge silenced him with an outstretched hand.

To Lizzie, "What is the nature of your information?"

"Miss Barnes came to California with a duly executed document by which her owner, Mr. John Horace Barnes, Sr., who was the present Mr. Barnes's father, set her free prior to his death. I saw this document with my own eyes. It described Rachel so accurately that no one could possibly doubt she is one and the same person to whom it referred. It was recorded with the court in Fairfax, Virginia, in late January of this year, although I cannot recall the exact date. It also bore the seal of Mr. Barnes."

Raised eyebrows. "May the court see this document?"

"No, because it was stolen by Mr. Barnes and destroyed as part of his scheme to whisk Rachel back into slavery."

"That is an outrageous and untrue accusation!" Barnes countered. "No such document ever existed."

"I am prepared to place my hand on the Holy Bible and swear to its existence," said Lizzie. "Are you prepared to do likewise regarding its nonexistence, Mr. Barnes? Are you so determined to conclude this travesty that you are willing to put your immortal soul in jeopardy?"

Her words gave him enough pause for her to continue, "You have already committed acts of theft, assault, and kidnaping for hire in order to assure my silence. I expect the judge would be interested in hearing where I spent Christmas Day and how I got there. Facts that Mr. Jonathan Collins... " She gestured in his direction. "... can surely corroborate."

"Enough," said the judge. He turned to Sheriff Coates. "Do you have anything to contribute to this?"

"Not really, Your Honor. There was considerable fuss over Miss Hamilton's accusations the other night, but I expect sorting it out would require more than this simple hearing. As for kidnaping—this is the first I have heard of it."

Lizzie forged ahead despite the judge having just silenced her. "I have been greatly misused by this man, Your Honor, but I am willing to disregard his misdeeds if he will but stand down where Miss Barnes is concerned. Either way, I plead with Your Honor to confirm her status as a free person of color."

He remained standing and nodded. "I accept your testimony regarding the proof of this woman's freedom. It shall be so recorded in Plumas County, and as long as she remains in this state, she shall be free."

Horace Barnes looked as if he were about to explode. "Your Honor, I object—"

Again the judge cut him off. "This matter is concluded, Mr. Barnes. I suggest you take yourself back to Virginia where you will no doubt find people more sympathetic to your cause. As for me, I despise the institution of slavery and shall do all within my power to rip out whatever roots of support still remain in the hearts of Californians. Now if you will all leave me, I have matters of true import to see to."

Lizzie whirled to Rachel, who had been forced to stand mute while her very fate was debated and decided. Sheriff Coates released her arm, and they embraced, Rachel silently weeping with relief. Jonathan stepped between them and ushered them out.

∞∞∞

They found Lucy Mae waiting outside the courthouse, her anxiety apparent. When she saw the happy smiles of those who emerged, she gave an unladylike whoop and led them all to The Southern Belle for a drink of celebration. Lizzie decided it was as good a time as any to broach the subject of her betrothal to Jonathan. She was surprised and relieved to have her employer receive the news with fatalistic stoicism.

"Might have known I couldn't keep you for long. Such a pretty little thing you are. Destined for much more than I could ever offer you. So good luck to you, little girl of the South. I still have my Black Nightingale to keep them coming in."

How long she would have Rachel's remarkable voice to call her own, however, remained to be seen. The two women discussed their futures in their room that night, and Rachel confided she would likely stay in Quincy until spring. She would save her earnings until she was able to return to either Sacramento or San Francisco and sustain herself as she resumed her former career, this time in the sunlight of assured freedom.

As for Lizzie, she and Jonathan spent many hours making their plans. She raised the possibility of remaining in Quincy until the spring along with Rachel, but he was adamantly opposed to the idea.

"I am determined never to be separated from you again. I refuse to tempt fate by leaving you here to face God only knows what possible evils. Further, Missy would never forgive me if I crossed our threshold without you."

And so it was decided they would depart together on December the twenty-eighth, exactly one year from the day Jack O'Rourke shot and killed the English earl, the consequences of which had changed Lizzie's life forever. Unconscious of this irony, she packed her belongings in a small trunk purchased with her unspent earnings. She left the grand gowns Lucy Mae had commissioned for her behind and took only the more modest ready-made dresses she had purchased on her own from the local mercantile, as well as the personal items similarly purchased. Jonathan hired a buckboard and driver to take them as far as Marysville, Jonathan's horse Shadow trailing behind, where they would board the stage to Sacramento.

Lucy Mae and Rachel came out to wave them off on a miserable, rainy day. Lizzie had already said her goodbyes to Rachel, but they had not been so very painful since they believed they would see one another again in the spring. Lucy Mae would brook no emotion, not even tendering the opportunity of an embrace, but stood looking solid and imperial as they climbed up, draped themselves with India rubber, and huddled under their umbrellas.

As the driver hauled himself up and took up the reins, Jonathan put his arm around Lizzie and said, "Well, my darling girl, the time has come. You are leaving a life filled with variety and amusement for one that will be boring and dull by comparison. I hope you will not come to regret it one day."

She stretched up to kiss him, then snuggled against him. "Do you remember telling me about the dog and the shadow? How greed led him to lose what he already had? I was truly like him, seeking something I already had within my grasp. I am through searching. My home is wherever you are."

His eyes misted over, and it had nothing to do with the falling rain. "How I love you, Elizabeth Hamilton."

He pulled her into another kiss, this one deep and exciting and full of promise. They barely noticed as the driver flicked the reins and started them on their way.

Watch for my next book:

Excerpt from
A Light Within

By Ann Nolder Heinz

Chapter One

Sacramento, California
December 27, 1858

"It is not fair!"

Cora Fielding's cry quivered with the full-throated indignation for which she had long been excoriated by her mama as unladylike.

Her twin brother Carl's triumphant smirk only infuriated her further. She ignored him and crossed the room to her father, freckled face red as a tomato, fists clenched in frustration.

"I am twice the student as Carl! I have memorized every medical book in the house despite having to spend hours each day attending to my position as tutor to the Isaacs children. When I am able to be present at the clinic, I anticipate what treatments you will prescribe before you speak a word to the patient. Why am I not as qualified to study medicine as any man?"

Richard Fielding sighed, his craggy face a mask of pity and frustration. "My dear child, you know very well in a world of my own choosing you would be free to follow your heart's desire. Indeed, I believe one day young women such as yourself will have that freedom. God knows, you are amply qualified, as you rightly say. But we live in the present age, and despite the prodigious efforts of Professor Rowell..." For emphasis, he lifted the day's edition of the *Sacramento Daily Union* from which he had just been reading. "...the faculty has decided people of your gender will not be admitted to the new school. And there is damn all any of us can do to change that fact."

Her father's use of profanity, normally so rare, told Cora as nothing else could the passion with which he held his convictions. That knowledge did little to quell her own outrage.

Carl sniffed with smug superiority, saying, "Father is, as always, being kind. But everyone knows the female gender is not in the least suited for the rigors of medicine. Not to mention its necessary assault on a lady's sensibilities over issues of physical delicacy."

"Horse feathers! I am not the one who fainted dead away at the sight of butcher Harper's nearly-severed hand dangling from his wrist by a mere tendon or two."

His cheeks, even more freckled than her own, flamed. "Why must you always throw that one weakness up to me? You know I was tired and ill when it happened."

"A few sniffles do not constitute an illness sufficient to cause such a humiliating debacle. You simply did not have the stomach for it!"

"Perhaps you should look to your own deficiencies before faulting others. Why do you suppose Herbert Roskam has stopped calling on you? You with your haughty airs and sharp tongue could not attract a proper gentleman if your life depended on it!"

"He stopped calling because I sent him packing. Who would want such a fool as that?"

"Please, children, do not bicker," said their mother, her tone shimmering with weary forbearance. "We are but one day past Christmas, and I refuse to allow this unpleasantness to ruin the lingering spirit of that holy day."

Cora felt an immediate stab of remorse. Maude Fielding sat bundled in a blanket in a rocking chair pulled close by the hearth, her diminished frame and pale complexion reflecting the close call she had recently had with pneumonia. They were lucky to have her still with them, and for Cora to have caused her such distress was inexcusable. She shot her brother one last angry glare and retreated to the stuffed chintz chair near the front windows where she had been sitting when her father roiled her day by reading aloud the dream-shattering announcement.

What a difference from that day earlier in the year when it was reported that Dr. Elias Samuel Cooper had managed to pull together a Board of Trustees and Faculty of Medicine in order to establish the first medical school on the West Coast. Dr. Cooper was not a figure without controversy, having inserted himself with bold arrogance into the medical community soon after his arrival from the East Coast in 1855. His widely-advertised series of anatomical and surgical lectures and demonstrations had earned him a reputation for self-aggrandizement. This plus an infamous malpractice lawsuit had led many in the profession to do their best to diminish his reputation. However, his success with the proposed school could not be denied, and many were enthralled with the prospect of students being able to pursue their medical studies here rather than traveling to the schools on the East Coast.

Richard Fielding had greeted this news with special satisfaction, for he had two prospective students in his own household. It had long been expected that his only son Carl would succeed him in medicine; Cora's similar aspiration had come as a surprise, dismissed at first, but given greater gravitas as her interest burgeoned during the years since their arrival in California when she was but a girl of sixteen.

For her part, Cora had prided herself on the perseverance that finally convinced her father of the seriousness of her ambitions, prompting him to serve as preceptor to her as well as to Carl so both could complete the required two years of study before they would be allowed admittance to a school of medicine. She had rested her hopes on the fact that the new faculty had not yet decided whether or not enrollment would be coeducational. One of the professors in particular, a Dr. Isaac Rowell, had been vocal in his belief that the school should be open to aspirants of both genders. However, his point of view had not held the day, as was just now verified in the *Union*'s account of the school's third faculty meeting held six days before on December 21st. Carl would be going off to pursue his studies in a few months' time while she stayed home in her dreary tutoring position, a fact all the more galling for her deep-seated belief that were he given a choice, he would not enter medicine at all.

Long before the family embarked on their difficult overland trek from Indiana in 1854, Carl's obsession with wood whittling had born witness to the fact that he had a true artist's gift when it came to creating figures of lifelike proportion. That skill would give him entry into any number of trades. Instead, he would bow to their father's wishes and become a physician whose lack of passion would assure a career of but mediocre dimension.

She sighed, her mood contrary to the room's cozy ambiance. The house with its attached medical office had been built shortly after their arrival when the City of Sacramento had just been declared the capital of California and was still shedding its infancy, crude planks and adobe and canvas being slowly replaced by sawn lumber and brick and mortar. In the years since, the house had taken on an aura of settled permanency with its white-painted exterior, green shutters, and yard graced by young oak and apple trees and flowering camellia plants. Likewise, the gradual acquisition of furniture and fixtures had transformed the interior so that it now reflected the professional stature of its master.

At this time of year, the parlor in which the family was now gathered took on a special aura of cheery hominess. The fire crackled around a freshly-laid log, candlelight brightened the rainy winter day, and the pine tree standing in the far corner, decorated with popcorn chains, colored ribbons, and little candles with burnt wicks, still gave off a fresh tangy odor. Having co-opted this charming custom from their father's German patients, they had gone to the surrounding hills to cut it just days before. It had been a true sight to see when they had lit the candles on Christmas morning and sung carols in honor of the day. This afternoon, however, the season no longer held any charm for Cora. Her inner person seethed with resentment even as she pondered the long path that had led her to this moment.

    She had felt the scourge of her gender from earliest childhood, all the more poignant for the freedom her twin brother enjoyed simply by virtue of being male. While he was outdoors with his friends playing stickball or hunting for frogs in a nearby stream, she was kept indoors at her mother's knee learning how to crochet, knit, sew, and any other skill deemed suitable for a young lady. While her brother went off to her uncle's school for boys in nearby New Harmony, Indiana, she learned her ABC's from books that implanted the importance of the female's role in the home, perfected her penmanship and writing skills, and practiced on the pianoforte, all with the purpose of one day attracting a proper gentleman with her feminine wiles. It was true that she had been allowed to enroll for two years, along with Carl, in The Sacramento Academy and Female Institute where her uncle taught on first arriving in Sacramento. However, the curriculum for the twins had been vastly different, again reflecting the cultural bias as to which subjects were suitable for girls and which for boys, the former being much less demanding than the latter.

    In the face of this seemingly impenetrable wall of expectation, she had rebelled in whatever manner she could. She had developed the habit of speaking her mind in a bold, direct fashion, eschewing the demure feminine reserve she had been taught. She had read her father's discarded newspapers and listened intently to any discussion among his male friends and colleagues in order to form her own independent opinions about matters of governance and politics. She read the writings of Elizabeth Cady Stanton as well as Harriet Beecher Stowe's popular novel *Uncle Tom's Cabin,* which led her to become a champion of the oppressed, whether of her fellow females and their status as second-class citizens or the Negro race and its hateful misuse by supposedly enlightened society

Her father had always looked upon her defiant views with forbearance, even admiration as they reflected much of his own thinking. Thus, when she persisted in her highest form of mutiny, her insatiable desire to become a physician, he was not only sympathetic but secretly delighted. Her mother, however, was more perplexed than judgmental. Nor had she given up hope for a more conventional path for her daughter, as evidenced by her ill-concealed pleasure when Carl's friend Herbert Roskam began calling on Cora.

He was a nice enough fellow, she thought as she brought his soft round countenance before her mind's eye. And his intent to succeed his father in the grocer's business assured him of an income sufficient to support a wife and family. His expectation of said wife's traditional role, however, had doomed his effort every bit as much as his lack of physical appeal. Cora had the same carnal appetite as any other young woman of twenty years, and she hoped one day to find a man who would trigger those feelings while at the same time valuing her for her independence and quest for self-determination. Alas, she feared her brother was right in his assessment that capturing such a man's fancy was highly unlikely. Her slight five-foot frame, flame-red hair, and freckled countenance hardly personified the day's standard of female pulchritude. Add her willful, bombastic personality, and even she had to admit that her chances of romantic success were scant at best.

She pushed the thought from her mind. The only thing that mattered now was devising a way to achieve her tattered but still passionate dream. There had to be a way.

Also by Ann Nolder Heinz

Fox River Valley Series
Wilt Thou Be Mine
Final Victim
Free Fall
Extreme Influence

Standalone
Last Stop Freedom
Refiner's Fire
A Light Within
Shadows of Time

Watch for more at www.fictionbookmates.com.

About the Author

Ann Nolder Heinz holds a Bachelor of Arts degree from the University of Washington with a major in Sociology. When she is not writing, she works as the office manager of her husband's civil engineering and suveying firm. They reside in East Dundee, Illinois, where several "depots" on the Underground Railroad were said to have been located.

Read more at www.fictionbookmates.com.

CPSIA information can be obtained
at www.ICGtesting.com
Printed in the USA
BVHW031500071118
532439BV00001B/68/P